FROM *LONDON* FAR

Michael Innes is the pseudonym of J. I. M. Stewart, who was a Student of Christ Church, Oxford, from 1949 until his retirement in 1973. He was born in 1906 and was educated at Edinburgh Academy and Oriel College, Oxford. He was lecturer in English at the University of Leeds from 1930 to 1935, Jury Professor of English at the University of Adelaide, South Australia, from 1935 to 1945, and lecturer in Queen's University, Belfast, between 1946 and 1948.

He has published many novels – including the quintet *A Staircase in Surrey* (*The Gaudy*, *Young Pattullo*, *A Memorial Service*, *The Madonna of the Astrolabe* and *Full Term*) – several volumes of short stories, as well as books of criticism and essays, under his own name. His *Eight Modern Writers* appeared in 1963 as the final volume of *The Oxford History of English Literature*, and he is also the author of *Rudyard Kipling* (1966) and *Joseph Conrad* (1968). His other books include *Andrew and Tobias* (1981), *The Bridge at Arta and Other Stories* (1981), *A Villa in France* (1982), *My Aunt Christine and Other Stories* (1983), *An Open Prison* (1984), *The Naylors* (1985) and *Parlour 4 and Other Stories* (1986).

Under the pseudonym of Michael Innes he has written broadcast scripts and many crime novels including *Appleby's End* (1945), *The Bloody Wood* (1966), *An Awkward Lie* (1971), *The Open House* (1972), *Appleby's Answer* (1973), *Appleby's Other Story* (1974), *The Appleby File* (1975), *The Gay Phoenix* (1976), *Honeybath's Haven* (1977), *The Ampersand Papers* (1978), *Going It Alone* (1980), *Lord Mullion's Secret* (1981), *Sheiks and Adders* (1982), *Appleby and Honeybath* (1983), *Carson's Conspiracy*

(1984) and *Appleby and the Ospreys* (1986). Several of these are published in Penguin together with two omnibus editions, *The Michael Innes Omnibus* containing *Death at the President's Lodging, Hamlet, Ravenge!* and *The Daffodil Affair* and *The Second Michael Innes Omnibus* containing *The Journeying Boy, Operation Pax* and *The Man from the Sea.*

MICHAEL INNES

From *London* Far

Resolved at length, from vice and *London* far,
To breathe in distant fields a purer air...
London, A Poem

PENGUIN BOOKS

PENGUIN BOOKS

Published by the Penguin Group
Penguin Books Ltd, 27 Wrights Lane, London W8 5TZ, England
Penguin Books USA Inc., 375 Hudson Street, New York, New York 10014, USA
Penguin Books Australia Ltd, Ringwood, Victoria, Australia
Penguin Books Canada Ltd, 10 Alcorn Avenue, Toronto, Ontario, Canada M4V 3B2
Penguin Books (NZ) Ltd, 182–190 Wairau Road, Auckland 10, New Zealand

Penguin Books Ltd, Registered Offices: Harmondsworth, Middlesex, England

First published in Great Britain by Victor Gollancz 1946
Published in Penguin Books 1962
9 10 8

Every character in this book is entirely fictitious,
and no reference whatsoever is intended to any living person.

Printed in England by Clays Ltd, St Ives plc
Set in Monotype Baskerville

CONTENTS

PART ONE

PART TWO

PART THREE

Part One

THE HORTON VENUS

I

MEREDITH, had he ever discussed the affair afterwards, would have cited it as a singular instance of the operation of mere chance. That these precise words should have come to his lips just there and then was a freak of circumstance upon which all else turned; had they remained unspoken, the adventure would simply not have happened, numerous fates and fortunes would have been altogether different, and in time Mr Neff's Collection might have come to outrival the Prado or the Louvre. There was matter for sober thought in this. And Meredith would murmur certain Greek verses to the effect that hard beside each other run the paths of night and day – meaning thereby that a man's life is full of close shaves of which he is wholly unaware. The blade passes within a millimetre, but, because it is invisible, not a blink results.

If Meredith was reticent, Dr Higbed was communicative – and as his involvement had at one period been even more uncomfortable he was abundantly entitled to his say. That chance had in any significant sense entered into the inception of the affair his science constrained him to deny. He knew that when he himself whistled seemingly at random in his bath associations invariably substantial and frequently sinister unconsciously governed the choice of tune – so that after *Coming through the Rye* or *Rule, Britannia!* or *Old Man River*, for example, it was decent and expedient to avoid Mrs Higbed's eye; whereas *Spanish Ladies* was a propitious prelude to such mild marital raptures as professional sexologists enjoy. Possessing this deeper insight into the springs of human action, Dr Higbed was not likely to admit that Meredith's uttering the words he did was fortuitous. Here, he said, was but one little clank or rattle of the iron chain of Necessity, the endless running out of which into the abysm of Time constitutes the meaningless thunder men dignify with the name of History. But a greater point of interest lay in this: that the words uttered were in fact only an approximation to the words heard. What was said was odd enough, being the eccentric ejaculation of a discursively-minded professor. What was heard was so out of place that Meredith could by no possibility have uttered it – such impossibility being, of course, essential to the elementary safety of the system. And what had been forgotten by the contrivers of the system was a simple fact in psychology: that what we anxiously look for our eye will presently report with some confidence as seen, and what we are in earnest expectation of hearing our ear will sooner or later assert as uttered.

For all our waking lives – Dr Higbed, warming to his subject, would continue – we are hard at work imposing significance and form upon what comes to us as a mere phantasmagoria of sense; we cannot – and here Dr Higbed used one of those pleasing illustrations which had won him favour as a popular scientist – we cannot so much as squeeze closer to a pretty girl on a crowded bus without first constituting her both a girl and pretty through prodigies of creative exertion; likely enough, too, she is a plain Jill after all, since constantly we retort upon our senses with nudgings and wheedlings to give us what we want. And even – Dr Higbed would with increasing confidence pursue – to give us what we detest and fear, since so much of our unconscious life is a ceaseless striving after self-punishment. The neurotic sees as a lurid rash the tint and glow of healthy tissue. (Here Dr Higbed would stroll over to a mirror and view with some complacency his own radiant complexion.) The psychotic sees in the veins of hand and arm so many loathly worms burrowing to the bone. (Dr Higbed would bend back his palms and scan

8

his wrists, assured of observing no signs of age in the blue lines which ran there.) Now, the fellow in Meredith's tobacco shop was playing dangerous game. Each time the thing happened it might mean a trap, with the gaff blown and the place surrounded. To this ending he would look forward with mingled fascination and dread. And from any one of a hundred men in the day the significant words might fall. It was all-important that he should hear *aright*, but this – such is the tortuousness of the human mind – made it all the likelier that he would hear *wrong*. So that when Meredith, meditating on the poetry of Samuel Johnson...

Thus Meredith himself sparely, and Higbed with his practised fluency, on the genesis of the affair. Meredith's fateful words had been hardly more than reverie; he had not so much as intended a perceptible ripple upon the pond of casual talk; the result, nevertheless, was a veritable tornado for several unsuspecting people some thousands of miles away. This one might well call chance. On the other hand, the words were of a piece with the man; one of the major interests of his life echoed in them, however idly; and he often came out with things quite as odd. Here Higbed doubtless had the rights of the matter. But what has finally to be noted is neither chance nor fixed association. Rather, it is a fact of character. The paths of night and day sweep close together – but at their nearest a step remains to be taken. There is always a moment of decision, and it is through some assertion of the will that we either stay cautiously put or move from the old world to a new. So with Richard Meredith, a scholar in his fiftieth year. Suddenly a strange path opened – opened at the distance of one vigorous stride. Literally, it was like that; and literally – as if for further drama – it came in the shape of an unsuspected chasm at his feet. Meredith stepped forward and down.

It had been a good day. All morning pale autumn sunshine had filtered sparely into the great library, and the slowly moving shafts of light, like so many dial's hands, added their subtle emphasis to the sense – always faintly present in this book-lined silence – of time flowing massively over the labours of generations of men. The particles of dust that floated in the slanting beams had crept from the pages of manuscripts and books perhaps unopened since they lay in the hands of Housman, of Headlam, of Jowett – nay, conceivably of Porson or Bentley. Such thoughts as these Meredith was far from formulating – he was too busy for that – but the raw material of them brushed the fringes of his mind and contributed to the austere pleasure which workers in such places know. And when at lunch-time the farthest-creeping shaft of golden light touched his high forehead crowned with its untidy hair – hair darker by some degrees than it was to be after Fate had called him to more than one unexpected shore – Meredith stretched himself momentarily in the warmth. 'O Juvenal lord,' he murmured happily with Chaucer, 'O Juvenal lord, true is thy sentence.' And disregarding faint promptings towards the Express Dairy in which he was accustomed to eat a frugal meal, he bent lower over the ancient monastic catalogue on the desk. Excitement was mounting in him – excitement controlled by increasingly severe logical scrutiny as the possibilities of important discovery increased. Might this pointer conceivably lead to the actual recension by Nicaeus to which a subscription in the Leyden Manuscript refers? Was there a possibility of its being indirectly connected with the *scholia* of Epicarpius? In speculations such as these, recondite but blameless, the afternoon wore away. And at four o'clock, having marked certain tentative conclusions beyond which it would be ill-advised to advance without an interval for consideration, Meredith packed up – an operation which consisted chiefly in locking the Duke of Nesfield's manuscript securely in his despatch-case. For this valuable document, which he had now finished collating, he proposed himself to take down to Nesfield Court on the following day and return to Mr Collins, the Duke's librarian.

It thus came about – a circumstance on the inwardness

of which not even Dr Higbed could comment – that on this day of all days, when there was bearing down upon him perhaps the first thoroughly untoward incident of his life, Meredith was the custodian of some ten sheets of ancient parchment which were not only of the highest scholarly interest, but of very considerable monetary value as well. It was carrying this small fortune under his arm that he left the august seclusion of the inner library, passed through the great circular reading-room beyond, and presently found himself in the comparative brightness of a London October afternoon. A shower had fallen and heavy clouds were gathering; nevertheless, gleams of sunshine still caught the tops of the buses and reached down to the wet pavements at intersections; the smell of mouldering leaves, just perceptible through dust and petrol vapour, was like a faint echo of rural peace. Meredith remembered that on the morrow he would be travelling north, and reflected that if the weather cleared again the journey would be pleasant enough.

> Resolved at length, from vice and *London* far,
> To breathe in distant fields a purer air...

Juvenal once more – and as paraphrased by Dr Johnson he put the matter very nicely. Meredith crossed the street, dodging sundry lethal vehicles without being at all aware of them, and went in quest of some small shop that should provide a quiet cup of tea. After that he would walk by way of Shaftesbury Avenue and Piccadilly to the Athenaeum, and a couple of hours' light reading – perhaps in recent numbers of the *Journal of Classical Archaelogy* – would take him on to dinner-time.

> For who would leave, unbrib'd, Hibernia's land,
> Or change the rocks of Scotland for the Strand?

Well, Boswell would – and Johnson himself, for that matter, although he was here obliged to follow the Latin poet's swinging denunciation of urban life:

> Here malice, rapine, accident, conspire,
> And now a rabble rages, now a fire ...

There had been plenty of fire – void spaces round him as he walked witnessed to it – but not much in the way of rabble.

> Here falling houses thunder on your head ...

Yes, that decidedly. Meredith halted, peered into the first likely tea-shop, and descried with dismay two learned ladies of his acquaintance earnestly discoursing.

> Here falling houses thunder on your head,
> And here a female Atheist talks you dead.

Much pleased with this little joke, Meredith crossed the street again with another tea-shop in his eye. It was as he did so that he remembered being out of tobacco.

In all this Destiny was doubtless working – the object of Destiny being to bring Meredith into a certain unobtrusive Bloomsbury tobacco shop with Samuel Johnson's verses still running in his head. Not really a good poem, Meredith reflected as he gained the farther pavement; you could never have guessed on the strength of it that he would write so great a thing as *The Vanity of Human Wishes*. For a moment his mind went off down the resounding corridors of the later composition. But as he turned in to make his purchase and saw that the shop was empty he was thinking again of *London*.

> Their ambush here relentless ruffians lay...

Meredith became aware that the shopman was close beside him, stooped over a glass case in which he was arranging rows of petrol-lighters and cigarette-holders. A sullen fellow with a shifting glance and a nervous tremor over one eyelid, Meredith remarked as he gave his order – and the man somewhat rudely delaying to finish his job, he fell into an abstraction once more. The full title was *London, A Poem*. And similarly with Johnson's play; it was called *Irene, A Tragedy*. The age – in this how unlike the twentieth century! – had been fond of precise statement. Meredith looked round the commonplace little shop and noticed that it suggested nothing very brisk in the way of trade. Over sun-drenched houris in wispy bathing suits, entranced couples proposing tennis, firm but kindly-faced business men, dignified but mildly humorous clergy; over the larger-than-life pasteboard of all these devotees of nicotine, the London grime had settled and the London spiders had spun. But still the vicar clutched his glowing pipe, his other hand lovingly toying with the tobacco jar with the College arms. *For ever warm and still to be enjoyed,* thought Meredith, momentarily abandoning Dr Johnson for Keats. Matinée idols thrust forwards disproportionately large cigarette-cases in frozen gestures: *Bold Lover, never, never canst thou kiss.* Meredith smiled benignly at the sullen shopkeeper. *What men or gods are these?* he wanted to say to him. *What maidens loath? What mad pursuit? What struggle to escape? What pipes?* ... Meredith faintly chuckled at this, startling the man who had now leant over the counter to fish him out his two ounces of tobacco. An unknown brand – but, of course, one was lucky to get it. Nevertheless, Meredith looked at it suspiciously. Would it satisfy the massively discriminative business man, the approachable but public-school and Oxfordy vicar? Or was it of the kind –

> That leaves a heart high sorrowful and cloy'd,
> A burning forehead, and a parching tongue?

And Meredith was so startled at the appositeness of this final snatch from Keats's Ode that he spoke aloud and at random. Moreover – and here was Fate's final inconsequence, a riddle such as scarcely Dr Higbed himself might unravel – it was to Dr Johnson that he turned again as the obscure necessity for speech moved him. 'London, a Poem,' he articulated absently at the half-turned back of the tobacconist.

And the man stiffened, swung round, glanced apprehensively round the empty shop. 'Rotterdam's gone,' he said in a low voice. And, stooping swiftly, he tugged at a ring in the floor. A trapdoor opened and revealed a flight of wooden steps dropping into darkness.

'Quick!' said the man.

Meredith paused a second – but it was to take hold of his tobacco. Then he stepped down. A light flicked on at his feet as he did so. And the trapdoor closed above his head.

2

THE practical and everyday advantages of the exacting science known as Textual Criticism are admittedly few. To ponder the minute inaccuracies of long-dead scribes and thus penetrate through a corrupted text to the pristine meaning of a yet longer-dead orator or grammarian is a way of life not likely to be appealing to the actively inclined. And yet, in what was to be decidedly an active affair, Textual Criticism gave Meredith a good send-off, for it enabled him, between one rung and the next, to discover why the words *London, a Poem* should receive the inconsequent answer *Rotterdam's gone*. He had been understood to say *London's going*; and what he had exchanged with the sullen tobacconist was, in fact, a password and countersign. *London's going: Rotterdam's gone*. The second statement was as unchallengeable as it was melancholy. The first statement was an old guess and a bad one, since London, battered and beautiful, still very substantially existed all around him. An *old* guess; it was therefore to be inferred that the organization or racket or conspiracy – for certainly it was on something of the sort that he had stumbled – had been in existence for some time...

Thus far did Meredith's science take him. It could not at all tell him why he had himself done this extraordinary thing; why he should have thus unhesitatingly stepped into the melodrama so unexpectedly sprung upon him. But *was* it melodrama? Meredith, who was now more than halfway down the ladder, stopped, appalled. Had he come upon something merely sordid; perhaps upon a haunt of vice? Poised on the tobacconist's ladder, he remembered a fable current in the Cambridge of his day. One went into a tobacconist's shop (a *tobacconist's* shop!), put a pound note on the counter, asked for some unlikely purchase, and was immediately ushered –

Incontinently, a cold sweat broke out on Meredith's brow. In horrid trepidation he peered down what was now revealed as a narrow, white-washed corridor, dimly lit by small electric bulbs. Some twenty feet ahead it made a blank turn and disappeared – to open upon what? Had he not, in his innocence on the low life of the Metropolis, made a wholly embarrassing blunder? Meredith took a couple of paces forward, his mind unwontedly besieged by vivid, detailed and swiftly moving visual fantasies. His ignorance of the seamy side of modern London might be vast, but yet vaster was his knowledge of the seamy side of classical Rome. And this specialized information, for long sterilized and stored up for strictly learned purposes, now rioted before him in images of some vast Neronian lupanar, replete with everything that should satiate the farthest reach and curiosity of lust ...

How would one respond if one were by some black magic actually precipitated upon such surroundings – infinite artistries of the flesh amid a wilderness of marble and gold? The vision and the question hung before Meredith only for a moment and gave way to the drab conviction that he must indeed have broken across the threshold of a subterranean brothel. And again images stirred in his mind. Memories, thirty years deep, showed him a student hurrying through these streets, and men in shabby Edwardian clothes beckoning meaningfully from doorways, and one man – his features perfectly recalled as they hung etched against gaslight – inviting to a house 'where the girls danced on the table'. Meredith shivered. At twenty he had perhaps been a little tempted by these girls, but he had no wish to meet their granddaughters. Should he turn round and make for the ladder by which he had come?

London's going: Rotterdam's gone. Who, after all, would

think to choose such words as a passport to venery? Meredith's confidence returned. He thrust his two ounces of tobacco into a pocket, clasped his despatch-case firmly under an arm, and continued to advance down the corridor.

The floor was swept; the whitewash had been recently renewed; round the little electric bulbs overhead no cobwebs had been allowed to gather. This was in marked contrast with the dilapidated and rather dirty shop above. It suggested the environs of a hospital, or at least of some institution markedly functional and antiseptic – but whether in this there was matter that should further allay his apprehensions Meredith felt that he was without the data for knowing. He pressed on and in a low, shadowless light turned the corner. And there, very abruptly, he stopped.

Straight ahead, a lady reclined luxuriously on a divan. She wore a tiara and three strings of pearls; she had no clothes whatever; and she looked at Meredith with a steady and infinite enticement. This was embarrassing; but far more so was Meredith's instant knowledge that the lady – and the lady thus frankly posed – was familiar to him. He had met her like this before. Meredith, his worst fears thus copiously confirmed, was about to suppose himself an unwitting Jekyll whose Hyde familiarly haunted such places as this when he realized that the low light and his own apprehensions had deceived him. The lady existed only on canvas. In fact, she was the Horton Venus. And she had been painted by Titian just on four hundred years ago.

Meredith, now on easy and natural terms with what was thus strangely displayed, advanced with simple pleasure for a closer inspection. The Duke of Horton, he recalled, possessed amid his great collection of pictures two which were pre-eminent: Vermeer's Aquarium, a little miracle of virtuoso edges, of jewelled, mirrored, and refracted light; and this prodigal evocation and transmutation of some great courtesan of Venice, golden-haired, black-eyed, and of ample and resplendent flesh, over the

16

mastering of whose subtle planes and infinite dyes the artist had toiled through oblivious, torrid days. She lay on scarlet; behind her a great emerald curtain was drawn back to reveal an angry sky and a strip of mysteriously sun-drenched sea; upon the goddess herself scattered tints from this tremendous setting were at play with the ivory and rose and gold of the curved torso, the studied relaxation of the limbs. Meredith, when he had looked at the picture for some time, remembered that it ought to be at Horton House.

He had seen it before, and the Vermeer too – but that had been at the Italian and Dutch Exhibitions back in the thirties. Normally the Vermeer lived at Scamnum Court, the Duke's principal country seat. And the Titian lived in Town. But only –

And then Meredith remembered. Horton House was a burnt-out shell, and had been so these two years past. One of the last of the big raids had got it. And by what the Duke – grown old and obstinate – had chosen to leave there, exposed to the hazards of bomb and rocket, a good many people had been disturbed. That the Duke himself should stop on in the vast, almost deserted house (sleeping, it was said, very comfortably in an attic which he shared with his butler) was his own affair, but assuredly he ought to have sent away the Titian, and the Gobelin tapestries, and the famous Crispin Collection of cameos. Not but what (Meredith seemed to remember) the precious things were thought to have turned out safe and sound after all, the Duke having in fact tucked them away in cellars far below the level of the nearby Thames. But *this* cellar certainly had nothing to do with Horton House; it was hidden in the heart of Bloomsbury. Why, then, should the Titian be here – and stacked casually against a whitewashed wall?

Until he asked himself this question Meredith had been so absorbed by the great painting that he had not looked farther about him. Now he shifted his gaze – this with the intention of taking a comprehensive view of his surroundings – only to have it riveted once more on an immediately adjoining object: Almost blocking the corridor was an immense conglomerate of masonry and plaster, which would have looked like the disregarded product of some large-scale work of demolition but for the fact that it was held together by an elaborate system of steel rods and screws designed for the purpose. Meredith advanced several paces until he was in a position to examine the mass on its thither side. What he found was a fresco by Giotto. A very familiar fresco, which Meredith was accustomed to view as often as he visited Italy. The fact was astounding but undeniable. The Titian had travelled some five miles from Horton House. This formidable fragment of a thirteenth-century church had travelled some seven hundred from Florence!

London's going: Rotterdam's gone – Meredith began to see some appositeness in these cryptic phrases. Toledo had gone – years ago and as a sort of curtain-raiser on chaos. That put a big question mark against most of the world's El Grecos. Budapest had gone – which meant Caravaggios and Tiepolos. What had happened to the Rijksmuseum Amsterdam, with its host of Rembrandts; to the Mauritshuis at The Hague, with the Head of a Girl, and the View of Delft? There were people whose business it was to collect information on such matters – but Meredith suspected that it was all pretty fragmentary as yet. And other things must be pretty fragmentary too: marbles, bronzes, terracottas, great paintings, rare books, unique manuscripts – enough of these lay in scraps, rubble, dust amid the still-smoking ruins of Europe. Experts and connoisseurs had followed the armies; and, doubtless, carefully constituted commissions timelessly inquired. But sufficient confusion must remain to afford scope to a small host of depradators and thieves. Had not the crowning achievement of Botticelli been discovered lying in a granary or a stable? Meredith shut his eyes at the thought of it. When he opened them again it was to find that he was no longer alone.

Standing beside him, in fact, was Mr Spackman of the Department of Antiquities in a large provincial museum.

Spackman was well known to Meredith – indeed, they had been at college together – and a meeting with him was always mildly embarrassing. For Spackman, unfortunately, was never quite sober; with a man who is never quite sober learned conversation is virtually impracticable; and for conversation other than learned and impersonal Meredith had, with Spackman, no list at all. Civilities, however, must always be exchanged – and so Meredith, suspending for a moment the puzzling speculations into which his situation had led him, took off his hat. Meredith took off his hat (since this was a good academic custom and not to be abrogated even in a thieves' kitchen) and said pleasantly: 'Good afternoon, Spackman. How are you?'

But Spackman, who was muttering angrily to himself, appeared unaware of the greeting. He had been shambling forward and now stopped by a table where he proceeded to thrust into a Gladstone bag a massive and shiny object which Meredith at once identified as a something worse than mediocre Graeco-Roman bust. Spackman was trembling with irritation; the hinges of the bag kept shutting on his fingers; he swore under his breath in a fashion which Meredith found extremely distasteful. Nevertheless, Meredith advanced and took hold of the bag. 'Let me hold it while you get the thing in,' he said.

Spackman swung round scowling; then, as he recognized who it was that had addressed him, his expression turned to consternation and fear. The spectacle was far from pleasing; from an inebriate red, the man's complexion turned to something like a cadaver blue – but Meredith viewed it with much the satisfaction of a chemist who achieves similar results with a scrap of litmus paper. For here was what might be termed experimental verification of a working hypothesis – to wit, that this underground retreat was the business premises of some particularly enterprising receiver of stolen goods. And Meredith tapped pleasantly on the Gladstone bag which Spackman had now shut with a snap. 'Turned down?' he said interrogatively. 'Not a sufficiently high-class crib?'

This easy command of the jargon of larceny looked like

being finally unnerving to Spackman. His mouth fell open and he swayed like one about to sag nastily at the knees. But suddenly his gaze fixed itself rigidly on a spot beneath Meredith's left shoulder; he threw back his head and uttered a shrill, unsteady laugh; the laugh was followed by what could only be described as a confidential leer; he then picked up his rejected burden with an effort and staggered off down a side corridor which Meredith had not until this moment observed. With a nasty shock Meredith realized that what had arrested the attention of this old reprobate was his dispatch-case. Spackman had supposed it to be performing the same function as his own Gladstone bag.

And a yet nastier reflection followed. This abominable catacomb was fast becoming a sort of illicit annex of what is known in Nottinghamshire as the Dukeries. For there against the wall was the Duke of Horton's Venus, plainly filched from its proper métier of affording a refined aesthetic delectation to an aristocratic few. And here, in this same luckless dispatch-case, was the Duke of Nesfield's famous Juvenal manuscript, which a former Duke of Nesfield had astutely stolen from a monastic library in the Levant, and which appeared in the most present danger of being stolen anew. For Meredith was now aware of certain yet more disturbing facts of environment. He stood just where his corridor opened out into a species of lobby or ante-chamber scattered about which – and on chromium and plywood chairs which nicely combined a hint of opulence with the still dominant antisepsis – sat various displeasing persons clutching either bags, parcels, boxes, small crates, or even articles of *vertu* or connoisseurship frankly unwrapped. Clients evidently – and evidently there was quite a waiting-list. But this was not all. Hard by a farther door stood a heavily-built man in what had much the appearance of the type of sober livery favoured by banking establishments for their messengers and superior attendants: only this man (who was looking suspiciously at Meredith) visibly sported two impressive pistols in holsters on his hips. And hard by him, behind a simple but clearly expensive chromium and ebony desk, sat a young lady at once glamorous and severely secretarial. In front of her were two telephones, as also one of those box-like contrivances into which business magnates bark and snap and growl so impressively in Hollywood films. The young lady was flicking a switch on this instrument now, and evidently proposing to speak into it with the utmost haste. And her eye at the same time was fixed upon Meredith – upon Meredith and his dispatch-case.

Their ambush here relentless ruffians lay...

Dr Johnson and Juvenal had not been so far off it after all.

To be equal to such a situation as this, Meredith reflected, one has to think quickly. In romantic fiction, the hero invariably manages to do so; his mind – often extremely unnoticeable during other parts of the narrative – rises to the occasion and works like a flash. But unfortunately Meredith's own thinking, although tolerably reliable, was on the slow side. Could he now successfully bid the machine do double time? The case was sufficiently urgent. For an organization which left Titians and Giottos lying about its outer corridors was evidently Big Business of the most unchallengeable kind, and it was unlikely to pack up its chromium furniture and house telephones and fade away because intruded upon by an unwitting scholar.

Rather, it would be the scholar who would fade away. The man like a bank messenger would simply draw his pistol – and subsequently disguise the body as a case of bullion and remove it in a taxi. Here – unlike Titian's Venus – was something that Meredith had not encountered before: the prospect of being (as they say) taken for a ride. Or bumped off. And Meredith shook his head slightly – this because it occurred to him to doubt whether *to bump off* were any longer contemporary idiom.

As rapid thinking, this piece of philological curiosity was a bad start. But it had a marked and unexpected effect upon the young lady at the desk. For this abstracted shake of the head of Meredith's apparently struck her as an authoritative and inhibiting gesture. She abandoned the motion of speaking into her box and looked at Meredith expectantly, as if asking for more. And now Meredith frowned and his mouth set grimly in a thin line. This was because he had once more recalled his custodianship of the Juvenal manuscript, and was confronting the fact that it would in all probability go down river in the same sack as the body – or would conceivably, were its value discovered, go the way of the Horton Venus. Here was a thought very dreadful to Meredith; it added to the fatal affair a sort of second death. And so Meredith frowned and looked grim. And this too had its effect upon the young lady. She blanched. And the man with the revolvers, who had been lounging against the frame of a closed door, straightened himself into a statuesque and formal pose.

It was the man's movement that first caught Meredith's eye. For a moment he judged it ominous, a sort of equivalent of that 'on your marks' position that preludes athletic action. And then – and it was decidedly a matter of a flash – Meredith realized the situation. These outer guardians of the establishment were as apprehensive of him as he was of them.

Did they take him to be a detective-inspector from Scotland Yard, some notable scourge of hi-jackers and Black Marketeers, who would presently put a whistle to his lips and summon an overwhelming force of heavily armed police? Meredith would have liked to think that it was so, but modesty assured him that members of the Athenaeum do not readily suggest such a figure. Moreover, the quality of the apprehensiveness in the persons before him subtly but decisively negatived this reading of the situation. Rather, they were like –

And Meredith paused to remember. Yes, they were like undergraduates just about to come before a board of examiners for some *viva voce* test. Aided by this comparison – or rather, thought Meredith, by this intuitive perception of illuminating analogy – it was possible to make a bold guess. He, Meredith, was being taken for one of the bosses of the concern. And here, plainly, thought for the moment stopped and action must supervene. Only action, decisive and even inspired, would ever get that manuscript back to poor Mr Collins at Nesfield Court. Even as he entertained these reflections, Meredith found himself striding confidently towards the telephones, and the box for snarling into, and the man who carried – or was it 'packed'? – the guns.

Packed was indubitably correct – and even as Meredith reached this conclusion he heard a voice raised in harsh but not uncultivated reproof. 'Get these people out of here,' said the voice. 'If they're offering the same sort of rubbish as that fellow Spackman you're all wasting your time. Clear them out, if you please. Trade's over for the day.' And Meredith – for the voice was Meredith's very own – glanced round him in a menacing and authoritative manner. Anyone aware that this was the first occasion on which he had attempted to look menacing since leaving his private school would have been bound to admit that the learned pursuits to which he had given himself represented a sad deprivation in the annals of the legitimate stage.

And the effect was altogether satisfactory. The bank attendant jumped like a bullock stung by the gadfly in June and fell to circling the room with gestures of the largest menace. 'Gettahelloutahere,' said the bank attendant. 'Scram.' And the clients, who all seemed of a kind accustomed to being held of small account, picked up their inferior offerings and began an abject and obedient shuffling from the room.

The young lady at the desk looked helplessly from Meredith to her telephones and back again. 'Of course, we know they're a low lot,' she said apologetically. 'No class at all. It's just that we try to clean up that kind at the end of the day.'

'No doubt,' said Meredith. And he looked at the young lady as nastily as he could. 'As it happens, I'm feeling rather like a bit of clean up myself.' He began to contort the muscles of his face into the semblance of a horrible scowl. Then, glimpsing an altogether more refined conception of his role, he transformed this into a sweet and – as he hoped – wholly spine-chilling smile. 'A bit of clean up,' he repeated softly; 'just a little bit of straightening things out.'

The obscure displeasingness which Meredith contrived to insinuate into this simple metaphor spoke much for the vigorous tone of the most unpresentable regions of his unconscious mind. 'Of straightening things out,' he reiterated lingeringly. And the repetition, though indulged in after the manner of the political orator who requires time to think, was so effective that the man with the revolvers sank down upon a shiny chair and made gulping noises in his throat.

For the moment, Meredith judged, he dominated the room. Were he to order the gulping man to shoot the young lady dead the command would be unhesitatingly obeyed. Were he to order the young lady to stand up and sing the Jewel Song from *Faust* she would do so with the automatism of one in a heavy hypnotic trance. There was, in fact, only one thing that Meredith at this juncture had no chance of carrying off – and that was turning round and departing as he had come. For purposeful and aggressive advance was the essence of the part he had been driven to play, and were this to fail for a moment the illusion would snap. He would scarcely have passed the Giotto and the Titian before the end would come with a bullet in the back. His only safety – and the only safety of Mr Collins's luckless loan – was to continue marching breast forward as he had begun.

Meredith therefore advanced. He advanced upon the door which it appeared to be the young lady's function to guard, and as he did so he saw her hand hover over the switches of her box. 'You needn't announce me,' he said drily. 'We'll just make it a little surprise.'

The young lady's eyes widened in dismay. 'Mr Bubear is in cahnference,' she said – even in her consternation giving the right filmic intonation to this announcement. 'Mr Bubear is in cahnference, Mr Birdsong – '

Meredith blinked. It was extremely valuable to know

that he was Mr Birdsong: at the same time, and to one with mild feelings on descent and lineage, it had its disconcerting side. Birdsong at morning – he thought with one of his worst lapses into inconsequence – and starshine at night. It would be nice to be tolerably assured that he would ever know either one or other of these natural phenomena again... 'Is he, indeed?' said Meredith. 'All the same' – and his voice sank to an ecstatically sadistic whisper – 'I think we'll make it a *little* surprise.'

And Meredith threw open the door and took the second of his decisive steps into drama.

3

MR BUBEAR'S conference was with a female friend – a good-looking girl, but dissipated, Meredith judged; and with something in her eyes that suggested drink or drugs. He had the impression that she had been sitting on Mr Bubear's desk and leaning eagerly towards him – this after a fashion equivocally suggesting either business or dalliance – and now as she slipped rapidly back into a chair she gave Meredith a glance which was first appraising and then fleetingly surprised. Meredith had time to reflect that she was intelligent as well as pretty before bracing himself to meet the first shock of encounter with Mr Bubear himself. Mr Bubear was a pasty-faced man grown thin and dyspeptic in what was demonstrably a mistaken vocation; he would not last long, but meanwhile was sufficiently formidable by reason of the intense nervous energy he was pouring into the effort of holding down the job.

Meredith got as far as this in analysis while Mr Bubear blustered – standing behind his desk in a tremble and calling upon the Devil to tell him who was this. Adopting the technique that had proved so startlingly successful hitherto, Meredith made no attempt to think like lightning, but simply eyed his antagonist with an unkindly smile while arranging his ideas at leisure. This, however, was not so instantaneously effective as before. Mr Bubear's indignation at being intruded upon mounted. 'And who the Devil', he repeated furiously, 'are you? And what damned fool let you into this office?'

Meredith, who felt that this was a very improper way to speak in front of any woman, glanced by way of apology at the young person who had retreated to the other end of the room. When he looked back at Mr Bubear he found that he was being aimed at – 'covered' was surely the word – with a revolver, and that his unwilling host was at the same time urgently seeking information through the system of snarling boxes which connected him with his secretary in the outer room. The reply, more urgent still, consisted of a single word. 'Birdsong', the box exploded and hissed – and the gulps of the bank attendant could be heard as a faint accompaniment.

And at this Mr Bubear dropped his revolver, disposed an expression of revolting cordiality over his face, and advanced across the room. 'My dear Herr Vogelsang,' he exclaimed, 'how truly delighted we are to welcome you at last!'

To be transformed incontinently from a tolerably familiar Meredith to a totally unknown Birdsong had been disconcerting enough; now – and at the mere crossing of a further threshold – to be hailed as that Birdsong's Teutonic equivalent was bewildering in the utmost degree.

Meredith, however, clicked his heels in an appropriately Germanic manner, bowed coldly, and at the same time held up a hand which uncompromisingly forbade Mr Bubear's nearer approach. Then he pointed to a chair – quite an insignificant chair and remote from this now grovelling person's desk. 'Mr Bubear,' he said briskly, 'please take place.' The situation, he reflected, was becoming increasingly problematical, but a little stiffness in point of English idiom could hardly be out of the way.

Obediently Mr Bubear sat down – whereupon Meredith crossed over to the desk and sat down in its vacant swivel chair. Lying in front of him was now the weapon which Mr Bubear had just abandoned. This successful *coup de théâtre* he had by no means intended, and he looked from Mr Bubear to the revolver with considerable misgiving. Could he fire the thing? Could he discharge it with sufficient accuracy to hit Mr Bubear between the eyes, or in the stomach? And would this be at all helpful? Would it be at all helpful to take the less conclusive step of shooting him through the arm or leg?

These were questions outside the common run of Meredith's experience and required – like so much else in this extraordinary situation – a little reflecting on. Meanwhile, something had better be said – and it would be advantageous if a tone of reprobation could be maintained Herr Vogelsang therefore looked sternly at the agitated Bubear – whom he was meeting, he remembered, for the first time. '*Herr Bubear*,' he said chillily, '*es freut mich sehr Sie kennen lernen zu dürfen.*' He paused on this extreme of formality, which, whether intelligible or not, seemed to serve its purpose of having a further depressant effect upon the person to whom it was addressed. 'And the Titian,' he continued suddenly, 'the *sogenannte* Venus: you let it lie about like a sack of potatoes, yes?'

Mr Bubear raised imploring hands. 'But, my dear sir, the crate is being made at this moment! I assure you that every instruction is being attended to. And the painting stands, as you must have noted, well in our porter's view. A well-armed and resolute man, Herr Vogelsang.'

Meredith, with much artistic restraint, responded with some moments' silence and a smile in which nastiness was modified by absence of mind. Then he fell to tapping the desk slowly and gently with his little finger, and was pleased to observe that Bubear hung upon the sound as if it were a knell. 'Your porter', he said in measured accents, 'I do not greatly care for. And your man in the shop above' – Meredith paused and smiled again – 'must go.'

'But certainly, Herr Vogelsang.' And Bubear bobbed after the manner of a tailor of whom one has bespoken a new suit. 'Allow me to make a memorandum.' Bubear's shaking hand dived into a pocket and produced a note-book and pencil. 'He will be removed tomorrow and a reliable replacement made. There will be no difficulty.' And Bubear smiled ingratiatingly. 'A suitable incident shall be arranged.'

This was an unexpected disaster – and Meredith saw at once that the continued existence of the wretched tobacconist whose doom he had so lightly pronounced was a charge upon his conscience prior even to the safety of the Duke of Nesfield's Juvenal. 'You may let the man be,' he said sombrely. 'Give him work on – on the crates, and so forth. He may be useful later in some hazardous assignment. I will see that he is placed on the expendable list.'

Bubear bowed respectfully – plainly more impressed by the cold-blooded flavour of this than inclined to notice the nice turns of native English speech to which it ran. 'The Giotto', he said – plainly anxious to vindicate his stewardship somewhere – 'arrived very inadequately packed. And I have had a little difficulty in obtaining a sufficient quantity of wood wool. But this has now come, Herr Vogelsang, I am glad to say. The fresco, as well as the Titian, will be ready for transmission tonight. In fact, they will make the journey with the same consignment as yourself.'

'Um,' said Meredith – impressively as it turned out, but actually because he was too disconcerted to say anything else. He might have apprehended something like this. For if Mr Birdsong *alias* Herr Vogelsang had been expected it was likely enough to be by way of fulfilling some known programme. Which was awkward. So was the fact that there was presumably a real Herr Vogelsang, the imminence of whose arrival had alone made possible the strange misapprehension which had occurred. At any moment, in fact, Herr Vogelsang might walk in at one door, and Meredith himself would have to take what slender chance might be of getting safely out through another. At roughly similar situations one used to laugh unrestrainedly when visiting an Aldwych farce. But at the moment Meredith felt not at all like laughing. He felt only like getting away. And, provided he were able to take his dispatch-case with him, he did not at all care whether his exit was as undignified as any ever contrived for the inimitable Mr Robertson Hare.

But need it be undignified? Might he not leave with an air, even as he had come? Meredith took out his watch and consulted it with every appearance of leisured ease. 'The consignment,' he asked '– at what time does it leave?'

Bubear looked fleetingly surprised. 'At ten o'clock, Herr Vogelsang; the usual hour.'

'*Also!*' Meredith, who did not like that flickering surprise, put an extra dose of sinister inwardness into this harmless Teutonic expletive. '*Also – gut!* At nine I shall return, Herr Bubear. *Auf Wiedersehen.*' And Meredith rose from behind the desk and paused like one accustomed to obsequious attendance upon his occasions.

For a second's space uncertainty – what might even be dawning suspicion – flitted across Mr Bubear's pasty face, discernibly sweating under the nervous stresses of the interview. And then – what Meredith positively felt as a waft of cool air blowing in from freedom – the bluff worked. Bowing and scraping like a shopwalker of the old school, Bubear began to usher Meredith towards a door in the farther corner of the room. '*Zu Befehl, lieber Herr Vogelsang!*' he exclaimed – and paused in evident pride over this scrap of Germanic courtesy. 'May I venture to hope that you will honour me by joining in a light collation before your final departure?' His hand was on the door knob. 'By the way, you do not yourself wish to interrogate the prisoner?'

'The prisoner?' Meredith, much perplexed, contrived to speak coldly.

'An obstinate girl.' Bubear again betrayed that flicker of surprise. He turned towards the body of the room again. 'A very obstinate girl indeed.'

Meredith had forgotten the girl who had appeared to be sitting on the desk, and who had slumped so swiftly and quietly into a chair. But he looked at her attentively enough now. And the girl looked equally attentively at him. It was only for a moment. But what passed between them was full of obscure intimations. 'Ah, yes,' said Meredith softly – and more than ever before his whole soul, for some reason, went into sustaining his sinister role. 'Ah, yes – *das Mädel.* Your interesting little prisoner, my good Mr Bubear. You have been ineffective, yes? Let me talk to her, by all means.'

Bubear's hand fell from the handle of the door. Meredith returned to the desk. It would have been possible, he reflected as he sat down, simply to get away, and find a policeman, who would in turn have found more policemen. But in the meantime the real Vogelsang (or Birdsong) might have arrived, or through any of a dozen channels overwhelming suspicion might have poured in upon the hitherto hypnotized intellectuals of the man Bubear. In which case what might not happen to this girl – and to the Titian and the Giotto too – in the interval before effective aid could be marshalled? There was nothing for it – Meredith decided without any sense of heroic decision – but to stick it out. Juvenal and he (and he set the despatch-case carefully on the desk beside him) must sit on the wicket and continue to play for time.

He looked at the girl. He looked at her with an extreme of nastiness and no compunction – this because he realized that she was not deceived. She knew very well that he was not Vogelsang; even knew (Meredith guessed) that he was a mere outsider, strayed in by fatal inadvertence, and from minute to minute extemporizing a part. But what did *he* know of *her?* That his first impression of drugs and dissipation had been altogether wide of the mark; that she had appeared to be sprawling on Bubear's desk not in dalliance, but because Bubear had been bullying her; that she had slumped into a chair as she had because of some extreme of physical exhaustion. This, and that Bubear called her the prisoner – the obstinate prisoner...

As all this dawned on Meredith he looked down at the desk and absently pushed the despatch-case aside. For suddenly Juvenal seemed very unimportant and the one

30

fact really relevant to the situation was this: that somewhere on the desk still was Bubear's revolver, with which Bubear could be killed. There it was – and Meredith slid his hand towards it. He looked again at the girl and saw that once more she knew very well what he was about. She was sitting, perfectly relaxed, on one of the establishment's hygienic chairs, and it was evident that she was deliberately recovering what physical resources she could. Less evident – just perceptible, indeed – was the fact that she was shaking her head. The revolver might be a card in reserve, but this was not yet the moment to play it.

For the second time Meredith had the odd experience of hearing his own voice take charge of the situation without any apparent intervention of the will. 'Don't you think' – it was a gentle, almost caressing voice – 'don't you think you had better give in?'

There was a moment's silence. Meredith found that, although thus resourceful in utterance, he could now hardly trust himself to look at the girl. For she was haggard and heavy-eyed; her legs, carefully relaxed as they were, intermittently trembled; there was a tear in her dress. To save himself from grabbing at the revolver outright, he repeated, harshly this time: 'Don't you think you had better give in?'

The girl raised her head wearily. 'I've told him it's no good. I've told him and I tell you. I just don't know who intercepted your Consignment 99, or where the stuff was taken to. It wasn't our lot – see? It just wasn't Marsden's lot. There's still plenty of phoney traffic avoiding the main North Road, and plenty of hi-jacking of cargoes whose drivers can't afford to start shouting for the village copper. I don't know who took your Mykonos Marbles. Maybe it was folk who thought they were getting a good haul of Colonial burgundy or canned pork. Probably it didn't happen until right up in Scotland. Off to Moila yourself tonight, aren't you, to join forces with Bubear's boss? Perhaps you'll never get there with your precious news of what you've filched from the rubble of Berlin. Perhaps you'll be hi-jacked yourself and big boss Properjohn just won't see you ever. If he does – and feels like talking to you after your losing the marbles for him – just tell him they didn't fall to us, worse luck.' The girl paused. 'It won't be a very nice topic, will it, seeing that you'll be meeting him for the first time?' She laughed shakily but with convincing malice. 'Don't I just see it? "Chicago's going," you'll say. And Properjohn will answer: "Maybe so. But what you and Bubear have to explain, Herr Vogelsang, is why the Mykonos Marbles have gone." Isn't right? "Titians are nice," he'll say, "and shipments of Giotto frescoes are something new. But what Mr Neff and the others are really wild for is real, genuine archaic stuff. And Marsden's lot are coming forward with it on very keen quotes – very keen quotes indeed, Herr Vogelsang!" That's what Properjohn will say, more or less. And maybe he'll think to have what you call a nice little clear up. I hope he remembers your poor stooge Bubear here, not to mention your filthy porter and hellcat of a secretary.'

'Very obstinate, indeed, Mr Bubear; very, very obstinate, indeed.' Meredith, thus ingeniously flooded with vital, if still bewildering, information, spoke the first appropriate words that came into his head. 'And it appears that your situation is rather awkward. The Mykonos Marbles, above all things, should not have been let slip.' He looked sombrely at Bubear, who first advanced upon the girl as if with some venomous intention and then, changing his mind, made a gesture of despair and sank down on a seat. And Meredith nodded. 'That is right, Mr Bubear. Please take place. This had now better be left to me. For it does not seem that you have distinguished yourself, my friend. I think you were warned not to underestimate Marsden's men here. When I get to Moila all this will have to be discussed, you may be sure. And decisions will have to be taken – decisions, Mr Bubear.

Meredith paused and reflected that intimidation had its insidious pleasures. That Bubear had been taking it out of the girl was a sort of justification for taking it out of Bubear – but the exercise was gratifying in itself, like twisting the arm of a smaller boy. But this reflection (a

32

sure sign that he was being swiftly subdued to what he worked in) gave Meredith pause only for a moment. 'I had been looking forward', he pursued silkily, 'to contacting the chief of your organization. It grieves me much that I should have to take forward with me so unsatisfactory a report. And it is not the Mykonos Marbles only, as I think you very well know. There are other matters, Mr Bubear. *Nicht wahr?*' And Meredith gave his victim what he hoped would register as a penetrating glance. It had occurred to him that as the man was a scoundrel part of his scoundrelism was probably expended in double-crossing his employers, and that in Bubear's present state of demoralization a little in the way of shock tactics might penetrate to this. Meanwhile, Meredith glanced fleetingly at the girl. And, ever so faintly, the girl nodded.

'*Nicht wahr?*' repeated Meredith softly, and much encouraged by this sign of what he thought of as professional approbation. 'I think you know to what I refer, Herr Bubear? Allow me to make a memorandum.' And Meredith fished ironically about the desk. 'The matter will have to be discussed. I think it very likely that you will be removed and a reliable replacement made. There will be no difficulty. A suitable incident will be arranged.'

At this Bubear suddenly groaned, and then fell to gulpings much like those of the bank messenger outside. 'The figurines!' he cried out in despair. 'I implore you to believe that they were a private transaction which I felt myself entitled to make. The funds and resources of the organization were in no way engaged –'

Meredith had opened his eyes wide. 'The Tobermoray figurines!' he exclaimed. For he very well knew to what Bubear referred. These priceless objects had disappeared from the Marquis of Tobermoray's house some two years before, when a time-bomb had fallen nearby and a temporary evacuation had been enforced. 'You have the hardihood to assert, Mr Bubear, that the organization would countenance your making the disposal of the Tobermoray figurines a matter for your own private profit?'

33

And here, thought Meredith, is the crest of the wave. Now or never he and the girl must take advantage of its impetus to get themselves safely ashore. To delay would be inevitably to overreach himself; he would be driven to some long shot which would be hopelessly astray and precipitate sudden and irretrievable disaster for them both. Which was a shocking confusion of images, Meredith thought – and he was about to go back in his mind to the *wave* and see if something better could not be done with an *undertug*, when he once more caught the girl's eye. The eye held its unmistakable message: *we had better make a break for it if we can.*

But how could he propose with any plausibility to walk out with a prisoner for whom the gaining of the public street would mean security and escape? And yet plausible it must be made. Meredith stood up. 'And here, too, my friend, you have failed.' He pointed to the girl. 'I know the sort. You will never get anywhere with her that way. You shout at her, you slap her face – *hein?* And the result? She is one of Marsden's girls still. Now she will come with me and we shall talk. You are surprised? Pah! You are a fool.' He turned to the girl. 'Come, my dear. And where shall we dine? I think you will find that I know how to offer sensible terms.'

It was going to work. Bubear had betaken himself again to his bowing and bobbing; nothing was required but to get the girl on her feet and march out. And with luck they could be back with the whole of Scotland Yard within half an hour. The Titian, the Giotto, and whatever other monstrous thefts the recesses of the place concealed would be restored to their true homes, and all these deplorable people safely lodged in gaol.

With this pleasing issue of things before him Meredith stepped briskly from behind the desk. The girl rose to her feet and advanced towards him. At this moment there was a sound of confused voices outside; the door by which Meredith had entered was flung open; a tall figure, encased in a heavy greatcoat and carrying a dispatch-case, strode into the room. The newcomer took a rapid

34

glance around him, stopped, clicked his heels and stiffly bowed. 'Vogelsang,' he said.

4

HAD Vogelsang been feeling like Birdsong – Meredith reflected afterwards – he might not have chosen to announce himself in this bald but customary Germanic fashion. In which case Meredith would, during certain vital seconds, have had to give him the benefit of a doubt; for he might, after all, have been Scotland Yard's own vanguard sweeping into action. As it was, the truth was instantaneously apparent. The real traveller to Moila had turned up. He was looking with swift suspicion at the bogus one now.

In this crisis – *tanto in discrimine*, thought Meredith as his hand went out towards Bubear's revolver once more – there was only a single ticklish point to decide. The Titian, the Giotto, the Juvenal, and – no doubt – much else: the only faint chance of saving these lay in definite and instantaneous action. Unfortunately, that action would not be justifiable. Consider, thought Meredith, a burglar getting away with all your wordly goods; you might shoot at him if reasonably certain that the effect would not be mortal – but assuredly you would do wrong if you deliberately shot him dead. And so with Vogelsang – whom certainly it would be useless merely to wing. But if all this was clear something else was obscure. There was his own fate and – what he was bound to put first – the fate of the girl. If they were beaten in this desperate game they would infallibly be killed. In fact, he, Meredith, was the protector not merely of sundry masterpieces of art, but of at least one innocent human life besides his own. What then – and here lay the ticklish point – was the right ethical aspect of what might be termed *preventive homicide?*

Some fraction of a second before reaching this point in

his speculations Meredith had raised Bubear's revolver (an engine of which he had no understanding whatever), had aimed it, compressed the trigger, and shot Vogelsang dead. The body lay sprawled on the carpet and Meredith noticed that the effect was rather that of the sort of sensational dust-cover to be met with on railway bookstalls. There was blood, and what must be brains – and this on a carpet which, being genuine Aubusson, it was to be presumed Mr Bubear had detained by way of perquisite from his employers. Meredith felt sorry that he had spoilt this carpet. He also felt very sick. But neither of these things prevented his wheeling round upon Bubear and crying out harshly, 'You fool, it's the police!'

Bubear was puzzled. Probably he was terrified too. And, unfortunately, terror lent him wit. He ran to the body, stooped over it, and in a moment had straightened up with some weapon taken from the dead man in his hand. The tragi-comedy, Meredith saw, must at once reach a further pitch of bewilderment. 'Clear out,' he called. 'Clear out with that damned girl!' And, racing across the room, he pressed himself against the wall by the door through which Vogelsang had come, thrust his right arm through the aperture, and continued to discharge the firearm with which Fate had dowered him. As he was now facing the long subterranean corridor which led to the tobacconist's shop, the resulting echoes and reverberations were innumerable and yielded a most convincing impression of a large-scale gun-fight. He took a quick glance into the antechamber. The secretary was crouched under her ebony and chromium desk. The bank attendant was vindicating his character as a well-armed and resolute man by lying down behind the massive masonry of the Giotto. But from certain further passages over to the left the sound of advancing voices and running feet could be heard. Meredith slammed to the door, shot a bolt and raced back across the room. 'Dozens of them!' he panted. 'Why haven't you got away?'

Even as he spoke Bubear, who was fumbling at a farther wall, stepped back and revealed what appeared to be a small sliding panel masked by a system of pipes which ran down the brickwork. This he had pushed back, and he was now thrusting the girl through the narrow bolt-hole thus revealed. Bubear himself followed and Meredith tumbled through after him; the panel immediately closed and they were left all three standing in a narrow, white-washed corridor, dimly lit by small electric lights, and virtually identical with that through which Meredith had first come.

And here Bubear paused. 'But the police –' he began. He looked full at Meredith and the arm with Vogelsang's weapon stirred at his side. 'Why, you –'

'Look out!' The girl, who had moved a few steps in advance down the corridor, shouted in sudden apparent terror; Bubear, momentarily distracted, swung round towards her; Meredith, as if the concerted action had been long practised for performance on a stage, brought the butt of his revolver hard down on Bubear's head. Bubear made a nasty noise in his throat and fell on the ground. Meredith, not pausing to contemplate the issue of this second stroke of violence, took the girl by the hand and hurried forward. A distant hammering and thumping assured him that some assault had begun upon the room from which they had just fled.

The girl had taken the lead. She must, Meredith thought as he was swung down a side corridor and up a flight of stairs, be what is called an adventuress, and used to this sort of thing. Certainly for one who was to be presumed recently escaped from some species of third degree – But there again, surely, was an obsolete phrase. Perhaps *given the works* was correct, although it rather suggested being handed the complete plays of Shakespeare on a school speech day. For one so recently in a state of evident exhaustion, the girl was displaying a remarkable turn of speed. But then she looked a long way under thirty, and Meredith was forty-nine. Too old to take steep stone stairs three at a time – which was nevertheless what the present exigency required.

For now there were shouts not far behind them, and

seconds after they had reached what must be the first floor of this mysterious building the zip of a bullet past their ears suggested that momentarily at least they had been within sight of their pursuers. They raced down yet another white-washed corridor, swung round a corner, and found themselves in a dimly lit chamber of cathedral-like vastness, wholly void. The thud and echo of their footsteps as they crossed this was like the rout of an army through the colonnades of a deserted city.

Again there were shouts not far behind – and this time, it seemed to Meredith, less by way of mere hubbub and more by way of well-directed hue and cry. Moreover, there were answering calls from somewhere in front of them, a fact the sinister import of which even an amateur could appreciate at once.

But now they were once more in a white-washed corridor – a short one, this time, and from which they emerged upon a further low-lit chamber of an amplitude answering to the first. But whereas the first had been empty this was everywhere filled with uncertainly discerned rectangular masses, in some places scattered singly upon the floor and in others piled in towers and pyramids disappearing into a .dimness of rafters or girders overhead. It was like tumbling into a giants' nursery at night and scurrying forward through a prodigal disorder of building bricks abandoned at the end of a day's tremendous play. Meredith and the girl plunged into the recesses of this fantastic repository. But voices, purposeful and assured, were all around them. They were trapped. The girl, as if realizing that nothing remained but to fight it out, stopped short, gave a quick glance to see that Meredith still had Bubear's gun, and drew him swiftly into the complete shadow of two impending cliffs of the giants' play blocks. Actually, they were packing-cases, Meredith could now see. Was it possible – fantastic thought! – that they were all filled with masterpieces of the world's art? He was about to whisper an urgent inquiry on this when a quick pressure of the girl's hand restrained him. Somebody had run straight past their hiding-place, shouting an order as he went.

The girl was leaning forward, straining every sense. Meredith, acutely aware that his own respiratory and pulmonary systems were shockingly noisy contrivances, crouched motionless beside her. Fortunately, there was a great deal of noise round about. Meredith listened – and presently with something of an analytical ear. His conclusion was a curious one. He and the girl were doubtless the occasion of all this noise. But they were the object of only part of it. A hunt for them, that was to say, was going forward. But so was much else as well.

Hoists and derricks were in operation. Motor-trolleys of the kind which, in recent years, have come to add to the discomforts of a railway platform were clattering over the floor, some with trains of satellite trolleys behind them. Twice beneath their feet there was the roar and throb of a powerful petrol engine, and this was followed by the grinding of gears hastily thrown in and a rapidly diminishing rumble and rubbery shudder through the building. Heavy lorries, in fact, were pulling out into the safety of London. Meredith had a sudden intuition in the darkness of a multifarious and ordered activity all about him. A whole community had sprung to the performance of some complex evolution at a word. *Action stations* – but that was not quite it. *Abandon ship* – he had got it now. Mr Bubear's little branch of the mysterious Properjohn's organization had concluded that it was indeed the police and was hastily closing down. But meantime a sizeable detachment were out for blood.

Blood ... Meredith remembered that he had killed somebody. He had shot an unknown criminal called Vogelsang through the head as a sort of precautionary measure. And another criminal, Bubear, he had at least very decisively knocked out. These were definitive acts. That a little water would clear him of this deed was most assuredly untrue. But unspeakable as was his horror at having killed a man, the main result, he found, was to make him particularly determined not to be killed himself.

He felt cautiously over the revolver and tried to remember how often it had already been fired. Even if he were to be killed – and the girl too – there would be some satisfaction in selling life dearly. Meredith frowned into the darkness as he discovered in himself the strength of this conviction. It was sufficiently pagan; nay, magical, even – for did it not proceed from some obscure comfort in the thought of drawing vanquished enemies with him into the shades? Meredith found that his fingers were no longer exploring the surface of the weapon to any practical purpose – his ignorance, indeed, was too complete to receive any intelligible information from their reports – but were simply caressing it as a hunter might caress a cherished hound … At this moment the girl grabbed him by the sleeve and, doubled up, once more began to run.

Dodging round crates and shapeless canvas packages, he presently discovered that the thought of the hunter's hound had come to him through the simplest prompting of sense. There was, in fact, a hound on the job. Perhaps, indeed, there were two. A very terrible baying, interspersed with slobberings, sniffings, and growls, now mingled with the shouted orders and the warehouse noises farther off. And the primitive sound released some fresh spring of chemicals in Meredith's blood-stream. For the first time he felt afraid. It is true that fear came to him in a sudden apprehension of the true horror of Actaeon's story – the youth by Artemis transformed into a stag and torn to pieces by his own dogs. But although this was the image, the emotion was such as the rudest savage might feel. He was afraid. And he found that, although his joints were no longer supple and he had to run crouched near the floor, he was making better speed than the girl.

Nature had had its moment; nurture supervened. He stopped and turned acknowledging that the rearguard was his place. And as he did so he sighted the bloodhound – for it was that – not six yards behind her. There was more light now, but he must have imagined more of the brute than he actually saw: a slavering, lolloping creature grotesquely compounded of the filmic Pluto and early impressions of the Hound of the Baskervilles. Meredith

40

waited until the girl was abreast of him; then he carefully directed the revolver towards the oncoming creature and pulled the trigger. Unfortunately, the bloodhound did not respond at all as Vogelsang had done, but advanced with increased momentum upon the two of them. They dropped behind a packing case and it pounded by.

Again they ran, knowing that the creature was wheeling fast behind them. And now the noise was redoubled; a second animal was on the trail and bearing down upon them in flank. A moment later they had reached some boundary of the piled-up crates and packages and were stumbling helplessly across a nightmarishly empty floor.

The hounds were behind them, and so close that the chase seemed pretty well over. Meredith remembered that in his waistcoat pocket was a penknife with a blade perhaps two inches long. By no stretch of delirious hope could it be conceived as of the slightest avail, but Meredith fumbled for it as he ran, glancing down as he did so. The motion was almost the end of him, for it distracted his attention from his headlong course and a moment later a collision with a skeletal object, upright and unyielding, knocked most of the breath out of his body. Then he realized that they had attained at last a corner of this enormous chamber, and that what he had charged into was a narrow spiral staircase of cast iron disappearing into the darkness above. He shoved the girl against the lower steps and automatically she began to climb. He followed tumbling on her heels; there was a rush and snap as he did so; he felt the tail of his jacket rend and part; and then he was spiralling upwards free from immediate pursuit. There are few obstacles which a human being can negotiate and a bloodhound in full cry cannot. But a narrow spiral staircase is one. The advantage of bipedal progression comes into play at once.

They corkscrewed rapidly upwards – so rapidly that when Meredith glanced below him the floor appeared to rotate. The surface of the earth, he thought, must look like this from an aeroplane gone into a spin. But at least the two bloodhounds were becoming no more than dark

41

canine smudges, and the figures of several men who had now appeared from the shadows were foreshortening themselves with satisfactory speed. Moreover, no more shots had been fired, and although this no doubt merely signified that they were judged more valuable alive (for a time) than dead, it gave the affair for the moment the feel of a no more than slightly nightmarish hide-and-seek.

Two men were guarding the foot of the staircase, but making no attempt to climb it. The other men were withdrawing hastily, dragging the bloodhounds with them – a manoeuvre the motive of which would have been obscure had not, at this moment, a dozen powerful lights snapped on overhead.

And now the whole situation was instantaneously clear. The place was indeed a species of bulk store or depository of surprising length and breadth and quite astounding height; this interminable spiral staircase led up through several galleries apparently appropriated to the accommodation of lighter articles; and the men who were hauling off the bloodhounds were making for a large lift or enclosed hoist which also linked the galleries at the other end of the hall. Even as Meredith realized this, men and dogs gained their objective and the lift was shooting upwards on a course parallel to theirs. Meredith and the girl, however, had a substantial start, and as a result they gained the topmost gallery on one side in the identical moment at which the lift gained it on the other. They ran, pounding along an openwork, cast-iron floor such as Meredith associated with scientific penitentiaries designed by Jeremy Bentham. The men debouched and ran, together with the dogs, which appeared, however, to be conceiving a disrelish for the whole affair. The men ran, the dogs slithered and slobbered, Meredith and the girl ran until they abruptly saw that running was useless. There was no longer any possibility of keeping ahead, for the men had branched left and right, and whichever way they went it must be straight into the arms of their pursuers.

Or so it seemed – until beneath their feet a fantastic

prospect opened. Besides the lift and the staircase there was a third route down: a sort of giant slippery-dip which plunged earthwards in a dizzying succession of hairpin bends and was presumably employed for the easy delivery of objects of an altogether unbreakable sort. At this Meredith, whose acquaintance with fun fairs was something less than small, stared for a moment uncomprehendingly. But the girl had leapt to it without a pause, and Meredith followed. He had time only to see their baffled pursuers turn again for the lift, and to recall fleetingly Gallileo's formula for bodies moving freely on an inclined plane, when there was a shout from somewhere down below and the whole place disappeared in total darkness. Hurtled from side to side as his battered and breathless body involuntarily negotiated the hairpin bends, and plunging with a steady acceleration into a mere black pit beneath, Meredith profoundly felt the truth of the Virgilian assertion that easy is the descent to hell.

And now would come the bump. *Nunc animis opus, Aenea* – thought Meredith, his mind jumping some hundred lines of the poem – *nunc pectore firmo*. In fact, take a deep breath... He landed on what he suspected was partly a pile of old sacking and partly the girl. The girl and he scrambled to their feet and ran – this time merely from the habit of running, since in the pitch darkness which now enfolded them it was impossible to direct their course upon any rational calculation of chances. They ran and Meredith had the impression that the men were running too – there being no novelty in this except in the obscure impression that they were now running *away*. And upon this impression Meredith would perhaps have halted for better assurance had he not been momentarily unnerved by a new element in the monstrous confusions around him.

This was the shrill reverberation of a high-pitched electric bell which had begun to ring somewhere up in the darkness. The urgent sound had scarcely made itself heard when there was a banging of doors and clattering of feet dying away on distant corridors; and almost at the same moment Meredith and the girl stumbled over something at once soft and massive that lay in their path. The something dismally howled and simultaneously another something fell over them limply but weightily from behind. All this was accompanied by a doggy smell and Meredith, seizing upon so illuminating a scrap of sense-data, conjectured that he, the girl, and the bloodhounds had unwittingly involved themselves in a single complicated tangle. Moreover, they had done so on ground which felt oddly insecure; the floor was gently swinging and twisting beneath them; and Meredith, feeling this, threshed out in sudden unreasoning panic. Both beasts were now abjectly whimpering, and Reason would have told Meredith that as Hounds of the Baskervilles they had fallen altogether short. But Reason had for the moment nodded and Meredith's only instinct was to lay hold on some weapon with which he could belabour the slavering brutes about him. And even as this urgency came upon him his hand in the darkness closed upon what seemed the handle of some such implement as he required. The handle gave – but only some inches, and moving in an arc. At the same moment he was tumbled over again by one of the bloodhounds and the handle slipped from his grasp. And in the same moment, too, there was a deep purr as of some powerful mechanism coming into operation; the floor rose up and punched Meredith hard as he lay on it; a second later his whereabouts was evident; he, the girl, and the abominable if ineffective dogs were hurtling rapidly skywards in the lift.

Such contrivances, Meredith told himself with some confidence, stop automatically upon reaching a point beyond which they are not designed to proceed. But even as he formulated this conviction his mind misgave him. For what was in no sense an express elevator built to haul one up sixty storeys, the machine, even in the darkness, was perceptibly moving with an altogether untoward acceleration. Was it possible – A bone-grinding, nerve-shattering jolt, followed by a deafening confusion of breaking, tearing, and rending noises, interrupted Meredith's speculations. The world had turned topsy-turvy; he was spinning through space; he reached out and grabbed something warm, rough, and moist which even in this distracting moment he absurdly knew to be a bloodhound's slavering and protruding tongue. He was falling perhaps from the top of the building to the bottom, but his chief horror was at a nervous inability to relinquish his grasp on this plainly unavailing lingual support... Then another sense came into play. He was looking at the evening star.

Hesperus, alone in the sky, is not to be mistaken. Around that remote patin of light, single and serene, Meredith rearranged his impressions. He lay in open air with a London sky above him; his horizon was a low parapet of artificial stone; the girl stood beside him, pulling up her stockings; behind her was the disrupted remains of that sort of penthouse which on the roofs of great buildings houses the upper mechanisms of lifts; and lying at her feet, reposeful as if posing for Sir Edwin Landseer, were two large, sleepy, friendly bloodhounds.

Meredith sat up. 'Where', he said, 'is my curly-headed dog-boy?'

The girl let her skirt fall and stared at him. 'Whatever do you mean?'

Meredith passed a hand across his forehead. 'Dear me!' he said. 'You must please forgive me. I spoke quite at random. It was merely what Fuseli used to say of the young Landseer. Landseer, of course, drew animals admirably when very young.'

'I see.' The girl looked at Meredith anxiously in the early twilight. 'I'm afraid you are in a bit of a daze. Something must have hit you on the head.'

'I think not. I fear I have the habit of sometimes saying very inconsequent things. Indeed, it was just such a foolish utterance that gave me the *entrée* to our friends' stronghold this evening.' Meredith frowned. 'Do you know, I think I must be a little dazed after all? *Entrée* must be replaceable by some good straightforward English

45

word. But for the life of me I can't put my tongue to it. By the way, have you ever clutched a dog's tongue in the dark? It is a remarkable sensation, really remarkable.'

'I suppose it must be.' The girl now looked as if her mind on Meredith's intellectuals was quite made up. 'And now we'd better be going. Our perch here is still pretty unhealthy, if you ask me.'

Standing up, Meredith could now see farther about him. Landmarks familiar to him upon his diurnal academic occasions showed new and surprising proportions from this unwonted elevation. They were reassuring, nevertheless. 'Yes,' he said, 'I suppose we had better move on.' He crossed tentatively to the low parapet bounding the flat roof upon which they had been precipitated. 'Do you know, I can just distinguish Smirke's portico? It looks uncommonly impressive in the evening light. But, so far as I can see, we are on a sort of island block. Escape appears impracticable without descending again into the building. How fortunate that these animals have composed their differences with us. Do you know anything about firearms, ma'am? If our assailants follow us to the roof it will be useful to know whether the capacities of this weapon are exhausted.'

The girl took Bubear's revolver from his hand and looked at it. 'Its capacities', she said gravely, 'are exhausted, sir.' She looked about her. 'But I don't think anybody will follow us. And it's just because nobody has followed that I think we had better be off. Call the dogs.'

Meredith turned uncertainly towards the animals. 'Call them?' he said.

'Certainly. You wouldn't leave them to it, would you? And it looks to me rather hopeful over this way.' The girl had moved off to the farther side of the roof. 'Well, I see it's only a girder. I'd rather hoped for a fire-escape or at least a little iron bridge. Do you think you can manage it? I must say you've managed a great deal. And I'm frightfully grateful.' The girl paused. 'Sir,' she added seriously.

Meredith had followed her and the dogs had come at his heel without urging. 'Manage it, ma'am?' He peered

46

at the girl in the dusk with a gleam of humour. Then his voice sharpened. 'Manage *that?*'

The request was certainly formidable. For *that* was a short steel girder, with a flat top some six inches broad, which ran horizontally out from the building some three feet below the level of the parapet and met a farther building at about the same distance below a parapet of similar type. There were indeed, Meredith saw, several identical girders at intervals of some yards; presumably they were designed to give additional stability to the tall old buildings between which they ran; the relevant fact about them, however was that they spanned a chasm the recesses of which dusk was now rendering unplumbable. 'You suggest', said Meredith, 'that we had better get across one of these?'

The girl looked at a wrist-watch – a motion which Meredith had observed her make several times in the preceding couple of minutes. 'I'm terribly sorry.' The girl was sincerely apologetic. 'I'm terribly sorry, sir. But I think we better had.'

'I beg you not to.' Meredith frowned at having said a futile thing. 'If we had a rope perhaps I could help –'

'But we haven't. And I'll go first.' She advanced to the parapet and there for a fraction of a second hesitated.

Meredith laid a hand on her arm. 'Wait.' He swung his legs over. Three feet was a long way down. The girder, in fact, could not be reached while he was in any state of balance unless he turned on his stomach and lowered himself gently while feeling about with his feet. And the disadvantage of this was that he would then be facing the wrong way round – for to walk across the girder backwards would tax an acrobat. There was no help for it. Over on his stomach he must go and the adventure must begin with an awkward about-turn.

Having seen the necessity of these manoeuvres, Meredith proceeded to carry them out. He must not look down. As soon as he had managed the turn, he must look carefully but with no strained fixity at a point on the opposite parapet immediately above the girder and move steadily

47

towards it… And now he was over and his feet had found their hold. He straightened up, paused, turned. The opposite parapet was before him, perhaps ten feet away. Suddenly it came to him from some intuitive depth that looking straight ahead was not his particular line. For other people – yes. But he would do better after taking a good peer down… The muscles first of his neck and then of his eyes rebelled; he mastered them and peered; he saw the walls of the two buildings running down until they almost converged in the gloom. And as Meredith thoughtfully scanned this a hovering vertigo lifted and he walked briskly across the girder with a steady tread. Nor did the opposite parapet offer any difficulty. He had surmounted it before beginning to think how to do so.

'It's not bad,' he called back seriously – and wondered whether he should stand watching the girl or move out of sight. She was on the girder. An appalling conviction of powerlessness seized him. He dropped on his knees and vomited – as quietly as he could. By the time he had recovered from this irresistible natural call the girl was beside him.

'I don't think I could have done it if you hadn't shown me it could be done.' She laughed a little shakily. 'I suppose you are a member of the Alpine Club?'

'The Alpine Club?' Meredith shook his head seriously. 'The Athenaeum is the only club I belong to nowadays. Some of my colleagues have a fondness for mountaineering. But I have always known I had no head for it. Dear me! What of the dogs? They baulked at the spiral staircase. I fear that the girder –'

But the dogs – weirdly enough – had taken the girder. Somehow they had got down to it and were crossing sedately now. The girl watched them, fascinated. 'Ineffective brutes,' she said indulgently. 'More like goats than bloodhounds.' She glanced once more at her watch. 'These roofs carry on right to the end of the street. And we've got to make the other end at the double.'

They made it – the bloodhounds lolloping grotesquely beside them across the grimy London leads. Only when they were as far from Mr Bubear's repository as they could get did the girl stop and begin looking for some trapdoor or staircase that would lead them downwards. Nothing of the sort immediately appeared. She halted. 'I think', she said seriously, 'that we'd better take cover. You never know how these things will go.'

Meredith paused to see the girl drop securely behind a sufficiently massive chimney stack. Then he dropped down himself. But as he did so his glance travelled back the way they had come. Only an upper corner of the scene of his recent adventures was now visible. And even as he looked it disappeared, as if irresistibly sucked outwards and down. A cloud of smoke, a mass of flying debris and dust had taken its place, and in the instant of this appearance the shattering sound of the explosion followed. *And with a quaint device*, thought Meredith at his most random, *the banquet vanishes*... The reverberations died away into subsidiary rumbling scarcely registered by the outraged ear. The air was dust and fume. And suddenly Meredith cried out. 'The Titian!' he exclaimed in agony. 'The Titian and the Giotto –'

'I don't think we need worry.' The girl's face, now a battlefield of sweat and grime, was close to his. 'The birds are flown – in quite a little fleet of pantechnicons. And you may be sure that they've taken all that's really first-class with them.'

'You really think so?' Meredith peered at her hopefully. All of a sudden he looked about him and his face expressed horrified despair. 'But the Juvenal! The Juvenal, ma'am –'

The girl smiled. 'Sir,' she said, 'I brought it along with me.' And from the torn opening of her frock she produced what was to Meredith a miraculously familiar leather wallet. 'It wasn't difficult to guess it was important. But I'm terribly sorry I had to jettison the despatch case you had it in. It was just when we ran –'

'My dear young lady –' began Meredith. Words failed him. 'My dear,' he said, and kissed her rapturously on a sooty nose.

49

THEY came down to earth prosaically enough through an unfastened trap door and a staircase leading past sundry dingy offices. The demolition of which Mr Bubear's organization had engineered the appearance was sufficiently commonplace; a couple of blocks away nobody was at all disturbed. That Meredith and the girl ought to have gone at once and given an account of themselves was undoubted. But an unspoken agreement – perhaps to the simple effect that for the moment they had had enough – took them in the opposite direction. Their clothes were tattered and covered with dust; their faces were begrimed. This in itself excited little remark. But the fact that they were respectfully followed by a brace of bloodhounds did occasionally attract the curious eye, and Meredith, who saw no practicable means of casting off these now faithful companions, felt that it would be pleasant to find a taxi. That a bus conductor could be persuaded to harbour the creatures was unlikely, and the vision of them on an escalator and in a crowded tube was something wilder still... 'I wonder', said Meredith, speaking for the first time since they had gained the street, 'if by any chance we could find a cab?'

'Most improbable, I should say.' The girl replied briskly, but her voice was tired. 'I wonder what the creatures are called? Perhaps we might call them Giotto and Titian. Unless you would prefer Landseer and Fuseli.'

Meredith looked at the girl in alarm – for, having quite forgotten his own bemused reference to those eminent academicians, he found her remark as suggestive of mental derangement as she had a little time before found his. 'Are you sure', he said, 'that you feel fit to walk? We could report –'

'Quite fit.'

'Then perhaps I may escort you home?'

'Escort?' The girl looked at him quaintly and burst into

pleasant laughter. 'I'm so sorry – but somehow it sounded odd after all our caperings. And I haven't got a home in London, I'm afraid.'

'Nothing at all?'

'Quite nothing. Those people brought me here in a lorry, rather uncomfortably jammed up with a bad marble after the Capri Adonis.'

Meredith's brow darkened. 'The damned scoundrels!' And he looked about him as if a policeman had better be found at once.

'Well, I don't know.' The girl was philosophical. 'I asked for it, all right. And they weren't beastly. Just something between rough and –' She stopped. 'Good heavens, Titian's gone after a cat!'

Meredith went after Titian – an uncalled-for act of proprietorship to which he felt obscurely compelled. He returned dragging the animal by the collar. It was really an enormous brute, and more sheepish than ever. 'In that case,' he said – and paused in perplexity. 'In that case, we had better get something to eat.'

'Just that,' said the girl. 'And a bed.'

'Precisely so. That is to say – well, yes.' And Meredith stopped in the middle of the pavement and looked hopefully about him, much as if he expected Elijah's ravens to appear with pies, pasties, and a four-poster – or perhaps single bed-chambers chastely disposed on either side of the street. 'Exactly so. And at once.' He had been on his way, he remembered, to the Athenaeum. He had proposed to himself a little reading in the *Journal of Classical Archaeology*. And on the morrow he had been going to visit Mr Collins, the Peacockian old parasite who cared for the Duke of Nesfield's Library at Nesfield Court. These now seemed projects infinitely remote. And the immediate necessity was indeed a meal. 'At once,' Meredith repeated – and saw the girl, himself, and their attendant quadrupeds walking down Lower Regent Street and presenting themselves in those august apartments so notoriously thronged with 'noblemen and gentlemen distinguished as liberal patrons of science, literature, or

51

the arts'. The Athenaeum would have to be deferred. A restaurant was the thing – but again, they were decidedly grubby; and yet again, there were the dogs. 'I wonder,' Meredith heard himself saying – just as when he had spoken from some depth of mother-wit to Mr Bubear – 'I wonder if you would care to come and have a simple meal in my rooms, and sleep there if it would be convenient to you? Mrs Martin' – rather hurriedly Meredith came forward with this duenna – 'Mrs Martin, my landlady, although a trifle morose, is at bottom a motherly soul, I don't doubt. I am sure she would –'

'Lead the way.' Since he had abandoned addressing the girl as *ma'am*, she had abandoned addressing him as *sir*. 'Decidedly lead the way.' She was looking at him with remote amusement. 'After a square meal I'll be fit for anything. Mothering, even.' Her expression changed. 'You've been very kind. And terribly effective. But I make one condition: no fathering.'

'Fathering?' Meredith was perplexed.

'Look what we've been skipping through hand in hand. It makes us exact contemporaries, it seems to me. Thirty-two is your age – just as it is mine.'

'I see.' Meredith laughed, really amused at this fancy. 'But I'm afraid that the sort of activities into which I have tumbled are more likely to add to my years than to take away from them. The chute we went down, for instance. I should describe that as a definitely ageing experience.'

They had turned into a quiet square – or the remains of it – and as the last light drained from the sky the bleak and pure Augustan façades, the sudden void spaces, the blank party walls, and sprawl of shoring timber began to take on mystery from the night. 'I have no doubt', said Meredith, 'that you know more of what it was all about than I do.' (Was it not to be supposed, he told himself again, that the girl was an adventuress – or perhaps one of those hard-bitten but seductive female reporters who flourish in the tight places of Hollywood films?) He took soundings on this. 'I don't know if you go greatly in for that sort of thing –'

'Definitely not.'

'Ah.' Meredith felt considerably relieved. 'No more do I, as you may guess. And what strikes me about it is the special quality which comes from its being a hazard more or less unique to oneself. I suppose one was in as considerable physical danger on and off for years – but in group contexts, and that makes a world of difference.'

'That – and the suddenness. To be pitched into a fear-situation quite without warning is said to be particularly traumatic.'

'Precisely so.' Meredith, although aware of a faint and friendly mockery, was much pleased to find the girl possessed of a vocabulary of this sort. 'On the other hand, one does recuperate. Granted food, clothing, and shelter, the average human being can carry on indefinitely.'

'And a few familiar objects.' The girl now gravely supplemented him. 'One's own pipe or powder-puff or fireside stool may hold enormous solace. Which is why people dived for and carried away such ridiculous objects in the blitz.'

'That is very true.' Meredith was so struck by the interest of this that he stopped dead in the middle of the pavement. Titian and Giotto lay down and appeared to listen attentively. 'I remember once on an evening like this –' Meredith glanced round in the gathering darkness. 'But – dear me! – here we are. I had scarcely realized that we had arrived.' He turned and moved up a short flight of steps. 'Now, I have only to find my key – But, no – on second thoughts, I think we might ring the bell. It will bring Mrs Martin at once, and we can explain ourselves.'

'Yes,' said the girl, faintly amused again. 'We can do that.'

Mrs Martin had the proportions rather than the expression commonly thought of as motherly; she looked at Meredith with civil foreboding and at the girl not at all.

'Good evening, Mrs Martin; I am afraid you expected me to dine at my club.' Meredith, absent-mindedly endeavouring to remove an overcoat which he was not

53

wearing, very effectively displayed the ravages perpetrated upon his veritable garments by the unregenerate Titian or Giotto of earlier in the evening. 'But the fact is that my friend, Miss –' Only at this moment did it occur to him that the girl's name was unknown to him; and as she had retired some paces to the wardenship of the dogs there was no possibility of a convenient surreptitious prompting. 'The fact is that my friend and I have been involved together –'

'Um,' said Mrs Martin.

'– have been involved together in an exhausting incident –'

'Well, well,' said Mrs Martin.

'– and, being uncommonly hungry, would be glad of whatever your celebrated skill in such matters can put before us.'

'Well, well, well.' Mrs Martin, however, was mollified. 'There'll be somefink, I dare say.' She looked past Meredith and her expression became misdoubting. 'And would those be your friend's 'ounds?'

Meredith considered this for a moment. 'No,' he said; 'I hardly think that we may so describe them. On the contrary, indeed, they are my enemy's.' And he nodded innocently to Mrs Martin, who, presumably accustomed to obscure academic witticisms, let this enigmatic rejoinder pass. 'It would be not inaccurate, I suppose, to describe them as prisoners – or conceivably as booty. It is probable that they would appreciate being found a bone. Or two bones. And no doubt they can pass the night in the area or the basement.'

'Did you say pass the night?'

'Oh, decidedly so.' Meredith had an obscure feeling that there was something of chaperonage in the dogs; the evil constructions to which, as he feared, Mrs Martin was prone would be less colourable in the face of a party of four than of two. 'And, of course, my friend as well. Perhaps you can manage something on the second floor. You see, she can't get home tonight.'

'A pity,' said Mrs Martin.

'Because she doesn't live in London. She came to Town' – it would be politic, it occurred to Meredith, a little to harrow Mrs Martin – 'she came to Town squeezed up with an Adonis in a van.'

'Is that so, now?' It was deplorably plain that the vision conjured up in Mrs Martin's mind by this information was altogether impertinent to the matter.

'With a statue, that is to say. The Adonis of Capri.'

'The Adonis of the coal-cellar, I should have said.' As she uttered this severe witticism Mrs Martin looked more attentively at the girl. 'Well, well, well,' she added with sudden placidity, 'it mightn't be a bad thing if I began by turning on the barfs.'

6

IT was an hour later. Meredith, made philosophical by the rare indulgence of cutlets and sherry, leant forward and poked at a hospitable if diminutive fire.

'Despite your charming fancy', he said, 'I must lay claim to all the years that time has laid upon me. But the fact is that even at my age new facets of human nature are constantly being revealed to one. Here is a woman with whom I have lodged since some time before the war. During this long period my conduct has been almost painfully exemplary. And yet, upon the first occasion of my introducing a lady into the establishment in somewhat unconventional circumstances, all this goes for nothing. Mrs Martin at once supposes me fallen into immoral courses. What I say in the matter she unhesitatingly ignores. Only after a personal appraisal of yourself for which I must really apologize does she relinquish a thoroughly nasty view.'

Meredith laughed unexpectedly. 'And, having provided us with some very tolerable coffee, she is now, I don't doubt, investigating the *mores* of Titian and Giotto.' He laid down the pipe which he had just picked up from the mantelpiece. 'By Jove! Do you know I believe I have some cigarettes?' He jumped up. 'Ten cigarettes for you – I haven't the faintest doubt you smoke – and for me two ounces of tobacco which I bought in a commonplace little shop this afternoon. Do you know Johnson's *London*? "Their ambush here relentless ruffians lay". And "Here falling houses thunder on your head". It is extremely odd that lines so apposite should have been running in my mind as I bought the stuff. Yes, here are the cigarettes – and now let me find you a match. You and I, it is clear, have a tale to tell each other. And I think we might begin by exchanging names.'

The girl had curled up on a sofa and now looked at him through a perfectly defined smoke-ring which she had formed from her first puff of tobacco. 'Yes, Mr Meredith.'

Meredith laid down his pipe once more and looked at her in surprise. 'I don't think I heard Mrs Martin –'

The girl smiled. 'Martial,' she said. 'I used to come to your lectures on Martial at Cambridge.'

'Good heavens! That must be nearly twelve years ago.' Meredith was oddly pleased. 'You know, as simple, expository lectures they weren't at all bad.'

'And they seemed to be extempore. Which made me not so astounded at your dazzling performance this afternoon. Seconds after being dubbed Vogelsang you were piping like the veriest songster of the grove. But not before I had recognized you – and it was lucky that I did. Otherwise I should never have tumbled to it that you were on my side. By the way, my name is Jean Halliwell.'

'God bless my soul! Do you mean to say you wrote those papers on Minoan weapons in the *Hellenic Review*?' Meredith was so surprised that he had jumped up from his chair. 'And I took you for an adventuress or the sort of person sent out by newspapers.'

'I'm terribly sorry to be nothing so romantic. But I did write them and hope to write some more.'

'Of course you wrote them.' Meredith was quite confused. 'And I assure you that by "adventuress" I did not

56

at all imply – That is to say –' He caught Jean Halliwell's eye, recovered suddenly, and sat down again, chuckling, to stuff his pipe. 'I liked them. The *ordonnance* is markedly good. But I am bound to say that in some of your conclusions –' Meredith was once more on his feet, scanning the bookshelves which everywhere reached to the ceiling. 'I believe I could dig you out something by Salzwedel –'

'Which of us', asked Jean Halliwell, 'shall tell the first tale?'

And Meredith explained himself – with quite as much lucidity as if it were the *Epigrammata* of Martial that were in question. Miss Halliwell appeared to find it not at all odd that one should say 'London, a Poem' out aloud in a tobacco shop. 'London, a Poem,' she repeated appreciatively. 'London's goin'. Your tobacconist must have expected a visitor from the very highest circles. Not even the boldest and baddest baronets talk of huntin' and shootin' nowadays. The dropped *g* is confined to a few decrepit peers of the realm. I'm afraid he thought you were a duke – just another duke come to pawn a Gainsborough or Velasquez in a quiet way.'

'Do dukes pawn things to those people?'

'I doubt it. Anything like honest business would be abhorrent to the spirit of the firm. London, a Poem. How foolish of them to have a fellow with so defective an ear. And how foolish of the next lot of people to jump to the conclusion that you were Vogelsang.'

'Or Birdsong.' Meredith frowned. 'I'm afraid there is no doubt at all that I killed him. The – the appearances were conclusive.' (Brains, thought Meredith; brains as well as blood on that Aubusson carpet. He took a good pull at his pipe and discerned in the eddying smoke that his conscience was clear, after all.) 'It is not a thing one would willingly have done.'

'But, being done, it's all to the good. It gives us a line.' Jean Halliwell threw the butt of her cigarette into the fire. 'And now let me tell you about me. The story has points of similarity with your own. That is to say, I passed for a

57

time under false colours too. If I hadn't, I wouldn't know half so much as I do. Not that what I do know is enough. I think you'll find that we have lots to discover still.' She glanced fleetingly at Meredith. 'When we really get going on the job.'

Meredith looked startled. 'Do I understand that you propose –'

'But my introduction to the affair was not like yours. You pushed in without suspecting what it was all about. Although I suppose you must have suspected *something*.'

Meredith recalled his speculations when his eye had first fallen on the dimly lit Horton Venus. 'Well,' he said cautiously, 'my mind did turn over a few commonplace explanations. The reality at least had the charm of being out of the way. But do not let me interrupt you any more.'

'You pushed in without suspecting. I pushed in because I did suspect. And then, when it would have been healthy and possible to push out again, I gave a second obstinate shove. Lord knows why. And that was what I meant by saying that I had asked for it.'

Jean Halliwell paused as if to collect her thoughts and Meredith eyed her speculatively through his tobacco smoke. The horrible death of the creature Vogelsang, she had declared, was *all to the good*. Was so tough an assertion not disconcerting – even, perhaps (and Meredith picked a word from one of his obsolete vocabularies), a shade *un-maidenly?* Or was it merely clear-headed? Certainly the girl was that, and courageous as well. 'Go on,' he said softly.

'It began with my getting ten days' holiday and starting to help some people with a dig. You remember the fun some twenty years ago when all the Viking stuff was dug up at Traprain? Well, these friends of mine were on the trail of something similar in the Pentlands; and off and on they were digging away on some plan I didn't at all understand. You may guess I know nothing whatever about Danish and Norse antiquities. But I love a dig and I went up to help when I could. It was all pretty quiet; we had let out that all those hearty pits and trenches were an obscure sort of geological survey – and if the folk round about didn't believe that one they took it to be a hush-hush hunt for oil, which came to much the same thing. But then we suddenly got a bit of an advertisement. Sir James Presland, who lives in Edinburgh and is no end of a swell in that sort of archaeology, used to come out sometimes and give an eye to the affair. He gave a hand, too – for although he has a great white beard and must be about eighty he just loves going at it with a spade and pick – terribly recklessly, I may say, after the fashion of digging folk of that generation.

'Well, there was little doubt in the end that we were bang on the site. And out came Sir James brandishing his pick as if plumb determined to send it straight through a cinerary urn or a faience goblet. What he did put it through was a skull, and the skull turned out to be embarrassingly recent. In fact, the eminent Presland had unearthed some rather nasty mid-nineteenth-century rime. It was in all the sensational papers, and there was even a decent little column in the *Scotsman*. As a result, everybody knew just what was on and that quite a find might be expected any day. The publicity didn't seem greatly to matter, even though the dig had as often as not to be left deserted during the week. What we were likely to find might have considerable intrinsic value – there might be gold and jewels, that is to say – but the general impression would be that we were eager to dig up a few old swords and helmets... I'm afraid I'm making this story frightfully long.'

'You are making it distinctly intriguing.' Meredith chuckled at what he conceived to be his very modish use of this word. 'I would beg you not to retrench in any way what may appear to you to be the superfluities of your expression.'

Jean Halliwell gave him a momentary wary glance, such as elaborately facetious dons are accustomed to receive from their pupils. 'Well, we were working away one day – cautiously and without Sir James – and suddenly we came on the whole thing. The clue, whatever it was, had led to something very considerable indeed: piles and

59

piles of treasure thieved from all over the place. And there we were, four women and one man, ladling the stuff out as if from a bran pie. We had the use of a shed nearby and we stacked things there for the first night. We had arranged with the nearest police-station for a guard if necessary, and one of us went off on a bicycle and found the bobby assigned to the job. In the end we left both him and the man of our party camped in the hut until various transport arrangements could be made next day. The bobby was a decent chap in a dour Midlothian fashion, and two of his kids came along to see him settled in for the night. And our own man was a decent chap too – minus a leg which he had left in Lybia, but able to give a thoroughly good account of himself if there was trouble. It seemed all right.' Jean Halliwell paused. 'The next bit isn't at all nice.'

'They were attacked?'

'On the following morning there was nothing but a crater, bomb fragments, four bodies, and a lot of archaeological debris.'

'God bless my soul!' Meredith was horrified. 'But those things did fall just anywhere.'

'That is what everybody said. But just consider. That one of the beastly things should land not only just there but *just there on that particular night* is a very big coincidence. And why the bodies of *four* men – two of whom were never identified? It was a pretty hectic month that, one way and another, and I don't know that the technical check-up on the incident was particularly thorough. Anyway, I had to come back south and hadn't much time to think about it. But when I did think I saw more and more clearly that it was queer, and I wrote once or twice to the people who had been in on it. They had managed to collect quite a lot of interesting stuff from the rubble, but when I saw finally that these remains were far more scanty than was natural I definitely began to view the thing as a crime – a very ruthless and horrible crime planned by people with exceptional resources. Faking the death of four people by a particularly violent form of enemy action –'

'But why four?' Meredith found himself as absorbed as he was horrified by this further new world that was swimming into his ken. 'There must have been visitors –'

'Not a bit of it. You see, it wasn't just a matter of blowing up the hut straight away. Our men had to be overpowered, and all the best things removed, and *then* the incident had to be faked. Well, our men were armed, as I said. And, despite being taken by surprise, they gave a good account of themselves – which is why four bodies were finally involved... When I had eventually got all this sorted out in my mind I thought it was about time to go to the police.'

Meredith nodded. 'It most certainly was.'

'But I didn't. I went north again to scout round. You see, I was coming to think of it as *my* mystery. Just as now I'm coming to think of it as *ours*.'

'I see.' Meredith frowned into the fire and then turned to look soberly at the girl. '*Into what dangers would you lead me, Cassius,*' he quoted, '*That you would have me seek into myself For that which is not in me?*'

'*Good Brutus, be prepared to hear.*' Jean Halliwell had leant forward earnestly. '*I, your glass –*' She hesitated.

'*Will modestly discover to yourself That of yourself which you yet know not of.*' He shook his head. 'A few hours ago I had nothing more momentous in front of me than a quiet journey to a great house in Yorkshire. Now you are beckoning me heaven knows where – say out of Anthony Trollope into John Buchan. But proceed. You went north.'

'I went north and presently discovered a good many things. The nearest inhabited spot to the scene of the dig was a tiny village in a fold of the Pentlands, and, although it was nearly a year ago, the folk there remembered the night in question well enough. One of them told me in an incidental way that it was the night the furniture van had broken down just past the church. I was on to that in a jiffy, you may be sure. And it appeared that a great covered removal van had pulled up with engine trouble outside the village, and that the driver and his mate had been tinkering with it until after dark, and that the next

61

morning it was gone. Nobody had thought anything of it. It had been labelled with the name of a familiar Edinburgh firm.

'Well, of course I hurried off to those people – they were a big Princes Street shop – and I said that my grandmother's favourite Aberdeen terrier had been killed on the road on that particular night, and that my grandmother was a little weak in the head and believed that one of the firm's vans was responsible, and that for months I had been trying to dissuade her from going to law –'

'God bless my soul!' Meredith looked at the girl in astonishment. 'For one whose profession is penetrating to the truth in a very difficult historical field, you appear to have a quite remarkable command of fibs. It is clear that private detection might be your *métier* equally with classical archaeology.'

'Thank you very much. Well, I said various things of that sort and then the removal people obligingly looked up their books and showed me that none of their vans had been within ten miles of the place. I said that would cook grandmama's goose all right, and left. And it was just as I left that I was tipped the black spot.'

'You were *threatened?*'

'I got on a tram along with several other people. A couple of stops later, one of them – a man got up in the purest spirit of melodrama with dark glasses and a beard – brushed past me on the way out and hissed, "Keep out of it or it will be the worse for you." After that you can't blame me for rather feeling that I owned a real mystery of my own. And I told you I had been warned. In fact, I went on pushing in where it clearly wasn't healthy – which makes me feel that I must take a sporting view of the uncomfortable things which happened later.' Jean Halliwell paused. 'I'm like you,' she continued presently. 'If those people didn't have, besides a great deal of efficiency, a rich vein of sheer muddle I should be worms' meat at this moment.' She uncurled her legs from under her, stretched them out before the fire as if for Meredith's contemplation and her own, and nodded. 'Worms' meat,' she repeated.

'But I anticipate. And, really, the yarn is stretching out interminably.

'So let me hurry on. The problem was to get a fresh line on the criminals, since the scent of the Pentlands affair was a bit cold. Now, it could hardly have been an isolated enterprise. For simply to come by an eighth-century pirate hoard would not be at all an easy road to wealth unless one had an extensive connexion in the whole trade – the whole trade of illicit trafficking in works of art, that is to say. You probably know that there has always been such a trade and that the war produced quite a boom in it. Well, here were fairly large-scale operators, and they had a distinctive technique. Could I come on any trace of it elsewhere? Suddenly I remembered an extraordinary story that had been told me by a man in the A.M.P.C. here in town. It was about Horton House.'

Meredith sat up. 'And the Venus?'

'Well, yes – in a way. Some months before the house received a direct hit and was destroyed there was a very queer false alarm immediately after a heavy raid. A time-bomb had been located just between the house and the river, all the appropriate personnel turned up, and there was the regular evacuation – which meant, it seems, just the old Duke and a few servants. Everything looked quite as it should do when the Duke went off in a taxi – but when he got tired of sitting in his club and decided to go back and see if his Town house was still in existence he found that the whole circus had just faded out. Being an intelligent old person, he had decided within ten minutes that the affair was an elaborately planned screen for robbery. So he hurried about the house – a great barn of a place it must have been – and was astounded to find that nothing was missing. He even went down to a deep cellar where he had stowed his Titian. But here the lady was – vulnerable to attack, you might say, but safe and sound, nevertheless. Or so he thought. And of course he had to decide that his shrewd notion of a robbery was fallacious, after all, and that there had just been a glorious muddle. So he held his peace, feeling that to clamour for an investigation would merely be getting in the way. Now, what do you think of that? It struck me at once as a coup of a very high-class order indeed. There must have been masses of valuable stuff to lift for the asking. But nothing was actually taken except one extremely valuable painting – of which a copy had been prepared, at least good enough to stand the scrutiny of an old gentleman in a cellar. I don't doubt that the Duke knew the lady's every curve and dimple, but the light would be bad and the circumstances agitating.'

Jean Halliwell paused, perhaps to observe the effect of this sally on a respectable student of Juvenal and Martial. 'I don't know what happened when Horton House was really bombed, but I believe it is supposed that the Titian escaped. By that time, however, the real Titian was in hiding while awaiting disposal. And you and I are the only honest people who know its whereabouts – or its whereabouts three hours ago.

'So here was a not altogether dissimilar affair. At Horton House there had been another concealing of theft under cloak of a hazard of war. And these people were equally pleased with one of the world's greatest paintings or a collection of Viking helmets and Iberian bronzes. In other words, they were in business on a grand scale. And with uncomfortably large tracts of Europe in no end of a mess they were probably doing quite nicely too.'

Jean Halliwell stretched sleepily and yawned. 'But all this is just something I remembered and chewed over while sitting in a bedroom in the Caledonian Hotel and squinting up through a thick Edinburgh fog at the Castle. It didn't really give me a line... What was I saying?'

'That it didn't really give you a line.' Meredith was wondering whether he ought to ring for Mrs Martin and have this young person tucked up in bed. 'I'm afraid you must feel –'

'Not a line – just that. Well, it looked as if I were at a dead end. It was true that the gang – I had come to think of it as that – seemed to have a permanent representative in Edinburgh, and that he had got wind of my unhealthy curiosity quickly enough. But the Pentlands affair had been a single isolated operation, and it wasn't likely that there would be much more in the way of traces in – in what's it called?' – again Jean Halliwell yawned – 'in Midlothian. The best thing would probably be to pack up and come to Town. But – unexpectedly enough – that was done for me… How comfortable this sofa is. Warm, too, with your lovely fire.'

'I think, perhaps –'

'And now, after boring you a great deal, I come to the exciting part of my story. There I was … I was sitting in my hotel bedroom … and somebody … and somebody knocked at the door. Somebody –'

Jean Halliwell was asleep.

7

BUT to Meredith himself sleep did not come for several hours. He lay awake listening to the ebbing of the slender traffic in those quiet squares, rehearsing what he had in the latter part of this day experienced, speculating on what lay before him on the morrow. The girl belonged to his own world; at the same time, if not an adventuress, she was decidedly an adventurer. She had plunged into danger, and he could clearly read the fact that she proposed to plunge in again. Men of that sort, for all his retired life in colleges and libraries, Meredith had met in plenty. Such men had a daemon and must always be testing themselves in a tight corner, a strait place. But a female of this species was something new and required adjusting to; not the less so because there appeared no atom of the mannish in her composition. Jean Halliwell was for seeing her adventure through without help from the big armies of order and law. This, although she had but hinted it, he could discern. And he himself Fate had made a partner in her enterprise – unless he behaved at once in a sensible way.

Yet he had scarcely begun sensibly. It was altogether absurd to cast fragments of Augustan poetry at a tobacconist, even in Bloomsbury. It was ridiculous to walk into a parlour to which the spider was under some palpable misapprehension inviting one. It was entirely indecorous to bring two bloodhounds and a girl home for the night... Meredith turned over in bed and listened. Through his open window and from somewhere below came a faint and comfortable slavering noise, from which it was to be inferred that either Giotto or Titian was enjoying toothsome dreams. Yes, his conduct had been high-fantastical – and never more so than in the crazy impersonation into which he had been precipitated.

Meredith reviewed his brief career as Vogelsang. And as he went over the queer scene he detected (he thought) a tentative stirring of vanity within him. Really, he had brought it off not ill. Moreover, quite a new Meredith had come to birth in the affair – and it is pleasant – *intriguing*, as the young people say – in the later forties to turn a corner and come upon an alternative self.

Descrying this in his conscience Meredith endeavoured to harden his heart against adventure. But the unknown and problematical called to him, much as it often did from some ancient codex awaiting palaeographical elucidation. *Consignment 99 ... Marsden's lot ... the Mykonos Marbles.* The phrases knocked at Meredith's brain as mysteriously as the unknown hand had done upon the girl's bedroom door at the moment when she had broken off in her narrative. *Moila ... Properjohn ... Chicago's going.* Could Chicago go? – Meredith wondered as he felt the first approaches of sleep at last. Could he go ... go to Moila?

> For who would leave, unbrib'd, Hibernia's land,
> Or change the rocks of Scotland for the Strand?

Must he change the Strand – and Gower Street and Mecklenburg Square – for the rocks of Scotland?

> Resolved at length, from vice and *London* far,
> To breathe in distant fields a purer air...

66

Could Mrs Martin really have suspected him of *vice?*...
Meredith, too, was asleep.

And in the morning, pouring tea in a brocaded dressing-gown which he had years before discarded as a vanity, Jean Halliwell told the rest of her story. *The Times* was propped before her on the hot-water jug and on her left a Bradshaw jostled with the marmalade. Meredith looked in some surprise at the newspaper – simply because he had never, in that room, seen it propped in front of another person before. At the time-table he glanced with apprehension, conscious of a decision yet unmade. And then he looked at the girl.

Sleep had recruited her as rapidly as it might recruit a sick child, with the result that one was less aware of her good looks – which were there, nevertheless – than of an abounding well-being and vitality. Jean Halliwell would have been best described as hearty if there had not been a subdued play of sensibility over her features, discernible to the attentive eye. If obliged to define her briefly, Meredith decided, he would record her as a mature young woman in excellent fleece. No doubt this would be regarded as inadequate by an expert in such inventories, but it was as far as he could get without what he felt would be an impertinent appraisal of her charms... Meredith sat down before what Mrs Martin had provided, contrived with a momentary effort to fall into his customary abstracted inspection of the plane trees in the gardens outside, and prepared to hear what more the girl chose to tell.

'I suppose you have met Higbed?' she asked unexpectedly.

'The psychiatrist – or perhaps I ought to say the polymath?' Meredith chuckled. 'My own attitude to knowledge is very old-fashioned, I fear. Everything about something and something about everything is my generation's prescription – and although only the second part is nowadays at all feasible it is the first that is the more important. Providence, I sometimes think, has made the human span just long enough for the tolerable mastering of a single field. So the Higbeds, who are so fortunate as to know the greater part of everything, a little disconcert me, I confess. They are the modern Sophists, are they not? Only we on our side unfortunately entirely lack our Socrates. Or would you say that Whitehead fitted the role – or Dewey?' Meredith paused speculatively – and in doing so caught himself up. 'Dear me, what a lot of blather! Yes, I know Higbed. But surely he does not come into your tale?'

'Quite definitely. In fact, it was he who knocked on the door of my hotel bedroom that afternoon in Edinburgh. It was quite an accident; he had lost his own room and was going very cautiously to work finding it again. But as it happened I had met him in a casual way shortly before, and he recognized me at once. It's always gratifying to be taken notice of by a celebrity –'

'My dear, I think you should really have snubbed him. His views are unsound and his conduct at least questionable. I cannot believe that you would find his conversation improving.' Meredith delivered himself of this speech very firmly and reached for the marmalade.

Jean Halliwell looked at him with a sort of comical gravity. 'I'm afraid I didn't think of it like that. We went down and had a drink – which is worse and worse, I fear – and he talked a great deal. At first he talked just like one of his books, which was entertaining enough – though unsound, no doubt. But I could see that he had something else on his mind, and that he had collared me and was being fascinating only because he felt that was how the great big male Higbed should move about the world.' Jean Halliwell looked candidly at Meredith. 'Picking up superior girls in good hotels.'

'My dear Jean!' Meredith was startled into this address. 'Pray come to what he had on his mind.'

'Pantechnicons.'

'*What?*'

'Just that. Big furniture-removing vans. Mighty forms that do not live. Like living things moved slowly through his mind by day, and were a trouble to his dreams... You can't say that *my* conversation isn't improving. It is replete with apposite references to the great monuments of our culture. But there's the fact. The all-learned Higbed was scared of removal vans. They kept on following him round. Or so he had managed to convince himself.'

Meredith looked at Jean in perplexity. 'However did he come to make you this extraordinary confidence?'

'Quite suddenly. He was talking away about mandates, or micro-chemistry, or mysticism in Mandalay, and at the same time conscientiously eyeing my knees in a very lascivious way –' Jean paused. 'I'm terribly sorry. It's the fathering business that tempts me to say these things. Anyway, Higbed was jawing away like that when he suddenly did a sort of breakdown. Rather startling in one whose profession is breaking up breakdowns, in a manner of speaking. What happened was this. Mandalay or micro-chemistry incontinently died away on his lips, and he leant forward and whispered agitatedly: "Have you noticed what a lot of furniture vans have been about recently?"

'It would have been a queer enough thing to have said to one in any circumstances, wouldn't it? But, considering what I had just been on the track of, it was positively head-swirling. And my head swirled. "There *have* been a lot, haven't there?" he said. It was quite piteous. He had even forgotten to look at me as the great male Higbed should. But I hadn't quite forgiven him – I suppose I don't awfully like being fascinated in hotel lounges, after all – and I felt a bit vicious. "A lot of them?" I said. "Not a bit of it. They grow scarcer and scarcer, like whisky and taxis. I haven't noticed one for months."

'And that floored him altogether. "It's a neurosis," he whimpered. "It's a new and horrible neurosis. And I've got it bad!" For a minute he was quite weepy, and then he plucked up and started gassing about it. Nothing so interesting had come his way for a long time. He was suffering from the hallucination of being followed about by furniture vans. Plainly they were symbols of the maternal womb. But while everybody sought a return to the maternal womb, he had never heard of anyone being pursued by it. Yet here was a great uterine symbol dogging him about the streets first of London and then of Edinburgh. He had come down to give a lecture on the psychopathology of colour-blindness, and one of these vans had trailed him to Euston. When he got out of the train in Edinburgh there was another of them waiting.'

Meredith shook his head. 'I can't really believe –'

'It took a bit of swallowing. But I asked him a crucial question at once: had he noticed the name on the Edinburgh maternal symbol? And he had. It was the name of the perfectly respectable Princes Street firm that had been used by the bogus van in the Pentlands affair. I simply looked at Higbed and goggled.

'Higbed is no Titian. In fact, he would have made a very striking portrait by Sargent. It didn't seem possible that they were after him as a work of art – so what could this extraordinary story mean? If it hadn't been Higbed, a well-known public figure, I should have suspected that the friends of the bearded and darkglasses man were after me still, and that this yarn was some fantastic trap. As it was, the thing was either really a hallucination, in which case I had bumped up against an astounding coincidence, or it was a sober fact – in which case it was putting me on the trail again, however unaccountable it might be in itself. So what should I do? Obviously, test it out.

'"It's bad," I said; "isn't it? The sort of neurosis that leads straight on into something thoroughly psychotic." Higbed fairly slavered at that; he might have been Giotto in one of his most hangdog moments. "But perhaps", I said, "it's not too late to pull up. Or, rather, to let your-self go. Because I suspect the trouble is some sort of in-hibition. Probably you've been deferring too much to a narrow conventional morality. After all, there's nothing like moral purity for slipping one into the looney-bin." Higbed didn't quite know how to take that. So I gave him an amorous *œillade* or speaking look – one that would have utterly shocked Don Juan, if I may say so. And after a second Higbed registered it.'

Meredith fairly groaned. 'All this', he said, 'is worse than I could have supposed. Your involvement in the affair has put you to the most disagreeable necessities.'

'Quite so. Well, he registered it, as I say. And then I proposed a walkabout. We were to stroll through Auld Reekie's dusk together. Do you know Edinburgh? There is a hill just short of the village of Corstorphine which goes by the name of Rest-and-be-thankful. And through its bosky recesses there winds quite a lovers' lane. Delicately indicating all this –'

Meredith agitatedly stirred his tea.

'Well, we were to go there. I could see that it was all much too rapid for the great, big, predatory Higgy. Still, he was quite sure that he ought to be fascinated and compelled –'

'Abominable!' said Meredith.

'But, after all, the man's bread and butter is grounded in the conviction that Rest-and-be-thankful is something the sexual man just doesn't know. *Vénus toute entière à sa proie attachée* right round the clock. Anyway, we set out, romantically seated side by side on the top of an electric tram. It was dusk by this time, all right, and I sat staring straight ahead of me.'

'I am glad to hear it.'

'I mean that I didn't try to peer out and see if there was a great big pantechnicon following the great big amorist and me. That could wait. It waited until the tram stopped at the foot of an eminently respectable thoroughfare called Murrayfield Road. Along this lay our route to dalliance, and off we got. And there was the pantechnicon, sure enough. I was suddenly and utterly afraid.'

'And not unreasonably, my dear. These people had killed one of your friends and a policeman. What you were doing was incredibly rash. But, since you must have had a certain amount of intelligent anticipation, it was extremely courageous as well.'

'It was just what you might call bringing matters to a head. If pantechnicons had dogged Higbed through a couple of capital cities, it wasn't with a view to his summary liquidation. They wanted the live – the so terribly live and vital – man. Now they were going to get him, and I was going to be the pound of tea thrown in by the way. We walked up on the left of this Murrayfield Road, with the kerb on one side of us and a high stone wall on the other. When we were about a hundred yards, up the van turned in from the main road and followed us. I think Higbed heard the engine; anyway, he turned his head and saw the thing. "I'm seeing it," he said in a desperate voice. "It's coming up the hill." I looked round too and did my best to stare into empty space – which wasn't altogether easy, for really the great bulk of the thing looked uncommonly sinister and threatening. "How very interesting," I said. "There isn't even a shadow on the ground to suggest such a thing. I think we'd better hurry on."

'And now the van was pretty well abreast of us. On the one side of the road was this high wall. On the other were two semi-detached villas without a sign of life. I was just trying to imagine that I heard the footfalls of a bobby on his beat when the thing happened. The van stopped, enclosing us in a sort of canyon. Higbed gave a horrid yelp. "Don't be an ass," I said. "You're fancying things." And then the big doors at the back of the van opened and our capture was effected without the slightest fuss. No revolvers, no knocking on the head. We were simply hustled in. The road to Rest-and-be-thankful had passed, you might say, straight through Chicago.'

'Bless me!' Meredith looked at Jean with renewed astonishment. 'I thought I did something uncommonly out-of-the-way when I stepped through that little tobacconist's trap-door. But to lay yourself out to be abducted by known assassins –'

'The return to the womb. I must just have had a neurosis, like Higbed. And there he was – his uterine symbol suddenly materialized, and himself swallowed up in it as surprised as could be. Having myself had a Biblical childhood rather than a scientific one, I felt much more as if it were the whale, and Jonah's catastrophe had included an unknown *compagnon de voyage*. Not that the inside of the pantechnicon held anything to reinforce either suggestion. For one thing, it was brightly lit. And for another, it was just like an office in a high-rental area. Everything smart and very compact. Typewriter, filing cabinets, and two clerkly men sitting on each side of a desk. A little form was provided for Higbed and myself; it was meagre and moderately uncomfortable; just the sort of thing you would keep minor clients waiting on if you wanted to make them feel small.'

'I cannot imagine that any business could be successfully conducted –'

'You're behind the times. But that is less disturbing than being behind two stout wood and iron doors painted to look like the back of a furniture van. Higbed was gasping like a fish, and I suppose it was a bit of a shock to realize that he was in his right mind after all – if he did realize it, which I rather doubt. One of the clerkly men was looking at me with a good deal of disfavour. "I don't think we wanted a woman as well," he said – rather doubtfully, and fumbling in some sort of card-index the while. His companion was much more decisive. "We certainly don't want a woman," he said. "We have absolutely no occasion for one. It's an extremely awkward thing."

'There were two plug-uglies inside the van as well; they had done the greater part of the hustling. It was plain that they resented the second clerkly man's attitude a good deal. To my mind, they had done a pretty good job, and it was rather tough to blame them for landing their bosses with a slight *embarras de richesses*. But now the clerkly men were checking up on Higbed from a file. "It's him, all right," said the first. "But who would want a fellow like that?" "Who, indeed," said the second. "Can you see yourself leaving a thousand pounds in notes to get *him* back again? Blessed if I can." "It's nothing like that," said the first. "Lord knows what it is, but it's nothing like that. Perhaps he did a little double-crossing – something a bit too nasty to have him just dumped quietly in the

73

Forth for." And then he looked at me. "As for the girl,"
he said, "we'd better dump her there at once." "Oh,
decidedly," said the second. "Tell them to drive there
straight away. And get out a sack." And, sure enough,
one of the plug-uglies gave orders to the driver through a
little shutter, and the other fished out a sack from a locker.
"Here," he said – and it was the first word that had been
directly addressed to either of us – "get into this."

'I didn't feel too good. Compared with the inside of a
sack destined for the bottom of the Firth of Forth, that
furniture van was just all that the warm precincts of the
cheerful day could be. I even cast one longing ling'ring
look at Higgy. And at that moment the first clerkly man
– the indecisive one – took a good look at me. Not at all
an interested look – but, after all, he wouldn't have another chance. "Hold hard," he said. "I think that girl's
on the list." He turned to the other fellow. "Where's the
requisition book?" he asked. "I've got an idea you'll find
this girl's mug in it, after all." And the other fellow
fumbled in a drawer. Presently he was ransacking the
whole van. "That's funny," he said. "In fact, it's uncommon awkward. I don't often lose the requisition book"
And he took a squint at me. "But you're right," he said.
"She's there, for certain. I've got it! She's one of Marsden's girls." "Do you think so?" said the first man – a bit
doubtfully. "I don't seem to remember –" "Of course she
is," said the decided man. And he turned to me. "You're
one of Marsden's girls, aren't you?" '

Jean Halliwell paused and followed Meredith's gaze
thoughtfully out to the plane trees. 'Well, it seemed that
or the Forth. "Of course I am," I said. "I'm Marsden's
best girl." And after that, as you might say, the die was
cast.'

Meredith reached over and peered into the teapot. 'It
was a bold move,' he said.

'Well, if they had no occasion for a plain girl, Marsden's
girl it must be. And, if Marsden's girl at all, why not his
best girl? I certainly didn't at all know what I was letting
myself in for – any more than you did when you became

74

Vogelsang. But anything was better than a sack. My kittenish days, as you must have remarked, are long since over, and that sort of drowning just didn't appeal. So I became one of Marsden's girls and remained so until we did our bolt this afternoon. Indeed, I don't suppose it has yet occurred to them that I am anything else.' Jean Halliwell fished out her last night's packet of cigarettes. 'And that's all I have to tell.'

Meredith looked at her in perplexity. 'But my dear Jean – if my years may give me the privilege of calling you so – you have brought your astonishing narrative only to the point –'

'But the rest you can pretty well infer. Marsden is some rival racketeer in *objets d'art*. And he had lifted the Mykonos Marbles from the Properjon-Bubear lot – who must in turn somehow have contrived to lift them from their home in Budapest. That was why somebody of Marsden's was wanted who might be induced to spill the beans.'

'Spill the beans?' Meredith shook his head. 'Do you know, I believe your idiom in these matters is sometimes as obsolete as my own? And here, surely, is a sign of the instability of the times. Formerly, canting language was quite durable, and Robert Greene's foists and coney-catchers would have been substantially intelligible to Fielding's Jonathan Wild. But nowadays the language of criminals renews itself every lustre.' He shook his head and sighed. 'But this is typical of the futility of the scholar's calling today. We take refuge from unpleasant present facts in the mere fripperies of philology. And your predicament was certainly an unpleasant fact enough. If it were not that here you are safe and sound in this room, I could scarcely bear to think of it.'

'It was awkward enough.' Jean nodded soberly. 'I knew none of the things that I was supposed to know, and that those rather unscrupulous people were determined to learn. So the next few days had their actively displeasing side. And my return to Town was altogether lacking in amenity. Just what would have happened in the end I don't at all know. But then you walked in – and extremely grateful I am. Moreover' – and Jean smiled happily – 'the balance to date is all on the credit side. It was taken for granted that I knew so much that in actual fact I learnt quite a lot. Properjohn and Neff and Moila: I began a little to see how these fragments fitted together. We are in quite a strong position to plan our next move.'

There was silence in Meredith's book-lined room. Meredith took a long puff at his pipe. But unlike the pasteboard devotees of the weed among whom his adventures had begun, his expression was troubled. 'My dear,' he said, 'can you offer me a single substantial reason why we should not at once take this story to the police?'

'You know I can't.'

'We must consider what is at stake. Canvases by Titian and frescoes by Giotto, Hellenic marbles and Cnossos figurines, are by no means counters to be hazarded in a game of personal adventure. But it would be impertinent in me to lecture you on that.'

'We will spend the next couple of hours putting everything relevant on paper, and lodge the document with appropriate instructions at your bank. At the moment we should be thought mad as hatters. More attention will be paid to the thing if we never come back.'

Meredith smiled. 'You are trying to think of reasons, after all. But none will hold. There is nothing to take you an inch further in this thing on your own except some personal rule of conduct to which you happen to subscribe.'

'As you do, too. The trapdoor and Vogelsang attest it.'

'I confess that when I look into my heart I see that I would not willingly draw back. But I am an elderly man with nothing before me except editing Juvenal, probably by no means so well as I have already edited Martial. It is different with you.' Meredith had stood up and was looking very serious. 'Unless I am entirely mistaken you are not the sort of woman whom an aberrant psychic constitution prompts to live among the Turks or scale the Himalayas. You have your work, which is as good as any man's in your field. But you also have –'

'I also have you.' Jean Halliwell's eyes were suddenly

alive – with mischief and with more than mischief. 'I've got you! And of what other male can I say that? You are going to come. And Bradshaw is before us.'

He looked at her for a moment in very great surprise. 'I'm afraid it may be a bit out of date,' he said. 'Better confirm the times by telephone.'

8

THE morning had advanced. Meredith scanned the last of several sheets of foolscap, closely covered in his fine hand. 'I think', he said, 'that all the material particulars are there. And now we had better find out about Moila ... Yes, Mrs Martin?'

The landlady, who had provided breakfast from within a cloud of considerable reserve, was standing in the doorway with some shapeless object in her hand. She spoke with deliberation, her eye scanning the room meanwhile – much as if she expected further tattered but well-poised girls to have appeared in it. 'Mr Meredith, sir, and beg pardon for hinterrumping, but I would be obliged to 'ave your wishes on the 'ounds.'

'The hounds, Mrs Martin?'

'The 'ounds, Mr Meredith, sir – and very friendly-disposed they did appear to be. But now I must confess to apprehensials, sir. Sitting on each side of the kitchen range, they was, for all the world like a calendar from the grocer. But now one of them 'as gorn and been sick in the mews.'

'Dear me! I am extremely sorry. But the mews would seem a not unsuitable choice –'

'It's *wot* he sicked, Mr Meredith, that has gorn to give me the apprehensials, I confess.' Dramatically, Mrs Martin held a ragged garment up in air. 'If I were to say, now, Mr Meredith, sir, that this 'ere was your best jacket you would not denige of it?'

'Assuredly not. It is certainly the remains of what might be so described. But I assure you –'

Mrs Martin held the garment higher still and pointed to a large hiatus. 'What the brute sicked', she said, 'was *that*. And it give me a fair turn orl right.'

Meredith nodded placidly. 'My dear Mrs Martin, it is certainly true that the creature attacked me. But both it and its companion appear subsequently to have undergone a change of heart.'

'A change of 'eart?' said Mrs Martin, and held the garment higher still. 'I don't know that I ever 'eard –' She stopped as there was a clatter on the floor. 'Now wot –'

It was Bubear's revolver, dropped lucklessly from the pocket into which Meredith must at some stage of his adventures have dropped it. Jean stooped and picked it up. 'No call for more apprehension on this, Mrs Martin,' she said. 'It's been fired until it can be fired no more.'

'That's just what I used to say of my old man.' Mrs Martin was suddenly as emphatic as she was inconsequent. 'Lorst more jobs, 'e did, than the queen has bangles.' She stopped and stared. 'It wouldn't be a *gun*, now?' Her eyes widened. 'Mr Meredith wouldn't be going packing a gun?'

'Packing a gun? Dear me, no. I have no intention of taking a firearm with me.' Meredith smiled, suddenly understanding. 'Ah, *packing* a gun. I perceive, Mrs Martin, that you do not go to the cinemas for nothing. And – well – last night I was very decidedly packing a gun.'

'Which would be why, Mr Meredith, sir, there would be brains on your boots?'

'*Brains on my boots!*' Meredith recalled the Aubusson carpet and stared at his landlady in horror.

Mrs Martin nodded with paralysing placidity. 'They do say as how they splatter,' she said. 'They do say they splatter somethink chronic.' She lowered her voice. 'Mr Meredith, sir, and beg pardon for being inquisitial, but 'ow did you buy orf the police dorgs? Would it 'ave been wiv a chop?'

'Really, Mrs Martin, the matter was not quite as you would appear to apprehend. It is hardly possible to explain –'

'Wot I would 'ave you tell me, Mr Meredith, sir, is this: 'ow am I to explain the 'ounds when you and the young lady is gorn? For going I can see you are – and very natural too in the circumstantials. But the 'ounds will be inquired after, I don't doubt.' Her glance strayed to the desk at which Meredith had been writing, and to the substantial document which lay there. 'Lord a mercy!' she exclaimed. 'If you haven't been and wrote out a confession. Now just you be going and packing up unobtrusive like, and give that to me to put straight into the kitchen range.'

It was plain that Mrs Martin supposed her learned lodger to have committed some homicidal act – probably of the species *crime passionnel*. It was equally plain that she had no thought of being other than an accessory after the fact. Meredith looked at her in some perplexity. 'Perhaps,' he said – and knew that his words were to be without inspiration – 'perhaps the hounds will just go away.'

Mrs Martin shook her head despondingly. 'Would that I were Mandrake!' she said – and paused as if to admire this literary turn of phrase. 'Would that I were Mandrake Mr Meredith, sir.'

'Mandrake, Mrs Martin?' This was a reference altogether outside the circle of Meredith's cultivation. 'Do I understand you to refer to a plant of the genus *Mandragora?*'

'A magician, Mr Meredith – one as wot changes 'umans into 'ounds reg'lar. And I could say I had done that to you and Miss Halliwell 'ere.'

'Bless my soul!' Meredith looked mildly surprised at this Circean proposal. 'It would certainly be what might be termed a false scent. But I must assure you that you are altogether under a misapprehension. As far as I know, the police are not, in fact, looking for Miss Halliwell and myself; and I believe that none of the King's judges would hold that I had committed a crime.'

79

Mrs Martin shook her head sadly. 'Ah, Mr Meredith, sir,' she said, 'they all believes that until the black and fatal moment comes. Would you be liking a taxi, or would it be more curcumspecial to go out by the back?'

Meredith sighed. 'The back, Mrs Martin – by all means, the back. And I hope to return to you in a few days' time.'

'Um,' said Mrs Martin.

'If I do not, you will find that suitable arrangements have been made. And I would like to say that, despite an abstraction and reserve of which no one is more painfully conscious than myself, I have always greatly appreciated your kindly and competent ministrations.'

'There, now – if you aren't a regular gentleman!' Dropping Meredith's mutilated jacket and lifting up a crumpled apron, Mrs Martin wept. 'I know as 'ow there will be money in it,' she whimpered. 'My hexclusive story in the Sunday papers and a photograph as well – 'olding the 'ounds, as likely as not. But oh, Mr Meredith, sir, would that I were Mandrake!' And Mrs Martin ran blubbering from the room.

'Really,' said Meredith, 'it is hard to know how to take this good woman. Not only is she assisting us, as she believes, to cheat the gallows, but she is taking that course without thinking twice about it. And although in this instance it is all to our benefit, I cannot help feeling that the morals of the Metropolitan populace have been somewhat impaired by the times we live in.'

Jean Halliwell, who was endeavouring to take a comprehensive survey of her dilapidated person in two inches of pocket mirror, laughed aloud. 'Juvenal speaks!' she said. '*Resolved at length* – How does it go?'

'Ah! you have remembered Johnson:

> Resolved at length, from vice and *London* far,
> To breathe in distant fields a purer air …

Meredith paused. 'Well, I suppose that is just what we are going to do. The road to Moila lies right over peat and heather – to say nothing of some little part at least of the stormy waters of the North Minch. And, talking of Dr Johnson, he was there himself, you know, in 1773, or thereabouts. Boswell's is a very amusing account of the whole adventure. There may be considerable charm in following some of his footsteps.' And Meredith, momentarily seeing the hazardous escapade before him in the mild character of a literary pilgrimage, turned to search for an atlas. 'When he met Lord Monboddo and debated whether our ancestors had tails –'

'We shan't meet Lord Monboddo.' Jean had put her mirror away. 'But we do hope to meet the arch-conspirator, Properjohn. A prim and harmless sort of name, don't you think? But we may find ourselves rather wishing that we were Mandrake, nevertheless. That the distant fields will yield a purer air is altogether problematical.'

Meredith, now studying a map, chuckled comfortably. 'It will be an excellent plan to begin by making each other's flesh creep. And here is one way to do it: let us remember last night and the very sufficient alarms we experienced on the mere periphery of the business. And by that measure let us compute the kind of reception we are likely to receive at its centre.'

'Our arrival will at least be totally unexpected. For the gang must undoubtedly believe that we are dead.'

'I am inclined to agree with you in that.' And Meredith nodded – now gravely enough. 'In addition to destroying we don't know what compromising matter, the explosion was certainly designed to eliminate ourselves. But just what all these people made of the situation, it would be hard to say.'

'I think I'd risk saying that they had once more lost the requisition book. Of course, it's a terrifying organization and all that – but I have a kind of feeling that a pleasing vein of muddle runs right through it. Think of the absurdity of swallowing you as Vogelsang! Incidentally, and whether Bubear is alive still or dead, I'm banking a lot on that.'

Meredith frowned. He was now packing a suitcase – which with him meant beginning with a substantial layer

81

of books. 'You mean that he will want to keep mum about the whole thing?'

'Just that. He was careless, and as a result the real Vogelsang was killed and the whole depot or whatever it is to be called was abandoned and destroyed in a panic. He doesn't know what you were after; he doesn't perhaps *really* know whether you were the real Vogelsang or not; he just knows that *both* claimants to the name were killed – as was Marsden's girl before she gave any information on the Mykonos Marbles. Now, Bubear has been cheating his bosses, as we know, and ten to one it will be his instinct to obscure the discreditable truth of last night's junketings behind whatever fibs come first into his head. And there's one other point – a fact I gathered when I was picking up what I could. This Vogelsang, as far as personal acquaintance goes, was to be quite a new contact. Properjohn had never met him. There may be a strong card in that yet.'

Meredith, having half-filled his suitcase with Latin authors, had gone to seek pyjamas and socks. 'Your mind', he called from his bedroom, 'moves naturally to the tune of romance – or indeed of that strip-fiction in which you and Mrs Martin are both so well read. Or I ought to say *so well seen* – a capital use for an old idiom. For the effort of reading is unnecessary with such things, and hence their charm.'

'I'm making the effort to read Bradshaw. And it will be effort, I expect, all the way. To get on trains and to stay there. Likely enough, it will be corridors all the time.'

'All that.' Meredith reappeared with a safety razor and a tooth-brush. 'Moreover, our movements may be complicated by coming upon areas still under some species of military jurisdiction. I should imagine that those islands –' He broke off, his eye meditatively upon Jean. 'By the way … it rather occurs to me that your attire … I mean that if it is really cold –' And Meredith stopped, much confused.

'You mean I look as if I had come out of a rag-bag – and you would prefer to travel with something from a band-box? But that is going to be fixed right away. Mrs Martin is taking upon herself to lend me an outfit of her daughter Minnie's things. Are you nearly ready? I think I'll go and get into them now.'

'Minnie Martin's things?' Meredith appeared scarcely relieved. 'I really greatly fear –'

But Jean was gone. And Meredith crossed to the window and peered thoughtfully across the square. It occurred to him to count the plane trees; he had never done so before; he felt it unlikely that he would have the chance again. Then his glance strayed over familiar objects: a shelter, a ruined house, a great tank of water filmed with rust and oil. He turned at a sound behind him and found that it was Jean who had re-entered the room. Obscurely perplexed, he studied her as she stood fully equipped for travel. '*Minnie's* clothes?' he said.

'Of course.'

He shook his head. 'I always understood that clothes, although they may be very simple, must be *good*. To give a certain effect, that is to say. And I am sure that Minnie, although an excellent child –'

'You have been misinformed.' Jean produced the two inches of mirror once more. 'It's not the quality. It's the way one puts them on.'

'Is that so?' Meredith was interested and impressed. 'I am afraid that I know far too little of the *mundus mulierum*.'

'Unlike Higbed, to whom all things womanly are an open book.'

'Dear me! I had entirely forgotten him. Have you any idea of what befell the poor man?'

Jean shook her head. 'None whatever. We were separated quite early on. I have no more idea of what they did with him than I have – or these clerkly men had – of why he was wanted. Or requisitioned, as they liked to say.'

'Well, well!' said Meredith. 'I wonder if we shall meet him in Moila?'

Part Two

THE FLYING FOXES OF MOILA

I

THE Isle of Moila lies off the west coast of Scotland at a point not remote from Loch Torridon, and is separated from the mainland by the Sound of Moila, a shallow and stormy channel, treacherously strewn with submerged rock, which at its narrowest point shows a breadth of little more than a quarter of a mile. The coast is here precipitous, the island being but an outlying spur to the central massif of Ben Carron, from which some prehistoric cataclysm has sundered it by the narrow gash of the Sound. It thus comes about that the cliffs of the mainland are higher than, and dominate, those of the Isle – so that were warfare to be supposed in these well-nigh solitary fastnesses it would appear that a light artillery could quickly subdue the few hundred acres to which Moila extends and destroy whatever of human artifice had been here reared amid the solemn architecture of Nature.

But such building as Moila shows antedates by far the effective exploitation of gunpowder; and Castle Moila was for centuries second only to Tantallon in the impregnability which its situation conferred. For the westermost tip of the island is formed by a precipitous peninsula, somewhat the shape of a gaping beak or lobster's claw, to which the only access is by a short and winding causey dizzily poised above a seething sea some hundred feet below. On this peninsula the castle is built, its massive keep facing towards the island, and its two main courts occupying each a limb or jaw of the peninsula and crowning these naturally inexpugnable ramparts with a further *vallum* of frowning and crenellated stone. It thus comes about that from the inner embrasures of the building the prospect is of a small and secluded natural anchorage nestling within the foundations of the castle far below. Beyond this the view is of sea and the dimness of distant islands, with, however, the little islet of Inchfarr scarcely more than a furlong's length away.

The greater part of Castle Moila had been a ruin for centuries – and indeed anyone studying the beautiful series of steel-faced etchings of the building which Robert Billings included in his *Baronial and Ecclesiastical Antiquities* just a hundred years ago would suppose that no corner of it could remain inhabitable. A habitation, however, it has always been, and its tenant the hereditary Captain holding from the Marquis of Raasay. Only at the beginning of the present century, and when Fortune possessed this dignitary of another castle altogether more eligible for residence – substantially weatherproof, indeed – did this venerable disposition cease to obtain. The hereditary Captain moved out, taking all his possessions with him in three market wains and a governess cart, and Castle Moila was for a time delivered over to the gulls and the gannets.

These fowl had for centuries proliferated on Inchfarr (a fact, this, which was to be peculiarly fateful for the history we relate) and now upon the abandonment of the castle they extended the boundaries of their domain. Soon the dark and towering walls of the great ruin were everywhere white with their droppings, and gleamed like an inexplicable fantasy of snow against the long green rigs of poppy-sprinkled oats on the body of the island. And regularly once a fortnight in the tourist season there would appear from Oban a far-ranging paddle-steamer, its decks supporting some hundreds of trippers, two or three favoured rams or ewes in pens, and an old man who played Hebridean music on a xylophone. This argosy would thump its way cautiously between Moila and Inchfarr, and at an appropriate moment a long wail from its siren would start myriads of seafowl from the rocks and battlements to circle and scream in the air. Whereupon the paddle-steamer, its mission accomplished, would waddle round Inchfarr and head for home, while the passengers, their thirst for natural beauty slaked, would retire to a cold luncheon in the saloon. At irregular intervals, too, there would come a smaller steamer, decently propelled by a screw, and devoted to that transporting of flocks of sheep from island to island which is one of the few observable activities of the region. This steamer would tie up within the very foundations of the castle – up and through which and across the causey to the island its baaing and bleating cargo would then be discharged. For some years these were the only human activities that Castle Moila saw. Had there been anything to shoot on the island, the place might have been called a shooting-box and let to some guileless American. Had there been a stream to fish, some financier from Glasgow might have been found to sophisticate the ruins into a hydropathic or a hotel. As it was, the birds had it all their own way.

There came a time, however, when the hereditary Captain found his well-roofed mainland domicile increasingly embarrassed by the characterful behaviour of a number of elder sisters. When the finally disruptive moment arrived, two of these ladies – whose names were Miss Isabella and Miss Dorcas Macleod – flatly declined to retire to the dower house of the estate, maintaining that the great-aunt who held sway there was a witch. Whereupon the hereditary Captain bethought himself of what he held from the Marquis of Raasay, consulted with his factor on certain quantities of floor-board, wainscoting, and slate, with his grieve on a due provision of goats, pigs, and chickens, and, finally, with the Misses Isabella and Dorcas themselves on a convenient date for their early remove to the island. Then, and by way of graceful afterthought, he moved sundry Writers to the Signet, Advocates, and Solicitors to the Supreme Courts in Edinburgh to effect a transference of staff and baton. Miss Isabella Macleod had barely ceased coping with the more obtrusive impertinences of the gulls and gannets about her new abode when she was informed that the Marquis of Raasay had gained the Royal concurrence in a notable change in feudal tenure. She was herself hereditary Captain of the Castle of Moila.

To hold the office, however, it proved to be necessary that Miss Isabella should in person present the Marquis with a pair of velvet breeches yearly – and as this nobleman (with great public spirit) had agreed to govern one of his sovereign's remoter colonies, the feudal service thus required was not merely rather indelicate, but quite impracticable as well; and the matter was finally adjusted by the lady's despatching a substantial cheque annually to her overlord's bankers. Her purse being already in the straitened case usual with those offshoots of the Highland aristocracy who have failed to attach themselves in some way to the prosperity of the *Sasunnach*, the charge was a considerable burden. Nor was Miss Isabella's displeasure in any way mitigated when the Marquis from his antipodean retreat ingeniously turned himself into a Limited Company. That the descendant of an earl who fell on Flodden Field should be periodically in need of velvet breeches is in itself not probable; nevertheless, there was about the transaction a colouring of antiquity that had rendered tolerable even the compounding for it with a cheque that would have bought several complete wardrobes. But Limited Companies, while they live on cheques and indeed for them, are inconceivable in breeches, velvet or otherwise; and Miss Isabella never put her signature to this yearly quittance without following it with a Gaelic curse upon the composition of which, pacing her battlements in the long twilight of the Islands, she was accustomed to bestow considerable literary skill. But as the cheque made its way direct to Leadenhall Street and was there dealt with by a resident of Plumstead not particularly well-traded in tongues these careful exercises in a language admirably adapted for imprecation were taken to represent merely so many styles and titles which this remote Celtic lady thought proper to append to her name.

Moreover, no amount of cursing could mitigate the drastic effect upon the bank balance of the Misses Macleod. It was this that gave Mr Properjohn his chance.

Mr Properjohn, although a person of no particular nationality, might be classed as a *Sasunnach* – and it seemed very likely that he was himself a limited company as well. Moreover, he was – or had been on the occasion of his first appearance – a tourist, staying at a mainland hotel some ten miles away with an orthodox paraphernalia of brand new guns and rods (on the chance of making the acquaintance of the gentry) and golf clubs (on a calculation that he probably would not). Or so the inhabitants read him – and not the kindlier for his appearing in a kilt, something of a solecism even where kilts are worn, and very definitely so where they are not.

To be a tourist was to fall, in the estimation of the Misses Macleod and of their housekeeper, into a middling category difficult to deal with. Travellers – whom the ladies thought of vaguely as country gentlemen sequacious of Antiquities and the Picturesque, traversing the country in a chariot or a chaise – travellers were to be received at any time and shown over the castle by Mrs Cameron. Etiquette required that the Misses Macleod should be declared not in residence, and to maintain this fiction they would lurk for half an hour on end in a servant's bedroom or a privy. Should some mischance, however, actually bring about an encounter with a Traveller it was necessary that courtesies should be interchanged, and a glass of whisky and an oat-cake offered and discussed. Travellers were thus definitely of the eighteenth century.

Trippers belonged equally definitely to the twentieth. They used paddle steamers and chars-à-bancs. They moved in droves. The Misses Macleod had no doubts about Trippers. They were a menacing tide in no circumstances to be let break against the rocks of Moila.

Tourists came in between. Their aura was of Birmingham and the later Victorian age. It was known that people had been marrying their sons and even daughters to the children of Tourists for quite a long time. The

88

advent of a Tourist was thus regularly the occasion of anxious debate. And it was in this category that Mr Properjohn was provisionally placed when Hamish Macleod rowed him across to Moila in his boat.

Mr Properjohn, as has been mentioned, was wearing a kilt – and this attracted the eye of Miss Dorcas Macleod, one of whose favourite bedside books was the *Vestiarium Scoticum* of Sobieski Stuart. It was late afternoon and Miss Dorcas had been walking on the keep, whither it was her custom to repair at this hour in order to feed a small flock of pigeons who there led a somewhat harried existence amid the ocean fowl. The season was autumnal and the mists were chill. Miss Dorcas was dressed in a balaclava helmet and British warm abandoned by her brother, the former hereditary Captain, some twenty-five years before. Her figure was thus not particularly suggestive of the Celtic Twilight; pacing the crumbling battlements, she looked rather more like Marcellus or Bernardo about to meet the Ghost in a modern-dress production of the tragedy of *Hamlet*. And when Mr Properjohn came into view approaching the causey she halted as abruptly as if about to demand that he should stand and unfold himself.

The curiosity of Miss Dorcas was scientific rather than personal, for the fact was that the tartan sported by Mr Properjohn was unknown to her. Momentarily, indeed, she took that mingling of greens crossed by a narrow yellow line to betoken the approach of a Campbell of Breadalbane; and then – the darker green taking on a bluish tinge in the level light of early evening – she conjectured that the visitor might even be a Gordon. But then there was scarlet too, and what looked uncommonly like lines of ultramarine. Miss Dorcas was puzzled and disturbed. She set down the pannikin of breadcrumbs which she had brought for the pigeons and leant precariously over the keep for better observation. Meanwhile, Mr Properjohn (whose tartan had, in fact, been invented some six months previously by a tailor within reasonable hail of Savile Row) approached the castle and walked confidently across the drawbridge. He looked as if he were about to buy the place. And, as it happened, it was approximately this that was in his mind.

It would have been customary upon such an occasion for Miss Dorcas to make her way hurriedly to the castle's flagstaff and there lower the little standard which indicated that the hereditary Captain and herself were at home. The ladies would then have retired to their bedchambers – or to the kitchen if the day was chilly – and thus permit Mrs Cameron or the man Tammas to show the visitor round. But Miss Dorcas was so interested in the new tartan – the wearer of which, as she could now see, further sported an outsize dirk, or *skeandhu*, in his stocking – that she hurried down the long winding-stair of the keep, strode across the base-court and herself threw open the wicket in the great door of the castle. No sooner had she done this than she was overwhelmed with a sense of the temerity and impropriety of her conduct.

Mr Properjohn was passing somewhat apprehensively beneath the portcullis. At the same time he was calculating (as it happened) just what this might fetch if sold to a gentleman then engaged in rapidly assembling a medieval castle in the neighbourhood of Pasadena, Cal. Thus Miss Dorcas's confusion was for a moment matched by the visitor's abstraction and apprehension, and they looked at each other without speaking. Mr Properjohn wore a sporran of white horsehair and shining silver – including what appeared to be the representation of a camelopard rampant. At the sight of this garment, appropriate only to a parade ground or a ballroom, Miss Dorcas's heart further misgave her. And then Mr Properjohn raised his hat.

Mr Properjohn *raised his hat*, which is a motion so socially distinct from *taking it off* that Miss Dorcas at once apprehended the worst. Moreover, the hat being, as it happened, a glengarry bonnet, and Mr Properjohn fumbling with it while held suspended above his head, it returned to its resting place back to front, with the result that two broad black ribbons hung down on each side of

Mr Properjohn's nose. Miss Dorcas found this so very funny that she laughed unrestrainedly – so loudly, indeed, as to raise clouds of screaming gulls from the precipitous slopes of the causey. All this, together with the intermittent reverberation of breakers upon the rocks below and the farmyard noises which were never absent from the base-court, appeared to put the visitor to considerable confusion. It was with a view to relieving this, as well as atoning for her discourtesy, that Miss Dorcas mildly said: 'Good afternoon. I think that perhaps you are a Traveller?'

Now this (as the reader knows) was to falsify her own judgement in the matter and convey something of a compliment. Miss Dorcas was therefore much at a loss when Mr Properjohn – still from behind the two black ribbons – at once replied in the negative and with a good deal of offended pride. The fact was, of course, that by this form of words he supposed himself to be taxed with peddling refrigerators or vacuum-cleaners; and it is conceivable that he felt his acumen as well as his dignity to be assailed by Miss Dorcas's conjecture. For assuredly the vacuum-cleaner that could hope to cope with Castle Moila still lay in the womb of time, while a refrigerator would have been altogether misplaced there.

'My goot man,' said Mr Properjohn (being led altogether astray by the balaclava, the British warm, and the Hebridean ruggedness of Miss Dorcas's features), 'my goot man, I am the director of six, seven big large companies – some the largest biggest companies of industrial chemistry operating presently. So please permit you take my cart to your mistress. *Sogleich.*' And Mr Properjohn produced a square of pasteboard on which Miss Dorcas found inscribed:

AMOS WILLOUGHBY PROPERJOHN,
MANAGING DIRECTOR
Macrocosmic Chemicals, Ltd, Inc., and Prop.

Miss Dorcas studied this, and found at least the end of it as incomprehensible as the bank found her sister's curses.

And while Miss Dorcas studied Mr Properjohn's card Mr Properjohn studied the gulls – watching their multitudinous gyrations with such benevolent and indeed proprietary approval that he might have been taken, standing in this wild place in his Celtic habiliments, to represent that Angus of the Birds so beautifully celebrated by the late W. B. Yeats. And, unlike the Enoch Arden of an earlier poet, he appeared to find the myriad scream of these ocean fowl definitely to his taste. Almost, it might have been the chink of guineas on a counter that was sounding in his ear. As it happened, this was very much what it did, in fact, represent.

'I am afraid', said Miss Dorcas, 'that it is now some years since my sister has received.'

'Say!' What Mr Properjohn put into this interjection was a large and cordial interest – nor did he appear at all abashed by the revelation that it was a Miss Macleod who addressed him. 'But that's definite what I come about. Now onworts I promise your sister she receive regular as clockwork – *sempre!*'

Miss Dorcas was a good deal startled by this impertinence. 'Sir,' she began, 'I fear that some strange misapprehension –'

'In fak, quarterly,' continued Mr Properjohn. 'And you leave it to me I work it so it don't pay no taxes neither.'

'Do I understand you to suggest that my sister, Miss Isabella, is to receive *money?*' Miss Dorcas, whose quick grasp of a contingency so unlikely as this did her wits much credit, looked with entirely fresh interest at the exotic Mr Properjohn. 'And that your call upon her is in the capacity of a man of business?'

'Sure! *Véritablement!* Money from home!' Mr Properjohn exuded confidence and cheer. 'And there is no inconveniences – no inconveniences in the worlt. Even we are able to be of a liddle direk service – and you permit my saying service is the motto of our organization – and do ourselves a piece of goot the same time. And that is what service is, no?'

'It is a species', said Miss Dorcas drily, 'of which the rumour has reached us, I confess.'

'Then that's capital.' Mr Properjohn had added a large obtuseness to his aura. 'A little direk service in the way of giving the castle – your wonderful old castle – a goot clean up.'

'A clean up!'

'Exak so. And if you should care to replace this contrivance' – and Mr Properjohn gestured upwards at the portcullis – 'by a puttikler handsome front door, or even some the finest wrought iron gates including high-class heraldic device –'

'The portcullis was there', said Miss Dorcas, 'in the age of Prince Charles Edward, who passed under it in the year 1745. It was then perhaps six hundred years old. So I fancy it may last our time.'

'Six hundut years!' Mr Properjohn, who saw that he had been altogether below the mark in what he had supposed this feudal contraption might fetch in Pasadena, sighed with brief regret. 'But what we can do round abouts the castle is small matters. It's like maybe you got an odder island and we make a deal on that?'

'You mean Inchfarr?' It occurred to Miss Dorcas for the first time that this fancy-dress *Sasunnach* might be astray in his wits. Quite possibly he was bewitched – and conceivable by Great-aunt Patuffa of the dower-house. It was not at all improbable, when she came to think of it, that Great-aunt Patuffa had deliberately despatched him as a plague on Moila. The gold he offered would be fairy gold – and it would prove so. 'Inchfarr?' repeated Miss Dorcas warily.

'Inchfarr. *Jawohl*.' Mr Properjohn was emphatic. 'I understand your sister owns it?'

'Miss Isabella, the hereditary Captain, holds not in chief, but from the Marquis of Raasay.' Miss Dorcas spoke at once with dignity and caution. 'The feu is therefore subject to the payment of chiefery, as also of teinds to the Synod of Argyll. Subject to these, I have little doubt that His Majesty would be pleased to regard our holding as inalienable. Always supposing, that is to say, that we remained well affected to his Throne and Person.'

'*Par exemple!*' said Mr Properjohn – the more confidently in that this novel angle on the real-estate business both bewildered and impressed him.

'As there is little doubt that we should do. The present Pretender is a gracious and charming Prince, with whom my sister and I were privileged to dine in Rome some twenty years ago. But it is now several generations since we have had any doubts on the expediency of the Hanoverian Settlement.'

'Natchly,' said Mr Properjohn. 'I can say I met few several kinks myself and they looks like maybe lorts of creation you go in to them first. But start talking business and they acts like they were you or me.' Mr Properjohn paused on this reminiscence and his glance rose once more to the wheeling gulls. 'Peeutiful birts!' he cried with enthusiasm. 'Always at it even on the wink. Always industrials like the bees.'

2

THE fabrication of a mystery being far from the purpose of the present narrative, it will already be abundantly clear to the reader that Mr Properjohn (of Macrocosmic Chemicals, Ltd, Inc., and Prop.) was – ostensibly, at least – after guano, that valuable manure formed by the immemorial droppings of birds (or bats). Hence his pleasing enthusiasm for the industriousness of the feathered myriads of Moila and Inchfarr. And no doubt, had the bats of Castle Moila been numbered by hundreds of thousands (instead of merely by hundreds), he would have been equally lyrical about them. As it was, he now followed Miss Dorcas across the base-court with his gaze so elevated to the skies that he first stumbled over a recumbent sow and seconds later almost precipitated himself down the castle's oubliette. Had not Miss Dorcas – who was by no means disposed to let even fairy gold vanish into a dungeon – grasped him by the tail of his kilt he would undoubtedly have gone the way of Sir Mungo Macalpine (who had entered into an unfortunate dispute with a hereditary Captain in the later fourteenth century) and of Black Malcolm, a minstrel who had failed to commend himself to the ear (it was said) of a hereditary Captain's lady some fifty years later, and whose plaintive strains could still be heard issuing from the bowels of the castle on any tolerably calm night when the moon was full.

From the company of this melodious shade, then, Miss Dorcas just snatched Mr Properjohn, and led him firmly through the remaining offices to the superior parts of the castle. The man Tammas – who, with the slow motion effect common to all Island activities, was slitting the throat of a calf – paused in astonishment at the spectacle, so that he looked rather like Abraham when in doubts about Isaac, his knife poised in air. And Mrs Cameron – with even more of deliberation, she was wringing the neck of a rooster – stood so transfixed before the apparition of Miss Dorcas in familiar conversation with an outlandishly attired stranger that she bore much the appearance of Lot's wife at the fatal moment of taking a backward glance at Sodom – a Biblical occasion, as it happened, vividly commemorated in sampler work above Mrs Cameron's bed.

Mr Properjohn removed his eye from the welkin sufficiently long to take a passing glance at these retainers. 'I suppose', he said, 'that you keep a great many servants in a such place like this? Butlers and valets and five, six, ten hired girls?'

'We are waited upon by Mrs Cameron and Tammas. The needs of my sister and myself are extremely simple.' Miss Dorcas's reply was absent and betrayed no consciousness of offence. She was trying to think of anything – apart from the portcullis – for which this fantastically ill-informed person could possibly propose to part with a quarterly cheque. Could it be the Raeburn? There was no

95

chance whatever of her sister's being persuaded to sacrifice that. Could it be Uncle Alastair's Landseers? Miss Dorcas was dimly aware that Landseers were not quite what they had once been. Might Mr Properjohn, despite his commercial connection, be himself an artist and merely desirous of hiring a studio with superior marine views? But artists, Miss Dorcas was quite sure, do not wear the wrong sort of sporran and seldom talk about hired girls. There flitted through her mind the possibility that this unaccountable stranger, as a fugitive from justice – had he not said something about avoiding income tax? – and proposed to pay handsomely for asylum. Castle Moila had harboured plenty of such people in its time – commonly *gratis*, but occasionally for cash down. And a commercial man was, of course, peculiarly likely to be in such trouble. Yet there was something a little too obtrusive about Mr Properjohn for this explanation to fit – unless, indeed, he regarded his garish costume as a sort of protective colouring which should virtually compose him into the landscape of the Highlands of Scotland ... Miss Dorcas had got so far in her speculations – to little purpose, it must be confessed – when she became aware of her sister regarding her with a very minimum of approval from the steps of the banqueting-hall.

Mr Properjohn, having been at fault with his first Miss Macleod, was determined to make no mistake with this elder lady. Sweeping off his glengarry bonnet with a new and altogether more generous gesture, he contrived a blended bow and genuflection which might have satisfied the most stringent sense of feudal decorum. 'Goot afternoon,' he said agreeably to Miss Isabella. 'May I venture to express the hope that your Excellency finds herself in her accustomed peeutiful health?'

This was a species of address which Mr Properjohn had known to answer capitally in various corners of Europe – and particularly when he was conducting business in the Balkan countries (whether with kings or others) through the medium of an interpreter. As both the approach to Moila along the Glasgow and Mallaig line, and also the condition of the peasantry so far as he had been able to observe it, strongly reminded him of the wildness and poverty of those other outposts of Europe, it had struck him that this was the likely line to take.

'Bless me!' said Miss Isabella. 'Dorcas, what in the world is this?'

'An offer of for certain five hundut pounts a year.' Mr Properjohn interrupted deftly with what his Balkan experience told him was the next important point. 'And no inconvenience – no inconvenience whatever. We undertake we take special care that the machinery is puttikler noiseless and thoroughly safe –'

'A man from the paddle steamers!' Miss Isabella cried with indignation. 'I suppose, sir, that you wish to tie up in the anchorage? And to land trippers to prowl the castle? Let me tell you that it is not the policy of the Macleods to admit a superior force within their gates. Troth has been broken before this, and hospitality betrayed. Begone, sir!'

Mr Properjohn, while not penetrating precisely to the truth of the matter (which was simply that the hereditary Captain's mind was prone to slip rather suddenly into the past and out again), realized that the moment was critical. He put his hand first to a hip pocket – or to where a hip pocket would have been in a *Sasunnach* normally clad – and then to his resplendent sporran. From this he drew a cheque-book. 'The first payment', he said, 'being on the nail. *Ça ira!* Your Excellency need only say the wort.'

'Dorcas,' said Miss Isabella, 'is this person a *banker?*' And the hereditary Captain's gaze, which was penetrating and indeed a trifle wild, travelled past her visitor in what was distinguishably the direction of the oubliette.

'By no means, Tibbie.' Miss Dorcas, though a woman formidable enough in herself, spoke in some nervous agitation. 'Mr Properjohn – whom I wish to present to you – is a man of business. But not by any means a banker. Nor do I think that he is connected with the paddle steamers. It would appear that he has proposals to make to you which are in some way connected with Inchfarr.

And by drawing out his cheque-book he merely means to imply that the arrangement would result in the immediate payment of a sum of money.'

Miss Isabella, whose eyes had been narrowed on Mr Properjohn's tartan and gargantuan *skeandhu*, widened them abruptly at this. 'Stay!' she said commandingly to Mr Properjohn. 'We admit parley.' And, turning round, she led the way into the recesses of her castle.

Mr Properjohn took one last look at the gulls – for, having some artistry in his temperament, he had almost persuaded himself that they were indeed the end of his manoeuvres – and followed. His step was lighter and his kilt swung gallantly as he moved – gallantly enough to have done credit to the Black Watch or the Gay Gordons. For he had won the day and knew it.

Or perhaps it should be said that Mr Properjohn had won the evening. For the sun was now low in the western heaven; the precipitous rocks of Inchfarr, gleaming white at other hours of the day, were a dark silhouette against its broadening mass; presently the reddening disk would spill itself into a line of fire on the horizon and disappear. The castle was a place of sprawling shadows and fantastically eroded forms shot through by fugitive gleams of light like some vast prone skeleton in which fireflies danced. And Mr Properjohn, as if he were indeed a Traveller eager for the Picturesque, took the plainest delight in this romantically-accented gloaming, this Gothic twilight. His enthusiasm, if not always intelligent, was unflagging – and the more interesting for being absent-mindedly expressed in several languages. 'Peeutiful!' he exclaimed when viewing what remained of the vaulting of the banqueting-hall. '*Wunderschön!*' And '*Wunderbar!*' and '*Ausgezeichnet!*' he murmured as he was led up the interminable staircase buried in the wall of the keep; and when conducted to the dizzying *Aussichtspunkt* of the uppermost bartisan he declared that the sheer drop to the moat below was *effrayant* in the extreme. The Misses Macleod, who, like all good Scots, lived far closer to Europe than Englishmen contrive to do, were considerably taken with this pronounced if puzzling cosmopolitanism. They scarcely noticed that without a further word of business having been spoken they had themselves unprecedentedly conducted a stranger on the grand tour of Castle Moila – a tour the final stages of which had to be accomplished behind a flaming torch born aloft by the flabbergasted Tammas. '*Uomo da bosco e da riviera*,' said Mr Properjohn in appraising Tammas himself. '*Bel cecino!*' And on finding that Tammas was stone-deaf, very short-sighted, something crippled, and much astray in his wits, Mr Properjohn's enthusiasm rose to such a pitch that he gave him half a crown. This, although extremely surprising to everybody, was perhaps less curious than his pronounced approbation of the well-nigh grotesquely inconvenient living arrangements to which the Misses Macleod had been obliged to submit themselves in their island home.

It will be recalled that Castle Moila consists of two main courts, each occupying a limb or claw of the bifurcate peninsula upon which the building stands, these being linked together by the massive keep at that point where the castle faces the causey to the body of the island. The general form is thus that of a vast semicircle or half-girdle of stone, the inner face of which follows and crowns the great arc of cliff and scree which surround the deep and retired anchorage below. But on all this seaward side of the castle the ravages of past military science, as also of everpresent and eating Time, have been extreme, so that here are nothing but broken walls and roofless chambers, spiral staircases ending in air, and masses of masonry mysteriously impending over empty space, with darnel and thistle and sea-holly growing from clefts in the immemorial stone. Only on the extreme outer perimeter of the far-spreading pile is there a series of high and narrow chambers in which habitation is possible.

For the Misses Macleod, therefore, life in the castle was rather like life in the corridors of a railway train frozen into immobility while rounding a sharp curve and then pounded and pashed into debris in all its parts save the interminable concatenation of corridors themselves. And as all the inhabited parts of Castle Moila faced towards Moila itself and the mainland, and none of them towards Inchsfarr and the open sea, it was evident that the anchorage was no more under the observation of human eye than when the previous hereditary Captain had departed with his governess cart and Moila had been abandoned to the seagulls. It was after Mr Properjohn had satisfied himself of this, and had surveyed, from a hazardous perch on the crumbling Western Ward, the pitchy darkness of the deepwater inlet below, that he returned to his business proposals. By this time it had become plain that whisky and oatcakes must be provided, and it was while discussing these in Miss Macleod's solar – an apartment furnished in the Victorian taste, but always referred to under this finely medieval name – that Mr Properjohn explained about the Flying Foxes.

Mr Properjohn had successfully employed Flying Foxes – more technically known as a telpher span – in numerous parts of the world. If the Misses Macleod had ever visited the mining districts of Western Australia –

The Misses Macleod disclaimed being travelled after this fashion, but admitted to a voyage in the Adriatic in the course of which they were tolerably confident that they had disembarked and spent some nights at Spalato, which was no doubt the same place that Mr Properjohn referred to as Split. Miss Isabella seemed to remember that their hostelry had been called the *Grand Hôtel de l'Univers*; Miss Dorcas did verily believe that Mr Properjohn's Flying Foxes had there been within the field of observation from her bedroom window. Miss Isabella had no recollection of the Foxes, but her conviction as to the name of the hotel strengthened, and she was prepared to allow Miss Dorcas the Foxes if Miss Dorcas allowed her this. Mr Properjohn produced paper and pencil and showed the old ladies (for so we may now without ungallantry describe them) how Flying Foxes work. And although Miss Isabella's mind wandered away every now and then to the Forty-Five or farther, and Miss Dorcas's to plumbing (for Miss Dorcas had all her life longed for *drains*; the idea of them fascinated her; and on five hundred a year wonders might be possible) – although the old ladies, we say, listened only amid these distractions, Mr Properjohn yet contrived to make of it all a most friendly and informative evening. The Flying Foxes would approach virtually noiselessly from the mainland; they would sweep high over the castle above an ample provision of safety-nets; three pylons, or at the most four, would carry them on to Inchfarr. There they would be loaded with the guano – of which the deposits were so tremendous as to justify this machinery – and return as they had come. When they reached the mainland once more their jaws would open, the guano would fall into waiting lorries, and Macrocosmic Chemicals, Ltd., Inc., and Prop., would be inestimably furthered in the beneficent activities for which it lived. Moreover, there would be that cheque.

Flesh and blood – even that of a Highland aristocracy – is weak and frail. Less than a couple of hours before, the Misses Macleod had regarded as the most intolerable assault upon their just privacy the sporadic appearance of a paddle-steamer on waters nearly a league removed from their home. Now they were seriously envisaging the installation of an endless chain of gigantic buckets each one of which should whisk through the skies above them the accumulated droppings of whole generations of birds. The hereditary Captain and her sister, like Lord Tennyson in his prophetic poem, would see their heavens filled with commerce. And they had only Mr Properjohn's word for it that there would not rain a ghastly dew – to wit, ammonium oxalate and urate – upon such roofs as Castle Moila could still show.

The money appealed to Miss Dorcas. What appealed to Miss Isabella is obscure. Perhaps she saw in this tremendous contrivance a potential engine of war such as might have been invented by Leonardo da Vinci – an instrument for pouring a derisive ammunition upon the hostile forces of the mainland. Or perhaps she saw in it an equally ingenious means of provisioning her island were it blockaded by an enemy fleet.

Be this as it may, Miss Isabella closed with Mr Properjohn and asked him to stay the night. As Hamish Macleod and his boat had long since departed, the only alternative to this would have been a vigil under a clump of whins or in one of the more outlying ruins. Miss Isabella's invitation was thus a matter more of humanity than of hospitality. And as Miss Dorcas busied herself to find a bedchamber without broken windows, sheets without holes, and – most difficult of all – a sleeping-garment without the most obvious feminine suggestions, it is to be feared that her thoughts were less on the comfort these would bring to a benighted stranger than on boilers, towel-rails, drying-cupboards, hot and cold taps, baths, and water-closets. On these latter in particular Miss Dorcas had made extensive observations during her travels to Edinburgh, Paris, Rome, and other capitals. Like all who have given thought to this matter, she had been amazed by the multiplicity of forms which are to be found subsumed under the one governing idea of this convenience, and still more by the astounding variety of names which convention decrees should be imprinted on them. Her favourite she had found – curiously enough – no farther off than Fort Augustus. It was called the MacIsaacs. And as Prometheus had brought fire to men, so would Mr Properjohn bring a MacIsaacs to Castle Moila. So much was Miss Dorcas possessed by this sanitary reverie that she went to bed herself without once reflecting that Mr Properjohn's proposal – like the guano it concerned – was rather a fishy affair.

The reader, who perceives at once that the Misses Macleod were being *gulled*, will hardly forgive her for this obtuseness. But let him remember the opinion of the poet Butler:

> What makes all doctrines plain and clear?
> About two hundred pounds a year.

It is not otherwise with business propositions. And in the

Highlands of Scotland five hundred pounds goes a very long way.

3

SOME years passed. Miss Isabella received one hundred and twenty-five pounds quarterly. Workmen came from Glasgow and installed a MacIsaacs in the Postern Tower, a boiler-house in the Counterscarp, and a bathroom somewhat inconveniently located within the walls of the Outer Enceinte. The Flying Foxes worked regularly by day and intermittently by night as well. They had been put up in record time (Mr Properjohn's visit to Castle Moila had been in the early months of 1939) and by such an army of labourers that the Misses Macleod had feared a permanent neighbourhood of many employees of the Macrocosmic Chemical Company. This foreboding, however, turned out to be unfounded. On Inchfarr itself two ancient persons – presumably devoid of olfactory sensations – were installed in a tin hut from which, week in and week out, they showed no disposition to depart; and their efforts apparently sufficed to fill the maw of the Foxes as they arrived. At the mainland end of the line, where the Foxes voided themselves into large covered motor-lorries, an engineer and his assistant composed the only staff which appeared to be regularly required. And these two also lived a solitary life of their own, rarely emerging from a tall, blind building of corrugated iron which served both as their living quarters, an engine-house and a shelter within which this final stage in the despatch of the guano accomplished itself.

Thus life in the castle, bating small changes of routine dictated by the necessity of using the new amenities provided, went on very much as before. Miss Dorcas's mind had turned from drains to trenches, shelters, and tunnels, and she spent much time planning molings and burrowings through the living rock upon which Castle Moila stood – this with the very rational object of bidding defiance to Marshal Goering's *Luftwaffe* when it should choose to appear in force over the island and demand its capitulation.

Miss Isabella thought little of the *Luftwaffe*, and not very much even of the Forty-five, her mind having taken a definite turn from modern times and being much occupied with the daily exigencies of life in the fifteenth century. Miss Isabella, in fact, had got news of gunpowder, and she saw with considerable intellectual clarity how this disagreeable innovation was likely to affect the castle-owning class.

At other times Miss Isabella was sane enough and sat amid the grass and poppies and flag-irises of the inner ward, looking up at the passing Foxes with a faintly sceptical eye. And the ladies were still waited upon by Tammas – who slit the throats of the calves more slowly than ever – and by Mrs Cameron – who had now completed a sampler depicting Shadrach, Meshach, and Abednego bound in their coats, their hose, their hats, and their other garments, and cast into the midst of the burning fiery furnace. This devotional composition Mrs Cameron had caused to be glazed and hung opposite the kitchen range, thus achieving a pleasantly realistic flicker of flame across its surface on dull afternoons.

So much for the retinue of the Misses Macleod, which was augmented only by a lad called Shamus, red-haired, innocent of the English tongue, of an age indeterminate between eleven and eighteen, and of skill to control the petrol engine without which, as it had appeared, modern conveniences could not be installed in the castle. Shamus ate and slept in the Barbican, tended his engine, and three or four times a week went off in a rowing boat after girls. If a boat were denied him he would swim, which was very dangerous, and when returning would lay hands on any boat that offered. The nearest girls, as it happened, were Mr Properjohn's maids, and this amatory link alone united Castle Moila with its benefactor.

For Mr Properjohn had doffed his dressy sporran, acquired a great quantity of authenic Hunting Stuart tartan from which he caused to be made, not only a new kilt, but a great many window curtains, applied himself to a variety of books on grouse and geese, and had bought a shooting-box on the mainland some three miles away. Here he frequently resided, the comfort of an invalid uncle, and here he occasionally entertained parties of polyglot gentlemen considerably less well-entered in sporting matters than himself. There had been a deer-stalking which was vastly comic, and a sort of battue against the pheasants in which the bag had consisted of a gillie and the wife of the Reverend Mr Grant; and this was vastly comic too, although at the same time embarrassing and extremely expensive. By the less ribald inhabitants it was commonly supposed that the gillie had been an infralapsarian, that Mrs Grant had been engaged in converting him to sound supralapsarianism, and that Mr Properjohn himself, being sublapsarian to the core, had proceeded ruthlessly to the extirpation of heresy. The wiser sort, however, realized that such stories gain ready currency in a community doggedly Calvinist on the surface and sceptically Catholic below, and that the matter must therefore have borne some other colouring. But only the faintest rumour of these things reached Castle Moila, where Mr Properjohn never ventured to intrude, and the unsavoury operations in the air above which – despite his eagerness to initiate them – he now appeared to regard as of very little account amid the multitudinous undertakings of Macrocosmic Chemicals.

But still the Flying Foxes swung and bucketed past each other on their elevated journey, great iron contraptions hauled and supported by unending steel cables which ran from pylon to pylon across the sound, swooped low over the castle and lower still over the anchorage, and then ran out on a series of stunted pylons to the gleaming mass of Inchfarr. Had Mr Properjohn been interested, indeed, he could with a telescope have commanded a view of this farther terminus of his system from the tartan-swathed windows of his shooting-box on the lower slope of Ben Carron. But that he should be interested was, after all, not to be supposed, for one load of guano is very like another, and the whole process, although of inestimable value on the food-production front (a fact, it would seem, not without influence in bringing Mr Properjohn several official privileges), had very little of variety or excitement to recommend it.

On one occasion, it is true, the jaws of a passing Fox accidentally opened and precipitated upon the Western Ward enough phosphates to fertilize flag-irises and buttercups by the million. And on another occasion Miss Dorcas, having reason to visit the Great Ditches in search of certain medicinal herbs which she supposed to grow there, found a small marble faun, in a posture not the most decent for such an encounter, lying as if unaccountably dropped from the sky. Miss Dorcas suspected the *Luftwaffe* and Miss Isabella discerned some attempted enchantment by Great-aunt Patuffa. Shamus was called to dispose of this problematical object; was greatly shocked by it; removed it as if for instant consignment to the ocean and finally put it cannily by as something which might well draw money from an English visitor.

It was some months after this that two English visitors arrived. They were an elderly man with the shrewd but abstracted eyes of a scholar and a young woman sufficiently distinguished to carry off what was by no means a perfectly fitting coat and skirt. Hamish Macleod rowed them across to Moila. Shamus received them beneath the portcullis. That they were altogether strangers to the district was evident from the fact that they asked for Mr Properjohn. Shamus, whose ignorance of the language rendered him particularly sensitive to its intonations, thought that there was a shade of emphasis or resolution about the manner in which this name was pronounced. He took one look at the elderly man, rather more than that at the girl, and bolted for Miss Dorcas.

4

MISS DORCAS advanced across the base-court and observed that the Travellers – for they were decidedly that – stood engaged in rapid consultation. Miss Dorcas thought this a little odd. But her manners being Highland – which is to say perfect – she paused once to pick a buttercup, once to shoo away a sow, and so delayed an encounter until the conference was over. 'Good morning,' she said. 'Our man has no English, but I gather that you seek Mr Properjohn?'

The scholarly man bowed – which was eminently a Traveller's way of replying to such a question.

'Then I fear that there has been misapprehension. I am Miss Dorcas Macleod, and only my sister – who is Miss Macleod of Moila – and myself live in the castle. Mr Properjohn lives at Carron Lodge on the mainland.'

'We are exceedingly sorry.' The scholarly man made motions of withdrawal; at the same time he held with his companion a mute correspondence which Miss Dorcas did not fail to observe. And again she thought it a little odd. The stranger, however, was of polished manners, and Miss Dorcas judged it likely that he was a man of much observation – perhaps, indeed, of extensive views. And, having these good early-Georgian characteristics, he ought not to be turned incontinently away.

'The castle', Miss Dorcas said, 'is lonely. We must not part with these suburban civilities. Pray enter and refresh yourselves!'

'Thank you. My name –' And Miss Dorcas observed the scholarly man to hesitate and look at her fleetingly with quite remarkable penetration, so that she felt obscurely that she was a comma or a colon in a suspected place. 'My name is Meredith – Richard Meredith. My friend is Miss Halliwell. We are altogether strangers here, and stand a little in need of information with which it would be kind of you to furnish us. We will come in most gladly.'

'Then let us make no more ado.' And Miss Dorcas turned and spoke to Shamus in Gaelic – this for the purpose of giving orders that Mrs Cameron should bring whisky and oat-cakes to the solar. The girl called Miss Halliwell, she noticed, glanced at her with quick wariness as the unintelligible words were spoken; and she noticed, too, that as they crossed the base-court and rounded the great bastions of the Inner Ward, her companions kept well to the wall and looked with veiled apprehensiveness about them. No doubt they had been much bombed, Miss Dorcas thought, and were a little shy of the open. Miss Dorcas sympathized with them. Of late she had herself been uneasy when moving about the courts of the castle. She preferred being indoors – and most of all preferred thinking of tunnels, catacombs, and caverns. This troglodyte habit in Miss Dorcas, although doubtless the consequence of shocking goings-on among her brothers and sisters during their nursery years, had been exacerbated of late by the Flying Foxes. It was not so much the contraptions themselves, creaking and straining on their course overhead, as the oblique and sinister line traced by their shadows on the tussock-grass and clover and meadowsweet of the empty and desolate courts that now got Miss Dorcas down. The curve and swoop, the sudden fore-shortened or elongated wing-shadow of a gull, had here for many years given a rhythmic pleasure to her eye. Now the steady shapeless creep of these things filled her with obscure alarm.

Mr Meredith was glancing upwards. He was wondering whether it would be civil to remark upon the incongruous objects. Somewhat nervously, Miss Dorcas forestalled him. 'Your friend Mr Properjohn, as you no doubt know, carries out certain quarrying operations on the island of Inchfarr. The great buckets which you see overhead are the means of transport to the mainland.'

'Dear me!' said Mr Meredith, and peered again with a sort of puzzled attention overhead. 'And has there been this activity for long?'

'For a number of years. I seemed to remember that the

machines were in operation shortly before the outbreak of war.'

'No doubt', said Mr Meredith, 'it has been work of national importance.'

'We did it for money.' Miss Dorcas was uncompromising. 'Subsequently we learnt that it was useful – it is a fertilizer, you will understand – but it was for money that we let the things be put up. What would you think it was worth?'

Mr Meredith considered this carefully. He paused and surveyed the dark-honey-coloured stone that ran out like the two paws of a couchant lion round the anchorage; he looked back at the dull purple mass of Ben Carron and forward again to where, through a crumbled arch rising above a floor of poppy and ragged robin, blue-green water veined with indigo led the eye to a gleaming shoulder of Inchfarr. Then he had another look at the pylons and cables of the Foxes. 'A substantial sum,' he said decidedly.

'Precisely so.' Miss Dorcas was pleased. 'Your friend offered my sister a sum of money which – though with little knowledge of such things – I have subsequently felt unaccountable.' And Miss Dorcas looked from Mr Meredith to Miss Halliwell, her mind obscurely working. 'You must see our water-closet,' she continued – the more startlingly because in exactly the same tone – 'and our tiled bathroom in the Outer Enceinte.'

'We shall be delighted.' Mr Meredith spoke with a level voice and faintly arched eyebrows. It was his first indication that the lady who had received him lived something on the farther side of eccentricity. Castle Moila was famous alike in legend, history, and fiction. To these courts Magnus Barelegs had brought fire; Donald, Lord of the Isles, a traitor's promise; Macleod of Lewis a gratricidal knife. Here had come Prince Charles Edward, thwarted of a throne, and daughters of a hereditary Captain had offered him manchets and wine. Of these walls Walter Scott had dreamed, sitting in an Adam house in an Edinburgh square, and had peopled them with romantic and loquacious shades. Now Flying Foxes swept above them, and obscurely prompted an ancient gentle-woman to invite inspection of a bathroom and a privy. Meredith found this last association altogether incomprehensible.

'So out of Mr Properjohn's quarrying you at least got some solid and prosaic comfort?' It was Jean Halliwell who spoke, having found the concatenation of ideas less mysterious.

'There has been that to be said for it.' Miss Dorcas looked at the young woman with approval. 'To sell the sky above our heads for money in a bank would be unpardonable. To exchange it for a hot-water circulation was rational. But it appears that rational actions are not always quite the right thing. For now I know it was a mistake.' As Miss Dorcas spoke there came from overhead the creaking sound of a cable straining over pulleys, and a large black shadow crept out from a corner of the courtyard they were about to cross. Miss Dorcas looked another way. 'Of how my sister feels in the matter I cannot be assured. It must be confessed some years since she opened her mind to me.'

The idiom of Miss Dorcas, Meredith was thinking, suggested that the Misses Macleod must have enjoyed the attentions of a superior governess far advanced towards senescence when they were themselves scarcely in sight of long frocks. But this was a reflection of very minor interest. What was significant was this: that Moila, which ought to have been the lair of a ruthless foe, was actually in the occupancy of two harmless gentlewomen rejoicing in a tiled bathroom and a water-closet.

Or so it appeared. Meredith was not altogether unfamiliar with that species of romantic fiction in which persons of the most benign and estimable exterior, unreservedly respected by all good men, suddenly drop the mask and reveal themselves as being the very fiends whose abominable crimes have held whole regions in fearsome awe. Could Miss Dorcas be like this? And when they were shortly led into the presence of her sister, Miss Macleod of Moila, would that lady receive them with a frank and inhuman glee and incontinently hand them over to several naked Ethiopian executioners? Or would there simply be a furniture van waiting in the next court? *This castle hath a pleasant seat; the air Nimbly and sweetly recommends itself ...* But in some great chamber within there had been pacing Lady Macbeth, invoking no nimble air, but *the dunnest smoke of hell.* Was the elder Miss Macleod similarly engaged now?

'I envy you such a home,' Jean Halliwell was saying. 'The air is wonderful.'

Meredith felt inclined by some surreptitious act of natural magic to avert this omen. But Miss Dorcas was shaking her head in a manner comfortingly devoid of all sinister suggestion. 'There is a great *deal* of air,' she said. 'It is undeniable that the castle is *airy* – particularly where there is no roof. But we do not know that the quality is to be recommended. On the east coast of Scotland there is ozone. But here the atmosphere is commonly muggy. And this makes various domestic appointments particularly desirable. Drying cupboards, for example, well supplied with hot pipes. Of course, one could get away from it by burrowing.'

'By burrowing?' said Meredith mildly.

'Or tunnelling. I dare say you are aware that the London Tubes are full of ozone?'

'I have heard something of the sort said. But I imagine that to be because electrical –'

'And thus we may suppose that at a certain depth ozone would be obtained.'

It was evident that anything with which Miss Dorcas would positively interrupt a guest must be in the nature of an *idée fixe.* 'Of course one could travel,' suggested Meredith. 'A lateral progression, as it were, towards North Berwick or St Andrews, even if it involved a journey of a hundred miles, might be less laborious than the necessary perpendicular excavation in what appears to be the living rock beneath the castle.' Meredith paused happily on this; he observed that Miss Dorcas was one who would follow such a well-turned period; and this gave him confidence that she was a reliable sort of person after all.

'Do you, in fact, travel much?'

'Dear me, no.' Miss Dorcas's tone was surprised. 'The mode of life of my sister and myself is retired. The fact is that on the mainland we have a relative, our Great-aunt Patuffa, whom we do not at all trust. But we have been given to understand that her malign power will not extend over water. And for this reason we do not leave the island. Are you fond of Rome?'

'Extremely so.' Meredith found the transition as odd as the information which had preceded it. 'There is a professional sense in which it might be called my native city.'

'But one has so far to go in the summer.' Miss Dorcas was evidently moved to show that despite her present insularity she too was a citizen of the world. 'At one time my sister and I thought of domiciling ourselves in Florence. Our Uncle Archibald lived most of his life in Venice. He was a virtuoso.'

'A very nice place to live.' Jean Halliwell was ingenuous. 'But who told you that your Great-aunt Patuffa's power would not extend to the island?'

Miss Dorcas considered. 'I think it must have been our brother, the former hereditary Captain. He advises us to live permanently in the castle. But that, of course, was money.' Here was a subject upon which Miss Dorcas was evidently always uncompromising. 'Florence, I suppose, would have been not expensive. But Castle Moila is unchallengeably less expensive still. Pray have a care in mounting the steps. They frequently work loose, I fear, and Tammas has even less readiness in such repairs than was his formerly. I do not doubt that you will find Mr Properjohn's house admirably appointed.'

'I think we ought to explain that Mr Properjohn –' Meredith thought better of this opening and paused. 'We are climbing, are we not,' he said, 'to a considerable height?'

'The solar is my sister's favourite room. It stands, of course, above and beyond the banqueting hall, and was constructed so as to catch the southern sun. Such places are nowadays called sun-traps, I believe. But I think I ought to explain that my sister –' And Miss Dorcas in her turn paused on this. 'You have known Mr Properjohn in a business way?' she asked.

'Neither of us has ever set eyes on him.'

'Indeed!' Miss Dorcas's last doubt about the Travellers were dissipated. 'I wonder if you would be so kind as to pause by this balistraria for a few moments? I confess to finding the winding staircases more fatiguing than formerly. And there is a word that I should like to say before joining Miss Macleod.' She paused and looked up, startled, as the light from the narrow window by which they stood faded as if at a sudden eclipse. 'Dear me, it is only one of the Flying Foxes again! This is the point at which they come closest to the castle. When the plan was first discussed we were given the impression that they would by no means swoop so low. But, of course, a certain gradient has to be maintained, and it would be expensive to give the pylons a greater elevation, no doubt. Now, what was I saying? Yes, to be sure. I simply wished to warn you that Tibbie – my sister, that is to say – is now far advanced in years, and her mind tends to dwell more and more upon the past.'

'It is a thing very common', said Meredith, 'upon the approach of old age.'

'I suppose it is.' Miss Dorcas sounded doubtful. 'And I must admit that I find my own girlhood returning to me more and more. Most of it was spent with relatives on my mother's side – at Glowrie Castle. Does either of you know it, I wonder?' Miss Dorcas was wistful. 'There are wonderful dungeons – some of them, it is said, nearly fifty feet below the surface. We used to go there in secret and play all sorts of odd games. I know they were very exciting. But, curiously enough, I remember very little about them.' Miss Dorcas had begun to climb again, a perplexed frown on her face. 'Sometimes I think there was something that it is important to remember ...' She broke off and threw open a door. 'But this is the solar. Tibbie, I have brought visitors – Travellers – whom you will be sure to welcome. They are Miss Halliwell and Mr Meredith, and have been misdirected while seeking Mr Properjohn. They have business with him, but I understand' – Miss Dorcas added this rather hastily – 'that they do not enjoy his personal acquaintance. Pray let me introduce you to my sister, Miss Macleod.'

The solar was a large room of undressed stone, with a groined roof and a flagged floor. Three narrow windows with deep embrasures faced south – and these, through a mysterious skill often to be found in such buildings, flooded the entire apartment with a very sufficient light. It was possible to see at once that there were threadbare patches on most of the rugs; that to sit on some of the chairs or lean on some of the tables would be to court immediate disaster; and that of the innumerable ornamental objects with which the place was crowded a substantial majority were sadly in need of dusting. On the walls were a number of steel engravings of Biblical subjects in massive mahogany frames, several ancient oleographs after Rembrandt, a number of Arundel prints (recalling Florence and Rome), several original Landseers (*the curly-headed dog-boy*, thought Meredith absently), and – dazzling distinct from all these – a Raeburn portrait over the great empty fireplace. It was on this that Meredith immediately fixed his eye. An old lady erect in a high-waisted gown, with grey hair under a filmy cap, looked directly at him with dark and penetrating eyes – with the ironic sadness, too, of one who remembers her own great beauty long departed.

A superb Raeburn ... Meredith, realizing that his glance had remained longer than was civil upon what was but an inanimate object after all, turned in some confusion to greet the lady of the castle. The result was comical. His eyes flew back to the portrait and at the same time he uttered an audible exclamation of surprise. For it

114

seemed there could be no doubt of it. The lady whom
Raeburn had painted somewhere in the last years of the
eighteenth century was now advancing to receive him
from a corner of the room.

It was, of course, a trick of family resemblance – and
partly, too, that Miss Macleod of Moila a little dressed the
part. But Meredith's impression had been so obvious that
there was nothing to do but refer to it. 'I cannot be the
only one', he said as he bowed over Miss Macleod's hand,
'to have been immediately struck by a resemblance –'

'It is always remarked.' The old lady before him had
faintly flushed. 'The portrait is of Flora Macleod – that
Lady Flora Macleod who raised a regiment for Prince
Charles Edward in the Forty-five. To every man who
came out she offered a kiss. She was eighteen then. My
brother has her portrait as taken at that time by Allan
Ramsay. Her hair is dark and falls in ringlets. And in it
she wears a white flower.'

'That must be very striking, too.' Meredith allowed
himself another glance at the Raeburn – almost as if to
make quite sure that it was still there. For it seemed just
the sort of thing near which Mr Properjohn would affect
to find a time-bomb, or for which he would send a brightly
painted furniture van. And Mr Properjohn was not many
miles off. Indeed, by his subordinates he appeared to be
thought of as Mr Properjohn of Moila, and this island
with its solitary castle was supposed by them to be the
place at which he was to be met. But that might be only
a loose manner of speaking, for all that one had to go on,
after all, was what Jean had managed to pick up in
distinctly harassing circumstances. Could it be possible
that these impoverished gentlewomen were in some comparatively innocent manner his accomplices? It was
evident that everything tended to strike them in decidedly
an old-world guise: might they believe, then, that they
had lent themselves simply to a little romantic smuggling
after the fashion of the age of Scott and Burns? In a way,
indeed, the activities of Mr Properjohn and his associates
were no more than that – except that they operated on

the largest scale, that their smuggling was *out* rather than *in*, and that they stood in some definite, if as yet undefined, relationship to certain late enemies of the King. And in that there surely lay a crucial point: the thing had been going on nearly all through the war. Incredible that in such circumstances the Misses Macleod would play any conscious part in irregular comings and goings off the coast of Scotland. The conclusion was clear. Mr Properjohn with his Flying Foxes was carrying on under their noses (or rather some way above them) a nefarious traffic of which they were entirely ignorant.

Having arrived at this view of the matter, Meredith felt decidedly better. The reckless adventure into which Jean Halliwell had led him was having an unexpectedly propitious beginning. Instead of walking straight in upon the enemy, they had come unexpectedly upon neutral territory; were perhaps even now conversing with future allies. And unless some effective spy system were in operation round about (a thing, unfortunately, by no means unlikely) they had gained this vantage-ground unbeknown to their adversaries. Indeed, if Jean had been right in her calculations as to the likely conduct of the man Bubear, Mr Properjohn even now knew nothing of the confused events which had led to, and followed upon, the death of Vogelsang. And, even if he did, he must suppose that both Vogelsang's mysterious impersonator and the girl who had been kidnapped as belonging to Marsden's lot had perished shortly after Vogelsang himself, as a consequence of the demolition of Bubear's abandoned warehouse.

And now the elder Miss Macleod was speaking again – and with every appearance (despite what her sister had averred) of being perfectly well posted on the passing moment. 'It is strange', she said, 'that you should have been directed to Mr Properjohn here at the castle. But we must not complain of an error, however unaccountable, which has brought us the pleasure of your company for an hour.'

This, thought Meredith, was very good. It was on the

positively courtly side of courtesy (as befitted a hereditary Captain); at the same time it most decidedly excluded any rash expectation of luncheon. Nor could the intimation have been better timed, since it coincided with the entrance of Mrs Cameron bearing whisky, port, bannocks, and that peculiar species of currant cake, miraculously supercharged with currants to the virtual exclusion of cake, which most travellers associate with afternoon teas partaken of on balconies fronting Edinburgh Castle. This respectable collation must soften any disappointment felt by wayfarers hoping for more substantial entertainment later.

Meredith accepted whisky and bannock, took another good look at Miss Isabella, and decided that it was time for matters to be a little developed. In the Macleod idiom, it was time for him to open his mind – or something like his mind – to the ladies. 'Properjohn?' he said. 'Ah, yes. Clearly, we have got absurdly off his tracks. And I must explain that Miss Halliwell and myself can definitely be described as *on* his tracks. The man is a malefactor, I am sorry to say.'

'A malefactor!' It was Miss Dorcas who responded – and in a markedly startled tone. Then she picked up a decanter. 'Miss Halliwell, may I offer you a glass of port wine?' She looked warily at Meredith. 'Do I understand you to suggest that Mr Properjohn is possessed of a malign influence?'

'A malign –?' Meredith was momentarily at a loss. 'Oh! I understand you. But it is not anything of an uncanny nature to which I refer. The plain fact is' – it would be too abrupt an announcement, Meredith felt, to declare to the Misses Macleod that their territories were virtually occupied by an enemy – 'the plain fact is that he operates a black market.'

'Black magic!' Miss Dorcas set down the decanter with a dangerous bang, so that a cloud of dust rose from the table. 'Then it was Great-aunt Patuffa after all!'

'*Market*, Dorcas.' The elder Miss Macleod was tart. She turned to Meredith. 'These are matters on which we are poorly informed, but of which we are not ignorant. And what you say may, I suppose, be true. And yet a black market in guano is hard to suppose. Moreover, I have some reason to believe that the undertaking is entirely regular. My man of business has made inquiries, and understands that the product of these operations on Inchfarr is very well reputed in the rural community.'

It was at this moment that Meredith saw what was, after all, sufficiently obvious. The Flying Foxes carried guano from Inchfarr to the mainland – but they did this merely to provide a chain of conveyances moving the other way. The Horton Venus would pack into one of these great contrivances readily enough; and so, quite possibly, would that great mass of masonry which bore the monstrously purloined Giotto fresco. The system, indeed, was exquisitely simple. Because guano had to be transported from Inchfarr to the mainland, and thence despatched in lorries to a railhead or elsewhere, a regular and unchallenged traffic, ostensibly in empties, had to operate in the other direction. What happened on the farther side of Inchfarr, and how from that point onwards the smuggling process could possibly avoid detection in such times as these, Meredith was far from being able to imagine. But that was not, at the moment, his affair. All, surely, that was needed now was some substantial verification of his suspicions. Once this was achieved, Jean Halliwell and he simply could not, as a personal adventure, carry the thing any further. The law would have to be invoked. And that would be that.

In fact, it might be rather dull. Meredith looked first at Jean, who had been for the most part silent and watchful since they had entered the castle, and then at the two ladies, its wardens. None of them it occurred to him, would act much by way of sober calculation. Of Jean this was already abundantly proved. Miss Dorcas, although she spoke in the precise idiom that her far-off governess had taught her, was discernibly under the sway, if not of Great-aunt Patuffa, at least of some other influence equally out of the way; one felt that at any moment her behaviour might become decidedly odd. As for Miss Isabella, her conversation, although wholly rational so far, was altogether belied by her eye. It was an eye, Meredith told himself, accustomed to look out – and with fanaticism – upon a world of its own imagining. Something like Don Quixote's eye ... And now Meredith looked once more round this ancient chamber – so ancient as to belong rather to the heroic than to the feudal age – with its steel engravings and Victorian furniture and Raeburn portrait of the old woman who had once worn a white flower in her hair. And, doing this, he obscurely but powerfully felt something like Don Quixote's world close – or better, perhaps, open – around him. He doubted whether that programme of a quick peer at Mr Properjohn's proceedings followed by a rapid appeal to authority would realize itself after all. For there was something inordinate about the whole affair – there was no other word for it – and it would play itself out according to its own rules ... Which was no reason for not proceeding with cautious inquiries in an orderly way. 'Not', said Meredith, 'that we know a great deal about this Properjohn. Might I ask what impression he has made upon yourselves?'

'There is no doubt that he made too much.' Miss Isabella was decided. 'The truth is that in our retired situation we were a little thrown off balance by the appearance of a man of the world.'

'Properjohn is that?'

'After a somewhat *outré* fashion – yes. He wore a ridiculous tartan which greatly perplexed my sister. His mode of address was both vulgar and peculiar. But he had a certain cosmopolitan and polyglot charm such as one sometimes finds in persons of no breeding who have been brought up in half a dozen corners of the world.'

'I see. But you speak of him as one whom you have not met for a considerable time?'

'We met him but the once, when he came with his proposals for the guano. After that the matter was arranged by correspondence. He is a bachelor, it seems, and when he settled nearby we thought it not necessary to call. Nor did he again visit us. And, after this number of years, I do not suppose that he will find occasion to trouble us again.'

Miss Isabella paused, and turned inquiringly to where Mrs Cameron had presented herself in the doorway.

'Mr Properjohn,' Mrs Cameron said.

5

HAD Mrs Cameron announced Allan Ramsay, Sir Henry Raeburn, or the curly-headed dog-boy himself, she could scarcely have achieved a more pronounced sensation. Miss Dorcas dropped a bannock, Miss Isabella looked as if she would much like to summon a dozen armed retainers from the hall, Meredith jumped up positively prepared for fisticuffs, and Jean Halliwell seized a poker.

Coming hard upon all this, the entrance of Mr Properjohn was something of an anticlimax. He no longer sported tartan, spurious or otherwise, and favoured instead knickerbockers of meagre cut, an ancient leather-trimmed jacket of Connemara cloth, a deerstalker hat, and the sort of grey and droopy moustache commonly found on gentlemen who have been in the Guards a long time ago. Mr Properjohn, plainly, had been learning all the time, and was now able to put up what was, in patches, a thoroughly colourable effect. He walked across the floor as country gentlemen walk across each other's floors in the best Shaftesbury Avenue theatres. 'Miss Macleod,' he said, 'I hope you will admit this very belated call from a neighbour and old acquaintance. Miss Dorcas, how do you do?' Mr Properjohn paused upon all this as if to let it sound sweetly on his own ear. And his pleasure in the result was such that he suddenly became more expansively cordial all round. 'And how do you do?' he said cheerfully to Meredith and Jean. And then the country gentleman rubbed his hands together and glanced at the decanters. 'Well,' he continued, 'looks like maybe you got a whisky?'

Miss Dorcas (since along with this she had received something like a nod commissioning refreshment) reached for a glass. Miss Isabella performed introductions and with some severity of gesture indicated a chair. 'It is possible', she said, 'that your call is occasioned by some difficulty on Inchfarr?'

'On Inchfarr?' Mr Properjohns features, although naturally acute, radiated vagueness to all corners of the room. 'Oh, Inchfarr! Really, I have heard jally little about it – jally little indeed. But I should think it is goin' along very nicely.' He turned abruptly to Meredith. 'Live round these parts?'

Meredith shook his head. 'I have come for a little hunting,' he said.

'Huntin'? Now, by gad, do you know I haven't heard of that?' Mr Properjohn looked vexed. 'How jally! Natchally, I have shootin' and fishin' bang on my own land, and we've done a little deer-stalkin' too. But nobody told me about the huntin'. Foxes, do you mean?'

'It might be *Flying* foxes.' Just as in Mr Bubear's repository, Meredith's speech was suddenly prompted from irrational depths.

But there was nothing irrational in the eye he kept cocked on Properjohn the while. And Properjohn reacted at once – with laughter that cannoned so startlingly about the vaulted roof that one almost expected to see Landseer's *Monarchs of the Glen* and *Deer Browsing* to lift their antlered heads and bolt from their frames. 'Dam' goot!' said Mr Properjohn – and smothered this exclamation in a cough. 'Amusin',' said the country gentleman; 'most amusin', 'pon my word.' And he, in his turn, cocked an eye at Meredith. Was it a suspicious – or was it rather a conspiratorial – eye?

Meredith was in doubt. And so, it seemed, was Jean. She had been sitting in a window embrasure, her head sunk in a hand and her gaze on a remote southern horizon. Now she raised her chin and addressed the company at large. 'Has any of you seen this morning's paper?' she asked inconsequently. 'Kobe's going.'

'And Tokio's gone.' Properjohn was emphatic. 'Swept by fire from end to end.'

'In America', said Meredith easily, 'they say that Japanese art is in great demand among collectors. People like Neff, for instance.'

'Ah,' said Properjohn.

'And it seems a pity to think of it being all smashed up. Fujiwara lacquer and Arita porcelain lying around the streets. Kosé and Tosa paintings flapping about in the wind. Terrible, if you ask me. Think what you could raise for Kanaoka's *Waterfall of Nachi* if you had it to sell in New York.'

Properjohn was so moved by this that for the first time he reverted to his old polyglot manner of utterance. '*Schrecklich!*' he said. '*Quelle horreur!*' Again he hastily coughed. 'Very distressin' thing.' He shook his head. 'And to think you just can't get your hands on it.'

'It is to be supposed', said Miss Isabella equably, 'that these wicked but artistic people will have put their finer things securely away.'

'And it's wonderful what a lot of galleries and the like managed to do that in Europe.' Properjohn looked dejectedly into his glass – perhaps simply because it was empty. Then he set it down and rose to his feet. 'Miss Macleod, Miss Dorcas,' he said, 'jally to have seen you again.' His glance travelled to the decanter. 'And a deuced good spot.' It travelled farther to Meredith. 'Nice walks round about. Mainland, just over the head. Particularly jally in afternoon.' And Mr Properjohn picked up his deer-stalker hat, apportioned hand-shakes and bows correctly among the company, and left the room with the perfect deportment of a young lady fresh from finishing-school.

'Really an odd man,' said Miss Dorcas. 'And I fear he has lost what attractiveness he had. Do you know, it seemed to me as if he were endeavouring after spurious refinement?'

'It is strange', said Miss Isabella, 'that he should pay a formal call after all these years.'

'Almost', said Miss Dorcas, 'it is as if he were spying out the land. Which was the occasion of his previous visit too, after all.'

'I must explain that he was spying on Miss Halliwell and myself.' Meredith spoke frankly. 'He had heard of our arrival and wanted to make what he could of us. And just what conclusion he did come to I would very much like to know. He has virtually invited us to confer with him on the mainland this afternoon.'

'Hold to the castle.' The hereditary Captain was suddenly decisive. 'Stay to luncheon. Dine here. Spend the night, letting Dorcas find you what quarters she can. We know nothing of the forces he can muster in an hour. A sortie would be madness. But we are well provisioned and can defy them till the siege be raised. Shamus must pass through their lines and urge my brother to call out the clan.'

Miss Isabella, then, was uncompromisingly on the side of the angels. It was also evident that her sister had spoken by no means idly when she had mentioned her tendency to wander into the past. Not but what – Meredith felt – calling out the clan might be a sound way of dealing with Properjohn and his associates when the right time came. Miss Isabella's line of thought, moreover, gave promise of a larger hospitality than had been adumbrated when Mrs Cameron brought in the bannocks – and this too might have its convenience. So Meredith spoke approvingly. 'Yes,' he said, 'there is much to be advanced in favour of that point of view. At the moment a sortie would assuredly not be the right thing. But perhaps a reconnaissance might be ventured this afternoon.'

Jean was still balancing in her hand the poker which she had picked up upon Properjohn's entrance. 'The portcullis,' she asked, 'does it come down still?'

'Of course it comes down, child.' The hereditary Captain frowned at so ill-conceived a question. 'Only they may have ordnance.' She got up and strode energetically to one of the narrow windows. 'They may bring up bombards. And we cannot stand long against them.'

Meredith was covertly fingering his pipe in the pocket of his jacket. If only he could smoke, he was thinking, he might clear his mind sufficiently to distinguish in this business between sense and fantasy. Jean's question about the portcullis had been perfectly sober. Was it a fact, then, that they might really be besieged?

Had Consignment 100 or whatever it might be – with the Titian and the Giotto and Bubear if he had survived – turned up yet at the terminus of the Flying Foxes? Had Properjohn known more than simply this: that a couple of strangers had arrived at Castle Moila? And what was the state of his knowledge when he had hinted an appointment on the mainland this afternoon? Did he believe that he had exchanged his absurd sign and countersign with the expected Vogelsang? Or did he very well know...?

It was useless thus to string questions together in air. Perhaps some consideration of Properjohn himself might be more helpful. As a figure who should stride upon the scene carrying a massive aura of sinister suggestion, this supposed master-criminal was altogether a frost. As one resolved to pass for a local laird, his efforts were so inept as to be decidedly funny. But the pervasive vulnerability which this suggested might be an illusion; and Properjohn, away from this hobby-horse and on his own professional ground, might be astute and formidable enough. It was even possible – Meredith with some subtlety discerned – that the comic laird business might be in some degree at least a self-discounting device to render more confident adversaries whom he was concerned to lure rapidly into his grasp. Was it his aim to get the known impersonator of Vogelsang and the supposed girl from Marsden's gang safely back across the double barrier of the causey and the Sound? And, that accomplished, would there be waiting a furniture van, a requisition-book open at the appropriate page, and a couple of sacks into which clerkly men would mildly invite one to step? Meredith was back with his vain questions. For there was no answer – and could be none until that reconnaissance was indeed made in some three hours' time. Unless Jean and he were content to lurk in the castle until contact were made with the rule of law, there was nothing for it except another plunge into the unknown – which was what they had come for, after all. And Meredith turned to Miss Isabella. 'We shall be very glad to stay to luncheon,' he said. 'And then, in the afternoon –'

From somewhere outside the castle a long, melancholy wail broke the island stillness and drowned the words on Meredith's lips. It rose, hung for a moment strident upon the ear, ebbed rapidly away. And Miss Dorcas sprang up and clapped her hands. 'Tibbie,' she cried out, 'it's the *Oronsay!*'

Surprisingly, Miss Isabella too clapped her hands like a child. 'Captain Maxwell already! But – to be sure – I noticed this morning that it is the second Thursday of the month.'

The hereditary Captain of Moila, Meredith thought, seemed a good deal more reliable on the current calendar than on the centuries. And certainly a steamer was approaching the island, since it was now possible to hear the throb of engines. But was not the *Oronsay* a sizeable Orient liner? It seemed altogether improbable that such a giant –

Meredith's speculations were interrupted by much bustle around him. Mrs Cameron had come in with a tablecloth and a tray of silver; at the same time Miss Dorcas, now oblivious of Mr Properjohn, his Foxes, and whatever further problems, military or economic, he posed, was wrapping herself in shawls and bonnet for some excursion in the open air. 'Come along,' said Miss Dorcas – and her tone was animated and even gay. 'How fortunate that you should have come on a second Thursday! Tibbie, you had best not venture out of doors. But do you think that Shamus will have remembered to collect the flock? And will the cow be ready, I wonder?' She made sweeping gestures towards the staircase which wound directly into the room. 'But come along, or we shall be too late for the tying up.'

And Miss Dorcas and her guests hurried down to ground level and across a series of courtyards. It was noon and the Flying Foxes were stationary; those farther away, suspended on their almost invisible cables, were like great bats unnaturally hovering in air. A light breeze blew through innumerable cracks and crannies in the castle's outer walls, producing a sort of low whistling upon a score of notes which blended with the farmyard noises from the base-court and the beat of surf far below. Clover and sea-spray and dry grass scented the air. From somewhere startlingly close at hand the incoming steamer hooted again and a thousand gulls rose at the sound, their wings catching or eluding the sun as they wheeled and wheeled again. Meredith found himself quite breathless as the old lady hurried him towards the seaward and deserted side of their domain. 'Is it', he asked, as a third hoot rose seemingly through the very rock beneath his feet, 'one of the paddle-steamers?'

Miss Dorcas looked at him in dismay. 'But, dear me, no! My sister would be most upset at such a suggestion. There have been none of them for years, I am glad to say. This is the *screw* steamer – Captain Maxwell's, a most charming man. He is often kind enough to join us at luncheon and bring us a breath of the wider world. He is always full of news, and often he executes any small commission we may have ... Pray be careful!'

Miss Dorcas had been hurrying forward with such precipitation, and had come so abruptly to a halt, that Meredith had scarcely time to notice that another step on his own part would assuredly have been his last. For the party now stood upon a narrow platform of turf, scarcely three feet wide, between a crumbled but still gigantic bastion of the ruined castle and a precipice dropping from beneath their feet to blue-back water far below – a precipice so sheer as scarcely to afford more than an occasional nesting-place for Moila's omnipresent gulls.

And now the full natural strength of the castle on this seaward aspect was revealed. For from round the deep, natural basin below – save only at one point where a small landing stage appeared to have been hewn from the rock – this unscalable face of stone everywhere rose up to merge with scarcely a break into the western walls of the fortification. The actual height was not, perhaps, so very great, but assuredly it was sufficient to bar assault from the sea. Nor did there appear – immediately, at least – any practicable route by which communication with the incoming steamer would be possible – unless indeed one should make use of Properjohn's Flying Foxes, the span for which swept steeply down from the level at which Meredith now stood, and halfway across the anchorage turned to the horizontal at a height of some fifteen feet above the water, thence running on and out to Inchfarr on the support of two stunted pylons of latticed steel.

The *Oronsay*, viewed from above, was a tub of a craft not much less broad than it was long, of an actual size approximating to that of a wherry, and in its present situation diminished to the proportions of a clockwork toy. A boy lounged in its blunt bows preparing to cast a rope; on a little bridge near the stern stood Captain Maxwell, a bearded man of very much the same proportions as his craft; and, in between, the deck was exclusively occupied by several hundred black-faced sheep. The baaing of these, reverberating round the great cauldron of the anchorage, was redoubled as the *Oronsay* jerkily manoeuvred for position; the noise of this sent a cloud of gulls screaming into the air; at the same moment the lad Shamus mysteriously appeared on the landing stage below and started a voluble shouting to which the boy in the bows responded; Captain Maxwell took off his nautical cap, waved it above his head, and hallooed in a deep bass to Miss Dorcas; Miss Dorcas waved in return and uttered shrill, gull-like cries; the gulls, more disturbed than ever, swooped and screamed anew. It was evident that on Moila second Thursdays were special days indeed.

Dogs were barking. From below-decks appeared a shepherd in bright blue trousers and a faded tartan plaid. The screw gave a final thresh; the *Oronsay* emitted a fourth and triumphant hoot; part of a bulwark designed as a gangway fell with a rattle of chain upon the landing stage;

the sheep, amid much bark and shout, poured across and were instantly and miraculously swallowed by the living rock. The baaing and barking faded on the air. Captain Maxwell, after gravely consulting with some assistant in the bowels of the vessel, disembarked and disappeared in his turn, with Shamus following and carrying a large carpet bag. There was now no sound but the beat of surf from beyond the harbour – that and a muted bleating underground, as if from the flocks of Pan banished to a cimmerian gloom. Slowly the bleating gained in resonance and was presently a tumultuous baaing once more – but this time it proceeded from within the courts of the castle, from the towering walls of which it took to itself echo upon echo until the effect was of some vast antipodean sheep-run contracted to one narrow room.

Meredith, turning round to investigate, found the massive figure of Captain Maxwell at his elbow. So massive, indeed, was the master of the *Oronsay* that, standing on this narrow ledge, he appeared to overhang the void below like a structure hazardously built out on corbels. And this was only a reminder that the position of the whole party was precarious. But even as the thought entered Meredith's head Miss Dorcas brushed past him with no more concern than if she were a guillemot and shook Captain Maxwell warmly by the hand. 'It is not often', she said, 'that we have other visitors when the *Oronsay* comes in. Let me introduce you to Miss Halliwell and Mr Meredith. And only an hour ago we had a third visitor – Mr Properjohn from Carron Lodge.'

'And are ye telling me that, now?' Captain Maxwell cast a disapproving glance at the line of cables running out to Inchfarr. 'And it's no' so mony hours since I heard tell of him myself. Awfu' queer goings-on. Did ye ever hear tell of an English body o' the name o' Higbed, or such-like?'

'Higbed!' exclaimed Meredith.

'Aye – just that.' Captain Maxwell looked with some suspicion at the stranger. 'A daftie, it seems, and this Properjohn has the charge of him. But why should a man whose business is wi' birds' muck' – and Captain Maxwell jerked a mighty thumb in the direction of the pylons – 'take up wi' keeping dafties?'

The party was now moving back towards the inhabited part of the castle. Meredith and Jean exchanged glances. 'But this', Meredith began incautiously, 'is most extraordinarily interesting –'

'And is that so?' Captain Maxwell became instantly uncommunicative. 'I'm thinking it's grand weather for getting in the peat.'

'It so happens', said Miss Dorcas, momentarily remembering the untoward disclosures of earlier in the morning, 'that Mr Meredith is endeavouring to get on Mr Properjohn's tracks –'

'I'm thinking he'd better be careful this Properjohn doesn't get on his. Like on that daftie's.' For a second Captain Maxwell seemed tempted to expand on this theme. But caution again overcame him. 'Miss Dorcas,' he said, 'when folks comes speiring round after other folks it's as well to haud your tongue until you ken just where ye are. Especially in awfu' times like these. But here's Miss Macleod – an' looking more like Lady Flora than ever.'

The hereditary Captain had appeared on the threshold of the solar, and received what was evidently a customary piece of gallantry with suitable graciousness. 'Come away, Captain Maxwell,' she said, 'come away to where your place is waiting you. Boiled mutton – and I believe caper sauce, which we owe to your own good offices.' Miss Isabella had returned for the time to a strictly contemporary world.

'And fancy you remembering that, Miss Macleod.' Captain Maxwell tucked a table-napkin beneath his beard. 'Maybe Mrs Cameron will find another wee bottle in the carpet-bag. It's wonderful what can be picked up frae time to time by those wi' business in the great waters. Miss Dorcas, you'll find two taiblets o' bath soap each near the size of a futba'. And that's something there's no easy coming by the noo'.' Captain Maxwell exhibited considerable complacency over this. 'For them's right awfu' days. Well, Miss Dorcas, if you mon do it' – for Miss Dorcas had produced the decanter – 'it had best be no more than a dram. There's an auld minefield to navigate this afternoon. And the *Oronsay* has to berth at Glasgow the morning's morn.'

'But we hope', said Miss Dorcas, 'that the seas are now considerably safer than before?'

'Aye, they are that. The Sunderlands got on top o' the prowling vermin at last, and in the end in they a' came like a fishing fleet. But it was Sunderland for sub for mony a long day.'

'Sunderland for sub?' asked Meredith.

'Aye, so.' Captain Maxwell was sober. 'Awa' doon by Lorient and in the Bay o' Biscay. Each yin would get the other, sure as sure. For it's no' easy to get onything for nothing in war. But it was like a winning game at chess, for a sub costs more and hauds more crew than a flying-boat. There's no subs now, praise be. No but what the laddies look as if they were after yin this very morn in these waters – which is an unco queer thing.' Captain Maxwell shook his head and absently drained his glass. 'Awfu' times,' he said. 'D'y ken, Miss Macleod, that over on Larra there's to be a daunce in the ha' o' the Continuing?'

'The Continuing?' Jean rashly asked.

'I see ye canna' be familiar, miss, wi' Kirk affairs in Scotland. Some weeks syne they had a daunce in the ha' o' the Church of Scotland on Larra, and now they're to haud yin in the ha' of the United Free Church of Scotland Continuing. And what would the Auld Lichts, or them o' the Original Secession, think o' that?'

Miss Dorcas poured out another dram, which her guest promptly drained. 'But, Captain Maxwell,' she said, 'surely there isn't any harm in dancing. I remember that George MacDonald himself says "Dance, ye Highland lads and lassies, hurricanes of Highland reels". And George MacDonald was a very godly man.'

'Aye – maybe so. But it's no reels they'll be dauncing

on Larra; it's them twa-backed daunces frae England. No more than a dram, if ye please, Miss Dorcas.'

Meredith took heart from this third potation. 'You were mentioning Properjohn,' he said, 'and something about a man called Higbed –'

But this was to reckon without the charms of theological conversation. 'It appears to me', Miss Isabella interrupted, 'that there is warrant for the practice of dancing in the Bible itself. Do you not recall, Captain Maxwell, that King David is described as dancing before the Ark of the Lord?'

'Aye, Miss Macleod, I'll grant ye that. But no' wi' a pairtner. And I'm thinking ye'd be fair stammagasted to hear o' the Ark o' the Lord appearing on Larra. All they'll be dancing afore there is a bit o' a quean strumming on a piano and a daft loon bloring into a saxaphone.'

'I think you said that Higbed was daft?' Jean seized boldly upon this tenuous transition. 'I'm surprised to hear that. For, as a matter of fact, I could tell you quite a lot about him.' She paused hopefully on this bait.

'And is that so, Miss Halliwell?' Captain Maxwell, from above his raised glass, gave Jean a shrewdly appraising glance. 'I'm thinking Miss Dorcas said that you and Mr Meredith had come to these pairts for more than change o' air?'

'Decidedly more.'

'Ye'll easier get change o' air in the Islands than change o' a threepenny bit.' Captain Maxwell produced this venerable witticism with innocent pleasure. 'It was bad enough when the lairds were real lairds o' a sort and ever grabbing another bit o' land and turning folk awa' to Canada and such coarse places. But it's unco the war' noo when they're no more than London bodies after a salmon or a bit o' a bird. Would you be saying this Properjohn was a London body?'

'I should say he comes about equally from London, Chicago, Hamburg, Salonica, and Marseille.'

'And are ye telling me that?' Captain Maxwell was impressed – so much so that he absently pushed his glass towards Miss Dorcas and the decanter. 'And would ye say – begging Miss Macleod's pardon – that in a' this affair o' the birds' muck he was up to what might be expected frae such a heathen-like creature?'

'Yes, Captain Maxwell. Quite definitely so.'

'Then listen.' And Captain Maxwell drew his glass towards him and pushed away his plate. 'I'll be telling you about the daftie Higbed.'

6

EVIDENTLY by prescriptive right, Captain Maxwell filled and lit his pipe. Meredith took courage to beg the same privilege. And once he had the tobacco of Mr Bubear's inept assistant well alight he felt a larger confidence in face of the problems which surrounded him. 'Captain Maxwell,' he said at a venture, 'would this matter of the daftie Higbed have anything to do with a furniture van?'

'It would that.' Captain Maxwell took his pipe from amid his whiskers and looked at Meredith with respect. 'In fact, twa.'

'*Two* furniture vans!'

'Twa – and a muck lorry forbye. And a gentleman's library lying about the peat. And a travelling altar.'

'A travelling altar?' said Miss Dorcas. 'I don't think I ever heard of such a thing.'

Captain Maxwell puffed at his pipe and with marked leisure watched the smoke drift up to the dimness of the vaulted roof. It was evident that he was not without the arts of the raconteur. 'No more ye need have,' he said. 'For who would want to know a' the unco notions o' the piscies?'

'The piscies?' said Jean.

'The Episcopalians, Miss Halliwell. Scots wha haud in with the Church of England are Episcopalians – and that's piscies for short. Respectable folk enough, the most of them are – but awfu' superstitious and formal. Aye reading a bittock out o' a book, like a bairn with a primer, instead o' following the godly and inventive practice o' conceived prayer. But about the travelling altar I never heard tell mysel' until I fell in with the Reverend Mr Wooley two days syne.

'The piscies are none too many in these pairts, and their kirks are few and far between. So they have this Mr Wooley, a douce and learned minister enough, louping ower the country in a wee bit car, holding a service here and a service there – or maybe just a bit recitation-like out o' his prayer-book – whenever he comes up wi' ony members o' his scattered flock. Now, him and me's been long acquaint, for whiles he takes the *Oronsay* frae island to island. And many's the crack we've had on Biblical matters – and I maun say, for all his high-popery, that he hauds sound views enough on the Book of Judges.'

'Ah!' said Miss Dorcas. 'But have you tried him on the Apocalypse?'

'So a couple o' days syne' – Captain Maxwell ignored this invitation to digress – 'when I'd been up Minervie-way over a freight and was looking to get quickly back aboard, I was right glad when up he drove and offered me a lift. The seat beside him was piled high with parcels – for it's natural that with transport so bad as it is in these awfu' times he should carry more than spiritual sustenance to the scattered piscies, and the Word o' the Lord won't be less acceptable if it arrives along o' the hens' corn or a bag o' flour. Well, I was climbing in at the back when Mr Wooley stops me, polite but a wee bit shocked. "Captain," he says, "not there; that's the altar." And, sure enough, there on the back seat was what might have been a tombstone, wrapped up for delivery in brown paper. And he explains to me that it's consecrated by his bishop, and that when he gets to some gentry house he has a couple o' billies fetch it into the drawingroom, maybe, so that anything he could do in a kirk he can do there. A profane man would think it clean skite, I dinna' doubt.

But though I question sorely whether the Lord would be vexed ony should Mr Wooley drop his travelling altar accidently-like into Loch Carron, I haud wi' respecting the beliefs o' a' such lower forms o' Christianity if sincerely held. And I was to respect Mr Wooley the more before the journey was out.

'You'll be wondering what a' this has to do wi' Properjohn and his daftie, the poor chiel Higbed. It was thiswise. There was a haar in from the sea – as ye may mind well if ye were here by then – and the mist was heavy between the mountain and the loch. And I was speiring a bit about the *Codex Sinaiticus*, seeing that I had been reading Kenyon's *Handbook to the Textual Criticism of the New Testament* –'

'An admirable manual,' said Meredith. 'Particularly in points where Tischendorf –'

'– and seeing that he appeared to be well-versed in such grave matters. Well, Mr Wooley drove slow, and whiles I listened and whiles we argued, and then the mist grew thicker and Mr Wooley drove slower still. And when he came to the Epistle of Barnabas he clean stopped, and there we sat on the brow of a wee brae, with the haar eddying about us and this o' the *Codex Sinaiticus* to chew on. And then the haar lifted for the time and there were the twa great furniture vans straight below us, and Properjohn's muck lorry that I knew fine forbye. And there, lying by the roadside as I was telling ye, was enough books to grace the sanctum of Mr Wooley's bishop himself. There was something unco about it a' – there in that dreich and lonesome place – and for a while we sat gowking at it, as still as if we were a couple of bogles set up to scare the crows in a turnip field. And what was going forward was straight to see. A couple o' billies were getting the books out o' one o' the furniture vans, and a third was stowing them in the muck lorry.'

'Good heavens!' Meredith's indignation was not to be curbed. 'Some priceless library, no doubt, that those scoundrels were making away with.'

'Is that so, now?' Captain Maxwell puffed at his pipe,

and his tone was massively ironical. 'It's one way of making a bit o' sense o' the whole unco affair, I'll admit. But just it wasn't so. For I had more than a keek at those books a bit later. And they were mostly sets o' what the learned call journals. Some I mind the name of. There was the *British Medical Journal*, and the *Journal of Ophthalmology*, and the *International Journal of Psycho-Analysis*. A' fu' o' deep matters, no doubt But I dinna ken that priceless would be the word for it.'

'Very curious,' said Meredith, somewhat blankly. 'Very curious, indeed.'

'Aye, mebbie. But more curious was to come. For as we sat there with none heeding us there was sudden-like a bit o' stir and confloption by the second furniture van, and a door at the back was thrown open, and out came a ragged, dirty creature and began running up the brae. He was a full-fleshed gawpus and short o' breath – but up he came louping as if the deil were at his doup in the likeness o' a slavering hound. Begging your pardon, Miss Macleod.'

'Higbed!' said Jean.

'So it was to appear. Well, up he came, and after him loupit twa bodies it might have been out o' a bank or an insurance office –'

'That's right! The clerkly men.'

'– and after that again twa billies frae the lorry – right villainous creatures that I didn't like the ill sight of. Well, no sooner does the daftie see Mr Wooley's car than he scraiches out like an auld wife after a runaway calf. "Taxi!" he scraiches. "Taxi!" And the next moment he's up wi' the car and jumping in at the back. "Caledonian Hotel", he says – just as if he was at the Haymarket in Edinburgh and anxious to get himself to the other end o' Shandwick Place. It was fair uncanny. And afore either o' us could think o' fit reply up runs his pursuers. "He's a madman," one calls out. "And dangerous," says the other. At that the lorry billies joined in, sweering terrible, right regardless o' Mr Wooley's cloth, and making to haul out the poor daftie from where he was crouching on the travelling altar like the timorous beastie in Rabbie

Burns's poem. And at that the gawpus lets out a yammering as if he would outroar Satan's pandemonium. "I'm Higbed!" he scraiches, "I'm Higbed!" I don't think it occurred to either of us that he was trying to tell us a name; it was like as if I scraiched at you, Miss Halliwell, that I was stammagasted or some such, and you had no comprehension o' what I was saying about myself. "I'm Higbed," he roars again – and at that one o' the lorry billies puts in an arm and makes a grab at him. But man! you should have heard Mr Wooley at that moment.'

Captain Maxwell leant back and gazed at the vaulted roof of Miss Macleod's solar, as if the better to visualize a grateful scene. 'You should have heard him for sure. "Stop!" he cries in a terrible voice. "Mad or sane, the man's in sanctuary." "He's mad," says one o' the bodies frae the vans. "And dangerous. And it's our lawful duty to secure him." "He's in sanctuary," says the reverend. "Sanctuary?" says the body, "and what the hell might you –" And the reverend – he was syne a gran' rugby player and stands six foot three – the reverend reaches out and takes him by the shoulder and tumbles him into the ditch. "You profane rascals," he says, "have you never seen an altar before? Captain Maxwell, I'm thinking we'll drive on." And drive on we did – with the daftie sitting there on the altar and fair convinced that the empty moor about him was the populous and ungodly streets o' Edinburgh.'

Miss Dorcas, who had been brewing coffee in a percolator so resplendent as to be evidently, like the tiled bathroom in the Outer Enceinte, a gift of the Flying Foxes, looked up as if a sudden thought had struck her. 'Tibbie,' she said, 'does not all this sound much like the work of Great-aunt Patuffa?'

'Nonsense, Dorcas.' Miss Isabella was at her sanest and most contemporary. 'And we are to understand' – she turned to Captain Maxwell – 'that Mr Properjohn himself had hand in this?'

'That he had, Miss Macleod – as will presently appear. But here was Mr Wooley and myself driving down the brae, and these folk hurrying after, and the daftie havering in the back. And by the vans the reverend stops and has a good look at them – and such a look at the coarse creatures coming up ahint us that they fair stopped in their tracks. And at that we drove on again with the haar closing in around us. "My friend," says Mr Wooley presently – and courteous as could be – "who were those fellows we were talking to?" Well, he couldn't have got a dafter reply to his speiring. For "Nobody at all," says the creature Higbed. "I beg you not to suppose that I believe myself subject to a persecution. I am not being pursued or molested by anybody." "I'm glad to hear it," says Mr Wooley, calm as ever; "and I suppose there wouldn't have been a couple of big red furniture vans?" "Certainly not," says Higbed – and at that I took a squinny at him and saw that he was in a fair sweat o' anxiety to convince it might be us or it might be himsel' o' the truth o' so daft a speak. "It's a simple but ramifying and systematized delusion," he says. "There's sustained auditory and visual hallucination," he says, "but no reference or other symptom of mania." And at that he keeks out o' the wee back window, plainly fearing that old Hornie himself was on the tracks o' him. "I must frankly tell you", he says, "that I see myself as in the middle of wide moorlands. But there's nothing very surprising in that. For, as you no doubt know, my particular study has been in the psycho-pathology of defective vision with particular reference to the hysterias. And a man is very apt to be stricken down by what he specializes in, particularly if he has over-worked. This is no more than overwork" – says the daftie, fairly sweating the breeks off his posteriors by this time – "overwork and sexual repressions. The furniture vans are very sexual – very sexual indeed. Would you be so kind as to drive me to Devonshire Place?" "Devonshire Place?" says the reverend mildly. "I mean Moray Place," says Higbed – minding, it seems, that he was in Edinburgh and no' his natural London. "Moray Place, if you please, where I have a colleague very well able to treat a mild nervous breakdown like this."

'Well, it was an unco thing – and fair pathetic to see a body at once so daft and so gleg. For dafter he plainly was than ony nervous breakdown the faculty could show to their bit classes in Morningside – and yet right gleg and cunning to put the best face on his affliction. Sanctuary or no sanctuary, I doubted it hadn't been right to take the creature away from his keepers, unco-like though they had been, and clean unhyne that they should be transporting him about as if he were a sofa or a chest o' drawers. As it was, we had taken a fine bit o' responsibility by the lug, driving down through the haar from Minervie to the head o' the loch, wi' this unsonsie blatherskite crouching like an egg-bound hen on poor Mr Wooley's altar. But the responsibility didn't bide wi' us long. For no sooner had we got to the old ford below Duthie, where the reverend had to come nigh to a stop, than the daftie jumps out o' the car. "Is this Moray Place?" he asks, and the next minute he fumbles in his pooch, tosses half a crown at Mr Wooley like as if he was throwing a bit dog-biscuit at a tink cur, and disappears into the mist as quick as the bad fairy vanishing down a trap at the panto. "I'm Higbed!" I could hear him scraich – to whomsoever was taking a dander round Moray Place, no doubt. And that, although the two o' us got out and went searching and shouting about, was the last that either of us saw of him. But I'm thinking from what happened afterwards that the poor creature would have done better to stick to Mr Wooley's sanctuary a while longer.'

Captain Maxwell paused in his narrative. As he did so the *Oronsay* hooted from the anchorage below. The sound ebbed away amid a screaming of startled gulls. Captain Maxwell looked at the decanter, and found it empty. He looked at his watch. 'They're telling me to mind the tide,' he said. 'And I must be awa', for certain.'

'But I hope', said Meredith, 'that you have time to tell us what more you know about Higbed, and how you discovered that Properjohn comes into it?'

'I have that – but no' in what ye might ca' picturesque detail. Though it would make up fine into a fearsome story.' Captain Maxwell shook his head. 'For the poor creature fell into the hands o' a pack o' gomeril Highlanders. Begging your pardon, Miss Macleod. And I don't say that Shamus himself is no' a decent lad enough. But I've cruised and bargained among Highlanders half my days, and I know them for kittle cattle and unchancy chiels.'

'Compared with the phlegmatic Saxon,' said Miss Dorcas, 'the temperamental Celt –'

'Aye – but I'll be finishing what ye set me to, and we'll have a bit talk about the Celts the next second Thursday. Well, it's little enough I know, being no more than putting twa and twa together frae the talk o' a couple o' shepherds on the *Oronsay* this morning. It seems that a' yesterday this Properjohn was driving about the countryside in a great car, much as if petrol was something you could draw from the udders o' every cow in the country. He was looking for a sick friend, he said, one that had fairly lost his memory and was nigh demented, and who had been coming to Carron Lodge over yonder for a rest cure. Which was a good enough tale until the body Properjohn fetched up with Mr Wooley. He had a bit more explaining to do then – not that explaining appeared to be any trouble to him. His poor friend's car, he said, had broken down in some right lonely place, and them that had the charge o'him were sore put out until along came a flitting.'

'A what?' said Jean.

'A removal, Miss Halliwell – meaning those twa great furniture vans. Well, they got a lift frae them, and a message through to Properjohn himself. And Properjohn, because his own car was away, could do no better than commandeer one o' his own muck lorries to meet the vans at as near as they would come.'

Meredith laughed softly. 'It's what might be called a colourable tale.'

'But this Properjohn had more than that. The bit papers frae doctors and the like about his poor afflicted friend were all there to show the reverend.'

'You may be sure they were. But what about all those books? Did he come forward with any explanation of them?'

'That he did, Mr Meredith. A' this o' the breakdown and having to ride in a van like a kitchen dresser or a pianola upset the nerves o' his poor friend and syne made him right violent, so that no sooner had the van stopped than he fell to hurling out o' it whatever he could lay his hand to among a' the stuff that was being flitted. Which was mostly books – the same Mr Wooley and I saw lying about the heather. So Properjohn's story seemed reasonable enough, and by yesterday forenoon he had near a' the countryside right sorry for his poor daftie and climbing halfway up Ben Carron to find him and get him safely away to his rest cure with this right benevolent friend. And found he was. But no' before that pairt o' the tale that's a fair scunner to think on. I mean the daftie's scourging.'

'His *what*?' asked Meredith.

'Aye, I tell ye it was a most scunnerfu' thing – and a' a matter o' the false religion and Dark Ages-like notions that ye find in any Highlander ye take a scratch at. Ye mind I said there was to be a dance in the ha' o' the Continuing on Larra? But that's no' everything that decent kirk ha's is let out for in these awfu' days. Up at Dundargie they were having a Revival – a series o' meetings conducted by some coarse creature from America and never a decent minister within a mile. What do you think o' that, now, for a Moderator and a General Assembly to chew on ? A pack o' gorkie Highland chiels working themselves up to the Almighty alone kens what daftness, and this American scraiching Hell and a' its devils at them. And at that in comes the daftie – this same poor gouk Higbed. Ye might think he'd be just one more misguided enthusiast slavering over his sins like them on the penitent form. But his luck didn't take him that way.

'For it seems that he came into this ha' at Dundargie – which is a back-o'-beyond place enough – still believing the same unco thing: namely that he was a sane man walking the streets o' Edinburgh, but just a wee bit troublit with what ye might call hallucinations – like seeing nothing but peat and heather and here and there a bothie or shealin where rightly there ought to be the Scott Monument or Princes Street Gardens. And when he got into the shelter o' this kirk ha' the fancy took him that he had found the consulting-room o' his friend, the Moray Place medico. And he took all the silly folk gathered there for purposes o' false religious enthusiasm to be a pack o' patients far further sunk in daftness than himself. I'm thinking he was no' so far wrong. But naturally it was an attitude sore ill-likit.'

Meredith was looking thoughtfully at the ashes in his pipe. 'And the poor man's agonies,' he interrupted, '– for really they must have been that – sprang originally from a sound enough instinct to preserve his own sanity. He was dogged by great furniture vans. Such a thing – he argued – does not in fact happen. Therefore the furniture vans were the product of a disordered vision, and sanity would consist in keeping a firm grasp on this. Presently he was kidnapped and cast into one of these vans which he had assured himself were illusory. Unless he were to abandon his first premise – to wit, the non-existence of the things – the kidnapping must be illusory too and the result of his remaining senses taking the same sort of holiday as his vision. After that there was only one logical attitude to adopt. He was a sane man woefully and obstinately betrayed by disordered sensory perceptions. To admit that it *was* a moor and that these *were* furniture vans would be to take the final plunge into lunacy.' Meredith shook his head. 'When one realizes this rational motive in what have been plainly regarded as his worst ravings, the unhappy fellow's plight becomes positively harrowing. But I interrupt your narrative.'

'You do that.' Captain Maxwell had risen and was buttoning his reefer jacket. 'Only there's little more to tell. It seems that the folk who were being converted by this American creature had just got to that part o' the jiggery-pokery when they began seeing visions – which is things right edifying to read about in the Scriptures and harmless enough in poetry, but no part o' decent piety in these latter days. But here were the silly chiels, springing up one after the other and declaring that they saw St Columba in his wee boat or a great feast and dance in Heaven or the signing o' the Solemn League and Covenant or Nebuchadnezzar out at grass or a choir of angels attending some minister that died a while back in a special odour o' sanctity. Well, Higbed, it seems, listened a while to a' this stite about seeing one unco thing or another. And he thought – kind o' rationally enough, as you've just remarkit – that this was no more than some sort o' clinic o' his friend's in which he had fallen in with others similarly afflicted to himself. So up he gets in his turn to declare –'

Jean Halliwell had been staring at Captain Maxwell roundeyed. Now she interrupted him. 'How utterly grotesque!' she said. 'How grotesque and rather horrible.'

'Aye. It was what the author-billies might well call a macabre situation. "I see a great crowd o' the heavenly host," says one gorkie body, "haudin' in wi' the late reverend McCloskey o' Minervie." "I see King Solomon's Temple," says another, "and the twirly upper parts o' it is embellishit wi' knops." "I see a mean and rather dirty little hall," says Higbed, "and outside it what looks like a dreary bit of the highlands of Scotland." "I see men which have the mark o' the beast," says one, "and noisome and grievous sores." "I see an ill-favoured fellow on a platform," says Higbed, "and I should say that he drank." "I see a great cloud o' witnesses," says another. "I see about twenty uncouth persons of low intelligence in a condition of unwholesome excitement," says Higbed. And by that time, as ye can imagine, he had the others beaten fair to it. Some were for regarding the strange creature as abounding in a special grace, for a' the hard things he said o' them. But the revivalist, who was sore affronted at being called ill-favoured and accused o' the drink, listened for a while and syne declared that the man was mad. So Higbed goes back to his scraiching. "I'm

Higbed!" he roars. And at that the revivalist gets scared and says they must send for the police or a doctor. The folk think little o' that, though – and presently an old wife, a bit more enthusiastic than the rest, ups and says it has straight been revealed to her that our poor brother is possessed by seven devils. He must be manacled, she says, and live in straw, and be beaten till he hollars like a bairn sore breeched. And so they all fa' on Properjohn's poor daftie, and tear the jacket and the breeks off him, and at that the revivalist has his own vision – which is of the dock looming afore him, like enough – and he goes louping through the door and isn't seen again.

'So after that there's a clear field for those uncouthy Highlanders. And when they've fair paiked the daftie black and blue the old wife says yes, she's seen one devil flee out o' his gob and go limping off, and that leaves no more than six to expel after the same pleasurable fashion. And so they fell to it again, still having their bit vision o' the fifth angel sounding or Jeannie Deans throwing her stool at the bishop or John Knox preaching the head off Queen Mary at Holyrood. Regular sadistic it was, and whiles the old wife would say yes, there was another devil, and whiles she would say no, but she was mistaken, and to scourge him the sounder. It was the fourth devil that was right obstinate, it seems; they could no more get it out than a red-breast a worm too big for it on a frosty day, or a bairn digging at a winkle with a wee pin. And so they might have gone on, right crazed and savage and a disgrace to Scotland, until sundown or after, had it no' been for wee Georgie Black, the flesher's wean o' Dundargie, who comes running in to the shop where his father is quartering a sheep and says that somebody is killing a pig up by the kirk ha' and is fell unskilly in the art o' it. So up goes Black and finds these Highlanders thrashing away and with a right skimmering look to them as if they were idiot themselves by now. And there was Higbed nigh skirl-naked, and whiles roaring in simple agony and whiles expostulating as sane as could be. For there was something in the old wife's prescription after all, it seems, and the sore drubbing he had suffered was right clarifying to the mind. And Black was just coming to get the hang of the affair when up drives a great car hooting like a fire engine, and out jumps Properjohn full of wrath and commiseration, and this Higbed is carried off to his rest-cure not afore he needed it.'

Again the *Oronsay* hooted from the anchorage. And Captain Maxwell, having completed his narrative to the evident satisfaction of his own artistic sense, advanced to take a ceremonious farewell of the Misses Macleod. 'Awfu' times,' he said. 'Scourging at Dundargie and dancing on Larra. It's right comforting to think there's no' likely to be anything scunnersome on Moila.'

7

IT was three o'clock when Meredith set off on his recon-naissance. The *Oronsay* was hull-down on the horizon. Its decks, he had noticed, were crowded with white-faced sheep; and now the black-faced sheep were spreading over Moila. This mysterious exchange would no doubt be re-enacted in reverse upon the next second Thursday — and in the interval the castle would maintain its unbroken feudal solitude. Meredith, as he crossed the island under Shamus's guidance, found himself more than once turning round to watch the diminishing trail of smoke from the little steamer's funnel; before he reached the farther side all trace of this had vanished, and beyond the grey, eroded line of the ruined buildings was only the white gleam of Inchfarr, and empty sea already glittering beneath the westering sun.

An irrational sense of being left in the lurch seized Me-redith. Captain Maxwell was a reliable man. Moreover, being a Lowlander, he was thoroughly comprehensible. Meredith glanced with some misgiving at Shamus, with whom articulate communication was no more possible than with a Chinese, and who was assuredly no less inscrutable than the most impassive oriental. Not that the lad was himself by any means impassive, for he combined with slow movements and an expression sufficiently withdrawn a lively eye which seemed to converse with whatever it fell upon. Here again, however, was a language as closed to Meredith as was the Gaelic in which Shamus occasionally uttered a few absent words. Whether Shamus knew that Moila was besieged and that this was a foray upon enemy ground Meredith had by no means determined. Nor was it possible to hazard a guess as to how he would comport himself should some untoward situation arise – this if only because he had the trick of appearing now a grown man and now a child scarcely of years to hold a sheep-hook. But when he had rowed Meredith across the Sound in a cockshell whose gunwales came much too close for comfort to a choppy sea, and when they were climbing up through broken cliffs to the swell of the moor, his speaking eye appeared to hold its discourse with invisible but beckoning powers. It was the strain of Celtic mysticism, Meredith decided; and Shamus's vision was penetrating beyond the tangible and visible surfaces of nature to some superior reality beyond. Mildly pleased by company so little Saxon and everyday, Meredith held on his course to whatever fate awaited him.

The sea was only a faint murmur behind them; they trod heather and by old association the smell of it reinforced a rapidly itensifying sense of loneliness abundantly warranted by the landscape. For what now revealed itself was both monotone and featureless; Ben Carron itself had through some odd configuration of the ground flattened itself before them, and the infinite roll of the moor was unbroken even by those protuberances and nodosities which had once a little relieved the wearied eye of Dr Johnson. *Matter left in its original elemental state*, thought Meredith, *or quickened only with one sullen power of useless vegetation*. Marvellous writing. But the point lay in the absence of landmarks to which to relate oneself; it was this that quickly shrivelled one to the stature of a fly crawling

145

over the interminable curves of some small barren brownish-purple planet.

It was to be noted, however, that Shamus appeared not affected in this way. He walked with what was almost a rapid stride, his eye was on the horizon, over his set features played the ghost of a triumphant and not notably innocent smile.

Was it possible, thought Meredith – suddenly changing his mind about Shamus's being in communion with a transcendental order – was it possible that the lad was in the pay of the monstrous Properjohn, and very well knew what reception was being prepared for the stranger under his guidance? Chance or calculation had made this remote island the linch-pin of a ruthless and ramifying criminal organization; was it not likely that in the castle they would keep a servant fee'd? And Shamus – he had surely heard Miss Dorcas remark – was the most recently acquired of the hereditary Captain's retainers. Meredith glanced cautiously at the enigmatic youth striding beside him. There was an increasing purposefulness in his bearing – whereas his instructions had surely been merely to transport Meredith to the mainland and there give whatever attendance was required of him. Was this not a sign of the real state of the case? Properjohn, then, had known well that morning that it was an enemy with whom he was confronted, and now his agent was leading that enemy into a trap.

But Meredith had no sooner cast Shamus for this sinister role than he saw that it was a superfluous one. Properjohn had hinted at a meeting; the hint had been freely accepted; and now no particular leading into a trap was required. Were Properjohn's intentions immediately lethal, he had only to scan this barren space with a telescope and then manoeuvre himself with a rifle behind some convenient tump of heather. If, on the other hand, he hoped to get information by means of either ruse or threat, his obvious course would be to contrive what had the appearance of a casual encounter. Perhaps, then,

Shamus's part would come later, when there was question of putting the body of an intrusive scholar in a sack and rowing out with it by night somewhere beyond Inchfarr. Or perhaps this was all wide of the mark, and Properjohn even more doubtful of the true state of the case than Meredith. Perhaps he did indeed believe or hope that he was about to contact his new associate, Vogelsang. In which case the presence of Shamus, whether as enemy or ally, was neither here nor there.

And there was a point of comfort – thought Meredith, trudging deeper into solitude – in the absence of Jean. With the departure of Captain Maxwell, that monthly link with an external and contemporary world, the mind of Miss Isabella Macleod had again embraced the conception of a state of siege, and it had been only reluctantly that she had agreed on the strategic expediency of a reconnaissance. And that Miss Halliwell should go she had declared altogether out of the question. Lady Flora Macleod, with a kiss instead of the king's shilling, might have raised a regiment for Prince Charles Edward in the Forty-five, but she had not thought it proper to appear in person at Prestonpans or Culloden. Miss Halliwell, therefore, must remain behind the security of Castle Moila's portcullis. And Jean, since she already owed something to the hospitality of the Misses Macleod and recognized that their continued countenance might be vital, had reluctantly agreed. Which – thought Meredith – was a capital thing, for had he not already seen this young woman enjoy more than her fill of danger? For danger, it was true, she had made this journey to the Western Highlands of Scotland. But of danger – if it was possible that an alarmed and desperate Properjohn might indeed after a fashion besiege Moila – future acts held sufficient store. For this afternoon at least it was all to the good that Jean should rest in the wings.

Meanwhile from behind that farther clump of heather a rifle might at this moment be pointing at his, Meredith's, heart. To remove his mind from this speculation, he fell to considering anew the mystery of Dr Higbed, that eminent practitioner of psychological medicine and widely celebrated polymath of popular science. Not so widely celebrated, however, as to be a familiar name in these fastnesses, where the announcement of his identity had nowhere scored any very notable effect. Meredith tried to imagine himself roaring 'I am Meredith!' by way of invoking the special clemency of men or calling down the special favour of heaven. It occurred to him – disturbingly – that this was something which, after all, one does every day, Higbed's particularity consisting only in bellowing, under severe stress, what one commonly does no more than whisper to one's own secret ear.

Here, however, was not the point in the Higbed story that called for present consideration. Properjohn's business, and presumably the business of the late Vogel-sang with whom he was proposing to affiliate himself, consisted in the stealing, receiving, smuggling, and disposing of important works of art. But it was more evident than ever that Higbed did not come within this category – unless, indeed, he were ingeniously to be driven mad and then exhibited in some choice private Bedlam?

Both metaphorically and in point of physical motion, Meredith paused on this. Shamus halted beside him and, momentarily suspending his mute conversation with persons or powers in the middle distance, eyed this abstracted *Sasunnach* with what might, or might not, have been a sinister curiosity. It was remarkable, Meredith was thinking, to what bizarre thoughts untoward circumstances rapidly brought one. A wealthy collector of *recherché* lunatics in the interests of whose cabinet furniture vans prowled the cities of Europe from Edinburgh to Gorki; here surely was a conception that even the inventors of horror films might envy. That it should occur to a sober and ageing student of the classics while walking amid the severe beauties of Northern Britain spoke volumes for the unsettling effect of the past few days.

The Higbed problem must have some less picturesque solution. Was it possible that in the course of his practice as an analytical psychologist the unfortunate man had received – perhaps without at once understanding its significance – information endangering the whole vast organization of which Properjohn was the head or near-head? But if this were so a sack and the Firth of Forth would surely have ended the matter, and Jean's unfortunate acquaintance would not now be enjoying a rest-cure at Carron Lodge. Without further data, Meredith decided, continued speculation was futile; he was without hold on any thread leading towards a solution of the mystery.

But straight above his head – he now realized – were several stout cables leading directly over the sweep of moor before him. And even as he noticed this the cables swayed, a clank and creak was audible, and from behind the next rise appeared the now oddly sinister shape of one of Properjohn's Flying Foxes on its long journey to Inchfarr. There were, he calculated, not many of these weirdly impending contrivances: perhaps a dozen all told, so that when the system was in motion six were always travelling towards, and six away from, the island. But the size of each was considerable, so that it somewhat resembled (Meredith now saw) a covered railway truck suspended upside down, with the invisible upper side presumably exposed to the sky, and the lower so constructed as to fall open when required and precipitate its load into some conveyance stationed below.

Overhead the Flying Fox crept by. And at once – as if it were some piece of theatrical machinery operating a transformation scene – Meredith was aware that the landscape had changed around him. He had come to an elevation at which the sea was again visible; far out, two large aircraft were flying north; and on the remote horizon, obscure behind the broad glittering path of the sun, floated the ghosts of islands. In front of him the mass of Ben Carron had reared itself again in massive grandeur, its lower slopes sparsely clothed with larch and fir, its middle reaches bare rock and scree across which floated wisps of vapour, its summit lost in cloud. He was looking up a shallow valley through which ran a brawling burn; here and there the hurrying water stilled and deepened in a dark brown pool; the faint sound of its tumbling progress was drowned beneath the cries of peewits cutting their arabesques in air. And now two buildings were visible. High on one side of the valley at its farther end a white house, solid, low, and featureless save for a stunted and unmeaning central tower, stood amid a meagre plantation of spruce and pine. This must be Carron Lodge, where Mr Properjohn played the highland laird and where the unhappy Higbed was presumably immured. Along the other side of the valley ran the pylons which carried the cables for the Flying Foxes, and these ended not more than half a mile away in a raw and ill-proportioned structure of corrugated iron, high, unpainted, and – because windowless – displeasingly blind. Up to this building from beyond the valley, and ending before closed and solid doors, was a roughly metalled road along which there doubtless travelled those lorries which collected the guano and transported it to a railhead farther on.

All this had as its setting absolute solitude still. And here, then, was the nerve-centre of the conspiracy. It was amid these august presences of mountain and moor and ocean that frescoes from Florence and statues from Budapest, figurines from Cnossos and canvases from Venice, trundled out to sea against a counterweight of the immemorial droppings of birds. But what happened to them after they went bucketing over the battlements of Castle Moila? Meredith shook his head, never more vividly aware than now of the monstrous disorder of the world's affairs. A weary Canadian soldier, it was said, had made his bed on what turned out to be the *Primavera* of Botticelli. The manuscripts of Goethe had been found fantastically mingled with a nation's gold at the bottom of a mine. What had just passed overhead might very well contain the Horton Venus. ... And these confusions were the product of a diabolic possession of the European body politic such as posterity would find it hard to forgive. Again Meredith shook his head, distrustful of his own preponderant concern for stuff out of museums. After all, people – and by the million – had had a rougher ride than Titian's resplendent lady could ever suffer.

Suppose that all the world's Titians were up there in one Flying Fox, and the always unsound and now demented Higbed were in another. And suppose that he, Meredith, could preserve only one or the other from falling to destruction – what would be the right thing to do? William Godwin, the friend of Shelley, had maintained that it would be one's duty to rescue the philosopher Fénelon from a burning house before attempting to rescue Fénelon's pretty maidservant, or even one's own aged and blameless mother – this because the philosopher had more potential ability to benefit mankind than the prettiest girl or most estimable old woman. Was Godwin right? And if one had to balance the assured cultural importance of the Titians against the very doubtful benefits which a rescued Higbed might bestow upon posterity – Meredith knitted his brows over this obscure question. But had not Bishop Butler, long ago, evolved some argument to dispose of quandaries like these? And Meredith looked absently about him, rather as if expecting the bishop to rise up helpfully from the heather. The bishop, however, was nowhere visible. Nor was Shamus. During this fit of metaphysical abstraction the lad had disappeared – unless, indeed, he had been transformed into what Meredith now saw not forty yards before him: the figure of a man in meagre knickerbockers and a deerstalker hat, absorbedly engaged in casting a fly over a small and improbable pool.

Here, then, was the critical encounter, unavoidable and imminent. And Meredith realized that once more it was an occasion for the lightning brain. Hours ago he ought to have gone over every possible opening, every likely move. Instead of which here he was tramping absently up to the fellow while harmlessly but ineptly meditating *Political Justice* and *The Analogy of Religion*. Ought he at once to reassure the role of Vogelsang? Or – since conceivably Properjohn knew that Vogelsang was dead, but understood little concerning the visitor to Moila – would this be wantonly to give the game away? And, if not Vogelsang, then what? The question was urgent, And, unfortunately, the lightning brain altogether refused to act. What, at this moment, came into Meredith's head instead was that particular philosophical argument after which he had been fumbling some minutes before. Men are quite without the sort of prescience which can determine what amount of human happiness a specific action may ultimately achieve, and before the burning house conscience will be a surer guide than any attempts at utilitarian calculation. But it was, of course, someone earlier than Godwin that Bishop Butler was confuting ... 'Shaftesbury!' Meredith triumphantly exclaimed – and was aware of being almost up with Properjohn as he did so.

And Properjohn – who had hitherto maintained a sinister and commanding immobility by his pool – turned, dropped his rod, and threw up his hands in despair. 'Passworts!' he cried. 'Four, five, eight, ten passworts nobody tells me what. And natchly you reckon us ninny-ficient all alonk.' Properjohn looked much mortified and upset. Then his expression cleared; he kicked his expensive fishing-rod carelessly into the heather and took Meredith by the arm. 'Dear feller,' he said – and chuckled gleefully at this assuming of the laird – 'Dear feller, charmin' to have you drop in. Toppin' year, what? Birts deuced stronk on the wing, eh? Come up and have a peg.' And Properjohn marched Meredith off in the direction of Carron Lodge.

The moors were empty. Only the peewits looked down. Was it, or was it not, Vogelsang who was being thus hospitably led to entertainment? Still Meredith did not know. And still anything in the nature of brilliant improvisation failed him. So he walked in silence, waiting for Properjohn to speak again.

And Properjohn spoke, lowering his voice as if the heather might have ears. 'We gotta Titian,' he said. 'We gotta Giotto.' He rubbed his hands and spoke now in a sort of boastful whisper. 'Almost we gotta German next-pert, *echter Kunsthistoriker*, save us maybe thousands, knows hundred two hundred perhaps places fine valuable pictures hid about Germany, Holland, France. We sure almost got him, Vogelsang passes as Birtsong.'

'*Almost* got him?' said Meredith. 'Did something go wrong?'

'Shot.' Properjohn was laconic. 'All this too dam' big organization, silly passworts and nobody hardly knows who. Some trouble in London I don't yet get it just how.' He shook his head despondently. 'Same as I don't quite get you. You know Bubear?'

So here the awkwardness began. Yes or no – oranges or lemons? Meredith could see no principle on which to choose. 'Oh yes,' he said – and tried to make the utterance as meaningful and cryptic as might be – 'I know Bubear.'

'Sure,' said Properjohn – apparently acquiescing in what he took to be Meredith's tone. 'And now Bubear lost his face.'

'Lost his face?' Meredith was horrified by this drastic issue of the swipe he had been obliged to take at Bubear with a revolver butt.

'Lost his face in a crisis and blew up two three thousand pounds not so bad goods. But he did clear the Titian and the Giotto.' Properjohn's voice was again triumphant. 'We gotta Titian and a Giotto better almost anything we sent through yet. And about this Vogelsang passed as Birtsong now shot we get the faks soon enough. Bubear comes here tonight.'

8

DUNCAN *comes here tonight* ... But at Dunsinane, thought Meredith, this had been hard cheese on Duncan himself; whereas at Carron Lodge the victim would be a somewhat earlier arrival – one better seen in Martial and Juvenal than in the elementary precautions that should attend criminal investigation.

Vogelsang, then, was not only dead, but known to be dead, and Jean's sanguine calculations as to Bubear's reticence and duplicity had been all awry. Moreover, the adventure was repeating itself with slight variations, much as if it were a fairy tale. In London Meredith had met Bubear and had been mistaken for somebody unknown – with that unknown's imminent arrival threatening exposure. Now in Scotland he had met Properjohn and been mistaken for somebody else unknown – with Bubear's imminent arrival threatening exposure. There was something peculiarly paralysing about having to play the identical hazardous farce over again. Moreover, he was now without any assistance equivalent to Jean's prompting – and to this had to be added his sense that the real Properjohn, who lurked beneath the absurdities of the polyglot laird, was a more formidable adversary than Bubear had been.

They drew near to Carron Lodge. It was, Meredith thought, an uncomfortably isolated spot. As locale for a trial of wits, or for another bout of slapstick hue and cry, he would prefer Bubear's lately demolished warehouse every time. For one thing, Carron Lodge spoke of leisure and reflective quiet, which was just the sort of environment against which imposture could not hope successfully to stand. This time to carry off the necessary impersonation was utterly impossible – or at least it was so while the identity of the man to be impersonated was a blank. At any moment Properjohn might ask some simple questions which would end the matter.

For a moment Meredith meditated ignominious flight. After all, he now definitely knew that Bubear, presumably convoying the Horton Venus and the Giotto, was to arrive tonight. To make good an escape and at once arrange a little reception by the military or the police was plainly the rational, as it was the only hopeful, course. But was flight possible? That he could run faster than Properjohn recent experiences made him judge likely enough. But the moor was wide and shelterless, and so desperate a character would certainly be armed. Before Meredith had made ten yards the situation would be clear to his enemy, and this meant that before he had made fifteen yards Properjohn would be taking aim at him. And at fifteen yards, Meredith knew, a revolver in any sort of practised hand scores no misses. Flight, in fact, would be an altogether injudicious resort.

There were only two bright spots. The one was that Jean was for the moment out of it. The other was that he had not rashly claimed to be Vogelsang on the chance that Properjohn supposed him to be so. That would have been fatal indeed. It would have been fatal, he repeated to himself, frowning as he did so...

And even as he frowned he stopped, and confronted Properjohn with a half turn. Not without some difficulty his heels clicked together in the soft heather. 'Vogelsang,' he said.

'Hey?' Properjohn looked at Meredith with a startled eye. 'What that you say about Vogelsang passed as Birtsong?'

'I am Vogelsang, my good Herr Properjohn. And it seems to me that about this Bubear of yours we must have a little talk. Why should he direct me to that castle instead of to your known house? And why should he send you a fantastic story about my having been shot? There is much in this that I do not understand, my friend.'

'Hey –'

'And why do you not give the countersign?' Meredith, now that there had been abruptly revealed to him the only course in which a possible safety lay, felt quite his old self. He l ooked sternly at Properjohn. 'Shaftesbury,' he said deliberately, and let a deepening suspicion gather on his brow.

Properjohn raised both hands despairingly in air. 'They mean nothinks to me, quarter, half, three-quarters these passworts! Always I –'

'When the safety of other men is at stake,' said Meredith silkily, 'the forgetting of a password may be inconvenient – very inconvenient indeed, Herr Properjohn. Or *sogenannter* Herr Properjohn.' And Meredith let his right hand steal in a sinister fashion towards a pocket.

'But I am Properjohn!'

The man was really rattled. Just so, Meredith reflected, must Higbed have made his own claim to identity on these very moors. But although Properjohn was rattled, he too was edging a hand towards the pocket of his country-gentleman's jacket. And this might be awkward. Meredith therefore let his own hands drop to his sides. '*Also, gut!*' he said soothingly, and wondered if it would be judicious and colourable to drop into German – a language which Properjohn had probably the same rather uncertain command of as English. 'And perhaps you will prove it by explaining convincingly whom you took me for in the *Schloss* – the castle – of those old ladies?'

'Natchly I take you for Signor Pantelli, big Italian dealer goes across tonight!' Properjohn was indignant. 'Goes across sell two three Giorgiones account clients thinks better leave Europe a while.'

'Two or three Giorgiones!' Meredith in turn could not restrain his indignation. Was it possible that even amid all the vastness of the United States there could be men at once so wealthy and so crazily depraved as to give large sums of money for stolen pictures which they could never do more than hide away?

'But we gotta Titian.' Properjohn, his pride evidently piqued by what he had misinterpreted as excessive admiration in Meredith's voice, was boastful once more. 'We gotta Titian, we gotta Giotto –'

'And you've got a very treacherous and incompetent London agent.' It would not do, Meredith had decided, to let Properjohn get up again on too confident a perch – or not until much more information had been extracted from him. They were now on a low terrace that ran before Carron Lodge; this sinister dwelling, tricked in all its abundant bunting of Hunting Stuart, was about to receive

156

them. Meredith laid a finger on his host's shoulder and brought him to a halt. 'Yes, my friend! A very treacherous fellow whom we shall lay by the heels tonight. And I think it is this same Bubear who has let you suppose that I am responsible for losing the Mykonos Marbles to Marsden's lot – *hein?*'

Properjohn made a deprecating but guilty noise. 'I get a code telegram Bubear that way,' he said. 'Same as I get a telegram Bubear shot Vogelsang and the place blowed up.'

'The place *is* blown up. Make no mistake about that. But all the stuff he'll tell you was destroyed there went into his own pocket long ago.'

Properjohn let out a sudden wail, altogether inappropriate to a highland laird standing by his own threshold. 'But, Herr Vogelsang, Bubear's got the Titian, Bubear's got the Giotto! He's supposed bringing them himself tonight.' Properjohn's wail became a howl. 'Almost we gotta Titian, almost we gotta Giotto. And now –'

'I doubt whether it's as bad as that.' Here was a point, Meredith saw, at which caution and foresight were required. 'Small pickings are what constitute Bubear's line, and I don't think he could handle a Titian. Perhaps you remember a little matter of an Aubusson carpet?'

Properjohn stared. 'Sure. But I don't get how you know these thinks. Puttikly seeing –'

'Well, the last time I saw Bubear he was standing on it. And I don't doubt he told you it was lost in transit.'

'Exak that.' Properjohn was breathing heavily, and it was plain that he was much stirred by these revelations. 'Once I only get Bubear here –'

'But I dare say he's merely been taking what he regards as a fair commission.' Meredith, who was now well launched upon the part of a modern Iago, realized that the appearance of assuaging suspicion was here his most potent means of rousing it. 'What is an Aubusson carpet, after all? Or even two or three thousand pounds worth of second-rate stuff supposed to have been destroyed in a basement? You and I, Herr Properjohn, need take small account of such trifles.'

'Trifles! You call the Mykonos Marbles trifles?' And Properjohn tugged in a sort of frenzy at his gentleman's droopy moustache.

'Come, come. I didn't say he took the Marbles. I said you were a fool to believe his story that I was concerned in it. It is not possible greatly to admire the efficiency of your organization, my friend.'

'Why, our organization has made all the biggest most importantest deals for gentlemen thinking leave Europe since almost Stalingrad or Battle of Britain back of that. And nobody ever criticized fine, efficient service we give before.'

'Shaftesbury,' said Meredith inexorably.

Properjohn appeared much disposed to vary tugging his moustache with tearing his hair. 'Passworts!' he cried. 'I tell you passworts isn't efficient, is only kids' acting. Most likeliest it was dam' fool London's-going Berlin's-burning talk lost us those marbles to Marsden.'

'Ah,' said Meredith, massively oracular.

'Hey?'

'I suppose you weren't even told that they had got hold of one of Marsden's girls?'

'Certain I was told. Most all importantest things is told to me at once. But Bubear reports last code wire this girl lost dead.' Properjohn frowned. 'Vogelsang lost dead and this girl lost dead. Fishlike, huh?'

Meredith nodded. 'Very fishlike, my friend. I begin to think that, after all, this Bubear must be playing for large stakes. He knew I was bringing the girl –'

'*Hey?*'

'– whereupon he declares that we are both dead. And – mark you – he had carefully misdirected us to that castle. Do you think he meant us ever to leave it – *or to leave it the way we came?*'

This last was a reckless shot in the dark. But then the whole piece of mystification upon which he was embarked was so nightmarishly tenuous, so vulnerable to the first effort of coherent thought that Properjohn should achieve that Meredith was convinced of its being only a matter of minutes till disaster overtook him. His dive back into the role of Vogelsang had been shrewd enough. The species of return from the dead which it posited had thrown Properjohn off his balance; and this Meredith had been able to follow up with a good deal of convincing information and reference. But the imposture started more hazards than it could possibly circumvent. All that could be done was to play for a little more time on the offchance that some favourable opportunity for a bolt would present itself. And meanwhile the more Meredith drew upon his fancy the better. He knew various bells that could be more or less effectively sounded in Properjohn's head. On these he must ring the changes as rapidly as he could.

'You gotta girl of Marsden's?' Properjohn had led the way into his incongruous domicile; now they were standing in a flashy veneer and chromium room before what Meredith conjectured to be a cocktail cabinet.

'Certainly I have. Marsden's *best* girl. Didn't you see her?'

'And her eating out of your fist?'

'Of course.' Meredith endeavoured to look like one before whose sexy charms an enemy's retainers melted away. And this put him in mind of another bell that might be sounded. 'And what about Higbed, my friend! It seems to have been a matter of Shaftesbury again, does it not?'

'They let him get away for a bit, sure.' Properjohn was abashed. But suddenly he looked at Meredith with bewilderment and supicion. 'Say!' he said. 'Signor Pantelli, rather mean Herr Vogelsang, I don't get how you up on Higbed, seeing Higbed is no more than little private insurance-cover idea of mine.'

'I'm not up on him.' Meredith spoke rather hastily. 'I merely mean that it's known all over this district that you have been pursuing an escaped madman called Higbed. It seems to me a matter which might cause gossip, and into which the police would inquire. Please remember that you are asking me to associate myself with your undertaking, Herr Properjohn. And all I meet is muddle,

muddle, and again muddle! All over Europe I have note of hidden works of art of the first quality. Naturally, I expect an organization of the first quality to deal with them. Would you like six wax figures by Michelangelo –'

'*Hey!*'

'– or a large Leonardo cartoon? Would you like' – and Meredith became at once specific and reckless – 'the Van Eyk altar-piece from Ghent, the Mona Lisa –'

'We gotta Titian. I *hope* we gotta Titian. But the Mona Lisa!'

'– the Night Watch, the Burial of Count Orgaz –'

'But hey! That burial of the guy Orgaz is certain almost –'

'Never mind!' Meredith raised a distracting hand and found Properjohn obsequiously pressing into it a luridly tinted decoction from his cocktail cabinet. 'Never mind what you have been led to believe, my friend. *I know.* You have a customer wants an El Greco, a Velasquez, a Goya? I can point to the very spot where it can be procured – and with no more trouble than in shovelling the earth off a trapdoor to a cellar, or pushing past a bundle of hay in a barn. *But I expect efficiency.*'

'Natchly, your Excellency.' Properjohn was now bowing and bobbing after a fashion very uncommon in gentlemen in knickerbockers and Connemara cloth. 'Please excuse shockink mistake take our importantest almost Continental connexion for small Wop dealer Pantelli goes across tonight with two three dud Giorgiones!'

'Ah,' said Meredith. 'About this Pantelli. He may be turning up at any time?'

Properjohn nodded. 'Most any time. Which is why when I heard about a stranger being at the castle I thought well better call in case small Wop Pantelli gone direk there by mistake.'

'I see.' Meredith, having in a fit of high spirits hoisted Vogelsang to the bad eminence of one with whom plundered Leonardos and El Grecos were matters of everyday, was beating his brains for some further monstrous absurdity for which to barter small pocketfuls of time. So far nobody had appeared except Properjohn himself, and not five paces from where host and guest stood sipping their cocktails was a window giving almost directly on deserted moor. Would not his best course be to endeavour to catch Properjohn for a moment unawares, serve him as he had served the subordinate Bubear not long ago, and then bolt from Carron Lodge as quickly as he could? To do so would be to give an alarm which must inevitably send the whole organization to earth with a speed rivalling even that with which the London warehouse had been abandoned and blown sky-high. And as it would be hours before any effective force could be summoned to these fastnesses, the final result might be unsatisfactory in the extreme. But was not even this better than the certainty of exposure either within minutes (as was still overwhelmingly probable) or hard upon the arrival of Bubear later in the evening?

Meredith looked round for a weapon – and remarked that for the sanctum of one given to trading in Titians and Giottos this retreat of Properjohn's was singularly devoid of traditional beauties. On the walls, it was true, were several excellent sporting prints, but these evidently went with the knickerbockers and the moustache as part of the build-up of the laird. The carpet showed a senseless design of squares and cubes in half a dozen impure colours, and the several objects reposing on it spoke equally of *l'art moderne* in the depressing form in which this percolates down to cheap furnishing concerns. Connoisseurship, it appeared, was something from which, in his off hours, Properjohn was pleased to escape. The only articles suggesting any pride of ownership were the cocktail cabinet and a large model galleon in full sail, entirely executed in chromium plating and silver wire. It was when Meredith's eye fell on this last absurdity that his mind was made up. The shape was somewhat awkward and only the hull would be strong enough to do the necessary damage. Nevertheless, he was resolved. He would pick up the galleon and bring it down hard on Properjohn's head. And then he would make a run for it.

With this plan in mind Meredith edged towards the galleon – cautiously at first and then with a rapid swoop as he remarked Properjohn's attention to be occupied with mixing another drink. He had reached out for it, indeed, when an entirely new thought struck him. Somewhere in this house was the unfortunate Dr Higbed – an unsound philosopher, it was true, but yet a fellow man and even, in a fashion, a fellow scholar. For reasons utterly obscure, he had been dogged by furniture vans, kidnapped, and subjected to various trials and indignities which had, it would appear, temporarily deprived him of his reason. If Meredith fled now would there be any substantial chance of rescuing the unhappy man before he was carried off to some more secure hiding-place? Meredith saw that he must first hit Properjohn on the head and then hunt for Higbed. This obligation would enormously decrease his chances of getting away. Yet only if he got away was there any substantial possibility of crushing the abominable organization through the channel of whose Flying Foxes some of the major art treasures of Europe were being conveyed to madmen far less innocent than the imprisoned psychologist. Here, in fact, was the old dilemma once more – the dilemma, not of Fénelon or the pretty maidservant, but of Higbed or the Horton Venus (and much else). And Meredith was so struck by the force of his predicament that he was actually standing in meditation upon it, and with his arms held out towards the galleon, when Properjohn turned round again holding a couple of glasses.

Fortunately, Properjohn misinterpreted his gesture as one of unrestrained admiration. He cocked his head on one side. 'Toppin' little think, eh what, m'dear fellow?' Chuckling at this return to his favourite comedy of the laird, Properjohn held out a glass. Then his face grew serious and it was clear that he saw his guest once more against the background of a veritable promised land of Rembrandts and Goyas. Soberly he set down both glasses the better to make a formal bow. 'Better your Excellency come alonk see the boss,' he said. 'Not like small Wop

Pantelli dealt with efficient by me and not know any better than that I run it.'

'The boss?' asked Meredith stupidly – but feeling as he did so that a great light dawned. This grotesque Properjohn, so lamentably deficient in an aura of the higher criminality, was but a screen behind which moved superior powers. And these superior powers were on the premises. An introduction was imminent.

For now Properjohn had turned and was leading the way out through a farther door. His head showed a bald patch behind. Here, had Meredith still so desired, was the right target for the galleon. Alternatively, he could assay the pleasure of leaping upon Properjohn from behind and throttling him. Or he could simply try one tremendous kick and then race for freedom. But none of these proposals had any charm for Meredith at this moment. Not even the business of saving the art treasures of Europe was sovereign with him. Once more – as upon a fateful occasion in a tobacconist's shop – simple intellectual curiosity held sway.

Properjohn walked down several corridors and mounted a staircase. Meredith had a fleeting impression of a butler or factotum carrying a tray, of maidservants of a respectable but personable sort flitting about with the cans of hot water proper to this evening hour – of these and other fugitive evidences of a gentleman's well-conducted house. And then Properjohn had opened a door and momentarily disappeared; his barbarous lingo was queerly mingled with a cultivated voice in rapid question and answer; he emerged and gestured somewhat after the fashion of a Lord Chamberlain according the *grande entrée* to a visitor of consequence.

And Meredith entered an altogether different sort of room. Over the fireplace hung Vermeer's Aquarium – which all the world knows has its proper abiding place at Scamnum Court. There was one other work of art; Meredith after a single glance knew that it was by Praxitiles. And from behind a gold-inlaid desk which had once been Napoleon's there advanced an old man with a high forehead and silver hair. 'My dear Herr Vogelsang,' he said, 'we welcome you as from the dead. And welcome indeed, my dear sir, to the headquarters of the International Society for the Diffusion of Cultural Objects.'

9

WERE I from Dunsinane away and clear, Profit again should hardly draw me here ... But still (thought Meredith) curiosity might. For Don Perez Sierra y Campo (which turned out to be the name of his new acquaintance) was an altogether more interesting person than either Properjohn or the now imminently expected Bubear. For one thing, not even the English of the Misses Macleod of Moila was purer than that dispensed by Don Perez over his dinnertable. And for another, he proceeded to expound in this limpid medium a veritable philosophy of theft. More confidently than Autolycus justifying himself as a snapperup of unconsidered trifles did this polished gentleman defend his endeavours to carry away the greater part of the treasures of Europe.

'We regret the Mykonos Marbles,' he said, 'and are the more rejoiced to hear that you may find means to regain them from the man Marsden. Properjohn mentioned a girl whose – ah – friendship you have succeeded in cultivating; and who is, it seems, at the castle. I confess that the matter is obscure to me, but no doubt you will provide enlightenment as your leisure serves.'

'Marsden's girl', said Meredith, 'is likely to be useful in more ways than one –'

'Ah,' said Don Perez urbanely.

'– and I don't really care to leave her there. Particularly as Bubear, who appears unreliable, almost certainly misdirected us to the castle for some dishonest purpose of his own.'

'It is not improbable,' said Don Perez. 'Everywhere,

indeed, we may discern symptoms of widespread moral disintegration. I should have no confidence in the integrity of the man Bubear.'

'In fact, after dinner, it will be as well that I should go across and fetch her away.' Meredith dropped this proposal very casually indeed. 'May I congratulate you on your claret?'

Don Perez bowed. 'Mouton Rotchield, Herr Vogelsang, of a year which I confess indifferently good. Wine at least will here and there incarnadine to the last the ashen pages of the European decadence! And when this continent is no more than a fading history shall we not recall its vanished epochs primarily in terms of wine and flowers? Mouton Rotchield and the beautiful – if absurdly named! – roses of modern horticulture will seem one with the violets of Catullus and the vine-leaves of Anacreon. Let them give you a little more of this very tolerable Chateaubriand which they have managed to scrape up for us.' Don Perez paused. 'As for your suggestion of fetching the girl tonight, I counsel – nay, I judge – against it. That the Marbles should be retrieved is excellent. But we must not forget that there are plenty good fish in the sea! For example, you can doubtless suggest where several equally fine archaic sculptures can be rescued?'

'Assuredly I can.' Meredith spoke with sober confidence. Was this elegant scoundrel, he wondered, with all his Mouton Rotchield and his fiddle-faddle of Anacreon and Catullus, really a person of substantial antiquarian culture? He decided to make a cast towards finding out. 'Assuredly I can,' he repeated. 'What would you say, for example, to the Locri Fawn?'

Don Perez looked momentarily puzzled. Then, politely, he laughed. 'You are pleased to joke with me, Herr Vogelsang. But after all, it is natural that you should not wish to divulge these matters until we have discussed the terms of our association.'

This was not so good. For the Locri Fawn was a statue which existed only in a work of imaginative literature – and Don Perez had been right on the spot within seconds.

Meredith began to pine for the less well-informed Properjohn – who had not been admitted to the present refined repast. He wished, too, that he had not talked so much bold nonsense about the Mona Lisa and the Burial of Count Orgaz. And was Don Perez Sierra y Campo really taken in, as undoubtedly Bubear and Properjohn had been? Or was this excellent dinner merely the graceful preliminary to a gesture which should unequivocally invite one to step into a sack? Meredith took a sip of claret – for, after all, there is nothing quite like a great claret for sharpening the perceptions and subtilizing the mind – and resolved to play the game out. 'May I ask', he said, 'if you feel satisfied with your operations to date?'

Don Perez shook his head sadly – but not before he, too, had applied himself to his glass. 'The Society does what it can. But much, I fear, is bound to go down with the ship.'

'The ship?'

Don Perez looked courteously surprised. 'Europe, my dear sir.'

'You are so sure of its sinking?' With concentrated effort Meredith smothered in himself sudden anger. 'You don't think that it may, after all, right itself again? I am, I fear, no historian – except in the field of aesthetics, maybe – but such inquiries as I have made suggest to me that over and over again cultivated Europeans have despaired of the stability of their civilization. Theirs is the fated generation at last! But it has been all tommyrot every time.'

'But not this time, Herr Vogelsang! And the whole labours of our Society (to which I trust you are firmly resolved to ally yourself) are undertaken in the light of that conviction. As a civilization Europe is bankrupt. To contemplate it is to achieve what a distinguished compatriot of yours has termed *ein Blick ins Chaos*, a glance into the abyss. Everywhere public order perishes, and civil polity has become but a historical phenomenon.' And Don Perez paused on this beautiful cadence, evidently to let it linger on the ear much as he let the Mouton

166

Rotchield linger on the palate. 'It is sad,' he said, 'very sad – but at least our duty is clear.'

'I cannot help feeling that you take a very exaggerated view.' Meredith was much too indignant at this impudent perversion of truths which were indeed sad enough to be very careful in remembering his part. 'In England, at least, I see a great deal of public order – if anything, rather too much. And the Continent, after all, has shown immense powers of resistance to the very storms it has let loose upon itself. This is true, for example, of the artists and men of letters of France. It has been true of many scholars – and of many simple people too – in my own country, Germany. And resistance means resilience. I believe that the social order, or what you call our civil polity, must be altogether changed. But of our powers of recuperation I have no doubt whatever. Nor can I believe that you, Don Perez, who belong to one of the oldest of Mediterranean civilizations –'

'What you say interests me.' And Don Perez Sierra y Campo looked at Meredith as if it were true that he was very interested indeed. 'But we must not let the mere fact of being ourselves Europeans carry us away. Let us suppose ourselves to be New Zealanders, as was the man whom your great writer, Lord Macaulay –'

'Surely,' said Meredith calmly, 'Macaulay was an Englishman.'

'I beg your pardon.' And Don Perez gave a little bow. 'Whom *their* great writer, Lord Macaulay, pictured as musing over the ruins of London. Let us imagine ourselves, I say, to be New Zealanders. Or, better, let us suppose ourselves observers in Mars, such as one finds in the romances of your – of the English novelist, Wells.'

'By all means,' said Meredith, 'let us imagine ourselves to be Martians.' Don Perez, he was reflecting, certainly did not make these little slips at random. Either he *knew* – or he was attempting to unnerve a suspected man. 'Or let it be inhabitants of the moon – whom another Englishman, a poet, describes as betwixt the angelical and human kind. For what could fit persons so benevolent as you and

I, Don Perez, better than that? Thank you: by all means another glass.' And Meredith took the decanter and poured wine with a steady hand.

'Whether from Mars or from the moon,' pursued Don Perez, 'we can survey both sides of the Atlantic at once. On the one hand, we see the smouldering ashes of a million destroying fires. We see shattered cathedrals; whole cities surviving from the Middle Ages only to be flattened from the air; canvases, which enshrine not individual genius alone, but centuries and centuries of the very mind of Europe, huddled in salt mines or trucked about as some war lord's booty. It is a veritable *Götterdämmerung –*'

'Quite so,' said Meredith. 'And an *Untergang des Abendlandes*. And *Blick ins Chaos* we have already had.'

Don Perez slightly raised his eyebrows. 'But now for the other view! And it is veritably a case, as your great poet Shakespeare said –' Don Perez paused. 'For I think you will agree that Shakespeare has been conclusively proved to have been a German?'

'I see no harm', said Meredith dryly, 'in the simpler of my fellow countrymen believing so.'

'It is a case, then, of *looking on this picture and on that*. For we turn from this savage spectacle to the shores of North America and are at once greeted with the heartening spectacle of advancing culture and ordered progress! Here, and here alone, can we look to see the millennial achievements of western civilization revered, perpetuated, deepened, and renewed.'

'There may be something in what you say.' Perhaps because of the claret, or perhaps because of the moorland air, Meredith found this vein of eloquence in Don Perez decidedly soporific. 'I am not at all disposed to question the likely cultural predominance of the United States. It will issue naturally from an economic predominance: their Rome to our Greece.'

'Precisely so; most happily put, my dear Herr Vogelsang! And now consider how the cultural heritage of

Greece was transferred to Rome. Or, even better, consider how the surviving art and literature of the entire ancient world was secured for the modern world in the Renaissance period.'

'Ah,' said Meredith. 'Theft.'

'It often came to that. Manuscripts, for example, were rescued from neglect and decay amid a degenerate monasticism by whatever means best served. And have not we – benevolent Martians dipping down from space – a similar duty today? We must rescue what we can from the decay of Europe and transfer it to the security and just esteem of the United States. And I say *just esteem* advisedly. You have only to consider what they are prepared to pay.' Don Perez paused while his butler served an ice pudding and uncorked a bottle of champagne. 'For our wares', he pursued, 'are almost the only conceivable goods which our transatlantic friends cannot produce for themselves. And how vastly important they are in maintaining the intellectual and aesthetic equilibrium of a continent so vastly and rapidly expansive on the material side! It is our merchandise alone, my dear sir, that may usefully be called in from the Old World to redress the balance of the New.'

Meredith looked distrustfully at his champagne. Was it the extreme felicity of Don Perez's expression that was getting on his nerves? Or was it the knowledge that at this very moment Properjohn and a newly arrived Bubear might be getting matters straight in another room? 'You put the matter admirably,' he said, 'and I look forward with pleasure to our continued cordial association. But don't you think it a great pity that all this has to be done in so clandestine a way? It limits the market so. Just think how much better it would be if, say, the Metropolitan Museum of Fine Arts in New York were prepared to ask no questions of a benevolent Martian coming forward with a well-known Gainsborough or Raeburn.'

Don Perez Sierra y Campo sighed. 'Ah, my dear sir, there is a vision of enlightenment indeed! But can we doubt that the time will come, and that quickly?'

'Well, as a matter of fact, I doubt it very much.'

Don Perez shook his head indulgently. 'Herr Vogelsang, did anyone bother his head when Lord Elgin walked off with most of the sculptures from the Parthenon?'

Meredith sat up. 'Most decidedly a good many people did! He had to defend himself in a pamphlet which he called *Memorandum on the Subject of the Earl of Elgin's Pursuits in Greece*.'

Don Perez bowed – thereby indicating, it seemed, that he had been agreeably instructed by a fellow scholar. 'Very well! And doubtless we shall put out our own pamphlet one day – though I suspect that it will be an altogether more substantial monograph. *The Early History of the International Society for the Diffusion of Cultural Objects*. But my point is simply this. At present we have to rely on enlightened collectors who are prepared to keep their acquisitions in private. But in a hundred – nay, perhaps in fifty – years all this will be changed. For the populations of Europe will be no more than a peasantry and a wandering banditti. And thus when these works of art are brought forth from their half-century of seclusion men will no more think to inquire of their former owners' rights than they do of tom-toms and totem-poles in some museum of Polynesian anthropology.'

It suddenly occurred to Meredith to wonder whether Don Perez really believed in this remarkable Shape of Things to Come – which would mean, surely, that he was mad. And the thought of madness suggested something else. 'By the way,' he said, 'what are your plans in regard to that fellow Higbed?'

'Higbed?' Don Perez stared. 'You mean the psychiatrist and author of all those facile books? I have no plan in regard to him whatever. Except, of course, on no account to read him.'

This was interesting. It suggested that just as Bubear was by way of doing a little business behind the back of Properjohn so was Properjohn behind the back of Don Perez. Indeed, had not Properjohn said something to the effect that Higbed was a private speculation of his own?

This mystery there seemed no penetrating. And meantime would not Don Perez think it odd that his new associate Vogelsang should ask so random a question?

But Don Perez's mind was moving in another direction. 'Not', he said, 'that the celebrated Higbed is at all an exception in that respect. I seldom read anything fresh from the printing presses. Indeed, as I grow older I turn back more and more to my Homer and my Theocritus, to my Martial, my Juvenal, and my Horace.'

Meredith suddenly felt an uncomfortable pricking of the spine. Was it possible that this well-dieted rascal – who now seemed to be proposing to move on from champagne to port – not only knew who he, Meredith, was not, but also – And here Meredith came upon an interesting fact of mind. Between the disastrous consequences of being known not Vogelsang, and those of being known positively as Richard Meredith, editor of Martial and authority on Juvenal, there was surely nothing to choose. And yet the suspicion that he was *known* was infinitely more unnerving than the suspicion that he was *detected*. Was this not a survival of primitive man's irrational belief that knowledge of his name would arm his enemy with some magical advantage? Meredith was so taken with this discovery that he now spoke with very little notion of what he was saying. 'What put Higbed in my mind', he said, 'was again that fellow Bubear – who seems an altogether unreliable man. He told me –'

'To be sure.' Don Perez helped himself to port and stretched out his hand towards the walnuts. 'Bubear is altogether unreliable, we are agreed. And – dear me! – here he is.'

It was deplorably true. Had Meredith not fallen into a muse on the subject of primitive man, footsteps or voices might have given him some seconds' further notice of what was coming. For Bubear – as also, no doubt, the Horton Venus and the Giotto fresco – had arrived; here, already standing in the doorway, were both the displeasing person whom he had once hit on the head and his more recent acquaintance Properjohn. It was evident that the two had already been in fierce dispute; so much had Meredith's Iago-whisperings of earlier in the evening achieved. But now, surely, the end had come. For Bubear was raising an accusing finger. Denunciation was upon his lips.

'Ah,' said Meredith. 'I think you scarcely expected to see me again, my friend.'

Bubear was disconcerted. Properjohn was perplexed. Don Perez Sierra y Campo sipped port.

'Perhaps' – Meredith continued – 'you will explain to us about your friends the old ladies in the castle, to whom you were good enough to misdirect Marsden's girl and myself? And this story of having had to blow up your warehouse and much valuable property belonging to the Society? And a little matter of a carpet? And a very big matter' – for suddenly the memory of a valuable confession of Bubear's had returned to Meredith – 'concerning the Tobermoray figurines?'

Don Perez abruptly set down his glass. 'The Tobermoray figurines!' he exclaimed.

Meredith nodded. 'But certainly. Bubear appropriated them to himself. I found out. And because of that – But you have only to look at him, Don Perez. His guilt is written plain upon his face.'

It was certainly true that Bubear presented a picture of guilt. That the man whom he had believed blown to fragments in a vast explosion should have turned up here claiming to be Vogelsang still was a circumstance confounding in itself; but the raising of the fatal matter of the Tobermoray figurines was plainly a death blow. Bubear was ashen. Yet he endeavoured to rally. He licked his lips and spoke in a sudden high surprising voice. 'This man is a spy! Vogelsang is dead, I tell you, and this man killed him. He and the girl –'

Don Perez got quietly to his feet and held up a hand before which the voice of his wretched subordinate tailed into silence. 'Mr Bubear,' he said, 'this is idle talk. Herr Vogelsang, though you have been unaware of the fact, has long been personally known to me. He is my honoured guest tonight.' And Don Perez bowed suavely to Meredith.

Meredith bowed back. What fantastic game was now afoot? But Don Perez had paused only for a second. Now he continued to address Bubear in an even tone. 'So lies are useless. The carpet I would have let you have taken without animadversion; it is as if a servant removed a bottle of inferior wine or a dish of game. But the misappropriation of the figurines was a major breach of trust. Do I understand that you admit it?'

Bubear, who was now totally unnerved, made what appeared to be an affirmative noise. He also – what was to Meredith extremely unpleasant – slid to his knees and raised his arms in a grotesque convention of supplication.

'Very well.' And Don Perez made an almost imperceptible sign to Properjohn. 'Mr Bubear, you are dismissed from the employment of the Society.'

Properjohn's arm moved and there was a dull report. Bubear fell on the floor, quite dead.

10

BUT it would be difficult, Meredith thought, to say who had killed the man. For it was he, Meredith, who had revealed the incriminating matter of the figurines – and this in what was still no more than a frantic playing for time. If he had concealed that major peculation Bubear might not have been (in his employer's pleasant phrase) *dismissed from the employment of the Society.* Was he at all justified in what he had done? Meredith doubted it. Nor could the rights or wrongs of the matter be at all affected by its remoter consequences; by the fact of whether it did, or did not, enable him to retrieve the whole desperate situation.

And what, indeed, was the state of affairs now? Bubear, whose dead body was jerking with a last reflex on the floor, had been cut off in the moment of denouncing the false Vogelsang; and thus the chief danger which Meredith had been called upon to face was eliminated. Don Perez had claimed to be fully assured that it was indeed Vogelsang who was dining with him. But this he had done by means of a direct lie and with the obvious intention of driving Bubear to a confession of his treachery. Did he *really* believe that his guest was the director of some great German picture-gallery, proposing to do a deal on the basis of much valuable information on hidden works of art? Meredith had received more than one hint to the contrary. And this in some degree tempered his horror and dismay at Bubear's end. For it meant the substantial likelihood still of mortal danger. And in mortal danger a man cannot afford the luxury of a scrupulous conscience.

'And now we can all sit down.' Don Perez spoke in brisker tones than Meredith had heard him use so far. It was almost as if he was about to call for the minutes of the last meeting. 'Properjohn, you may take a glass of port.'

Properjohn (who was supposed to be the laird of Carron and the support of an invalid uncle) sat down meekly and with an ingratiating bob. Meredith sat down too, though with considerable effort. So far as he knew, he had never before proposed to take wine with a couple of murderers, and the notion profoundly revolted him. At the same time he became aware of an even more disturbing prompting deep in his own mind. Why, he thought –

> why do I yield to that suggestion
> Whose horrid image doth unfix my hair
> And make my seated heart knock at my ribs,
> Against the use of nature?

And the horrid suggestion was simply this: that he should repeat – perfectly deliberately this time – his technique for prompting Don Perez to murder. His revealing the matter of the figurines had spelt the end of Bubear. By revealing that Properjohn too was up to some game of his own in the mysterious affair of Higbed might it not be possible to have this other enemy *dismissed from the employment of the Society?*

Meredith's mind turned from *Macbeth* to the equally sensational story of *Little Black Quasha* – in which at a critical juncture the tigers (all save two) are induced to gobble each other up. Would he be justified in engineering a somewhat similar state of affairs in the ranks of the Society for the Diffusion of Cultural Objects? But Meredith saw that it was no good debating this ethical point with himself, for the idea of thus eliminating Properjohn had such a thrill of unholy enticement to it that he knew he must turn it down at once. And, anyway, Don Perez was markedly dictating the course things should take at the moment, and Meredith saw no present means of seizing the initiative.

'And first,' said Don Perez, 'what of the Italian – Pantelli, is it not? Has he arrived?'

Properjohn shook his head. 'Like maybe he got lost,' he said. 'Udderwise ought to be here long ago.'

'But I don't like this of people getting lost.' Don Perez was suavely severe. 'And I am unable to believe that Bubear had anything to gain by directing Herr Vogelsang to the castle. There is much that requires sorting out in all this.'

Properjohn looked worried. 'Looks like maybe something we don't figure right yet. But at least Herr Vogelsang not fishlike same as I thought he might be when I heard the castle having visitors.'

Don Perez sighed wearily. 'Unfortunately, Herr Vogelsang *is* fishlike. Or better, perhaps, he is a very fish.' And Don Perez looked blandly at his guest. 'Perhaps even the dolphin, my good Properjohn, the dolphin that is the king of fishes. But, if so, the king of fishes is in a net.'

And Don Perez Sierra y Campo made an almost imperceptible sign. It was a sign very freshly familiar to Meredith, who now turned to Properjohn and found himself looking down the barrel of a revolver.

'But for the moment you may refrain from shooting.' Don Perez sipped his port. 'The gentleman, after all, has never been in the employment of the Society, and our customary summary dismissal might not be altogether in order.'

'Like maybe it's not Vogelsang at all?'

'Vogelsang? This man killed Vogelsang. Or so you heard Bubear say, and it was one of his few statements lately that I see no reason to doubt. So you have admitted to our counsels, my good Properjohn, a dangerous and extremely inquisitive outsider. He has, it is true, a little wit, and I am not ungrateful for the evening's diversion. Did he not offer to find me the Locri Fawn out of Norman Douglas's incomparable *South Wind*? Still, this must be a warning to me of the hazards of employing a person like yourself, totally lacking in cultivation. I feel that the Secretaryship of the Society may shortly be declared vacant. It is inconvenient to have a man who does not recognize an eminent classical scholar when he meets him in a Scottish castle or on a grouse moor.'

Properjohn was a picture of dismay; his moustache, beaded with port, drooped more than ever, and this gave him the appearance of a discouraged cur. 'But, Don Perez, seeing he had Marsden's girl, I natchly figured –'

'I do not at all suppose the girl to be Marsden's. I suspect her to be the girl Halliwell, who was to be kept under observation because of her curiosity concerning the affair near Edinburgh. And this is Richard Meredith, author of a sound, if conservative, edition of Martial. He is an authority on the Latin epigrammatists and satirists in general. He made his first reputation, however, by a severe examination of the textual side of Wilamowitz-Moellendorf's *Platon*.'

'But hey!' Properjohn was indignant as well as dismayed. 'He talks big same as if it was his puttikler business collect art. The Night Watch, and Mona Lisa, and Burial of the Guy Orgaz –'

Don Perez pushed away his glass with an impatient movement. 'My good fellow, any educated man with his wits about him could contrive such talk.' He pondered for a moment. 'Am I not right in thinking that we have had a good many inquiries lately from American and other collectors prepared to interest themselves in Codices and ancient manuscripts generally?'

'Sure, that's correk, Don Perez.' Properjohn was plainly anxious to vindicate his secretarial efficiency. 'Bauernstern and Gedgoud and Homer S. Codcroft, some the biggest book-collectors ever operated, all going that way now.'

'Precisely.' And Don Perez turned to his guest. 'Mr Meredith,' he said, 'I take pleasure in offering you the position of Secretary to the International Society for the Diffusion of Cultural Objects. The emoluments of the office will be at the rate of five thousand pounds a year, together with a substantial commission. As for our late Secretary' – and Don Perez looked witheringly at Properjohn – 'he will be transferred to the Department of Crates and Boxes.'

'Say, Don Perez!' Properjohn turned the name into a sort of melancholy howl. 'I gotta Titian, I gotta Giotto –'

'Go away!' Don Perez was now holding a revolver of his own. 'Go away, my man, and get some practice with a hammer and nails. The Secretary and I have important business to discuss. And take Bubear's body with you. In fact, begin on a coffin. But don't use any of the superior woods.' He waited until Properjohn had lugged the corpse to the door. 'By the way,' he added, 'if it should happen that I want *two* coffins, I'll ring.' And Don Perez smiled pleasantly at Meredith. 'Now,' he said, 'we can talk.'

The President of the International Society, still with a revolver in hand, produced a box of cigars. Meredith – because the affair had become utterly dreamlike and unreal – accepted one. 'You don't seriously suppose', he said, 'that any stranger you encounter is likely to join your criminal organization for the asking?'

'For the asking?' Don Perez shook his head. 'Assuredly not. But five thousand a year is a different matter. You would be unlikely to come by that through the ordinary exercise of your profession.'

'But I come by quite enough. I have a salary, and rather more money of my own than a man ought, perhaps, to have – and then, you know, I am unmarried. So I am afraid there really isn't any inducement.'

'In five years you could have not just ample money, but a fortune. Very likely, Mr Meredith, your life would then surprisingly change. Forgotten or suppressed capacities for pleasure – immediate as well as intellectual pleasure – would be reborn in you. Your cellar would be incomparable. Unmarried as you are, you would find the world's most alluring –'

'I cannot understand how a man controlling what is evidently a large and successful organization can talk such nonsense.' Meredith was nettled. 'It is like a parody of Mephistopheles tempting Faust. Your own port, I may say, is admirable. But I finished with wine-cellars long ago.'

'At least you still relish a sound cigar.' Don Perez smiled urbanely. 'And you race about Scotland on hazardous missions with what is doubtless an attractive and intelligent girl. Is your heart then so little romantic? I suggest that the quadrangles of Oxford and the reading-rooms of great libraries have never quite satisfied you. Your generation was brought up under the shadow of Pater. As undergraduates you taught yourselves that your business in life was to burn with a hard, gem-like flame. Not the fruit of experience, you know, but experience itself, is the end. A counted number of pulses only is given to us of a variegated, dramatic life. How shall we pass most swiftly from point to point –'

'Stuff and nonsense!' exclaimed Meredith. 'If Pater passed swiftly from point to point it was no more than from his own rooms at Brasenose to those of some other don. And if he counted his pulses it was because he was rather scared of all the great husky undergraduates he had to scurry past on the way. Have you ever looked at a portrait of him? Only a man chronically scared of life would have hidden behind that immense moustache. And I don't think I'm particularly scared myself, even though

I've fallen into a den of thieves. Don't talk nonsense about Pater to me.'

What this speech lacked in logic it more than made up for in simple feeling, and after he had delivered himself of it Meredith felt much better. He even began to enjoy his cigar. The people who had paid for it – to wit, the lawful owners of sundry stolen works of art – would scarcely grudge it, he thought, to an honest man engaged in the task of restoring their property. Not that there now appeared to be the slightest chance of his succeeding – for here was Don Perez with, as it were, his grotesque proposal in one hand and a loaded revolver in the other. At any moment he might ring the bell and commission that second coffin.

'I don't suppose' – Don Perez, quite unruffled, seemed prepared for debate into the small hours – 'that you have ever much studied that aspect of the history of art which collectors call provenance? Who owned the picture last, you know, and who before that. The ideal is to trace it right back to the studio. Well, there are very few major works of art which have changed hands in what you would term an honest manner as often as in a dishonest one. Indeed, there is possibly no study that gives one a queerer angle on human conduct. Unless, of course, one takes jewels, in which I have never greatly interested myself. The history of great jewels is almost invariably one, not of simple theft, but of blood. Recently, and rather exceptionally, the Society acquired and disposed of the Taprobane Diamond. Not only had it been responsible, in its comparatively short career, for the deaths of three men and one very beautiful woman. On two other occasions, as I happen to know, its transfer had taken place amid such sinister passions that the immediate consequences were a good deal more horrible than simple homicide.' And Don Perez looked reflectively at that spot on his dining-room floor from which the disgraced Properjohn had lately lugged the body of Bubear. 'Yes,' he said, 'it would interest you to hear about that. But it is one of those stories which I must keep for my memoirs.'

Meredith was very willing that he should keep it. His cigar was not only stolen; it was, in a sense, soaked in blood. He took another puff at it. Unquestionably, it was just the same cigar. And from this Meredith conjectured that his nerves remained in tolerably good order. So why not, he thought, continue to play for time? It had been his role ever since this affair started. And even if the effort led nowhere – or led, rather, inevitably to a coffin or a sack – he might as well, as he followed that road, continue to exercise what acquired skill in delaying tactics he now possessed. It was the nearest he could get to that burning with a hard gem-like flame.

So Meredith watched the cigar smoke wreathing upwards and pondered. Should he make some tentative move towards closing with the offer made by Don Perez on behalf of the International Society? But that would be rash.

'What I haven't seen for a long time', Meredith said, 'is a really distinguished liqueur brandy.'

Don Perez rose at once. It is not easy simultaneously to play the gracious host and keep one's guest covered with a firearm. But this talented man had no difficulty in achieving it. Within a minute he had produced the brandy, poured it into two great rummers, and drawn a couple of arm chairs hospitably up to the fire. 'And now to return', he said, 'to the very interesting point of the morality of our proceedings. I will admit at once that there are aspects of the business which are liable a little to offend people like ourselves.'

People like ourselves. This was something for Meredith to digest. Perhaps there was a sense in which, if one regarded the community at large, Don Perez and he would appear to stand tolerably close together. Were they not both a sort of cultured parasite, each pursuing his own socially-irresponsible fancy? And what were those aspects of the business which might a little offend? Meredith half expected his host to be looking once more at the spot where Bubear had fallen. But Don Perez, his rummer cupped in one hand and his revolver conveniently disposed towards the other, was gazing mildly into the fire.

'For example,' said Don Perez, 'there is this Pantelli whom Properjohn has been expecting tonight. We have to work in with him, although I cannot approve his trade. Hiding all over Europe, as you know, are men stained with the most abominable crimes. They have taken booty of one sort or another with them – including works of art – and Pantelli makes a business of negotiating these for them in order to build up funds abroad. It is not a nice profession.'

'Decidedly not.' Meredith sniffed at his brandy. 'One would be very unhappy at conniving at the escape of murderers.'

'Precisely so.' Don Perez nodded gravely. 'By the way, Mr Meredith, I suppose it is quite certain that we shall not see Vogelsang – the real Vogelsang – again?'

As a quick home thrust this was not at all bad. 'No,' said Meredith. 'Nor Bubear either.'

Don Perez sighed. 'These necessities are sometimes imposed upon one out of sheer pressure of brute fact. *Necessitas non habet legem*, as Sallust observes.'

'Publilius Syrus,' said Meredith mildly. And even as he made this donnish correction there came upon him one of those obscure promptings to which he had been intermittently subject ever since his adventures began. 'This Pantelli', he said, 'appears to be concerned at the moment with a couple of reputed Giorgiones. Just how is he going about it?'

'Very sensibly.' Don Perez spoke without hesitation – and this made Meredith feel that the sack or coffin must by now be in the next room. 'Very sensibly, indeed. He has paid us a substantial commission in advance and we have agreed to take him straight to Neff's man – who is at present, I believe, in Tampico – and he will then make his own deal. Neff, as you may have gathered, is the biggest collector we have contacted so far.'

'And the Giorgiones themselves?'

'We ferried them some time ago and they are waiting at Depot 10. Pantelli has only to send a cable, *Herbert ill expect George only*, and we will have them forwarded on to Neff's own place.'

181

'I see. And did you think of *George only* – and all those passwords about London and Berlin – yourself?'

'As a matter of fact, I did.' Don Perez Sierra y Campo looked faintly abashed. 'Properjohn, I know, disapproved. But Properjohn has gone – only, I assure you, to make boxes and crates – and the passwords remain. A little romantic mystification suits my taste. And now I think I shall make coffee.'

It must, Meredith felt, be getting uncommonly late. What was happening at the castle? Was it not likely that Don Perez, even before he sat down to dinner with the man he pretended to accept as Vogelsang, had ordered some assault upon it for the purpose of seizing a girl who now knew far too much about his organization? Jean had already narrowly escaped the Firth of Forth. Meredith was determined that she should escape the Sound of Moila. So he must either get clear at once from the head-quarters of the International Society or continue to play for time and occasion by affecting to be drawn towards its President's outrageous proposal. 'I cannot see', he said, with an irony which he tried to make sound uncertain, 'that I am at all fitted to discharge the responsible office you suggest for me. It would appear chiefly to require a first-hand acquaintance with low life and criminal practice.'

But Don Perez, after pausing to look slightly pained, brushed this aside. 'I design', he said, 'a radical change in the scope of the duties. You must not take Properjohn as a criterion. Indeed, I think we must have you called Secretary-General, with several men like Properjohn (although more efficient, of course) working under you. The fact is that our superior clients like to feel that they are in contact with an organization characterized by a little polish, erudition, scholarship – that sort of thing. Hitherto I have been obliged to carry all that myself. But you ...'

And Don Perez talked on. He must, Meredith reflected, have a thoroughly stupid side to him or he would scarcely imagine that a middle-aged man with whom orderly living had become second nature was to be won over by a little blarney and a little wine. There was, of course, the further point that it was acquiescence or death, but this only made the man's proposal the stranger. For what reliance could he propose to place upon an associate who had entered his organization under duress?

And suddenly Meredith saw that the answer to this was simple. The first job the new Secretary-General would be given would be of the kind from which no turning back was possible. It would not be some bit of minor organizing from which he could bolt with his denunciations to the police. It would be the perpetration of an absolute crime which would put him in the power of the Society for ever. Likely enough, he would be required to seek out his predecessor Properjohn amid his blameless crates and boxes and murder him, like an incoming priest or king performing his unholy ritual in *The Golden Bough*. Yes, that would suit Don Perez's taste even more than the passwords. And all this decidedly made the prospect no more encouraging. If he were invited to liquidate Properjohn, the game would be at an end.

Meredith looked at his host and found him still at a full tide of easy eloquence. He was talking so eloquently that it was reasonable to suppose that at the moment he had nothing important to say, and here then was a good opportunity to take fleeting stock of the situation, particularly in its physical and topographical aspects. Don Perez's dining-room (since he was, after all, the invalid uncle of the Laird of Carron) was in a separate group of rooms on the first floor. Which meant that liberty lay not merely outside its windows, but some twenty feet below them. Or perhaps – for the whole building, Meredith remembered, had little elevation – no more than fifteen feet. And although underneath these particular windows there might lie a flagged path, or a rockery, or even some sort of area or basement, the reasonable chance was that there would be a flowerbed or grass. Once landed there – and the drop should hold no terrors for one who had graduated from Bubear's warehouse – there was a whole moorland into which to vanish. If necessary, one could go right over Ben Carron and find the fairly sizeable town which lay somewhere on the other side. But it would be better to take the risk of making straight for Moila, of somehow getting across the Sound, and of endeavouring to hold the castle until help was summoned.

There was the wretch Higbed, of course – but Meredith no longer considered that his first duty lay in endeavouring to rescue him. The man could scarcely have been dogged by furniture vans and brought all the way to Carron Lodge or its environs simply to have his throat cut; and Properjohn's little plan for him, whatever it was, must be reckoning on the live man and not a corpse. Higbed therefore, though conceivably uncomfortable, was presumably safe for the time. Meredith looked at the windows.

Or rather he looked at the curtains – not here of Hunting Stuart – which concealed them. It was conceivable that the windows themselves were heavily barred or even that armed retainers lurked in their recesses ready to jump out and aid their employer.

Meredith looked at the doors, of which there was one at each end of the room. That through which he had come gave upon a tolerably long corridor and a flight of stairs leading down to a hall. As a means of escape, he distrusted this altogether. The other, through which an elaborate dinner had been brought, presumably led to a servants' staircase, a hatch or perhaps a lift, and then to sundry offices. And this, too, Meredith did not care for. In fact, a window was the thing.

At this point he became aware that Don Perez was pouring out more brandy – which Meredith by no means proposed to drink – and had returned to the particularly idiotic theme of those enchantments of the flesh which were to open up before the new Secretary-General. How, Meredith wondered, could a clever scoundrel be so absurd? But it would be well to display himself as a little moved by these seductions. 'Well, I really don't know,' he said. 'I'm getting a bit old for that sort of thing.' And

Meredith looked at Don Perez glumly enough, since he felt that a particularly nasty piece of play-acting lay in front of him. He remembered his embarrassed speculations as he first walked down Bubear's whitewashed corridor, and the extremely disconcerting quality of his confused encounter with the Horton Venus. Perhaps Don Perez, in his Mephistophelean role, was going to draw a curtain and reveal some modern Helen of Troy who should stand as bonus to his first year's wages. For was anything too fantastic to be conceived of in this bizarre retreat?

But Don Perez, it seemed, had no exhibits. He simply talked. He talked women. He kept on talking women with all the freedom and erudition of an Aretino. And presently Meredith was wondering whether there was not something in this absurd-seeming technique after all. Might it not be like the apparently crude repetitiveness of modern advertising – in other words a scientifically valid means of penetrating to and influencing the subliminal operations of the will, the very depths of the mind? Might not this sort of sustained talk, suitably compounded with old brandy, not merely seduce but permanently condition even a mature personality? For it was a sort of suggestion therapy which had the hidden ape and tiger on its side. As in the skilled indoctrination of cruelty to the abominable possibilities of which the world had recently awakened, a little would go a long way.

And here Meredith found he had hit upon a very interesting speculation, and one to which he was able to give an altogether objective regard. For the simple truth was that not even the Aretino of the *Sonnets* – and certainly not Don Perez Sierra y Campo himself – could hold a candle in all this to Meredith's virtuous old Romans once they were in their slippered and smoking-room vein. Meredith therefore (who had thought he might be obliged, like Dr Johnson on a substantially different occasion, to remove his mind and think of Tom Thumb) found him-slef listening to Don Perez with substantial, if academic, interest. It was like watching a slightly inferior examination candidate cover familiar ground – not an absorbing activity, but one offering reasonable scope for the exercise of the judgement.

Don Perez seemed presently to feel that this Temptation of St Anthony was not going too well. Imperceptibly, he abandoned the more curious and esoteric aspects of his subject. It was as if the chambering and perverse whispering, the little lurid fires of a score of deviant lusts, faded on the air and left it warm and golden: Giorgione's or Titian's or Palma Vecchio's air – that or the air of Arcady. And now the theme was pagan – carnal and innocent at once – and the evocation all of the eternal pursuit of beauty through the groves. Here, said Don Perez, was the archetypal and sovereign activity of the male, immortally enshrined in the exquisite mythology of Greece. Apollo hunting Daphne, Syrinx fleeing from Pan: here is the basic pattern of human life, where all pleasure lies in man's triumphant pursuit and capture of the loath and trembling maid.

Don Perez had got so far when Meredith became aware of some altogether untoward disturbance in his host's well-regulated house. A moment later the door from the offices burst open and there bounded into the room his late companion Shamus – a Shamus juvenile, dishevelled, panic-stricken, disrobed. And behind in hot pursuit, blind as if through some maened frenzy to all propriety of demeanour and place, poured the so-lately decorous maidservants of the Laird of Carron.

Not Apollo and Daphne, not Zeus and Semele, not the Rape of the Sabines, Meredith thought. Not this but the rout of Thracian women about to rend their Orpheus limb from limb and send his gory visage down the burn, down the swift Carron to the Moila shore. Here was that with which the Celtic eye of Shamus had conversed, here was the riddle of his disappearance solved, and here was tumultuous evidence that the precocious lad, dispersedly amorous, had mixed his dates or bitten off more than he could chew. The archetypal male, thought Meredith – and was aware of himself as adding to the uproar his own largest laughter. Shamus made for the farther door, the

Bacchantes streamed behind with rumpled aprons and flying hair. And Meredith realized that by this outrageous intrusion of fact upon phantasy Don Perez Sierra y Camp was for the moment utterly distracted. The opportunity, then, had come. He ran for a window, tore aside its curtains, thrust up a sash, and leapt over into darkness below.

11

Since he knew that Don Perez's dining-room was on the first floor, and had indeed made careful calculations as to its height from the ground, this leap – Meredith thought as he fell through space – was a sadly amateur affair. Presently he would be picked up with a broken leg. And because he had rejected the allurements of the living Aphrodite he would be put in a sack and consigned to the waves from which the offended goddess sprang.

This classical thought (which was certainly the result of Don Perez's table-talk) had scarcely run its course when Meredith discovered with some surprise that he was running too. Over his right hand there was trickling what he guessed to be blood; his right knee hurt; in his right side there was an uncomfortable sensation of twist or sprain. These inconveniences were the price of having forgotten to lower himself at full length before dropping: an elementary art which he had been taught (he now remembered) when commencing fire-fighting not many years ago. But he could get along fast enough – faster than in pitch darkness, it was at all judicious to go. But then if Macbeth's physician did, in fact, ever get *from Dunsinane away and clear* he most assuredly made for cover in the remains of Birnam Wood with a haste which little regarded the chances of taking a tumble in the heather.

Meredith ran. Remembering what he had been taught by games masters at his private school, he ran without looking over his shoulder. His speed was the better because he was going downhill, and because he derived from this an elementary sense of direction. A downward slope must lead him to the burn. And the burn, he knew, headed for the sea in what was roughly the neighbourhood of Moila.

There was no moon, and in a wide deep arc to the west the sky was overcast; only behind him, and trailing southwards from the Great Square of Pegasus, ran a broad river of stars unimpeded by cloud. Don Perez's dining-room had been brightly lit; for a time the darkness seemed absolute; and Meredith was brought up hard and painfully by what must be the stone wall bounding the garden of Carron Lodge. He scaled this and was among larches. The soft carpeting of their needles felt beneath his feet and their dark mass overhead gave him a momentary sense of security. Then their trunks gathered round him like the bars of some maze-like cage traversed in dream; at first so many stationary presences dimly discerned, they seemed to take motion to themselves as he zigzagged gropingly among them; soon they were a nightmare machine of obliquely gliding perpendicular bars, designed to advance, to buffet and to withdraw. The larches hit out at him and hit again. He dodged one only to find another coming up in flank or from behind. For a bewildering space he was both Meredith and the lad Shamus – Shamus with the maenad women menacingly about him. By an immense effort of the will he stopped dead and considered the fact – which somehow seemed altogether surprising – that he had momentarily lost his head. He could not recall that this had ever happened to him before, even in childhood. But had he not embarked on this mad adventure on the theory that a man does well at fifty to find what new worlds of experience he can? Provided, of course, that he is capable or coping with them in a reasonably efficient way. Which meant, for the present, eschewing reflection in favour of a precise use of the senses. Meredith listened.

The burn could not be far away. Beneath its dominant monotonous flow it harboured a myriad tiny accidents of sound, of varying ripple and eddy, and these were like an urgent whispering pitched just beyond the range of an anxious ear. To imagine in this nocturnal murmuring a sinister purposefulness, a network of menacing dispositions stealthily made, was easy enough. It is only civilization and security that rob the face of nature of an abundant and fearsome animism: demons yelling in the storm, slumbering giants in the swelling contours that ring a familiar plain. Meredith listened once more. A man's voice called out somewhere behind him and there was an answering shout from farther back. The pursuit had begun.

Carron Lodge (as had been startlingly evidence) held several women servants. These, although not without well-developed hunting instincts of their own, were unlikely to join effectively in a chase over the heather, or to be at all in the confidence of the International Society. Of menservants Meredith had seen only one, and there was a limit to the number that Don Perez (or Properjohn) could colourably maintain in an establishment of so moderate a size. And the night was dark and the moors were wide. Unless the headquarters of the Society ran to bloodhounds – and to bloodhounds altogether more pertinacious than Bubear's had been – it seemed to Meredith that he had a chance of getting clean away. And the chance would be strongest if he moved inland. By turning away from any sustained ascent, he could avoid going dangerously high on Ben Carron; and by walking through the remainder of the night he could make himself into a mere needle in a haystack so far as any immediate power of search could extend.

And yet Meredith felt he had better aim for Moila. It was true that the enemy, by a swift deployment of part of his forces, could easily enough cut his own uncertain route to the coast. But, even so, the Sound was long, the island beyond it sizeable, and there seemed no reason to regard a successful return to the castle as hopeless. How, then, should he proceed? The burn was his only guide, and this the enemy knew. Assuredly, then, they would press down it with all the speed they could contrive. This meant that there were two feasible plans.

He could *follow*. That was to say, he could go off downstream with sufficient disturbance and definiteness to set his pursuers well on that track, and then he could double back and become the cautious pursuer himself. Or he could *keep up*, moving away from the burn on one side or the other until almost out of earshot, and guiding himself by its murmur or by whatever noise the enemy made. Meredith decided on this second course. And he decided – this with some idea of bloodhounds in his mind – that he would begin by crossing the burn. He would then move westward at whatever seemed the best distance from its southern bank.

He was still in the larch wood. And again there were voices, this time on the edge of it. He moved quickly through the last fringe of trees, and it seemed to him that he now avoided their unyielding trunks less by sight or touch than by the exercise of an emergency sense summoned for the purpose. He climbed a wire fence that twanged alarmingly in the stillness as he too-abruptly let it go. At once there was a shout from the larch wood. But he knew now, with the confidence of a former visual impression sharply recalled, that before him lay broken but unprecipitous ground falling straight to the murmuring Carron. He would wade some fifty yards in water and then make the climb from the farther bank. For the first time he looked behind him and saw that he had already dropped a considerable distance. A bright glow showed where several lights must be burning in Don Perez's stronghold, but the house itself was invisible behind the trees. If he saw it again he hoped it would be in company with the assembled strength of the county constabulary. And Meredith ran for the burn.

Bounding o'er the heather is an athletic exercise frequently described in song. The actuality is not easy, even in daylight. And darkness makes a tumble certain every so many yards. The stuff is either curiously elastic and acts like a smooth but swift pneumatic brake, or it is absolutely strong-rooted and resistant, bringing one down at once. Meredith, by trial and error, quickly found the sort of out-thrusting, high-stepping stride best suited to this invisible terrain; it was no doubt the kind of movement that Captain Maxwell of the *Oronsay* described as *louping*. And presumably his pursuers could *loup* too; moreover, they would have torches to light them on their way.

Again he looked behind him. And, sure enough, some two hundred yards back several short beams of light flickered here and there, probing the heather. The Lodge had come into sight again as a row of dull lights behind Properjohn's absurd tartan curtains, with here and there a brighter shaft from some unguarded window. But it was another and fainter illumination that held Meredith's gaze – one faintly suffusing the eastern sky, cloudless and starry in a great band across the moor. There could be no doubt of it. The lowest stars were paling. Presently there would rise an untimely midnight moon.

And a moon, Meredith remembered, something like threequarters full. Unless the eastern heavens clouded over, visibility would presently be substantial. This, surely, must be far more in favour of pursuers than pursued. It robbed him of what had hitherto been an almost certain last resource, that of simply staying put and moving no farther than was required to avoid one wandering torch or another. But meanwhile there was perhaps half an hour to go before the actual moonlight came. And already he had gained the burn. He was wading in it something more than ankle-deep.

Suddenly, and in the middle of speculations wholly cool and confident, he found that his sense of direction had left him. The bank was steep; neither stars nor hint of moon nor Lodge was here visible; he was standing in this brawling little stream and could feel the stir and thrust of it about his calves – nevertheless he was unable to tell which way it flowed, or even in which direction lay its banks.

He cursed his own confused and urban senses. He bent

and experimented with dipping first one and then another finger in the water. No certainty resulted. It was like that sort of sudden waking-up in which his bed or bedroom was for seconds mysteriously disorientated and he had a disconcerting sense of the universe as turned inside-out. Meredith wondered if he was losing his head again – and even as he did so direction returned to him. The burn thrust strongly against his legs with a prompting there was no mistaking. He turned and moved off downstream. But only to halt – more abruptly than he had done yet.

Fifty yards below him a great beam of light had sprung into being against the darkness. It looked like a small searchlight. Perhaps it was only one of those peculiarly powerful spot-lights which form part of the equipment of large cars. However this might be, the shaft of light cut the burn like a knife and ran far up the farther bank. There was no road that way.

He turned – half expecting what he saw. At an equal distance upstream another great beam spanned the water. Meredith saw that the situation was very bad. And where he had before been merely cool he was now angry as well. He was furious at the odds against him – at the resources the rascally Society could bring to bear against a single law-abiding citizen in these solitary recesses. There were voices again now – incisive, almost triumphant – and among them he could recognize the cultivated accents of Don Perez – the same that had discoursed on the violets of Catullus and the vine-leaves of Anacreon. And at this memory Meredith's indignation against the pretentious and spurious scoundrel mounted even higher. But indignation, he told himself grimly, is not in itself an adequate reply to rifles, revolvers and searchlights. Where did his best chance lie?

The two beams of light radiated from a centre some two hundred yards away, and he was thus caught in a funnel the blinding sides of which it would be fatal to attempt to cross. And at any moment these sides might contract, the two shafts of light sweeping towards each other and raking the intervening stretch of burn and lights were mounted on motor vehicles, and although these could manoeuvre somewhere on the farther bank he doubted their being able to cross the burn without a considerable detour. Thus the further he could get in the next few minutes the less powerful would be the beams presently hunting for him again, and the larger the sector of moor over which they would have to play. Meredith ran straight ahead. And he was aware that the ground beneath his feet, though rough, was level.

But it ought to be rising. Had he turned, then, without noticing it, so that he was still following the burn? This could not be, for the sound of the water was growing faint behind him. And the only other explanation was a blessed one. He must have found the opening of some gully or minor valley that here joined the main valley of the Carron. And if this took an early turn or two in its course and did not rapidly rise to the general level of the moor it meant that he would be secure from those groping fingers of light until their reach was exhausted. Meredith looked overhead. The sky was now ever so faintly suffused with moonlight. It was just possible to discern that he was indeed in a sort of narrow canyon. And no sooner had he concluded on this than he was brought up with a jolt against earth and rock. This sunken way had turned sharply. Fortune could have brought him no better gift. He went ahead steadily, the ground rising only gradually beneath his feet. Overhead there was now an irregular play of light and darkness. The searchlights had been moved and were raking a wide arc of moor. But he was safe from them here – and safe not merely when lurking but when moving away from them with the best speed he could summon. His confidence grew.

Distance was hard to reckon. He had gone perhaps a quarter of a mile from the burn, which it had looked as if he would never do alive again. Unfortunately, he had been thwarted in his plan of making immediately for the coast by way of the Carron. The burn could no longer be heard and he judged himself to be moving somewhere between north and east. Moreover, the ground had begun to rise sharply, which meant that the little gully must be moor. The inequalities of the ground, it was true, and more particularly the slope down to the burn and up again, would leave numerous pockets of darkness in which he would be momentarily secure. But if he had to get along by diving from one to another of these the hide-and-seek would be desperate enough. And even as Meredith, still standing in midstream, confronted this fact the searchlights swept simultaneously towards him.

The two beams of light swept remorselessly towards him, like a scissors closing upon some helpless insect at the will of a wanton boy. He watched, fascinated, as clump after clump of heather sprang first into silhouette, then into full definition, and then abruptly vanished into the darkness beyond. Another thirty degrees and he would be like one of those tumps of heather himself – and no marksman could ask for a simpler target. The burn was here perhaps eighteen inches deep. His best chance would be to submerge himself in it as best he could. And Meredith was about to fling himself face downwards in the water when first one and then the other light faltered and vanished.

There was an angry shout, a voice cursing in reply, and the unmistakable sound of a self-starter being tugged and tugged again in the effort to turn over a sluggish engine. As he had conjectured, the lights were mounted on lorries or cars. And they had been so sited that some intervening rise masked them just as they came to bear on the vital sector where Meredith stood. Once more the International Society had muddled matters at a crucial moment. Presently, no doubt, they would find more favourable ground. Meanwhile Meredith ran – ran without thinking twice about it, since running was now pretty well his *métier*. As naturally as if he were making his way through a lecture-room to discourse on Lucretius or Virgil, he scrambled from the burn and dashed straight ahead. The powerful flattening out to the moor. He moved more cautiously, conscious that the beams of light, though very faint now, were closer above his head. And presently the immediate darkness withdrew. A wide, dimly discernible horizon was about him. The searchlights were still at play – but far behind him, and he could see that they were not such powerful affairs after all.

He lay down, breathless and feeling again the discomfort occasioned by his rash leap from Don Perez's window. But it had been worth it. He had got away.

Meredith lay and watched the little probing, uncertainly circling lights. A deadly menace only a little time ago, they now seemed an altogether futile and inadequate challenge to the immense and saving darkness about them. And on this the lights themselves seemed ready to agree. For they went out even as Meredith watched them. And neither could any pursuing voices be heard. About him there was nothing but silence and darkness, with that great band of stars to the north and east, and in the clouded sky above a barely distinguishable sense of the moonlight to come.

The moonlight might be awkward yet, but a little reflection could make an ally of it as well. For when it came Meredith would have a shadow as company. And if he regarded that shadow as the hand of a great clock pointing to noon, and himself moved steadily towards nine, he could scarcely go far astray in his quest of the island and its beleaguered castle. Pleased with this Boy-Scouting aspect of his new life, Meredith set off. But he was scarcely on his feet and moving when he was constrained to pull up and listen. A new sound – or rather a medley of sounds that invited disentangling – was coming to him over the moor.

Two motor engines: that was it. And during several minutes in which he intently listened the noise neither rose nor ebbed. There were two cars or lorries, and they were neither approaching directly nor drawing directly away. The place was too solitary to let him suppose with any reason that these were not Don Perez's forces still. Could they manoeuvre with any freedom over the moors? Meredith doubted it – unless, indeed, these were some species of tank-like vehicle that were on the hunt for him. That gentlemen now trundle over the wilds of Scotland in such contrivances in order the more effortlessly to come up with grouse or deer was a vagary of modern sportsmanship unknown to him. And he was therefore less apprehensive than he might have been.

But that there were two cars of a sort somewhere prowling the darkness was a conclusion which did not in itself complete the analysis of what was now coming to his hearing. Mingled with these, but yet coming from a different and (he sensed) higher quarter, there was a thin vibrant sound, like the plucking of a great string on some note almost beyond the compass of the human ear. Not dissimilar distant auditory effects one had been uncommonly suspicious of in urban places not so very long ago. Could they be firing – firing at some supposed refuge where he lay – with a weapon silent in itself, but the projectiles from which produced this strange twang in air? He frowned, dissatisfied. And then, suddenly, he was aware that the motor engines were very much nearer.

He was aware, too, of a new factor in his environment, and one thoroughly puzzling on this great expanse of open moor. Close in front of him there rose what appeared to be a high square crag – an obscure form which was at first like a great hole cut in the heavens, a black void space swept clear of stars, but which then immediately revealed itself as a substantial and menacing mass not fifty yards away. Meredith stared at this, perplexed. And as he did so the queer vibration above his head swelled to a loud hum with clanks and creakings intermingled. And at the same moment, too, part of the mass before him seemed to detach itself and plunge towards him, as if some gigantic bird of prey had launched itself from its eyrie to hurtle like a thunderbolt upon its prey.

And that, of course, was it. Here, once more, were the Flying Foxes of Moila.

12

WITH the departure of Captain Maxwell in the *Oronsay* and of Meredith and the lad Shamus for the mainland tedium and suspense had beset the castle. The hereditary Captain retired to a late-afternoon repose. Miss Dorcas, after providing Jean with a copy of *Life and Work* (which appeared to be a journal devoted to the views and occasions of a Presbyterian clergy), applied herself to the science of tunnelling as expounded in the *Encyclopaedia Britannica*, where she was endeavouring to master the complicated third phase in the construction of the Boston Subway. Mrs Cameron could be heard singing metrical versions of the Psalms in the banqueting hall – a chamber to which she regularly repaired for this exercise because of the extraordinary resonance it provided. The man Tammas, impressed by the unwonted hospitality to which his employers seemed inclined, was killing a calf in the base court with more than his usual ritualistic deliberation. In none of these activities was there much cheer, and even those comparatively skittish pages in which *Life and Work* broke into a serial story failed to make Jean feel other than bad. To sweep up Richard Meredith himself and carry him off on a joint adventure was one thing; to sit tight among a gaggle of ancient women while letting him depart on a reconnaissance of the utmost hazard was quite another. Jean wondered how she could have brought herself to do it – and found the answer in the simple fact that Meredith, after all, was running the show. She would not, for that matter, have asked him had she been other than certain that he would. But now here she was relegated to a role as circumscribed as even the true Teutonic Vogelsang could have desired.

Küche, Kirche, Kinder ... Of *Kinder* Castle Moila knew nothing – unless the Misses Macleod in their old age were tending a bit that way. *Kirche* was represented by the ululations of Mrs Cameron and the sober reading in

Life and Work. But *Küche* at least suggested a feasible exploration. And if she had been invited to inspect a privy and a tiled bathroom it was not presumably discourteous to have a look at the kitchen and the other offices as well. Idly prompted to this investigation, Jean left the solar and fell to wandering about the castle.

The domestic arrangements of Moila turned out to hold little of interest, Mr Properjohn's cheques having achieved most of the amenities commonly found in a well-appointed villa – the only difference being that these were built into the manifold vastnesses of the castle rather after the fashion of so many swallows' nests plastered about a barn. Mrs Cameron's kitchen, though by no means on the small side when absolutely regarded, had once been a fireplace and nothing more. The laundry was much like anybody else's, except that it was fifty feet high. There were few passages or corridors, and such as there were extended to little more than two feet in breadth while being apparently as topless as the towers of Ilium. The room in which Jean was to sleep was admirably appointed for some sixth of its length and then merged into a vaulted chamber of undressed stone, dimly discerned – so that inhabiting it would be rather like playing in some cosy bedroom scene with the curtain up upon a gigantic and deserted auditorium.

Half an hour of this wandering proved mildly unnerving, and Jean was soon feeling much like Lady Macbeth somnambulating through a set executed on a scale worthy of Mr Cecil B. De Mille. The open air in the first chill of evening would be less oppressive. Miss Dorcas was clearly of another opinion, and had left the Boston Subway only to take refuge in the New York Rapid Transit Tunnel. Jean, after one or two polite remarks which the depth of Harlem River rendered altogether inaudible, climbed to the battlements of the keep. Here was the ruin's highest accessible point, and she had some hope that from this vantage ground she might be able to descry Meredith returning trough the fading light.

The sun was touching the horizon and below her the

curve of the castle was like a monster's jaw cast on a desolate shore and jagged with carious teeth which cast elongated shadows across the empty courts and the darkling waters that flanked the causey. The sea was calm and a fading silver; Inchfarr was a white ghost; Moila was very quiet and empty, sparely traversed by blackfaced sheep that nosed their own distorted shadows; beyond the hidden Sound the mainland spread featureless beneath the obtuse mass of Ben Carron. Carron Lodge was the only visible habitation, and a dark line winding past it marked the course of the Carron burn. Perhaps this watercourse offered the easiest route to the coast, and a man following it would move unseen. It was possible that Meredith might in this way be hidden and yet nearing the island.

Jean stood very still by the parapet. Her glance, so absent as to be wholly unperturbed, travelled down the sheer wall of the keep and the almost as sheer precipice to the dark arm of water that curled round the castle's north-eastern side to break upon that narrow neck of land which linked island and stronghold. Doubtless the portcullis was down and her own security entire. But Richard Meredith – and for all the world as if something as familiar as the North Library of the British Museum were his objective – had gone off to meet the people who had murdered their way to that Viking hoard among the gentle Pentland hills, who had grotesquely hounded the wretched Higbed to distraction, who were familiarly disposed to put inconvenient people in sacks and drop them in the sea. And it was her doing that a mild and markedly courageous man had gone on this fated errand. She herself had discovered a taste for danger which gave her no shadow of moral distinction; it was a mere indulgence, such as rock-climbing is in a person who unaccountably finds relief and expression that way. But Meredith had no need of danger, or anything but a disregard of it when it was incidental to arriving at a truth. And she had used the mystery of Bubear and Properjohn and Moila to draw him into an escapade in which –

though she had not thought of it so – there was almost a certainty of the greater hazard being his.

She looked up again and across to the mainland. Nothing moved. The Flying Foxes were stationary. Only the line of pylons which bore them could be felt by the imagination as a hostile force advancing – this because of their direct and purposeful stride towards the castle in a mathematical line which the wandering Carron served to emphasize.

There was a pylon just beyond the causey. And the nearest of the great suspended cages was not more than a dozen yards away; it hung at the level of these battlements like a coach on some invisible big dipper or scenic railway, hovering before a downward plunge. And such a plunge was just what it would, in fact, take when the endless conveyor-belt of which it formed a unit moved again. Jean frowned and turned to circle the keep. Here the system dipped and swooped down through the courts of the castle to a lower level, as if in a hurry to reach the sea. Jean remembered a visual impression from earlier in the day. Within the anchorage the Foxes ran so low that the little *Oronsay*, had she crossed their path, would have fouled their cables with her funnel, but in order to cross the open channel to Inchfarr they rose again and were borne on pylons markedly taller. Why, then, should they ever dip lower than need be? Surely this extra fall and lift was a meaningless addition to the footpounds, or whatever might be the proper technical term, required to move these heavy contraptions between Inchfarr and the other terminal point some way back upon the mainland?

Jean descended from the keep and made her way to that perilous spot on the western side of the castle from which she and Miss Dorcas had watched the arrival of Captain Maxwell. It was a mere ledge of turf beneath a mouldering but gigantic bastion of stone, and in the fading light she trod with care. Clouds were banking in the west against a red afterglow that grew deeper and burning as she watched, and above was an immeasurable dome of lustreless steel. The gleaming white of Inchfarr had changed to a dark floating presence, insubstantial as a phantom wreck on ghostly waters, and the anchorage was deepest indigo shot with fire. Of the little landing-stage, set in fullest shadow beneath the cliff, nothing could be seen. No gull cried. No sound of lapping wave rose from below. Jean looked again at the sunset, almost as if the pervading silence might there be broken by the crackle and roar of flame. And against that vast conflagration the clouds were swelling, falling apart, and dissipating themselves, like the members of some vast animal body sprawled amid cremating fires. Jean shivered and turned back. The castle, black and immemorial and tumbledown about her, seemed no longer a place of security. Its bulk, the endlessness and variousness of its lurking recesses and dizzying coigns, the grotesque disproportion between its massive enduring strength and the few lives, feeble and burning to the socket, that it harboured: these things oppressed her suddenly, so that she felt as if the gathering darkness was coming down like a physical weight. And then she heard a bell.

Ring the alarum-bell. Murder and treason! Banquo and Donalbain! ... But this, no doubt, was no more than Mrs Cameron summoning to dinner. Jean hurried through the dark courts, at last forced to acknowledge to herself that night had come. Was there a chance that Meredith had returned while she had been restlessly prowling?

But Meredith had not returned, nor Shamus either. The Misses Macleod were alone in the solar, and both might have been described as *en grande tenue*. The hereditary Captain showed bare and ancient shoulders beneath a flowing cloak of threadbare velvet. And in her hair was a white flower – such as the Lady Flora had worn, Jean remembered, when painted by Allan Ramsay as a girl. Miss Dorcas was in a black gown bespangled with sequins, so that if in the uncertain light of the solar one looked at her with narrowed eyes she was strangely metamorphosed into the appearance of a distant city, glittering in the clear air of some sub-tropical night. But if the light in the solar was feeble it was sufficient to reveal the disconcerting absence of any sign of a meal. Was this, then, to be partaken of in some more formal apartment? Jean had scarcely asked herself this question when the man Tammas entered in a costume which could be obscurely distinguished as including white stockings, outcrops of lace, and wisps of golden braid. He carried a lantern which he proceeded to elevate in a solemn manner in air. Miss Isabella took Jean's arm. Miss Dorcas fell in behind. Tammas made a bow and uttered some formula in the Gaelic tongue. Whereupon the procession wound its way from the solar – the Landseers, the Arundel prints, the Biblical engravings, and the Raeburn looking impassively down the while.

They were out in the open air – which, after the fashion of the Islands, was at once muggy and chill. Jean looked upwards and saw that only in the eastern sky were there stars; she looked behind and saw Miss Dorcas uncertainly drifting – a sort of Rio de Janeiro become mysteriously unstuck and eddying beneath the Corcovado in a velvet night. Where were they going? The Misses Macleod were a little mad. Tammas was more than a little mad. Mrs Cameron was given to religious enthusiasm and so, in Jean's view, was on the thither side of sanity also. Was it possible –?

The party entered the banqueting hall. This vast chamber, Jean very well remembered, was substantially open to the sky. It contained nothing but benches and the solitary piece of furniture which the late hereditary Captain had neglected to take with him upon his remove: an oaken table some forty feet long. Of this, one end appeared to be more exposed to the elements than the other; grass was sprouting from various clefts and fissures and the intervening surfaces were covered with lichen and moss. The other end showed a snowy tablecloth and gleaming silver, lit by a handsome Aladdin lamp.

It would be difficult to decide whether these preparations could properly be described as for an *alfresco* meal. Certainly they were for a chilly one, and Jean wondered whether the lesser evil would be tepid soup or no soup at all. It is characteristic of an aristocratic culture to sacrifice comfort to style, and Versailles and Schönbrunn are as little designed for a rational cosiness as is the boiled shirt into which the *sahib* proverbially changes in the jungle. But seldom, surely, could the principle have been carried further than in this resolute frequentation of a family dining-room which had been definitively blitzed centuries ago.

Miss Isabella had taken the head of the table, and was looking round her as if puzzled by some unidentifiable gap or hiatus in her surroundings. Then her brow cleared. 'Of course!' she said. 'We no longer *have* a chaplain. Dorcas, is not that so?'

'Certainly it is so, Tibbie.' Miss Dorcas had moved some way from the lamp-lit table in order – Jean suspected – to eject a stray hen. Her voice, therefore, issued mysteriously as from a distant coruscation of lights – Cape Town from the sea, Adelaide from the Mount Lofty ranges. 'I dare say that with the money from Inchfarr a decent man of moderate learning might have been obtained. But the bathroom and the hot water seemed to come first.' She turned to Jean. 'Our Uncle Archibald, who was a virtuoso and lived in Venice, was insistent upon sanitary standards not then readily procurable in that beautiful city. He used to remark that godliness came next to cleanliness, and the force of the epigram has remained with me all my life. May I ask if you hear squeaking?'

'Squeaking?' Jean was startled, but considered it polite to listen intently. 'Well – yes, as a matter of fact I do.'

'Tibbie, Miss Halliwell hears squeaking.' Miss Dorcas was highly pleased. 'The sound comes, of course, from the bats in the belfry.'

'The belfry?'

'The alarm bell used to hang directly above our heads. Have you ever remarked that it is of belfries that bats are peculiarly fond? But we are delighted that they should be audible to you. As you no doubt know, the sound is commonly not distinguishable by older people. It is a long time since my sister or I has heard it.' And Miss Dorcas spread out a table napkin with complacency. As some would count among the pleasures of their table a consort of viols and be solicitous that their guest should adequately hear the music, so were the Misses Macleod, it appeared, disposed to feel about Moila's bats.

Jean looked at what Mrs. Cameron had placed before her. It was soup – and by some hidden resource scaldingly hot. *Ring the alarum-bell ... Banquo and Donalbain ...* For the first time in her life, Jean felt the possibility of hysteria rising within her. Helplessness was its cause. For here she sat, consuming bean soup in one of the more ruinous parts of this ruined castle, while Miss Dorcas discoursed on the virtuosity of her Uncle Archibald and the acoustic properties of bats – and while the chances of Meredith's ever returning to Moila grew more slender with every tick of the clock.

She wondered whether the old ladies, who had been convinced earlier in the day that the castle was indeed besieged and Meredith embarking upon a dangerous military operation, now remembered anything about the matter. Or was it only Miss Isabella who had held these romantic views? Jean watched Tammas, resplendent in his livery, but smelling distinctly of calf, take away the soup while Mrs Cameron brought forward herrings baked in a plentiful oatmeal. Yes, it was Miss Isabella who went in for a sort of time travelling, while Miss Dorcas confined herself to imaginary prowlings in cellars and caverns ... Abruptly Jean realized that she must be uncommonly sleepy to have to set about disentangling things in this way. Perhaps it was the Island air – this and the fact that only under the roof of Meredith's Mrs Martin had she known a full night's sleep for some time.

Tammas was now pouring out what proved to be claret – and it seemed that the proper way to drink this was with the addition of hot water from a silver jug. Jean looked carefully at the jug – it was so very old as to merit an archaeologist's attention – and saw that it was swimming slightly before her. So was Miss Dorcas, who now looked like Cairo when one comes in by air at night. Probably the claret, even thus curiously diluted, would make her sleepier still. Or was it a bogus sleepiness – a mere neurotic trick to dodge the strains of the evening? This was so humiliating a notion that Jean plunged into random speech. 'I was very interested in the sheep,' she said. 'I mean at the way in which they came up from the anchorage. It was almost as if there was a way through the bowels of the earth.'

'But there is!' Miss Dorcas was animated. 'A fissure winds from the landing-stage through the heart of the cliff and emerges through an outcrop of rock in the base court. Through it Magnus Barelegs came –'

Miss Isabella lifted her head. '*A furore Normannorum*', she said in a high voice, '*libera nos.*' For seconds she looked apprehensively but commandingly round her dusky domain. Then her eye fell on Mrs Cameron. 'Ah,' she continued mildly, 'a gigot. Tammas, let the ashet be placed here.'

'– when he fired the castle. Almost nothing was left.'

Jean looked as grave as she could at the mention of this ancient calamity. *Deliver us from the fury of the Norsemen.* And let us have a *gigot* on an *ashet,* thereby unconsciously demonstrating that even on this barbarian fringe of Europe our culture is substantially French And Jean, much as if she were Meredith himself, was so pleased with this little history lesson that for some moments she scarcely attended to Miss Dorcas continuing to describe this curious and fatal back door to Castle Moila. Indeed, it was the hereditary Captain who roused her by speaking once more in that strident voice which betokened her sliding back among her ancestors. 'But it ought to be sealed. Dorcas, there is a grille at the entrance to the Seaway. Has it not been closed and bolted? The enemy may find it as Magnus did.'

'The enemy, Isabella?'

'To be sure, child! Have you no memory, no wits? Do you not recall that our guests are pursued? That one of them even now is ventured out among the foe? The portcullis is down; why, then, is not the grille to the Seaway closed?'

And why not, indeed? thought Jean. It was a material point, and in a siege it would be Miss Isabella who would have her wits about her. But now the old lady was looking round the hall in a puzzled way once more. Was she again thinking of the missing chaplain?

'Dorcas,' said Miss Isabella, 'where is Black Malcolm?'

'Black Malcolm, Tibbie?' By this more than commonly welldefined piece of madness on her sister's part Miss Dorcas seemed to be put decidedly to a stand.

'But, to be sure, we no longer *have* a bard. These are straitened times.' The hereditary Captain turned to Jean. 'I should like', she said in her milder voice, 'to tell you what it occurred to me to say this year when signing my name to the Marquis's breeches.'

'I should like to hear it very much.' Jean, who was without the key to this (in fact) wholly rational statement, took it as a sign that Miss Isabella's condition was rapidly deteriorating. Or perhaps it was the claret and water.

'But unfortunately a sufficiently forceful translation of the Gaelic – one, that is to say, suitable for our table and your years – fails to suggest itself to me ... Hark!'

Jean harkened. At first she could hear nothing but the squeaking of the bats. Then she heard a creaking – which she ascribed to the shoes of the man Tammas as he advanced down a stone corridor bearing whatever was designed to follow the gigot. A bat flew down out of the darkness and fluttered across the table – a contingency which Jean had for some time expected, and by which she was correspondingly not at all alarmed.

But now the hereditary Captain had sprung to her feet. The incongruous light of the Aladdin lamp showed a glint of battle in her eye. She leant forward and spoke in a tense whisper. 'I hear them,' she said. 'I hear the long ships. They are nosing their way into the anchorage.' Her voice sank till it was barely audible. 'The Viking ships. The ships of Olaf the White. They are rowing with muffled oars. But – hark! – the rowlocks creak as they swing.'

And again Jean hearkened, while Miss Dorcas fiddled uncomfortably with her claret and Mrs Cameron deliver-

ed herself audibly of the Lord's Prayer. There could be no
doubt now that the mysterious creaking was coming from
somewhere far out in the night. And it might indeed have
been oars – many oars creaking down the sides of a long
black ship ...

For a moment Jean held her breath, the illusion com-
pletely mastering her. And then she realized the simple
truth. Once more, it was the Flying Foxes of Moila. Out
there in the darkness, and at this late hour of the night,
the whole system had begun to move.

13

In the darkness, Meredith knew, two cars of a sort were
prowling nearer, and just overhead one of the Flying
Foxes was beginning its long journey to Inchfarr. It was
demonstrable, therefore, that the high square crag which
had appeared before him was nothing other than that
displeasing structure of corrugated iron which housed the
controlling mechanism of the system and served to conceal
whatever operations were carried on at this end of the line.
Was there an authentic commerce in guano? Meredith
thought it quite likely that there was. With the present
needs of agriculture it was even possible that it paid for
itself, and thus cut down the overheads of the International Society.

And 'overheads' was the word. In that roomy contraption which had a minute before lunged menacingly
at him and then passed on harmlessly through the middle
air there might well be concealed the Horton Venus itself.
And how – it suddenly occurred to him to wonder – had
the rascally Don Perez possessed himself not only of this
but of the Duke of Horton's other treasure, Vermeer's
Aquarium – the painting which had graced his glorified
thieves' kitchen on the other side of the burn? It could
not be denied that the Diffusion of Cultural Objects was

207

being prosecuted with considerable success. And if Meredith himself was a cultural object – and he had, after all, a reasonable claim to that title – it seemed likely that he would soon be very effectively diffused himself. For now something altogether menacing had happened. The searchlights were at play again – and this time there were three of them disposed in a triangle of which he was roughly the centre.

Do triangles have centres? As he questioned himself on this point Meredith dropped to the heather and burrowed in it. What had happened was clear enough. The enemy had never been in substantial doubt as to his route, and by bringing up two cars with three searchlights between them they had contrived what was this time, not a cone, but a veritable cage. And the heather here was not really first-class for burrowing in; in fact, it was decidedly scrubby. Only one factor in the situation suggested the slightest comfort. Not only Meredith himself, but that tall and sinister shed lay within the three intersecting beams of light. By making for that and what lurking places it might afford, he could at least prolong the chase for a time. And one never knew. In adventures of this sort, after all, it was always at the last moment that unexpected but conclusive succour arrived. The lower slopes of Ben Carron appeared an unlikely trysting place with the Flying Squad. But there was nothing in favour of giving up. So Meredith ran.

Meredith running – Meredith thought – was becoming decidedly *vieux jeu*. Meredith swimming or Meredith flying – or even Meredith crawling painfully through some tunnel of the sort delighted in by Miss Dorcas Macleod – would surely constitute a welcome variation. Nevertheless, Meredith continued to run, with the result that a blank cliff of corrugated iron was presently directly before his nose. From beyond it came the deep throb of a powerful engine, but this did not obscure the fact that there were now shouts in the darkness behind him. Shouts also were in the *vieux jeu* category – despite which Meredith did not at all contrive to feel bored. He ran round the building as fast as he could, and found nothing but a pair of vast double doors, forbiddingly closed. Whereupon he ran round again – in this being about as rational as a mouse attempting to escape into a closed biscuit tin – and did in fact find an entrance after all. This was no more than a place where a corrugated iron panel had been forced back, perhaps by some heavy accidental pressure from within. Meredith bolted through the gap. In this, no doubt, there was not much rational plan either. He was simply resolved to keep going to the end. But it so happened that as a means of keeping going the move could by no conceivable resource have been surpassed. For he had taken no more than two steps forward in an uncertain light when he felt himself hit by something like a cyclone rapidly developing from below, and this was followed by a powerful impression of being carried obliquely upwards through the air.

The moment was bewildering. Meredith's heels were higher than his head, and he was pervasively bruised. It must therefore be accounted considerably to the credit of his intellectual capacities that he solved the problem of this involuntary levitation as rapidly as if it had been some elementary issue of textual science encountered in the security of the British Museum or the Bodleian.

The Flying Foxes formed an endless chain. From this it followed that at one terminal point they must move obliquely upwards and at the other obliquely downwards – in this being like the cars on a giant wheel in a fair. If it were at the mainland end that the upward motion occurred, and if it were to be supposed that he, Meredith, had tumbled into a Fox thus rising, an adequate explanation of the phenomena about him would be attained.

In other words, he was now on his way to Inchfarr.

As if to confirm this startling but cogent hypothesis, the metal surface upon which he reposed momentarily quivered and swayed, and then perceptibly changed direction. It had reached the limit of the arc upon which it turned, and after travelling upwards and outwards it was now travelling upwards and inwards instead. Presently it would level out and begin its long trundle to the sea. But for the moment Meredith and his conveyance were still within the shelter of the tall shed into which he had bolted with so surprising a result. Looking upwards, he could see a criss-cross of girders, amid which burnt a single and crudely brilliant electric lamp. The light from this grew as he mounted upwards. His immediate surroundings became distinguishable and he was surprised to find himself a centre of interest for four deeply sunburnt small boys.

The boys were naked – which was absurd in such a climate – and they regarded him fixedly and (he suddenly felt) very much as if about to commit some mild nuisance against his person. Alarmed by this, Meredith abruptly changed his position – and thereby discovered himself to be slithering in a shallow trough or basin of bronze. The Flying Fox swung higher to a fleeting point of maximum visibility. And Meredith saw that he was sitting in the middle of a fountain – mercifully dismantled – and that the four sunburnt boys were in fact so many bronze *putti* curiously cast in the Baroque taste. He had tumbled, not only into a Flying Fox, but into a Cultural Object as well.

Nervously – and rather like a naiad exploring the limits of her domain – Meredith clambered to the lip of the fountain and glanced about him. Undoubtedly he was in a Flying Fox – one which contained not only this elaborate waterwork, but a number of small packing cases also. Loading, presumably, must proceed on the lower level. At the mainland end this particular Fox was dealt with and dismissed; just how it would be received at the termination of its journey was a matter impossible to conceive. Meredith, now at ease with the four *putti* much as, on a previous occasion, he had been at ease with Titian's Venus, settled himself comfortably in the curve of the fountain and felt for his pipe. Unless – as was wildly improbable – the fantastic truth occurred to his enemies, he was pleasantly secure for a good twenty minutes or half an hour. And to one whose habit has become running like a hare before closely pursuing hounds such a space is as infinity held in the palm of the hand. So Meredith stuffed his pipe with tobacco – the fateful tobacco still – and as he did so the *putti* departed into shadow, the light overhead vanished, and a draught of cold air told him that his skyey progress had begun.

The motion – except for certain jerks when the Fox negotiated a pylon – was rhythmical and not displeasing. By clambering from his fountain and mounting a packing case, Meredith found that he was just able to peer out upon the world like a baby first getting to grips with the sides of its crib. The moon was up and the sky was clearing; he could see Carron Lodge gleaming behind its larches, and in the west Venus was sinking towards the sea. It was extremely peaceful. The moon rose higher and its beams, lipping the edges of the Fox, caught the topmost curls on the heads of his bronze companions. Meredith smoked on. The moonlight crept down the finely modelled noses of the *putti* and caught their delicately dimpled cheeks – so that one by one the naked little boys seemed to break into an enigmatic smile. Their own position was certainly un-toward, but even more so was their human companion's. Meredith, however, was not disturbed. The faint creaking of the Flying Fox held its own sufficient music for one who had suffered so long the cultivated conversation of Don Perez Sierra y Campo. And only once during its dream progress down the line of the Carron could another sound have been heard. It was a long deep chuckle. Meredith was thinking of Shamus and the maenad maids.

14

At least there was a fire in the solar, and after the chill solemnities of the banqueting hall it was cosiness itself. Jean sat on a low stool directly before the flames, the Raeburn looking dispassionately down on her through flickering shadow. On her right Miss Isabella sat bolt upright in a high-backed chair, listening to whatever the constant drift of the centuries through her mind suggested to her ear. On her left Miss Dorcas was murmuring over the encyclopaedia once more, wholly absorbed in the pioneer construction of the Waterloo and City Railway. Had Mr Properjohn proposed to convey guano from Inchfarr, not by an extended telpher span, but by a submarine tube, life at Moila would have taken on an altogether different emotional colouring for this wistfully troglodyte lady.

But Mr Properjohn had chosen Flying Foxes – and these were moving now. Jean's ear, strained to catch some distant sound which might suggest Tammas or Mrs Cameron welcoming back Richard Meredith, could hear at long intervals the creak of one of these contrivances making its sinister way through the darkness. To Miss Isabella the sound was sometimes from the oars of the Vikings as their long ships crept into the anchorage below, and sometimes from the rude axle-tree of some primitive piece of ordnance which this or that early king of Scotland was bringing to bear against the recalcitrant chiefs of Moila. To Jean herself the sound spoke of a problem solved, but solved too late. She looked from one to the other of her hostesses, wishing to speak of Meredith – to suggest that with Tammas or alone she make her way to the mainland and find what help she could. But Shamus and Meredith, she knew, had taken the only boat harbouring on this side of the Sound – which meant that at least until morning she was marooned as effectively as ever was Ben Gunn or Robinson Crusoe.

And the hereditary Captain, reasonably app oachable by day, by night plainly departed down the long corridors of history. Her sister, too, departed down corridors of her own, fading away into obscure intestinal explorations with the St Gotthard or the Mont Cenis for guide. Neither of these old ladies, she guessed, was any longer aware of her presence. To test this Jean slipped from her stool and tiptoed from the solar. Neither stirred.

But solitude she did not want, and Tammas she unreasonably distrusted. There remained Mrs Cameron. Jean made her way to the kitchen.

Mrs Cameron had finished her labours and was sitting, comfortably enough, before the opened range. Behind her Shadrach, Meshach, and Abednego showed equally comfortable in their burning fiery furnace. Open on her lap was a large volume seemingly of a devotional character. And she was drinking claret and hot water.

'I hope', said Jean, 'that I'm not disturbing you too much?' Mrs Cameron was looking so devout that she was apprehensive of being asked to join in extemporaneous prayer.

'Nay, you're very welcome.' And Mrs Cameron tapped the open page before her. 'Might I be asking if you ever read the general observations on vegetables?'

'I beg your pardon?' And then Jean, glancing down, saw that Mrs Cameron's devotional book was nothing less than Mrs Beeton's monumental work on household management. 'Well, no – I don't think I ever read that bit.'

'Are you telling me that?' Mrs Cameron, much pleased, drew up a chair for her guest, set a pair of steel-rimmed spectacles on her nose, and began to read aloud with serious emphasis. '*The Animal and Vegetable Kingdoms*', read Mrs Cameron, '*may be aptly compared to the primary colours of the prismatic spectrum, which are so gradually and intimately blended, that we fail to discover where the one terminates and where the other begins.*' Mrs Cameron paused. 'Perhaps', she said, 'you would be taking another drop of the claret?'

'No, thank you.' Jean looked at the clock ticking on the mantelpiece and stirred restlessly on her chair. 'Mrs Cameron, do the Flying Foxes often work at night?'

'*So far as is at present known, the vegetable kingdom is composed of upwards of 92,000 species of plants.*' Mrs Cameron sipped her claret. 'The Foxes? About once a month, Miss, this year or more.'

'Would it have something to do with the tides?'

'And very likely it would.' Mrs Cameron spoke absently;

she was running her eye appreciatively down Mrs Beeton's erudite page. '*Birds, as well as Quadrupeds, are likewise the means of dispersing the seeds of plants. Among the latter is the squirrel, which is an extensive planter of oaks; nay, it may be regarded as having, in some measure, been one of the creators of the British Navy.*' Mrs Cameron glanced over the tops of her spectacles. 'Now, if that isn't a wonderful thing!'

Jean nodded. 'Talking of navies,' she said hastily, 'has Miss Isabella been imagining those Viking ships for long?'

'Creeping into the anchorage?' Mrs Cameron considered. 'Only since she took to wandering.' She settled her spectacles more firmly on her nose. '*In the Vascular System of a Plant we at once see the great analogy which it bears to the veins and arteries in the human system –*'

'Wandering? When does Miss Isabella wander?'

'At night and when the Foxes are working, Miss Halliwell. The creaking of them disturbs her, I think, so that she can't sleep, poor dear. And then she takes a lantern, maybe, and wanders the castle in the dark, which is no safe thing to do. Even to the cliff's edge she'll go, and be staring down at the anchorage. It's then mostly she hears the long ships – and sees them too, she says; dark shapes with here and there a glimmering light.'

'Do you think she really sees them?'

Mrs Cameron looked surprised. 'And what for no? Even Tammas can hear Black Malcolm singing in his dungeon. And why shouldn't Miss Isabella, that is for ever peering through the years, see the dark ships of Magnus or Olaf?'

'I suppose there's no reason why she shouldn't.' Jean rose. 'I think I'll go outside for a little fresh air before going to bed.'

Mrs Cameron raised a delaying hand. '*The Root and the Stem finally demand notice. The root is designed, not only to support the plant by fixing it in the soil –*'

Jean slipped to the door.

'*– but also to fulfil the functions of a channel for the conveyance of nourishment.*'

The night air was chill. The moon was up.

'It is therefore furnished with pores –'

Jean closed the door behind her. The sky had blown clear and there were stars. Venus was setting in the west.

The base-court was two broad panels of moonlight bisected by a dark bar of shadow cast from the keep. The only sounds were of a pig scuffling in straw and small waves very faintly breaking far below.

An outcrop of stone ... Jean could see that in the farther corner of the court one of the massive inner walls seemed to rise up from a raised foundation of living rock. There must lie what Miss Isabella had called the Seaway – that deep fissure through which Magnus Barelegs had come long ago, and Captain Maxwell's bleating cargo that very morning. And there was a grille. The hereditary Captain, anxious for her castle's strength, had ordered that it be closed. But had Tammas obeyed? Jean thought it unlikely. Cautiously, and traversing the great shadow of the keep as one who fears an ambush, Jean crossed the court.

The aperture yawned before her. All that evening she had carried an electric torch in her bag – in Minnie Martin's bag. She shone it now. An irregular, steeply sloping passage with sheer sides – some work of Nature, perhaps, enlarged by human hands – wound into darkness, chill and smelling indifferently of sea and sheep. Jean slipped past the open grille – a massive barricade enough – and plunged down the cleft, her torch waving before her. Bats flapped. The smooth stone beneath her feet was slippery with the droppings of sheep. Behind her now the opening through which she had come was no more than a dimly moonlit patch upon the darkness. She moved on, only to halt abruptly at a heavy grating sound that echoed dully down the walls. She turned. The opening which seconds before had been a single splash of faint radiance was now a criss-cross of dark lines. Someone had closed the grille.

She had switched off her torch and now she stood very still pressed against the unyielding rock, her heart pounding. For a moment a massive shadow further obscured the

215

distant light. There was the sound of footsteps, progressing surely in the dark. And then a man laughed – a strange man.

It was Miss Dorcas's world, but turned to nightmare. Jean forced her limbs to move and pressed on down the pitchy passage. The man laughed again. It was the laugh of one who follows a secure quarry. She gritted her teeth. At the other end was at least the landing stage, the anchorage, the sea. If she could only make that she might conceivably have a chance to swim for it. She stumbled and fell heavily, bruising her knees, so that involuntarily she cried out with pain. The man laughed once more. Jean felt cold as ice, impossible to say whether with fear or rage. She turned – or was by the curve of the passage bumped round – a corner. Before her was the faintest possible radiance – an effect only perceptible because of the utter darkness from which she had come. The anchorage lay before her, a deep well unplumbed by moonlight or favouring stars. Only two dull red lights glowed near the surface of the water. She took a few more steps forward and was in open air.

Low-pitched voices murmured in the night. One light was moving. And across the centre of the anchorage lay a long, low shape, with immediately above it another dark mass suspended in air. Jean, poised to dive, hesitated while taking another glance at this obscurely significant thing. And as she did so a hand fell upon her shoulder from behind and the laugh sounded anew. '*Guten Abend,*' said a low ironical voice. '*Wie geht es Ihnen, gnädige Frau?*'

Jean turned. 'Who are you?' she asked steadily. 'And how did you come to be in the castle?'

The man kept his hand on her shoulder, spoke again in German, checked himself. 'We usually send someone to the head of that passage, to see that all is quiet in the ruins. Tonight I went myself – and it was not.' He paused. 'You are fortunate.'

'Am I?' Jean had detected something oddly sombre in the stranger's voice. But this did not obscure the fact that he had laughed when she fell. 'At least I haven't been driven daft, like poor Higbed.'

'Higbed?' The stranger was at a loss. 'I know nothing of him – nor of you either. But plainly you have been more inquisitive than is discreet. You were bound to be caught. And your good fortune consists in having been caught by us and not by them. They are common criminals, you know – no more. They would simply have dropped you into the sea.'

'What nonsense!' Jean, who thought it politic to scout this indubitable truth, tried to catch a glimpse of her captor's face. 'And you?'

'At first we were their employers. They were mere cogs in a system by which we got as much foreign currency as we could. But now that it is all over they have turned the tables on us. We are a mere ferry-service – and perhaps we might be called pirates, too.'

'Well, you know, you were always that, after all.'

The stranger dropped his hand to his side. 'We are broken soldiers, surplus war material – what you will.' His arm shot out again, but this time only to point to the dark low streak on the surface of the anchorage. 'She sank a British cruiser. And now she carries away the treasures of Europe to satisfy the vanity of –'

'I know all about that.' Jean found the noble melancholy of this German ex-sailor not particularly appealing. 'But surely you can't keep so complicated a thing as a U-boat in commission all on the quiet – as those other people do their furniture vans?'

'Obviously not.' The man standing in the darkness laughed again. 'She becomes more absurdly unseaworthy every week. Quite soon now she will submerge for the last time. The moment will come to surface, *gnädige Frau*, and surface she will not. I wonder what, on that occasion, will be on board? A crate of Russian ikons, perhaps, and the better part of some great private collection from Poland or Belgium. That will be sad! And I, since I am her commander, shall be on board too. Sad, again. And you –'

'I?' said Jean. 'But didn't you say I was fortunate?'

'Why, yes. Your watery grave will now not be a solitary one, after all. But here is the boat.'

A tiny dinghy with muffled oars had glided up to the landingstage, and for the first time Jean fully realized that she was about to say good-bye to Moila. The prospect of indefinite voyaging in an unseaworthy submarine was not pleasing, and less pleasing still was the thought that it must be in the hands of men very little under even the remnants of decent discipline. They were defeated enemies engaged in what might be called a blind-alley profession of the queerest sort. It was rather like being pitched into Jules Verne's *Twenty Thousand Leagues under the Sea*, which she remembered as about a super-submarine manned by outlaws. 'I suppose', she said, 'that you are Captain Nemo?'

The effect of this question was startling. Even in the darkness the man beside her could be seen to give a perceptible jump. 'I am Captain von Schwiebus,' he said, and hesitated. Then his voice broke out harshly: 'Who gave you that? From whom did you have that sign?'

Jean's head swam. Could this conceivably be the password business again? Captain Nemo was the first nickname with which anyone of mildly literary inclinations would think to dub the piratical von Schwiebus; could it be that such a person had rashly embodied it in some system of signs and tokens? If so, Richard Meredith's original role had now devolved upon her, and there was opening before her the first possibility of some obscure deception. Jean moved deliberately towards the dinghy. 'Captain von Schwiebus,' she said mockingly, 'how funny you are. More absurd, even, than they suggested to me.'

Von Schwiebus savagely kicked what might have been either the dinghy or the man rowing it. '*Bitte*,' he said roughly, '*nehmen Sie Platz*.' But his voice was uncertain – and to the uncertainty Jean hastened to add by stepping in with alacrity. Her shaken captor followed and dressed the boat. '*They?*' he said. 'Who are *they?*'

Jean laughed. She did her best to make the sound as disturbing in its kind as had been von Schwiebus's own laugh in the Seaway. 'What is wrong with many Germans', she said, 'is nothing particularly Germanic. It is simply reading too much Byron. Why is so mediocre a poet celebrated all over central Europe? And you, my dear Captain, devoured him. The fluency of your English attests it. And I was told how you delighted in the outcast hero role.'

Von Schwiebus breathed heavily. This, then, was mockery that went home.

'But it inclines you to suppose that every man's hand must be against you. Why did you behave in that ridiculous way in the fissure – shutting the grille and trying the effect of Satanic laughter? Didn't it at all occur to you that I might be not a spy but – well, one of the common criminals, as you pleasantly put it?'

Von Schwiebus swore at the man who was rowing. And Jean was aware that although he was nonplussed by this line at which she had dived something else was on his mind as well. He was looking at a wrist-watch. 'Be pleased to explain yourself,' he said abruptly.

'Dear me, no. All this is much too amusing. But I assure you that matters will explain themselves in time.'

'As time will be abundant,' said Captain von Schwiebus, 'that may well be so.'

Jean's heart misgave her. The retired hero was not so easy to rattle. And there is something particularly discouraging in the prospect of playing for time during an interminable voyage beneath the North Atlantic in an obsolete submarine. Still, things had seemed pretty hopeless before now. And for time, therefore, she would continue to play. 'I suppose', she asked carelessly, 'that you have met our excellent Mr Neff? He has been buying stuff from Marsden's people, I am sorry to say. But perhaps he will take the Horton Venus. Are you freighting it this trip, by the way?'

'No, I'm not.' By this knowing talk von Schwiebus looked like being quite impressed. 'The quality this trip is poor. Indeed, it includes an Italian.'

'A live Italian?'

'I understand so. But as he has failed to turn up on time, he may well be dead.' Von Schwiebus paused.

Perhaps', he said suddenly, 'you know his name?'

'Yes – perhaps I do.' Jean was not much struck by the success of her endeavour to put an enigmatic quality into this. But while she was still casting about for something more forceful the dinghy – it appeared to be a mere wood-and-canvas affair – bumped gently into the side of the submarine. She looked up and saw that the dark mass which had impended over it was gone. One more Flying Fox, in fact, had continued its bogus journey to Inchfarr.

There was a moment of confusion, the grip of strong hands, and she was standing on a narrow cat-walk amid a group of silent men. They were peering intently into the east, and one of them was glancing at a wrist-watch as von Schwiebus had done. She realized that the submarine was in a hurry to get away – perhaps because of some factor in the tides, perhaps because Captain Maxwell's Sunderland laddies were still in the air and safety demanded gaining deep water soon. A man with a shaded torch and a sheaf of papers had come up to von Schwiebus and in his low rapid German Jean caught references to the Italian and to the fountain. This latter was altogether mysterious – but perhaps, she thought, they had been alternating Byron with Mr Charles Morgan's mysterious love story. And now von Schwiebus said something about herself, the men parted before her, and she saw that she was being invited or required to descend an iron ladder that ran perpendicularly down through a hatch. The submarine was already low on the water, so this would mean that she was sinking below the surface of these chill, faintly lapping waves. There was something peculiarly unnerving about the necessity – much as there must be about a first parachute jump, she thought – and she stopped to give one last look at the upper air. At the level on which she stood all was absolute darkness and this continued until, seemingly immensely high above her head, the great black curtain became a ragged semicircular silhouette against a moonlit sky. That jagged line marked the ruined ramparts of Castle Moila. And Jean turned to the hatch indifferently. For it was as if she was already miles beneath the sea.

A low exclamation halted her. The waiting men had swung again to the east. She stood, unnoticed, and followed the line of their gaze. A small dark shape had appeared above the battlements; it grew larger and dropped lower, obscuring now one and now another star. Within seconds it had disappeared into the impenetrable darkness encircling them. Something began to vibrate directly overhead. The shape appeared again, startling close and low. It slowed down, and as it did so there was an intermittent creaking -- such a sound as might be made by many oars swinging in the rowlocks of a long dark ship ...

Jean wondered how the Foxes could be so accurately stopped directly above the waiting submarine -- and wondered too how they could be unloaded while hovering still in air. The men were hurrying forward and only von Schwiebus remained beside her, his eye fixed on his watch. There was the sound of laboured movement forward, a dull clang of steel, stifled exclamations. Jean glanced at von Schwiebus. He was frowning into the darkness and appeared to have forgotten her. Perhaps it really did go against the grain with him to be casting this loot --

Jean ceased to speculate -- it being revealed to her suddenly that it was now or never. She must jump and swim. She must jump, and then swim heaven knew where -- out beyond the anchorage perhaps and round to a less precipitous shore. It was the thinnest of chances -- but she must take it, *now*.

She braced herself to spring. And as she did so the men forward parted, and for a fatal second she was rooted in astonishment to the deck. The submarine -- she saw in the uncertain light of a low torch -- appeared to have been invaded by a number of small naked boys. And the next instant she saw something queerer still. A familiar figure was striding up the deck, and in front of it moved a little red glow as from a sweetly smoking pipe. The glow disappeared -- much as if some second thought had led to the hasty discarding of so Anglo-Saxon an object -- and Richard Meredith advanced into a fuller light. He made straight for von Schwiebus and took him by the hand.

'Pantelli!' he exclaimed with Latin exuberance; 'I am Signor Pantelli and arrived just in time.' His glance turned to Jean and for a moment genuine amazement flooded his features. Then he threw himself forward. *Mia carissima sposa!* he exclaimed, enraptured. 'My dear, dear wife!'

Part Three

DOVE COTTAGE

———————

I

THE lakeside home of Otis K. Neff tilted, slid, turned upon itself, and momentarily disappeared as the huge flying-boat banked and circled in order to land against the wind. Foamflecked water pistoned upwards, hung suspended, fell abruptly into nether space just as the waters of the Gulf of Mexico had done hours before. They were climbing again. 'Jes' impossible,' said Mr Drummey. 'A whole blame regatta all over the place.'

Richard Meredith peered downwards and saw that what he had taken for larger flecks of foam were the sails of yachts dispersed over a great area of water. He also saw once more the abode of Mr Neff. 'Does he really *live* there?' he asked. 'It must take him an uncommonly long time to get around.' In the Old World, he was reflecting, there were persons whom heredity and the pressure of custom constrained to live in structures of similar size and elaboration. But everything that lay below here Mr Neff had, it seemed, caused to be built himself. He had taken so many score acres of wooded lakeside and started from dot. Now there was this. And again Meredith incredulously peered. 'Extraordinary!' he murmured.

'It sure is a beautiful home.' Mr Drummey did not take his eyes from his instruments. His voice was expressionless. Nevertheless, Meredith was aware that he liked Mr Drummey, and that Mr Drummey was no more astray in the matter of evaluating Mr Neff's splendours than a whole committee of editors of Juvenal and Martial would have been. 'A swell home,' said Mr Drummey. 'It must be wonderful to feel you own all that after coming up the hard way. Hold on, there's another turn.' His eye was on half a dozen gauges at once. 'Jes' get yourself a home like that and you can be certain you've made good. If you get doubts in the night, you simply switch on the lights and start planning another wing. Architect yourself, perhaps – Signor Pantelli?'

The intelligence of Mr Drummey was of the sceptical order. And the two young men who assisted him to navigate this aerial leviathan were discernibly sceptical too – much more so than the sombre Captain von Schwiebus had been at first. 'An architect?' said Meredith. 'Dear me, no. I deal in pictures, and that sort of thing. And it's an important moment for me to meet so big a collector as Mr Neff.'

'Ah.' Mr Drummey was looking down with distaste at the yachts that were keeping him air-borne longer than need be. 'I've been told he buys a lot – and I've ferried some for him, too. Yet somehow there aren't too many on show down there.' And he jerked a thumb in the direction of Mr Neff's swell home. 'I've sometimes wondered if he kind of misers them.'

'Misers them?'

'Treats them as if they were a store of gold beneath his mattress. There's a story he has a whole gallery he never speaks about, and won't let other folks speak about either.'

'Dear me,' said Meredith. 'I hope he will have something to say about my Giorgiones.'

'Giorgiones?' Mr Drummey leant forward to turn a switch, offered some technical remarks to one of his assistants, and then looked full at Meredith. 'Surely there aren't so many of those around?'

'Very few indeed, Mr Drummey. But I've got three. And as soon as I contacted Mr Neff's agent in Tampico and heard there was a chance of a deal I wired to have the pictures sent along. They ought to be down below there now.'

224

'I see. Well, we'll be going down now. Perhaps the Signora had better have a piece of barley sugar. Nothing like glucose.'

'I certainly don't want barley sugar.' Jean Halliwell was gazing absorbedly downwards. 'You know,' she said, 'it's utterly monstrous, of course. But it can't really be said to be in bad taste.'

Mr Drummey raised an eyebrow. 'Peddling Giorgiones?' he asked.

'Mr Neff's house. It ought to be a howling horror. But really it's more like a vast, polished, and at the same time high-spirited joke.'

For the first time Mr Drummey laughed. 'Ever been to Beverley Hills?' he asked. 'Crammed with darn fool people believing they're living in one sort of solemn museum-piece or another. Tudor mansions, chunks of Versailles, Spanish Mission – all that. And really they're all inhabiting good jokes. Just the architect having a little fun.' Mr Drummey spoke absently, and while giving Jean a glance so swiftly appraising that she felt like an oil-gauge or a speedometer. Suddenly he put out his chin like one whose mind is made up. 'Say,' he said, 'what is all this, anyway?'

The Signor and Signora Pantelli looked at each other. They looked at Mr Drummey and – more doubtfully – at his silent assistants. 'I understand', said the Signor cautiously, 'that this is Mr Neff's private plane, and that you are all employees of his?'

'Yes.' Mr Drummey, as if to give leisure for a little confidential conversation, was beginning a lazy sweep of some ten miles' radius in air. 'And we've known some darn tight squeezes through the arms of the law. Eh, Joe? Eh, John?'

'Sure.' Joe and John spoke in concert and without taking their eyes from their several tasks.

'Faithful servants of the firm,' said Mr Drummey. 'Straight enough, in a way. You can't work for someone big without putting through a few pretty cheap-looking deals.'

'Dear me!' Meredith was perplexed. 'I should have imagined that to hold rather of working for someone small.'

'You can't', Mr Drummey, ignoring this, continued, 'work for a man at all without backing him against others of his own sort – can you? Wouldn't be honest. And that naturally lands you with some pretty low jobs to do. You carry on while you can.'

'You don't stick your head out,' said Joe.

'On the other hand,' said John, 'you don't close your eyes.'

'You have to watch for the limit,' said Joe. 'And we kind of feel that while ferrying fake Wops is one thing –'

'Fake Wops!' Meredith, though most irrationally, was extremely indignant.

'– abduction is quite another.'

'Abduction?' Jean looked at Joe in astonishment. 'You don't really think I'm being abducted?'

'I do not.' Joe frowned, apparently feeling that he had delivered this opinion more confidently than was polite. 'Though you'd be worth it every time.'

'It was an Englishman,' said Mr Drummey. 'Jes' the other day. He was scared plumb mute, it seemed to me. But I guess he wasn't making the trip anything like willingly.'

Jean sat upright. 'Did he tell you he was Higbed?'

'He did. He came scrambling through a lot of crates aft there, looked as if they might be full of books. And "I'm Higbed," he says. And at that the man Flosdorf – he's one of Neff's secretaries – leads him off and gives him a drink. Kind of nasty feeling about the whole thing.'

'And mysterious,' said John. 'Seemed as if Neff wasn't to know. Flosdorf had this Higbed and the crates landed way down by what's called the Belvidere, and told us to keep our traps shut.'

'Did you happen', Meredith asked, 'to notice anything about this Higbed's physical condition?'

'Bad.' Mr Drummey was decided. 'Looked as if he'd been dragged through somewheres several weeks on end.

Which makes it queerer the way I saw him two or three days afterwards. Sitting by the lake sleek and pleased as anything, puffing at a cigar and watching some girls bathing from a boat. Really watching them, if you know what I mean, but doing it open and unashamed. Might have had some theory he was being only fair to himself that way.'

'Well, it's Higbed, all right.' Jean glanced at Meredith. 'The dafty in abeyance and the great male Higgy uppermost, once more. But it's difficult to see what it all means.'

'Difficult to see what fake Wops mean.' And Mr Drummey looked at Meredith inquiringly. 'Talking?'

'Sure – that is to say: Yes.' Meredith was momentarily confused by this impertinent intrusion upon another idiom. 'A little talking would probably be an excellent thing.'

'Then we'll jes' take another turn round the block.'

And gently Otis K. Neff's flying boat banked and began to describe a farther county-wide circle in air. Its hub, the lakeside home of Otis K. Neff, showed still like a small, towering city far away below.

'So this von Schwiebus really believed you were Mr and Mrs Pantelli?' Mr Drummey looked swiftly at Jean. 'Quite early I figured it you two couldn't be married.'

Meredith smiled. 'Well, with von Schwiebus the deception did not, in fact, continue for very long. He must always have been suspicious, and in the end he just found out. Perhaps Miss Halliwell and I were neither so Italianate nor – ah – so conjugal as we ought to have been. We were exposed, and von Schwiebus reported to the scoundrel Don Perez by wireless.'

'By wireless!' John, whose business was radio among other things, looked at Meredith wonderingly. 'They could do that?'

'Apparently so. And although at the time it appeared to seal our doom, in point of fact it has been an altogether fortunate circumstance. It means that at the headquarters of the International Society they are still quite unalarmed. A little dispirited, perhaps, but nevertheless feeling quite secure.'

'I don't get all this.' Mr Drummey was frowning at his instruments. 'For here you are, making a come-back as the Pantellis – and free as air, more or less.'

'But that is only because of the misadventure that befell the submarine almost immediately afterwards. You must understand that as yet you have by no means heard the whole story.' Meredith looked apologetic. 'I hope that this is not occasioning an altogether unreasonable expenditure of petrol? Perhaps you would prefer to land in some quiet cove –'

'The firm can stand the gas. And when you're up it's best to stay here. It's the getting up that takes it out of the old crate.'

Jean, who was eating barley sugar after all, tucked a chunk into her cheek. 'And it's just like that with submarines. It seems they can always go down, but they won't always come up again. Particularly if they haven't any longer got proper dockyards and so on behind them. Right at the start von Schwiebus told me that one trip soon his craft would just refuse to surface. And they have to surface, you know, for the engines to do some sort of breathing exercises every now and then. Well, the fatal occasion had come. They worked all the proper machines, but the submarine just stayed put. So after a time they worked some other machines that released rafts and things on the surface. And then they got into a sort of life-saving contraptions and let themselves out through an escape hatch one by one. But there weren't any left over for Mr Meredith and myself, so we were left on board.' Jean sucked at her barley sugar. 'Kind of caretakers,' she added.

'They did that?' Mr Drummey relieved his feelings by soaring several hundred feet in air.

'As a matter of fact, von Schwiebus tricked them into thinking he could get us out too. So it wasn't the fault of his crew at large.' Jean spoke as if she felt that she had come to something really important at last. 'I expect they were very decent men, really.'

'I expect they were.' Mr Drummey climbed higher. 'All fond of mother. Go on.'

'There we were – for quite a long time.' Meredith continued the story. 'It became very stuffy. No doubt you have read descriptions of people in such a plight.'

'Sure.'

'After a time – a good long time – I fell to wondering whether there might be a revolver somewhere about. Miss Halliwell, I believe, had the same idea, and we both rummaged round. But nothing of the sort was to be found. So we just waited. But insensibility appeared to be a long time in coming. The situation was one which it seemed more and more futile to prolong.'

'Sure.'

'The submarine was, of course, bewilderingly full of mechanisms of every sort. And it occurred to me – perhaps merely because my mind was clouded – that by manipulating some of these it might be possible to open a hatch, admit the sea, and have done. The moral issue –'

'Sure.'

'Eventually I must have been blundering round in a frenzy, turning a wheel here and tugging at a switch or lever there. But the only result was to set going some powerful engine which made the whole craft vibrate and merely increased our discomfort. And this went on for what seemed an eternity. Eventually there was added a gentle but somehow very sickening rocking motion. It was Miss Halliwell who sensed its possible significance. She tried the hatch by which we had first descended into the interior of the vessel. It was designed to open upwards, so that the pressure of the water had, of course, made it immovable. But this time it opened easily. We were looking at a blue sky.' Meredith paused. 'There can be little doubt that I had succeeded in coaxing the machines to achieve what von Schwiebus and his crew had found impossible.'

Joe and John glanced at each other doubtfully. But Mr Drummey gave an impassive nod. 'Jes' that,' he said. 'What could be more likely? And then you started up all the other motors, hoisted an improvised white ensign, and sailed your prize into port.'

'Dear me, no. To begin with, and after that one incredible glimpse of sky, we both lay insensible for some hours. The abrupt change of atmospheric pressure was doubtless responsible. When we came to consciousness again the submarine was rocking gently on an empty sea. We had a meal.'

'Now, that's what I call sensible.' Mr Drummey was sincerely approving. 'And I'm beginning to think we could all do with one ourselves.'

'There is little more to tell. Alone on this derelict craft, with no other companions than four small boys rather beautifully cast in bronze, our situation was both alarming and untoward. But I think I am right in saying that our principal feeling was of a delicious sense of security. Even if we drowned we should now drown in a more or less ordinary way. Jean – Miss Halliwell – found a collapsed rubber raft, and this we were provident enough to inflate and place on deck. Fortunately so, as it turned out. For late in the afternoon, and without any further interference with the engines on our part, the submarine sank. We had just time to get in the raft and row out of danger's way when the vessel turned on its side and disappeared. I regretted the fountain and whatever else of beauty might be on board. Nevertheless, I was glad to see the thing go. And that evening we were picked up by a British tanker. Our adventures seemed to be at an end. I don't know whether I explained that it was by the notion of adventure – childish as it must seem – that Miss Halliwell and I had originally been prompted to set out.'

'I guess you didn't altogether miss your mark.' Mr Drummey stared thoughtfully at his passengers. 'But now here you are again: The Pantellis in their well-known adventurous role once more. What sense is there in that?'

'Very little really, Mr Drummey.' It was Jean who took up the tale. 'We ought just to have thrown in our hand and contacted the police. Only Fate came along on that tanker and gave us a great nudge – a sort of monstrous hint. You see, the tanker proved to be bound for Tampico – and Tampico was the place where we knew Pantelli had been going to contact somebody from Mr Neff. It just didn't seem right not to carry on through the next round. And we had one enormous advantage. The submarine was lost and, whether von Schwiebus was saved or not, the conclusion would be that his prisoners were drowned. That was what Mr Meredith meant by saying that at the headquarters of the International Society Don Perez and the rest would be dispirited, perhaps, but not alarmed. Moreover, as it had been a fake Pantelli who had appeared at Moila, it was not impossible that the real man might have decided to make Tampico some more comfortable way than in a lame-duck submarine. So why shouldn't we go right ahead and act on that?'

'It seems all crazy to me.' Mr Drummey was exasperated. 'And I'm not sure I get the present situation yet.'

'But it's simple enough! Pantelli was to cable Don Perez from Tampico to have the Giorgiones forwarded to Neff. If we did that cabling from Tampico and heard that the pictures were being delivered it would mean that Don Perez was taking it for granted that the real Pantelli had somehow turned up at Tampico as planned. Whereas, ten to one, the real Pantelli is being held by the military authorities somewhere on the Continent. Perhaps he's dead. We've come to realize that people do die.' Jean paused. 'Anyway, that's how we acted. Fortunately, Mr Meredith has a brother who's with a British mission in Washington –'

'Sure he has.' Joe nodded emphatically. 'All Englishmen have brothers with a mission Washington-way these days. Sisters too.'

'– and he got us money and so on in no time. So now we've come on to sell those Giorgiones to Neff. We're going to view all the paintings and what-not were ever stolen for him, and make an inventory of them, and finally do a real clean-up.'

'A clean-up?' Meredith frowned as if in some effort of memory. 'Do you know, that is what I said I was going to do in the beginning? When I was being Vogelsang, you remember, and trying to intimidate that poor fellow Bubear.'

2

MR NEFF (who had made most of his millions between two wars) frequently and movingly declared himself to be a man of peace; and to mark this spiritual conviction he had given his country home the unassuming name of Dove Cottage. A beautiful little golden dove with rather expensive ruby eyes lived in a niche over the front door. It would pop out (this by means of a simple adaptation of the photo-electric cell) and brood symbolically over any visitor who approached, while at the same time there would float down from above the muted strains of massed choirs singing the 'Jerusalem' of William Blake. This transcendentalized cuckoo-clock Mr Neff had thought up entirely by himself.

In addition to believing in peace, Mr Neff believed in progress, and his architect had been instructed to express the spirit of progress in his plans for a beautiful home. The architect at the time of receiving his commission had been improving himself by extensive reading in the works of Freud; and it chanced that in the course of these studies he had just come upon a very celebrated place. This is the comparison of the human mind with the city of Rome – as the city of Rome would be were every phase of its development preserved intact, the Rome of each succeeding age being simply superimposed upon that preceding. If this development after the manner of geological strata was the way humanity chose to get along, might it not be possible (Mr Neff's architect thought) to erect a veritable allegory of progress simply by building in sober fact what Freud had struck out by way of brilliant metaphor? Not, indeed, a Rome upon Rome – that would be laborious and perhaps a shade too costly as well – but a fantasia which should superimpose typical examples of one architectural epoch upon another?

From this bold conception rose Dove Cottage. Baby-

Ionish or Assyrian in those deepest foundations which housed only the multitudinous engines upon which the life of the Cottage depended, it rose at basement level to a species of insanely proliferating Norman crypt which provided store-rooms, and garage accommodation for the two or three hundred cars liable to turn up when Mr Neff was entertaining friends. Then (and serving for the main domestic offices) came a slightly reduced replica of Hampton Court. No choice could have been more judicious than this. For Hampton Court, being long, low, restrained, and flat-topped, is an excellent basis upon which to erect something striking. And to fulfil this latter function Mr Neff's architect had picked on Wollaton Hall, a somewhat enlarged version of which would give approximately the accommodation Mr Neff required. Wollaton Hall can scarcely be called restrained; it displays a sort of passionate prodigality of balustrades, pilasters, pedestals, crestings, busts, and medallions in the improving upon which Mr Neff's architect rather exhausted his energies for the while – with the result that what crowned each of the four angle towers was merely a small Queen Anne mansion in the severest taste. And, having achieved this, Mr Neff's architect (who did not at all care for the nineteenth century) felt that he was about through. He therefore moved direct to the central tower of Wollaton Hall and boldly clapped upon it something austerely functional after the fashion of Le Corbusier. This topmost flight of fancy was always something of a white elephant until Mr Neff applied to it his own inventive genius and installed the swimming pool to which not a little of his just celebrity was owed.

It was to the swimming pool that Mr Flosdorf whisked Meredith and Jean in an express elevator which was appropriately embellished with a massively-sculptured Ascension after Bernini. Mr Flosdorf, rocketing his guests and the Ascension skywards, explained that Mr Neff was invisible and would so remain until evening. Evening was the time at which the great man's aesthetic sensibilities were strongest and soundest and at which he commonly elected, therefore, to buy art. Did Mr Neff buy much art? Mr Flosdorf cautiously admitted to Signor Pantelli that his employer bought a fair deal: most of it, however, he gave away to museums, convents, and orphanages. Mr Neff was extremely charitable. Only last week he had given the Aquatic Club a fine Ingres of a lady standing beside a bath. He had given an El Greco to the Elks and several Alma-Tademas to the Sisters of St Joseph – which was particularly fine, seeing Mr Neff liked Alma-Tademas almost best of all. If Signor Pantelli knew of an Alma-Tadema to throw in with the Giorgiones he might find that he was doing himself a bit of good that way... And this was the swimming pool. They would find plenty of new bathing suits to choose from over there. The water was probably about right, but the temperature could be shifted ten degrees either way in just under the same number of minutes. And Mr Neff was rather proud of the dressing-rooms. He had thought them up himself.

The dressing-rooms, Meredith found, projected upon corbels from the main mass of this final eyrie of Dove Cottage. All six sides appeared from within to be of perfectly transparent glass; and thus while disrobing or disrobed one had an extensive view, not only of several hundred square miles of woods and lakes, but of the swimming pool itself and its immediate surroundings. Viewed from the outside, however, the dressing-rooms were so nearly opaque as to satisfy the strictest demands of modesty. This ingenious method of squaring the exhibitionistic instincts with decorum struck Meredith very much, and altogether unfavourably. He was hot and sticky; nevertheless, it was some minutes before he could bring himself to prepare for a dip; when he finally did so it was to find the swimming pool itself a good deal odder than the dressing-rooms.

It was a large circular tank some fifty feet in diameter by twelve feet high. The weight of water it contained must have been tremendous. Nevertheless, it simply rested on a flat roof much as if it were a goldfish bowl.

Like a goldfish bowl, its sides appeared to be of glass. And, like a goldfish bowl, it contained fish.

Jean was already pressing her nose to whatever astounding plastic substance sustained this gigantic aquarium. Meredith did the same. The fishes – monstrous, and distorted monstrously by the curve of the tank – swam slowly by. Or, facing outward with gobbling mouths and faintly working fins, they stared sightlessly out over the tops of distant forests or into cloud. Suddenly Jean gave an involuntary backwards leap. A great fish had turned slowly over on its belly within inches of her. 'But only look!' she cried. 'It's a shark.'

It was certainly a shark – and a shark, as was immediately apparent, sparring with an octopus. And now the whole pool revealed itself as being like this. Numerous great fish swam round angrily snapping at each other in their restricted space, or contentedly swallowing little fish which dashed themselves in terrified shoals against the plastic in the hopeless effort at escape. Octopodes floated like vast tennis balls half ripped to ribbons. Creatures that were all spikes and spines diverted themselves by stabbing and lacerating neighbours less formidably armed. Crabs, with one great claw clinging like jockeys to rainbow-fish or perch, with the other dug out and devoured great collops of their steeds as they swam. And all this was as visible as if pierced by a searchlight. As in the poem (thought Meredith after his literary fashion), one *saw Too far into the sea, where every maw The greater on the less feeds evermore.* One also saw Mr Flosdorf, who appeared to be swimming about amid this submarine carnage unconcerned.

But, of course, the point about Mr Neff's swimming pool was that it consisted of a tank within a tank. One climbed a ladder, walked rather nervously across a well-protected gangway, and was presently swimming securely enough within a sort of envelope or sleeve of fish-life. In Mr Neff's view, fish-life was peculiarly well calculated to illustrate progress – particularly on that side of struggle, supercession, and rugged individualism which is one of the most salutary revelations of the evolutionary hypothesis. So now Mr Flosdorf swam about within a great ring of sharks and dog-fish, and presently Jean and Meredith were doing the same. The water was just right; being chemically treated, it was also peculiarly crystalline and peculiarly buoyant; one could lie on it as on an exquisitely sprung bed, with blue sky above, fish-life round about, and below stratum beneath stratum of architectural history.

It was all slightly fantastic, Meredith reflected as he and a large bottle-nosed shark swam deliberately towards each other on either side of the invisible plastic barrier. Perhaps by this time not only the Giorgiones but the Horton Venus had arrived down below. Perhaps Don Perez had decided to part with Vermeer's Aquarium and Mr Neff was now the owner of that as well. Perhaps he was thinking up striking ways of utilizing his new property – bringing Vermeer's marine creatures up here to jostle with his own or converting the Titian into a gigantic lampshade or waste-paper basket. Much struck by the possibility of these horrors, Meredith felt that there was no time to be lost. In the middle of the pool was anchored a small raft, and upon this Mr Flosdorf was now hospitably preparing drinks. Meredith swam towards it and climbed out of the water. 'I suppose', he said, 'that Mr Neff's pictures keep you busy pretty well all the time?'

Flosdorf looked startled and wary. But then he nodded. 'That's right,' he said. 'Job depends on them, if you'd like to know.'

'Ah.' Meredith was sympathetic. 'Makes it all a bit ticklish, doesn't it?'

This was an arrow sent obscurely into the dark; nevertheless, Meredith felt that it had scored some sort of hit. Flosdorf took a hasty drink and looked cautiously around him. 'See here, Signor Pantelli,' he said, 'are you trading those Giorgiones on your own?'

'Not altogether. I've been working in with the International Society a good deal.'

'That so? Know the folks?'

'Dear me, yes. I know Don Perez very well. Failing a

bit, I'm afraid. Losing grip on details. Properjohn's the coming man. By the way, he sent you his regards.' Fibs, Meredith found, always tended to come jerkily at first. 'Yes,' he continued more fluently, 'the control is really falling to Properjohn. The last time I saw him he had just been promoted to run another important department.' And Meredith, seeing in his mind's eye the fallen Laird of Carron amid his crates and boxes, nevertheless nodded at Flosdorf with the largest conviction. 'A really clever fellow and sees a good long way ahead. And I think he's been uneasy about Neff for some time.'

'Uneasy – hell!' Flosdorf replenished his glass. 'It's like picnicking on a volcano and waiting for it to erupt.' He looked round frowning, as if conscious that he had given too much away. 'Where's your wife? Poured her out a drink.'

But Jean had disappeared. Perhaps, thought Meredith (who believed that he was rapidly gaining knowledge of the *mundus mulierum*), she had been drawn away to a contemplation of the remaining bathing suits. He turned again to Flosdorf. 'By the way,' he said, 'how's Higbed?'

Flosdorf jumped. 'Higbed?' he said. 'I don't know what you –'

'Come, come. Properjohn's little insurance policy.'

'I tell you I don't –'

This time it was Jean's voice that interrupted Flosdorf's protestations. 'Come out!' it called. 'Come out and over here. There's somebody I want to introduce you to.'

3

IN a sheltered corner of this uppermost thrust of Dove Cottage a man and a girl were sun-bathing. Screened behind a great sheet of glass, the couple were as yet unconscious of being observed. The man was middle-aged, in rude health running somewhat to flesh, and he was simultaneously enjoying the remains of a cigar and a thoughtful study of the girl's knees. Habit apart, there seemed to be no reason why he should not study the superincumbent parts of her anatomy as well, for the girl was stripped for bathing to a degree which Meredith could not at all approve. This, as much as her expression, gave her an eminently vacant look; she might have been a cover girl waiting for slabs of letterpress to be disposed about her, together with a price tag in the region of 15 cents. As something of the sort the man appeared content to regard her through wreaths of cigar smoke. And this, Meredith could not but obscurely feel, was unjust to the girl, who was very well habituated to stepping off the page and becoming a perfectly actual little wanton. Meredith had just arrived at this conclusion (which displays his *mundus mulierum* as expanding rapidly) when Jean stepped round the glass screen. 'Hullo, Dr Higbed,' she said. 'How are you?'

Dr Higbed, whose contemplation of the cover girl's knees had grown exceedingly absent, immediately disposed his features into an expression of practised lasciviousness. This he then proceeded to smooth away behind the urbane mask of the social man. And having completed this ritual tribute to the great male Higgy he rose and bowed. 'How do you do?' he said. 'Do you live here? I have an idea that we have met –'

At this moment Flosdorf hurried up. 'Say!' he called. 'What are you doing here, anyway?'

Higbed was offended. 'Going to have a swim,' he said. 'I was brought over by Miss –'

'You darn little dumbell!' Flosdorf turned upon the girl in a sort of panicky fury. 'Who gave you leave to let him out of the Belvidere? Wasn't it your assignment to keep him there, quiet and happy? And what could be simpler than that?' Flosdorf cast upon Dr Higbed a fleeting glance of considerable penetration. 'Easier than eating candy – and you fall plumb down on it.' He pulled out a watch. 'Don't you know sometimes Mr Neff comes up here right now? Go and hold him off – any way you can think of.' And Flosdorf looked round positively wildly. 'I'd better get a car to take you back to the Belvidere straight away.' He turned and hurried off, propelling the girl before him with uncompromising thwacks on one of the few draped portions of her person. Presently there was a rapidly diminishing whir as Flosdorf, the cover girl, and the Ascension hurtled precipitately downwards.

'Odd,' said Higbed. 'Decidedly odd. But, of course, it's natural that the husbands mustn't be let know.'

Jean stared at him. 'What was that?'

'Nothing – nothing at all. But, you know, I'm sure we've met before – and more than once?' Higbed peered at his late fellow captive in what had all the appearance of honest perplexity. 'Nice part of the States this, don't you think? Mild climate for the time of year.'

'My dear sir' – Meredith now came forward – 'I fear that you are still considerably distraught. Anything that we can do –'

'Distraught? I've no idea what you are talking about. I have just been remarking that this is a very pleasant part of the world. Nice people, too.' Higbed reached for his drink. 'Enjoying myself, I must say. Relaxation from a great many duties and responsibilities. Always kept rather too many irons in the fire. As a matter of fact, I'm Higbed.'

'That', said Jean, 'is what you told the Highlanders who were trying to cast out the devils. Don't you remember?' She walked slowly round Higbed. 'Doesn't seem to have left any weals or scars. Seen any furniture vans lately?'

'Surely', added Meredith, 'we are not mistaken in supposing you to have been abducted?'

'Abducted? Nonsense! Can't think what you mean.'

'Dr Higbed, when we last heard of you it was as the prisoner – for it was certainly that – of a criminal called Properjohn. And Properjohn has definite connexions with the monstrous establishment upon which we are at present perched. Do I understand you to assert that you are here of your own free will? Pray explain yourself.'

'Explain myself!' Higbed, who had been beginning to remember to eye Jean speculatively about the knees, looked indignant at Meredith. 'I am here, sir, in professional attendance upon a patient. You must be well aware that the position of a psychiatrist is often a delicate one – and particularly when his eminence' – Higbed coughed – 'when his experience is such that he is consulted by persons of note in a community. I am afraid that I cannot discuss my present responsibilities more fully.'

'Do you ask us to believe', said Meredith, 'that your professional services were so keenly desired by a person on the other side of the Atlantic that he caused you to be dogged by furniture vans through the streets of London and Edinburgh – and indeed to be so harried that you took temporary leave of your senses?'

Higbed looked elaborately puzzled. Then he looked as elaborately comprehending. 'Miss Halliwell!' he exclaimed. 'I knew the name would come back to me. And I am very sorry to know that your old trouble has returned.'

'My old trouble! Why, you –' Speech momentarily failed Jean – chiefly, perhaps, because Higbed's glance was conscientiously appraising as well as sympathetic. 'I'm going to dress.'

Meredith watched her march off. 'Dr Higbed,' he began, 'I am bound to say –'

'Sad case – very sad case indeed. Nice girl – but definitely suffers from delusions about men to whom she is sexually attracted.' Higbed shook his head and looked at Meredith. 'Has she had any delusions about you? Probably not.'

'I had better say at once –'

'A sadistic trait, of course. Fantasies in which the beloved is subjected to all sorts of indignities and humiliations. And these reveries are presently believed in as having actually occurred. Hence the poor girl's notion that I have been thrashed by Highlanders, and so on. But why Highlanders, I wonder?' And Higbed's expression became that of one who ponders a problem of superior scientific interest. 'There is an interesting point of symbolism about that.' He shook his head again and sighed. 'It is some years since Miss – Miss Halliwell, did I say? – consulted me. The analysis was broken off at an unfortunate point. You are no doubt familiar with what we call a transference –'

'You may as well know' – Meredith had altogether unwontedly raised his voice – 'that the story of your being soundly thrashed by Highlanders I had from a very hardheaded Lowlander, a captain in the Mercantile Marine. And that he was indulging in sadistic fantasies about the beloved, or had ever effected a transference of his affection upon you, Dr Higbed, I am quite unable to credit. In short, sir, you have attempted to evade an explanation by a monstrous aspersion of Miss Halliwell's character such as only your noxious and multifarious scribblings make me willing to believe you capable of perpetrating.' Meredith paused for breath upon this indignant period. 'And now you had better return to the disreputable young person who was instructed to treat you like eating candy.'

But much of this Higbed appeared not to have heard. 'Of course,' he said placatingly, 'there is always a substratum of fact upon which such fantasies are built. And it is true that I travelled here not altogether willingly in the first instance. I had received, under circumstances which were somewhat obscure, an invitation to attend a wealthy patient in America. The fee proposed was not unsatisfactory, but, nevertheless, I was obliged to decline. I had a great deal of work on hand, so I turned it down. Well, they wouldn't take it, and put – um – considerable pressure upon me to come. And in the end I came. I'm bound to say I don't regret it – don't regret it at all.'

Meredith had with considerable difficulty restrained himself during this explanation. 'You mean', he asked, 'that you find the patient interesting?'

'Patient?' Higbed looked momentarily blank. 'Well, I haven't yet met her, as a matter of fact.'

'Her?'

'Or, rather, I haven't met them.' Higbed, who had downed several drinks in the course of this conversation, lowered his voice confidentially. 'For I should imagine it to be a syndicate. After all, even for wealthy folk a good deal of money has been involved: for instance, they seem to have provided a whole professional library for my use. So I imagine it must be several women. And their husbands, of course, have to be kept in the dark. That is why there has been a certain amount of concealment, and why that fellow Flosdorf gets in such a fuss. I have no doubt, my dear sir, that you find it rather out of the way. But I assure you that in my profession there are delicate situations which must be courageously met.' And Higbed's features assumed an expression of monumental decorum.

For a moment Meredith was less angry than bewildered. 'But how', he asked, 'can a syndicate of wealthy women require your services as a psychotherapist? It doesn't make sense.'

'Ah!' Higbed took a pace forward and placed his hands before his bare pink torso in the attitude of one who grasps the lapels of a coat. This was evidently his public-lecture manner. 'Maladjustment!' he said. 'Maladjustment, with its terrible toll of consequent neurosis. The white woman's burden.' He paused and tapped Meredith displeasingly on the naked shoulder. 'Did you ever meet a Cherokee squaw with agarophobia?'

'I've never met one at all.'

'Or a Chinese woman addicted to fetichism? Have you ever known the happiness of a Hindu wife to be ruined by persistent zoophilia, or a female Mundugamor or Tchambuli to suffer from Pygmalionism?'

'From *what*?' Meredith was startled.

'Pygmalionism – exclusive sexual attachment to statues or pictures. It is an increasingly prevalent disorder in modern society.' Higbed, apparently unaware of how much this information struck Meredith, raised an admonitory finger. 'And all these troubles result from the ignorance of Western man, for centuries unlettered in the art of love.'

'I suppose that Pygmalionism –'

'Read the *Kama-Sutra*, my dear sir. Read the *Ananga-raga*. Read the *Perfumed Garden* of the Sheik Neffzawi. Or, better still, read my own recensions of these invaluable works. To guide our thwarted and inhibited modern sisters –'

Not even Don Perez Sierra y Campo had been quite so bad as this. 'Are you under the impression', Meredith interrupted, 'that you have been brought here at the instance of a group of women who propose to install you as their tutor and – and feeder in licence?'

'In sexology.' Higbed smiled complacently. 'The *ars amatoria*, my dear sir, of a happier age. A certain amount of skilled instruction by a world authority. What proposal could be more blameless – more laudable, indeed? A few studious weeks. A comprehensive course of instruction – of course, purely on the theoretical side.'

'I'm afraid you've got it wrong.' Distaste had faded from Meredith's mind and he found himself of a sudden quite amiably disposed to this unfortunate man and his fantasies. For fantasies he sensed that they were: confronted by the maenad women and when not protected by his lecturer's dais, the learned Higbed would come off even more poorly than the Misses Macleod's Shamus. Moreover, he was barking up altogether the wrong tree. For the professional purposes for which he had been brought to Dove Cottage, no amount of information on the Sheik Neffzawi's *Perfumed Garden* could have the slightest relevance. 'I think you will find', said Meredith, 'that in these speculations you are being betrayed by your own versatility. It is in some other capacity that your services are required. And I really don't know about a few weeks.'

'But certainly it is to be for only a few weeks! I have been assured that I shall be back in London –'

'Dr Higbed, you cannot surely place any confidence in the assurances of people who have taken – well, such extremely drastic steps to contrive your attendance here? At the moment you appear to enjoy a fair measure of

243

freedom. I urge you – nay, I beg you – to escape from this grotesque and sinister place and seek the security of the local police.'

Higbed smiled indulgently – and then this expression was replaced by one of conventional concern. 'The security of the police? Are you quite sure, my dear sir, that you are not coming yourself to harbour mild feelings of persecution? I have known quite bad cases to begin with an irrational solicitousness for the safety of others.'

'I repeat that I greatly doubt the few weeks.' The sun had disappeared and it was now unpleasantly chilly on the topmost perch of Dove Cottage; nevertheless, Meredith continued to wrestle with this insufferable man. 'Did you ever read the tale of the kidnapped expert?'

'I never heard of it.'

'There are a great many versions. I believe you will find one or two in the Sherlock Homes stories. Something goes wrong with a hydraulic press used by a gang of coiners and a skilled engineer has to be called in. But of course, he must never be let go again. You follow me?'

Higbed appeared to follow. For a moment his confidence visibly flickered. 'Nonsense!' he said. 'Mere melodrama.'

'But then the affair has taken you through a good deal of mere melodrama already, has it not? And I can well imagine the services of a psychiatrist being required in circumstances where a mere assurance of professional secrecy would not be a sufficient guarantee of safety to the patient or his associates. You might be required to deal with the psychological aftermath of some horrible crime.' Meredith paused. 'You have agreed to remain here partly for profit, no doubt, and partly through certain ridiculous and illusory expectations of conducting something between a female academy and a harem. Actually, you will be required to treat, not a gaggle of women, but a single man. I suppose him to be what I should call mad. And his continued madness is of a nature to endanger certain of his employees and, it must be said, accomplices. It is they who first approached you unsuccessfully in London

244

and later went the length of kidnapping you. It is they who have later squared you with luxurious treatment. But when you have served their turn – and equally whether you succeed in your professional treatment or fail – I judge it very likely that you will simply be put in a sack and dumped in the lake. Please think it over. Good afternoon.'

And Meredith, taking one glance at Higbed and seeing that no more could be done, walked off to change. Dusk was falling. The swimming pool of Otis K. Neff was shadowy. The sharks appeared to have gone early to bed.

4

A COUNTRYMAN of Mr Neff's has cited as an example of the oddities of the human mind the persuasion that rich men judiciously vindicate their grandeur by inhabiting structures so vast that they can only appear to infest them like vermin. But the image thus evoked by Thoreau of minute creatures crawling painfully down interminable corridors Mr Neff had in at least one important particular very successfully modified. Down the corridors of Dove Cottage it was quite unnecessary to crawl, since every corridor took the form of two gigantic conveyor belts. Along these belts Mr Neff, Mr Neff's guests, and Mr Neff's servants were effortlessly fed to their appropriate destinations just as if they were so many nuts and bolts in a well designed assembly plant. It is conceivable that Thoreau would have considered nuts and bolts thus marshalled and promenading as of even less dignity than rats or lice. But Mr Neff simply did not look at the matter in this way. He had applied himself rationally to the problem of cutting down the number of foot-pounds of energy daily required of one who would inhabit a Wollaton Hall expanded to occupy an area indentical with that of Hampton Court.

Or not quite rationally. For what had set Mr Neff upon this particular innovation had, in point of fact, been a dream: a recurring and harassing dream in which he everlastingly plodded down inconceivably gorgeous and elaborate vistas without ever getting anywhere that he really wanted to go. That it is better to travel hopefully than to arrive was decidedly no part of Mr Neff's philosophy, and this dream (which Dr Higbed would certainly have found interpretable at several different levels of experience) worried him a good deal. Presently it invaded, too, his waking consciousness, until at length as he plodded about his Cottage he was frequently doubtful as to whether he were dreaming or not. By constructing corridors in which he never did anything but stay put, Mr Neff, like the Deity on the occasion of Creation, firmly divided night and day. In his dreams he might endlessly toil through corridors still, but during his waking life the corridors should as endlessly toil past him.

It is no longer motion cheats your view, thought Meredith as a remote coign of Dove Cottage hurtled towards him, *As you near it the land approaches you*. He stepped with quite practised agility from his conveyor belt to a turntable, was swept in a wide arc round a spacious hall, fed into another corridor and presently deposited before double doors which gave upon a suite of rooms. Certain embarrassments with which a submarine had confronted an inadequately married couple were most prodigally obviated here. There were two bathrooms, two bedrooms, and an intervening *salon* the proportions of which would have made it entirely suitable for an ambassadorial reception. He crossed this with some impatience and knocked at a farther door. 'Jean,' he called, 'I think I've made it out.'

'Made it out?' Jean appeared in an evening gown which Meredith felt to be decidedly exotic. But then, of course, as between Tampico on the one hand and North Oxford or the environs of Cambridge on the other there must be substantial discrepancies in a matter so mutable as that of feminine *couture*. 'You mean about Higbed?' Jean asked.

'Yes. The fact is –' Meredith hesitated. 'Well, did you ever happen to hear of something called Pygmalionism?'

'Of course.' Jean looked surprised. 'It's a fancy name for iconolagnia.'

'For *what?*' Meredith was quite perturbed by this readiness in the field of sexual pathology.

'Iconolagnia. The element of non-aesthetic pleasure in the contemplation of gods in fig-leaves and goddesses barely in that. Of course, it has to be an exclusive interest. Anyone can get an occasional faintly carnal pleasure from a painting, can't they?'

'I suppose they can.' Meredith nodded uncertainly. 'You know, when I first saw the Horton Venus in Bubear's passage I took it for a moment to be a real woman. And then when I realized that it was a painting I experienced a distinct pleasurable surprise. Would you say that was iconolagnia?'

'Of course not.' Jean was reassuring. 'That was just a mixture of modesty and artistic appreciation. It's obvious that Neff hasn't any modesty to speak of. Are you suggesting that he hasn't any artistic appreciation either?'

Meredith looked round the vast salon in which they stood. 'I should think it demonstrable that he hasn't a scrap. But the point is this. Higbed has deluded himself into the belief that he has been brought here by a group of women anxious to make – um – certain recondite studies in which he supposes that he might assist them. Whereas in point of fact I judge that the explanation must be quite different. And, curiously enough, it was his making some chance reference to Pygmalionism (for he blathered a great deal, as you might expect) that set me on the track of it. When you come to think of it, any man who spends vast sums of money on secretly buying and hoarding stolen paintings must be pretty mad. No true love of the arts could lead him to do such a thing.'

'I disagree.' Jean was suddenly very much the person who had written those papers on Minoan weapons in the *Hellenic Review*. 'Think of all the immemorial stories of dragons stealing and guarding human treasure – which

247

meant jewels and armour and utensils finely wrought: the equivalent, in fact, of everything that we now think of as art. Why did the dragons do it? It wasn't iconolagnia or Pygmalionism, we may be sure. The fact is that the creatures had robust aesthetic sensibilities and liked beautiful things just for their beauty. At the same time they were loathly worms, inhuman and utterly without morals, and they didn't care two hoots whether they came by all those beautiful things honestly or not. And I'll bet it's just the same with Neff. He's a dragon – a horribly powerful modern dragon with oil interests and railroad companies instead of fiery breath and yard-long talons. And he just gathers all these beautiful things and sits on them for the sake of sitting.'

'That's just it!' Meredith interrupted as rapidly as if he were countering a colleague on Martial, 'For the sake of sitting, and not for the beauty of the things in themselves. It's like being a miser, as that admirable young man in the flying-boat suggested. And the activities of the miser are based as you know on a certain morbidity of development. He is a person whose notions of love and possession haven't progressed beyond those of a very small infant. Now, Neff collects pictures and so on not quite in that spirit, but somewhere near it. They don't minister to his sense of beauty, nor just to his sense of power and opulence in any ordinary way. They have become love-objects. It's like women doting over toy dogs, or men senselessly keeping half a dozen mistresses hidden away in different parts of a great town.'

'Well I'm blessed!' Jean was looking at Meredith in the frankest surprise. 'But go on.'

'Of course, it's disconcerting and repellent.' Meredith was by now so satisfied with his discovery that he made this statement in a rather perfunctory way. 'Still, it's a reasonable hypothesis, and certainly the only one I can think of as covering the facts. Neff's going hungrily round secretly possessing himself of picture after picture is a sort of perversion – a streak of madness which has now begun to spread. And all those people who have been his pimps and procurers have become afraid of some open scandal which would expose this whole monstrous trade in stolen masterpieces. So some of them – Properjohn and Flosdorf, for instance – decided that he must be cured or controlled by some suitable psychological treatment. But they daren't risk bringing in an American doctor openly, and so they kidnapped an English one and are holding him against the critical moment.'

'But I don't know what you mean by the critical moment.'

Meredith hesitated. 'Think of the man who keeps all those mistresses – and who, because of some sense of guilt, keeps them absolutely secretly. Or think of the miser with his hoard. Each has a counter-impulse to *tell*, to let people *see*. I've read cases of such men finally inviting their friends –'

'Good heavens!' Jean was looking more surprised still. 'Do you mean that as Neff gets loopier and loopier about these artistic fetiches or whatever Higbed would call them he is likely to invite his friends and rivals in a big business way to peer at them through keyholes?'

'Well, something like that. He's liable to give the game away somehow. And not just as a matter of simple reckless-ness or boastfulness, since there would be no point in bring-ing in a Higbed to combat that. The impulse Higbed might be able to deflect or resolve must be, broadly speaking, a pathological one – like this Pygmalionism, or treating pictures as erotic counters. I've said it's very disagreeable.'

'What is much more relevant is that it's very incredible. I don't believe a word of it.'

'Very well!' Meredith was quite nettled. 'We will take it that Neff is a simple amateur of the arts. At the same time, we know that Higbed, who is an accomplished psychiatrist, has been brought here, willy-nilly, as what Properjohn called an insurance policy – and because, in the fellow Flosdorf's words, purveying stolen pictures to Neff is like sitting on a volcano and waiting for it to erupt. I invite you to connect these facts on any theory other than my own.'

'And I invite you to wait until we see Neff – which I suppose we're going to do at dinner. Is he the Old Dragon, swinging the scaly horror of his folded tail? Is he the New Pygmalion, dreaming of biting succulent gobbets out of the Horton Venus? The way he handles his eating irons will show.' Jean, who was fiddling with her hair before a huge mirror, turned round as if a thought had suddenly struck her. 'Those Giorgiones of ours – have you seen them?'

'Yes. Flosdorf has had them unpacked. I should judge them to be fine paintings of that period – but whether actually by Giorgione or not I am, of course, without the connoisseurship to say.'

'But you can say whether they are iconolagnic? Giorgione could be when he tried. Think of the Sleeping Venus at Dresden.'

'As a matter of fact, they are not. The severest puritanism, that is to say, could not regard them as in any sense improper pictures.'

'I see.' Jean paused. 'And do you remember something we learnt right at the beginning: that Neff had turned keen on archaic sculpture?'

'Dear me! yes.'

'Well, wouldn't you say that archaic sculpture represented rather a severe taste in the New Pygmalion? Would anyone think of biting gobbets out of the Proserpina of Chiusi, or of peering through a keyhole at the Apollo of Delphi or a Canopic urn? And although the iconolagnic Neff might very well give an El Greco to the Elks how could he bear to part with that Ingres to the Aquatic Club? Your theory seems to me feebler and feebler the more one looks at it. In fact I think it would look much better if it stood on its head.' And Jean, who appeared quite to have forgotten her own reasonable suggestion of waiting to see what acquaintance with Mr Neff might produce, nodded emphatically at Meredith.

'Stood on its head? If I may say so, there is no more barren controversial trick than standing the other man's theory on its head.' Meredith looked very severely at Jean. 'And, anyway, I don't see how it can be done.'

'Nothing simpler. You say Higbed is here to make Neff sane. I say he is here to make him mad.'

'I just don't understand you.'

'Well, it's like this. Clearly enough, Neff is extremely eccentric. Look at this house and those horrible fish. And it might very well be to the interest of powerful people about him to drive him some stages further into downright madness. To get control of things, you know, or to prevent defalcations from being discovered. Of course, if they were sufficiently unscrupulous they might simply liquidate him straight away. But with a man holding such immense interests it is easy to imagine particular circumstances in which a good, certifiable madness would be preferable. You will agree to that?'

'Within limits, yes.' Meredith was cautious. 'But I don't at all see –'

'It's as clear as a pikestaff! For can you imagine anyone better able to drive a man mad than Higbed?'

'And that, no doubt, is why they started by driving Higbed himself mad. Just to give him a vivid sense of the effect required. I think your idea is utterly fanciful.'

'It's not nearly so fanciful as your Pygmalionism, Richard Meredith.' And the author of papers on Minoan weapons tossed her head in a not altogether scholarly way. 'For why Higbed? Higbed is a psychiatrist. But quite a large body of men are psychiatrists. What then distinguishes him from these? The fact, I should say, that he is thoroughly unscrupulous. Bring him here forcibly and, ten to one, he can be corrupted – a thing you probably couldn't predict of a single other skilled man in his profession. Very well. That points to his being brought for the most sinister purpose. And what is the most sinister purpose such a man could fulfil? Clearly that of using his knowledge of the mind the wrong way round – getting some hold on Neff (who is hypochondriac, likely enough) and edging him imperceptibly into the madhouse. You see? And I would say that my argument amounts almost to a demonstration. And even if it's only a hypothesis it's miles better than yours. Don't you think?'

'I do *not* think. In fact, your argument (as you are pleased to call it) is an outrageous piece of sophistry.' Meredith spoke with the most convinced emphasis. 'And I would say further –'

'I beg your pardon, sir.'

Both Meredith and Jean swung round, startled. Framed in the doorway stood an impeccably filmic butler such as it was inevitable that an establishment telescoping Hampton Court, Wollaton Hall, and four Queen Anne mansions should own. This functionary bowed with a freezing grandeur. 'Mr Neff's compliments, sir,' he said, 'and he hopes that the Signora and yourself will dine with him at eight o'clock.'

'We shall be very happy.'

The man bowed again and left the room. Prompted by a common impulse, Jean and Meredith moved to the door and peered after him. Standing perfectly still and bolt upright, Mr Neff's butler was receding rapidly upon his conveyor belt. He was like the detached figurehead of some ancient and haughty ship borne by a strong current towards the horizon.

5

But the encounter with Mr Neff (Meredith felt afterwards) had much the feel which those must experience who participate in a head-on naval battle. For Mr Neff, surrounded by a whole flotilla of auxiliaries, was first sighted at a distance representing almost the extreme length of the Cottage, and as he rapidly advanced he had the appearance of an admiral issuing from his bridge all that multiplicity of orders which must prelude an engagement. Actually, Mr Neff was conducting a conversation with a business associate in Johannesburg, and this was why an attendant stood beside him on the conveyor belt dextrously paying out a telephone cord as Mr Neff and his entourage were propelled forward. On each side were girls with open writing pads, behind were two menservants carrying a variety of garments (for Mr Neff was as yet but imperfectly attired) and behind this again was a little posse of important-looking and well-dieted gentlemen – presumably clients or familiars of Mr Neff – whose attitudes wavered between the largest confidence and a covert uneasiness at their overwhelming surroundings. And as this line of battle moved rapidly towards Meredith and Jean, so did those two move rapidly towards it. It is well known that the issue of modern naval conflicts depends upon split-second decisions; the moment comes at which the order must be given, the appropriate deflection achieved, and the enemy brought instantly and fatally within the rake of one's fire. And some such lightning strategy, Meredith felt, there ought now to be. Only on Mr Neff's conveyor belts one was much less manoeuvreable even than a battleship; in fact one was little better than a tram.

As you near it the land approaches you ... And Mr Neff was eminently *terra incognita*, territory virgin and unexplored. He liked Alma Tadema; he had given an El Greco to the Elks; all else was unknown. Was he a Dragon? Were his hoarded pictures a sort of megalomaniac version of the row of Pin-up Girls favoured by the simple G.I.? And, if so, had his attachment to those empty images of desire reached a point of embarrassment only to be coped with by a kidnapped psychiatrist? Or did he appear to be one who by the same psychiatrist could cunningly be driven mad? Of all these probabilities it should be possible to make some lightning provisional assessment now. But Meredith found so disconcerting a quality in the spectacle of a group of men, at once gesticulating and standing as stock still as waxworks, advancing like so many tin soldiers in an ambitiously mechanized window display, that he was unable to set about any appraisal whatever. He saw only what was patent for any observer to see: a small, hurried man, either dynamic or merely fussy according as to how one chose to take him, and very fairly representative of the not very interesting class of captains of industry.

Mr Neff – Mr Drummey had said – had come up the hard way. And he had not, Meredith presently judged – come up quite tip-top. He had not acquired the tricks of quiet and reticence which mark your magnate who has been born (as the poet adequately puts it) lapt in a five per cent Exchequer Bond. Mr Neff – as his domicile and his swimming pool might be held to presage – abundantly asserted himself, and in this he was like lesser and less secure members of his magnate breed. Immensely successfull he had quite obviously been, and yet, equally obviously, he was not quite what he would fain imagine. What then, was the flaw? Certainly it could not consist in a willingness to help himself to other people's property: for in that, after all, lay the very essence of the part. But might it somehow lie in the fact that prominent in that property were sundry works of human craft pre-eminent for beauty, and purveyed to their present illicit owner by the International Society for the Diffusion of Cultural Objects? There was the fact that Mr Neff was after his own queer fashion artistically creative; he had thought up the swimming pool, and the brooding dove which introduced Blake's 'Jerusalem', and the general idea of a country home which should symbolize the spirit of progress. There was the possibility –

But these were reflections far too slow for this hurrying moment. Mr Neff had tossed the telephone to the man paying out the cord, barked a couple of sentences at each of the girls with writing pads, snatched his tuxedo and a hairbrush from the attendant valets, waved Jean and Meredith off their conveyor belt, and with an agile leap landed beside them. The rest of the party proceeded on its way, rather like a convoy of harmless merchant vessels suddenly abandoned by a darting destroyer, and the owner of Dove Cottage was immediately isolated with his new guests. 'Mr and Mrs Pantelli?' he barked. 'Pleased to meet you. Keep quiet.' And he waved them once more on to the conveyor belt. 'Not one dam' word – see?'

This was discouraging, for the pleasure which Mr Neff

could experience in meeting persons whom he thus peremptorily forbade to converse must surely be of the most conventional sort. It was true, Meredith reflected, that Jean was decidedly pleasant just to look at, but this was scarcely a fact that should warrant a really courteous host's demanding that she keep her mouth shut.

But now Mr Neff spoke again. 'Talk!' he said.

Meredith looked at him in astonishment. 'But you have just required –'

'That's better.' Mr Neff nodded approvingly and jerked his thumb forwards. 'Talk natural-like, so those folks won't be wondering. But don't talk art, or buying art; just keep mum on it – see? Too many people have been hearing this story I collect art big. Take Gipson there' – and Mr Neff indicated what appeared to be the most consequential of the group forging steadily ahead before him – 'Gipson keeps on leading round to pictures how I don't like. Curiosity. Taking liberties with a man's private interests. And it's all wrong this story I collect art big.'

The idiom of Mr Neff, it occurred to Meredith, was distinguishably akin to that of the disgraced Properjohn. Perhaps this pillar of progressive Americanism, like Homer and other great men, had also a dubious ancestry amid many cities. Meredith glanced at Mr Neff, thinking to discern if there were also some physical resemblance to Don Perez's demoted controller of crates and boxes. And as Meredith glanced at Neff it so chanced that Neff glanced at Meredith – with the result that the latter found himself with several pieces of intelligence to review.

The eye of Mr Neff was by no means mad; rather it was shrewd and calculating. But it was also irascible. Indeed, there smouldered in it the hint of certain wrathful fires which might well make Flosdorf or another quail. Mr Neff might be a man of peace; he might own a gold and ruby dove; he might be fond of massed choirs proposing to build Jerusalem in England's – or Michigan's – green and pleasant land. Nevertheless, he was a dangerous man, very well able to turn from such laudable constructive

255

assertions to a simple raising hell. But this was not all – or indeed what was chiefly striking – in Mr Neff's eye.

For the eye so far was alien to Meredith's experience – and yet Mr Neft's eye was a familiar eye as well. In precisely what the familiarity consisted he found himself unable to say; it was an eye, so to speak, on some fringe of his own world which he could not at the moment further define. But now it appeared necessary to talk, and Meredith boldly decided to talk art despite the ban which Mr Neff had placed upon it. For he had, after all, no intention of really selling someone else's Giorgiones or near-Giorgiones to this unscrupulous collector, and there was the less need therefore of deference or tact.

'But it's quite plain', said Meredith, 'that you do collect art big. Just look at all that.' And he pointed to the panelled walls which were flowing smoothly past them on either side. As far as the eye could see these were hung with etchings: Rembrandt's etchings to the number of several hundred. 'No wonder your friend Mr Gipson keeps leading round to pictures in a way you don't like.'

'But we must put something on the walls; it wouldn't be natural not. Suspicious.'

What Properjohn – thought Meredith – would call fish-like. 'But it is suspicious,' he said aloud, '– hundreds of thousands of dollars worth of Rembrandt hanging along a corridor.'

'It strikes you that way?' And Mr Neff looked fleetingly and with a queer distrustfulness at these ranked master-pieces. 'Flosdorf arranges all that: the pictures we give away and the pictures we hang about the place for folks to see. Clever at it, I've always thought. Quiet and in good taste. Nothing to catch the eye, but the quality right. Same as if you had a custom-made suit with a neat pin stripe – nothing loud or dressy.'

'I see.' And Meredith looked again at the labours of Rembrandt thus likened to the products of a discreet tailor. 'No doubt they are quiet in one sense. On the other hand, a good many of them are highly dramatic – perhaps a little too much so.'

'For instance,' said Jean, 'look at that one – the Blinding of Samson.'

Mr Neff cast a rapid glance up the corridor to where the rest of the party were just disappearing on a turntable. 'Well,' he said, 'look at it.' And grabbing the arms of his two companions he jerked them off the conveyor belt in front of the etching. 'Look at it,' he repeated – and proceeded to do so himself, squarely and with no apparent disposition to speech. Samson in his agony confronted the three of them.

But presently Mr Neff did speak. 'Take Goya,' he said. 'Goya did a whole heap of things much like this – people maiming and torturing each other in some war way back in history. I got the whole lot of his stuff in a folio upstairs. It's not what you could put on a wall; not if you are a man of peace same as I am. But the point is that you're wrong about Rembrandt and his having too much drama. Goya's got that, but this hasn't.' Mr Neff made this pronouncement quite without absoluteness; indeed he frowned over it like an anxiously open-minded professor. 'Or so it's always seemed to me, Mrs Pantelli, after looking a good many times at both. And why? It just seems that this Rembrandt got more art all the time. It's the way the lines go across the paper.' Mr Neff offered this accurate if unsurprising information much as if it were his own unassuming contribution to aesthetic theory. 'That and how the light come here' – he made a curiously subtle gesture – 'and here. And I'll tell you another thing. Hang this upside down so you'd think it couldn't make sense, and you'd find it still looked somehow as if it had been put together on purpose. Now that doesn't work with the Goyas – or not with many of them – because I've tried with them often enough. And why is this Rembrandt still most the same van Rinjn even if you hang him topside down? Just because he got more art all the time. Step back folks, or we'll be late for the soup.'

They resumed their progress. Meredith was as persuaded of the essential soundness of the observations just offered as he was surprised at Mr Neff's making them.

'About Rembrandt again,' he said curiously, 'would you say he had more art all the time than even Alma Tadema?'

For a moment Mr Neff stared; then he burst out into large laughter. 'Art's tiring,' he said. 'Art's the darn'dest tiring thing I know. Ever felt that?'

'Well, I think I know what you mean.'

'And there's nothing like that Tadema if you want a break. I bought dozens of him just to have a bit of a joke now and then. Dirt cheap, too.' And Mr Neff laughed again. 'Not that I let Flosdorf in on that. Mean nothing to him. Clever man, of course. But he doesn't understand art.' Mr Neff lowered his voice. 'Doesn't even really know that art is beautiful. Kind of queer, isn't it?'

Meredith considered. 'I suppose it to be not uncommon.'

Mr Neff shook his head. 'It's wonderful', he murmured, 'how art *is* beautiful. Keeps on surprising me every time.' He looked from Meredith to Jean with the largest innocence. 'But about having only quiet things showing, so as not to have too much talk. You'll find it the same in the dining-room here. Just cartoons by Leonardo and Raphael, and things in soft chalks by Dürer. Nothing striking. All plain, nothing coloured.' Again he lowered his voice. 'Say,' he said, 'I'll do for you folks what I don't often. I'll show you the coloured ones tonight.'

'Thank you very much.' Meredith looked with increasing wonder at his host. 'I suppose a good many experts and connoisseurs come here?'

Mr Neff nodded. 'Yes, sir,' he said – and his more assertive self abruptly returned to him. 'Only to see what's on show, of course. It's modest and not striking, as I say; still it's brought big museum men and critics to the Cottage more than once.'

'With your fondness for these matters, you must find conversation with them very interesting.'

'And they do too.' Mr Neff was now frankly assertive. 'It's a remarkable thing. We talk art and understand each other.' His voice rose in sudden, surprising triumph. 'We understand each other all the time.'

6

MR NEFF, then, was a Dragon after all – a Dragon with pronounced if untutored aesthetic sensibilities and no morals whatever. He knew that art was beautiful. And he helped himself.

Nor was he altogether a solitary Dragon, crouched un-yieldingly upon his hoard. For although that part of it which was twopence coloured was securely hidden away, over the penny plain residue he was in the habit of con-versing with authorities, and of finding satisfaction in the exercise. Indeed, it had become clear that in this was the man's peculiar pride. And Meredith, as the tedious banquet to which he was set moved elaborately forward, considered the implications of this.

Mr Neff had come up the hard way, which meant that he had battled towards affluence with no pause for any-thing that could be called cultivation, with no glimmering intimation of what does in fact really constitute the good life, without access to that traditional body of philosophy, literature, art which a little serves to unsensualize the mind. And yet Mr Neff had never belonged quite sheerly to his type, had never been wholly and simply the Acquisitive Man. The queer streak of restless inventiveness which had evoked his home, his dove, his swimming pool, his conveyor belts would have been creativeness in a more genial environment. Almost, in fact, Mr Neff was an artist. Almost – but not quite.

And then Mr Neff had been got at to collect. Don Perez, Properjohn, Flosdorf: these or others (and the story was common enough) had for their own advantage set him to buying art. But Mr Neff (in this unlike most magnates who are induced to walk into the dealer's parlour) had not merely bought art. He had discovered it.

And at once some ever-present sense of inferiority was relieved. He was no longer merely a Merchant – the wealthiest of whose order all human testimony massively declares to be inferior to the poorest Scholar, the most meagre Artist. For his understanding of this new world of values was intuitive and immediate, and by this understanding his life was raised to a higher plane. He knew that art is beautiful – and this was more than his purveyor of pictures, Flosdorf, really did. When people who lived unchallenged upon this peak of culture came to look at the Leonardo and Raphael cartoons, the Dürer drawings, and the Rembrandt etchings, they had the same understanding as himself – in essence the same and no more – of what turned upon the way the light fell and the lines went across the paper. The *outré* Neff, assertive and uneasy, abundantly aware of the absurdity of his Cottage with its dove and sharks and octopodes and moving platforms, discovered that Nature, after all, had endowed him with the purest and most exact aesthetic taste. And to this discrimination, therefore, he had hitched the most powerful impulses of his abundant ego. His self-esteem, although it feigned to be, as of old, wholly implicated in the Big-Business game, was actually packed in this new, single basket. He knew that art is beautiful; and so he could not have enough of it. Honestly or dishonestly, he bought it up. And somewhere in this fantastic building, then, was the Dragon's hoard. Meredith and Jean were to be led to it that night.

Arrived thus far, and obliviously eating caviare for the first time in years, Meredith came back to the problem from which he had set out. Why Higbed? Why was that ill-treated but assuaged psychiatrist now kept lurking on the outskirts of Dove Cottage, like an ambulance or a fire-engine on the fringes of an aerodrome? What could the explanation be?

Across Mr Neff's elaborately laden board Meredith caught Jean's eye, and discerned in it a glint of provisional triumph. Certainly the stocks of Pygmalionism and iconolagnia had fallen low, for the nature of their host's interest in the plastic arts was evidently as irreproachable as Ruskin's had ever been, and a good deal more relevant. Indeed (thought Meredith, going into a learned reverie) there might be rather more reason for suspecting that

Ruskin had made love-objects of pictures than there was for supposing that Mr Neff did so. It was, of course, not inconceivable that Mr Neff in all this led a sort of double life; that his secret collection sometimes satisfied his sheer artistic sense and at other times ministered to delusions or obsessions. It was not necessary to suppose that he would fain bite collops from the Horton Venus, or that he struggled with a temptation to invite his acquaintances to inspect her through a keyhole. Some less specific confusion might easily be dangerous to the employees who had criminally brought the collection together. Art was something new to Mr Neff; if his mental balance was naturally poor might it not have become a focus of attention so compelling as intermittently to usurp reality? Moving in a necessary secrecy and solitude amid a hundred resplendent evocations of the Renaissance, his eye constantly conversing with the glowing pastorals of Palma and the resplendent palaces of Veronese, travelling down the Venetian vistas of Canaletto and Guardi –

Meredith became aware of the grossly alliterative nature of this speculation and looked suspiciously at the wine-glass beside him. The stuff, whatever it was, had nothing of the qualities of Don Perez's noble claret; it was far from clearing the brain; it favoured the silent composition of bad prose. But the point was this: might not Mr Neff, endlessly communing in his silent and secret gallery with all those potent memorials of another age, come imperceptibly to step in among them – or let them step from their frames like the deceased baronets in *Ruddigore?* And might not this be a likely road to sporadic delusions of grandeur to the control of which a Higbed might appositely be called – his patient one who had persuaded himself that he was a pope or a doge, a Borgia or a Medici or a Montefeltro? And Meredith, much taken with this new idea, looked up the table at his host. He looked up the table and sighed. For Mr Neff, somehow, did not look like even the most intermittent Borgia or Sforza or Gonzaga. He had the appearance of being altogether unintermittently Otis K. Neff.

It was evident that others besides Jean and Meredith had wind of the hoard, and that one of these was Mr Gipson. He was a dwarf of a man – it is dwarfs, after all, Meredith thought, who traditionally search out the hoards of dragons – but of those present at Mr Neff's table tonight it was he who seemed to approach nearest to the status of a colleague rather than a client. Mr Neff was disposed to talk business, with occasional explanatory asides to Jean on the magnitude of the interests involved and the infinite guile required in the handling of them. But the mind of Mr Gipson was running on art. Almost certainly he had no notion that art was beautiful. But he was plainly confident that there must be something to it – probably money – if it was being covertly trafficked in by his astute friend. Mr Gipson therefore, without at all knowing what the attempt would reveal, was doing his best to look through the keyhole. And Mr Neff was opposing him. In fact, the Dragon – in this wholly unlike the man with half a dozen mistresses hidden about a town – had no disposition to let anyone glimpse his riches. If the Pantellis were to be let in, this was no doubt in order to impress them with the singularly little consequence in which the owner of so extensive a collection would regard a mere two or three dubious Giorgiones.

'Neff,' said Mr Gipson, 'I wonder you don't think to brighten this place up. A bit sombre, to my mind.'

'That so? Take a drink.' And Mr Neff turned back to Jean. 'Yes,' he said heavily, 'nowadays it's Time Factor all through. When I started it was Business Efficiency, which meant buying more comptometers and having your files so that only the Business Efficiency folk could handle them. But now it's Time Factor that's the secret. You saw me on the long-distance before we sat down? That was Jo'burg. And what they said means I leave for the Coast six tomorrow morning. Drummey's out there on the lake tuning up now.'

'Dear me!' Jean was impressed. For there must be a genuine complexity about operations in which a message from Johannesburg sends a man shooting off to the shores of the Pacific. 'And shall you be there long?'

'Mightn't even get there. A radio might come when we were an hour out meaning it might be best to turn round and meet a man for dinner in London.'

'I see.' Transport was evidently a very different thing for Mr Neff to what it was for his clandestine friends of the International Society. No furniture vans, no Flying Foxes, no interminable crawling obsolete submarines. Just up in the air with Mr Drummey and to all intents and purposes you were on your own magic carpet. 'Do you often –'

But now Mr Gipson got going in earnest. 'Take that drab picture,' he said; 'the one with the two women and the two kids fooling in a rockery.'

'That's a Leonardo,' said Mr Neff quickly.

'No doubt it is. I don't say it's not high-class. But I do say it's drab.'

Jean twisted round. The Virgin and Child with Saint Anne and the infant St John the Baptist (for it was these that Mr Gipson had described) were indeed posed before a vast grotto. There could, Jean supposed, be few more precious objects in the world than this unknown conflation of the Virgin of the Rocks and the Royal Academy cartoon. But the charcoal on brown paper, sparely heightened with white, was no doubt on the drab side.

'Nice enough for a corner of your billiard-room,' said Mr Gipson.

Mr Neff flushed and for a moment looked Renaissance enough – for the temper of some orgulous despot glinted in his eye. 'Nice enough, hey?' he said. 'If you'd care to know, that cartoon is the one mentioned by Lomazzo as having been in the possession of a guy called Aurelio Luini. And now it's mine. I bought it fair and square from a bankrupt Graf in Hungary a bit before the war.'

'I don't care whether you bought it from a giraffe or not.' And Mr Gipson, as he produced this childish witticism, guffawed loudly. 'I don't care whether you bought it from a dromedary. It's drab.'

'Very well; it's drab.' And Mr Neff turned away to another of his guests. 'About what I was telling you,' he said.

'Time Factor again. I locked that option in my safe just sixteen minutes before the news broke.'

'And it's not only drab. It's odd.'

Had Mr Neff, it occurred to Meredith, exercised a little control over what he received in return for large cheques to his wine merchant, Mr Gipson might not have been so absolute. Or was he, perhaps, like a skilled *picador* enraging his bull?

'It may be by Leon Ardo or Tom Ardo or Dick Ardo,' pursued Mr Gipson. 'But it's odd, all the same. And I suppose you paid a tidy sum for it?'

'I paid', said Mr Neff, breathing heavily, 'a lot more than you could ever put your hand in your pocket for, Jeff Gipson.'

'I don't say you didn't. I've known folk interested in cattle would give any amount of money for a two-headed calf. And that's just what that picture is.'

'Jeff Gipson –'

'Don't you get mad. Just look and you'll see it's that. It's not two women at all. It's one woman with two necks and two heads.'

This was an acute observation on Mr Gipson's part, and it set his host momentarily at a stand. But Mr Neff now looked so exceedingly angry that Jean though she would attempt a little pacification. 'But that', she said, 'is because Leonardo when he was a child didn't know whether he had one mother or two. That's why the Virgin and St Anne are sort of fused together. Also when he was an infant he had an adventure with a bird, and so he keeps on putting the silhouettes of birds into his pictures without ever being aware of it.'

But this scientific information, with which Dr Higbed himself could not have been more ready, was not well received by Mr Neff. 'Mothers?' he said. 'Stuff and nonsense! When those great painters are at their easels they aren't thinking of Mother, same as we might be with the second Sunday in May coming along. Not even with the underside of their minds, they aren't.' And Mr Neff pointed a confident finger at the cartoon. 'It's the mass', he continued, 'and the planes and the edges. And getting the draperies monumental and to look like some great mystery. A mystery that kind of draws you right into itself.' Mr Neff checked himself abruptly. 'And so much for your two-headed calf, Jeff Gipson.'

'Well, well,' said Mr Gipson. 'If you don't know a whole heap! And all I say is, bring out a coloured one and brighten the place up. Looks like you might be a mortician with all that dingy stuff around.'

'What d'you mean by dingy stuff, you ignorant cuss?' And Mr Neff gestured largely round his dining-room. 'What Berenson say – hey? What Borenius and Fry say – and Bredius and Brinkmann and Venturi?'

'Never met 'em,' said Mr Gipson. 'And no more did you.'

'And what you mean bring out a coloured one?' Mr Neff had risen to his feet in his wrath. 'What you mean by it, you Jeff Gipson?'

'Kidding everybody!' said Mr Gipson witheringly. 'Kidding folk you collect art big! Kind of hinting and having your stooges whispering. Bring out a coloured one from the pictures you haven't got. That's what I mean.'

'Who says I don't –' Mr Neff checked himself just in time. 'Hell!' he mumbled. 'What is all this, anyway? I don't go in for pictures any. Know what I like. A few quiet things you see about, like that Leonardo. Don't attend to them much. Flosdorf picks them up for me when he has nothing better to do and hangs them about the place.'

Far down the table Meredith could see that the assistant thus invoked was mopping his brow with a silk handkerchief. And certainly to have his employer's illicit hoard thus nearly betrayed in anger to the wily Gipson and a heterogeneous collection of guests must be harassing enough. It was something which might, indeed, be described as sitting on a volcano. But where – and once more Meredith approached the heart of the mystery – where, in this simple scheme of things, did Higbed come in?

7

THE question was soon to have its sufficiently dramatic
answer, and Meredith was to realize that long ago he
had been given more pointers to it than one. Indeed, if he
and Jean had set out looking, not for adventures, but for
clues, they could quickly – he was to realise – have assembled the elements of an orthodox mystery around
themselves. But his mind had not been working this way,
and when the revelation actually came he was a good
deal slower than Jean to tumble to it. Perhaps this was
because he had been constrained to drink rather more of
Mr Neff's deplorably untrustworthy wines. Or perhaps
it was because he was finally misled by what appeared to
be the implication in certain observations of Flosdorf's.

In stoutly asserting that his artistic possessions ran to
no more than a few Leonardo and Raphael cartoons, some
hundreds of Rembrandt etchings, a like number of
drawings by Holbein and Dürer, together with such other
exhibits of a quiet, drab, or monochrome nature as Flosdorf had hung about the Cottage, it was evident that Mr
Neff had been obliged to make a herculean effort of self-
denial. To dissemble for the purposes of some business
manoeuvre his power or holdings in a dozen companies;
to deny that the dove or the conveyor belts or the sharks
and octopodes were children of his own brain: these
would have been acts of abnegation as nothing in the
comparison. For although Mr Neff might pretend still to
a consuming satisfaction in the contemplation of options
locked in a safe or in the lightning execution of plans
prompted by long-distance calls to Johannesburg, his
heart was in truth in none of these things. Wholly and
utterly he was a collector and a lover of the old and
beautiful things he secretly owned. To deny the existence
of these must have been a severe trial to one who had long
and largely indulged himself in habits of ostentation.

The guests had been disposed in the billiard-room – the

same to a smoky corner of which Mr Gipson would have relegated the Leonardo – and it soon became evident that their host was seeking an opportunity to slip away with the Pantellis. Perhaps he wanted to conclude the deal on the Giorgiones before packing his bag for London or the Pacific Coast next morning. Or perhaps, having so heroically denied his riches to the world at large, he was the more anxious to display them to persons who could be trusted in their own interests not to give away the secret.

But it became evident too that the prospect of this confidence threw Flosdorf more and more into a nervous flurry. He talked absently to those least important of Mr Neff's guests whom it was his duty to entertain, and was plainly getting so hot under the collar that it was almost possible to fancy that one heard the hiss and bubble of the threatening volcano across the length of the room. Once or twice the agitated man made dives at Meredith, and eventually he ran him down behind the insecure shelter of a whisky decanter. Flosdorf raised this in air, as if knowing that the perturbation written upon his features had best be concealed from the company at large.

'Keep your mouth shut,' Flosdorf said.

'I beg your pardon?' Meredith was so startled at having this abrupt injunction flung at him twice in an evening that for a moment he thought he must have misheard.

'He's taking you and your wife in to see all that stuff. I'd stop him if I could' – this Flosdorf displeasingly snarled – 'but I can't. Don't say a word. Remember the old fool is the goose who lays the golden eggs.'

'Of course,' said Meredith. 'I'm not likely to forget it when I'm busy selling him three fake Giorgiones, am I? You back me up over them and my wife and I will be as discreet as you could wish.'

Flosdorf nodded and passed a glass – much as if this frank avowal of villainy had greatly raised Meredith in his estimation. 'That's right,' he said. 'Live and let live. After all, the world would be a poor place if we weren't prepared to lend each other a helping hand. And it's eating candy, after all. Just don't talk.' He hesitated. 'You see, a good deal of the stuff in there is a bit different from what he thinks. Naturally so.'

'Oh, quite naturally so.' Meredith considered. 'But about all those experts and connoisseurs who have been about the place: has he never taken any of them through?'

Flosdorf looked horrified. 'You're crazy!' he said. 'Once let him think it's safe to take anybody through that we haven't got in our pocket and we're done for.'

'You mean they would give away the fact that it's all stolen?'

'Naturally they would. Seems all those high-ups in art – even most of the dealers when you get high enough – is plumb honest. But even suppose an expert who didn't much care where the pictures and stuff come from. Soon as he opened his mouth in there –'

'Hey, you – Flosdorf!' This was Mr Neff calling. 'Get that option out of the safe and show it to Mr Gipson. I've got to take Mr and Mrs Pantelli round the place soon as I've been through to Barcelona.' And as Flosdorf went off obediently in one direction his employer disappeared in another.

Meredith took advantage of this respite to seek out Jean. 'Do you know', he said, 'that I think I've made it out?'

Jean looked at him doubtfully. 'Haven't you said that before?'

'Perhaps I have. But this is very much simpler. I have just been speaking to Flosdorf, who is thoroughly apprehensive about what is going to happen when we are taken in to see the pictures. He says that if we don't keep our mouths shut we shall kill the goose that lays the golden eggs.' And Meredith repeated his recent conversation. 'Now, what do you think of that?'

'But it's you who are thinking. You've made it out.'

Meredith hesitated. 'Well, I suppose it to be like this. One very special circumstance governs such a clandestine collection as Neff's. No person really well informed on artistic matters can be let in on it. Eminent connoisseurs come and look at the honestly acquired cartoons and things displayed around the house, but, of course, they can't be let into the secret of the hoard. Still, the fact that they accept and are impressed by what is visible must have the effect of reassuring Neff on the importance and worth of all that is *not* visible – the dishonestly acquired masterpieces he has hidden away. But, my dear Jean' – and Meredith lowered his voice – '*are* they masterpieces, after all? Surely that is the question! Neff, quite evidently, has a real flair for art: an enjoyment of it and a sort of intuitive understanding of its governing principles. But, of course, he is no sort of connoisseur – and yet the vanity he has acquired by finding himself on equal terms with connoisseurs so far as simple appreciation goes will no doubt have given him a quite ill-grounded conceit of himself as judge of the authenticity of a picture. Yet, while he has been shelling out his money, Flosdorf and the rest have been gulling him all the time. That's the explanation. The pictures will prove not to be authentic Old Masters at all, but simply competent copies, such as you see nice old women sitting and painting in all the galleries of Europe. Copying Day at the National Gallery. Earnest girls in short hair and painty overalls laboriously reproducing Hobbema's Avenue. They are the true purveyors of Neff's monumental collection.'

Jean shook her head. 'I don't see it at all. For surely it's quite certain that the pictures Don Perez and his Society deal in are genuine enough. And they sell to Neff.'

'Do they?' And Meredith looked positively cunning. 'Isn't it likely that they keep their genuine wares for buyers better informed? Here is Neff as pleased as Punch with his flair for art; ready to buy what's brought along as recklessly as he buys his wine. Only there's this difference: the wine will sooner or later be presented to the palates of all and sundry, and eventually judged according to its actual worth. Whereas the paintings disappear for good and all, and only Neff himself and the unscrupulous Flosdorf ever commune with them.'

Jean considered. 'Isn't Neff unscrupulous too?'

'Well, yes – of course he must be. Only I seem to have taken rather a liking to him. I was puzzled by his eye. There was something familiar in it. And of course the explanation was that it is, in a way, quite a scholar's eye. He has had all those solitary times with the things he has collected – great monuments and milestones of human culture. For they remain that even in copies by nice old women or crop-haired girls.'

'No doubt,' said Jean. She was standing near the door of the billiard-room and appeared to be giving some of her attention to noises coming from outside.

'And I am sure that the frequentation of great art must breed a certain dispassionateness. Don't you think?'

'In Neff? Well, as a matter of fact I don't.' And Jean threw open the door.

Mr Neff was carrying on his telephone conversation with Barcelona not ten yards away. The two girls with writing pads were beside him as before, and the man who coped with the machine and its flex stood by. But this time, evidently, things were not going so well. Barcelona, unlike Johannesburg, was far from standing well in Mr Neff's regard. In fact, Mr Neff was bellowing into the machine as if it were necessary to outroar all the to-and-fro conflicting elements of the Atlantic Ocean. His features were contorted with fury; his complexion was a blackish blue; he danced with rage as he spoke. The effect was faintly comical and markedly improbable, like a conventionally exaggerated representation of anger in a strip cartoon. And even as they looked, Mr Neff gave a final howl of rage, pitched the telephone violently from him so that it shivered into fragments, snatched the writing pads of the girls and tossed them in their faces, gave a vicious but ineffective swipe at the male attendant, leapt upon a conveyor belt, and hurtled away. And all this (Meredith was bound to reflect) over merely commercial matters from which the heart of the man had long been substantially weaned. Whatever had gone wrong in Barcelona was not matter which really touched the core of Mr Neff's vanity.

And Meredith looked seriously at Jean. 'Well,' he said, 'it is possible that dispassionateness is somewhat too definite a term. But I still have a sneaking fondness for the ruffian. And I still think it probable that I've made it out.'

'I don't accept your new theory any more than your old one – the iconolagnia and Pygmalionism.' Jean shook her head decidedly. 'Indeed, it's distinctly weaker. It's weaker because it altogether fails to account for Higbed. If the expected trouble is just Neff's finding out that a lot of the pictures are copies and fakes, whatever is going to be the good of poor old Higgy? Can you see him coping with the sort of outburst we've just watched?'

'I don't think I can. Still, that must be the idea, all the same. They're afraid that Neff will go absolutely mad with rage; that he will rush out and give the show away –'

'Give what show away?'

Meredith frowned. 'Why, all this of buying stolen pictures, of course.'

'But surely if the pictures are no more than copies after all, there can be no dishonesty in Neff's owning them, and consequently no show to give away.'

'My dear Jean, this is merely another of your quibbles, as you very well know. Doubtless there is a mingling of stolen pictures and mere replicas. And, as I say, Higbed is being retained as one skilled in the treatment of mental disturbance to cope with whatever insane burst of fury attends Neff's discovery that he has been duped.'

'I tell you it just won't do. And you haven't really very perfectly defined what you called the one special circumstance governing Neff's clandestine collection. It isn't that no really well-informed critic is ever let in on it. It's that *nobody* is.'

'Nobody?' Meredith looked perplexed.

'Nobody but Neff himself, and Flosdorf, and perhaps one or two people in with Flosdorf. We are the catastrophic exceptions there, which is why Flosdorf is so worked up tonight. Can we keep our mouths shut – even if we do know that Neff lays the golden eggs? Flosdorf doubts it. And why? Because we are going to be really surprised.'

Meredith considered this thoughtfully. 'Well,' he said, 'it must be admitted that the affair has already brought us more surprises than one. It may well be that another is in store. But of just what sort of surprise are you thinking?'

'A big one – really a big one this time. We are going to be led by Neff, regularly swelling with pride, to view his collection. And the collection won't be there.'

'Won't be there!' Meredith stared. 'You mean it will have been stolen?'

'Not a bit of it. I mean it never has been there. I'm not sure, of course, that there won't be frames. But I'm quite sure that there will be no pictures ... You remember the story of the King and the Invisible Clothes?'

'My dear Jean, I cannot conceive how Hans Andersen –'

'He was persuaded that he had been made the most gorgeous clothes, and that to himself alone were they invisible. And so he was tricked into parading before his subjects in his shirt – something like that. Well, with Neff and his pictures it's rather the same. The pictures aren't there, but Neff is convinced that they are. He goes in and gloats over them and gets all sorts of lovely and refined aesthetic sensations. But it's from bare walls or empty frames.'

'I see.' Meredith was reduced to simple sarcasm. 'And have you yet arrived at any notion as to how this odd state of affairs is brought about?'

'Dear me, yes! Are you at all familiar, I wonder, with the more recent developments of medical hypnotism?'

'Really, if you must make up a tale of a cock and a bull –'

'I assure you they are some of them extremely odd. Take the training of air crews. When that had to be speeded up it was found that with a certain degree of hypnotic control and a set of earphones a man could be very successfully taught in his sleep.'

'I don't believe it.'

'It's absolutely true. The earphones whispered away at him all night; the physiological and psychological effects of sleep were not in the least impaired; and the next morning he had eight hours' hard learning securely in his head. With regular hypnosis you can do almost anything. And, what's more, hypnotic states can now be super-induced upon sleep. Sleep comes first, then the hypnosis, and so the subject may know nothing about it.'

'And you seriously suggest that Neff –'

'And, of course, you know how stage hypnotists can make people do and actually believe the most absurd-seeming things. But there's always one condition. The thing to be done, however absurd it may seem, must always satisfy some unconscious wish of the person hypno-tised. If somewhere I own a powerful unconscious death-wish, then I can be hypnotized into going and lying down at the bottom of a tank of water –'

'I doubt it. I think you would find that mere specific gravity would keep you bobbing up again.'

'And who's quibbling now? The point is that Neff quite powerfully wants to have lovely feelings among pictures, adventures of the soul amid masterpieces. Which definitely means that he could be hypnotized into seeing pictures on a bare wall, just as a hungry man can be hypnotized into eating a non-existent meal.'

'And you suggest that quite regularly –'

'Just that. The masterpieces were real, and they were worth millions. But nobody except Neff himself and Flos-dorf was ever to see them. Secure a hypnotist, therefore, capable of getting at Neff in his sleep, and you can safely carry the masterpieces off one by one and sell them all over again to other Neffs elsewhere.'

'I see. And then you have only to secure another hypnotist and you can repeat the process all over again.'

'I never thought of that.' Jean appeared seriously im-pressed. 'But now you see the point of Higbed. After all, this invaluable hypnotist might just die in the night at any time. Whereupon the hypnotic suggestion would slowly fade; Neff would see his imaginary pictures more and more faintly; and at last he would just be looking at the wallpaper. Rather the situation of Alice and the Cheshire Cat.'

'I never', said Meredith, 'judged *Alice in Wonderland* a very probable story.'

Jean ignored this. 'And so there had to be a second string. No doubt Higbed has made some reputation for himself in the hypnotic line. It's right up the street of psychiatrists again, since so much narcoanalysis has come in.'

'I must say that you are extraordinarily glib. But of all the sheerly cobweb theories or hypotheses ever put forward to account for a group of known facts I judge that yours must be –'

'Now, then, folks, come along.'

It was Mr Neff who spoke. Making the round of the Cottage on his conveyor belts must have rapidly restored his equanimity – for now here he was come up behind them in the benignest manner.

'Come along, Mr and Mrs Patnelli,' said Mr Neff – and glanced rapidly across the billiard-room to see that the unspeakable Gipson was securely engaged. 'We'll go in to the coloured ones right now.'

8

AND the coloured ones were there. Mr Neff threw open a door, flicked a switch, and Jean's hypothesis of the King and the Invisible Clothes was instantly dissolved into the air from which it had been formed. Interminably down either wall of a gallery resplendent with marble and gold hung masterpiece upon masterpiece of European art. For Mr Neff had been a purchaser on an imperial scale, and of everything to which Don Perez had murdered and swindled his way the cream had clearly flowed into this one stupendous room. The International Society for the Diffusion of Cultural Objects had been altogether mis-named, since it had here achieved such a concentration as had never, perhaps, been known outside Europe before.

Mr Neff, then, was far from communing with wallpaper or empty frames – unless, of course, his visitors had now been unwittingly hypnotized too. But if Jean was astray in her reckoning so equally was Meredith, since it was abundantly obvious that neither nice old ladies nor crop-haired girls displayed their handiwork here. Nearly all these pictures Meredith knew – and some of them so well that every crack and every missing flake of pigment was familiar to him. Whatever Mr Neff had spent, he had received value for his money. Here his surroundings, like those of a somewhat kindred spirit, the First Grand Thief of Milton's poem, far outshone the wealth of Ormus and of Ind.

And Mr Neff knew it. A strange mingling of pride and humility irradiated the man as he shut the door behind him and turned to his guests. 'I guess we'll take a quick turn round first,' he said. 'Just give you an idea of what you'd most like to see.' He paused. 'If I could just bring that Jeff Gipson in here!' he breathed. And then he chuckled. 'Flosdorf is dead scared that sometime that guy will get me mad.'

'I'm sure you never get mad,' said Jean. 'One turns so dispassionate once one realizes that art is beautiful –'

'And would you say, Mr Neff' – Meredith interrupted hastily – 'that Flosdorf is dead scared about anything else?'

Mr Neff stared. 'Now, that's a strange question. For Flosdorf has sure been kind of scared for a long time about I can't figure what. And keeping some sort of hanky-panky in the background, too. Scurrying people away. Sometimes I've thought it was just he couldn't keep girls out of the house, although he has a place called the Belvi-dere, not half a mile away, he can do what he likes. And when he's scared about I can't figure what I think it's maybe just his nerves bad because of too much girl. But sometimes I think there's something back of that. Now,

this afternoon when I was starting to go up for a swim –'
Mr Neff checked himself. 'But come along, Mr and Mrs
Pantelli. Waste of time trying to figure out Flosdorf when
I can show you Masaccio, Spinelli, Uccello –' Again Mr
Neff stopped short. 'Masaccio!' he exclaimed. 'Now, if
that isn't darned queer. It's just come back to me how
Flosdorf started being scared. It was one day when we
were talking about the little Masaccio over there by the
Mantegna ... *hey?*'

For Jean had sharply exclaimed. But now she shook her
head. 'I'd just noticed one that is particularly beautiful,
Mr Neff. But you were saying that Flosdorf –?'

'Plumb scared as we stood there. Just as if he'd gotten
a sudden shock. Paid less for it than he said, maybe, and
thought I'd cottoned on to it.'

'That would be it.' Jean was looking at Mr Neff with
sudden fascinated interest. 'That would be it, Mr Neff.
But let's go round, like you said.'

They went round – effortlessly, since a conveyor belt
circumlocambulated the gallery. It was a very superior
conveyor belt, having every appearance of a costly
parquetry. And its speed could be regulated from a little
dial carried in the hand, somewhat after the fashion of the
instrument by which lazy people control the radio from
an armchair. Everybody knows that there is something
peculiarly fatiguing in tramping about a picture gallery.
Mr Neff's system, so excellent an innovation about Dove
Cottage in general, was here particularly well-conceived.
Physical effort being obviated, the soul was the more free
for its adventures amid masterpieces.

And an odd adventure among masterpieces was about
to transact itself. But Mr Neff and Meredith, at least,
were unaware of this. They went round the gallery together, conversing in a really friendly way. It was true
that the pictures compacted here ought rightly to have
been scattered over Europe from Paris to Odessa and
from Oslo to Naples. But Meredith (recalling how soldiers
had slept unwittingly on the Primavera of Botticelli) was

so pleased to see them all safe and sound that he could not at the moment find it in his heart to hold Mr Neff in deep approbrium. Besides, had not Mr Neff a scholarly eye? Already Meredith had forgotten the little matter of his host's displeasure with Barcelona.

And with a rather touching mixture of naïveté and conscientious reading Mr Neff was explaining the mysteries of the coloured ones. 'It's the grey tones,' he said solemnly. standing before a melancholic Hapsburg by Velasquez; 'it's all in the grey tones, Mr and Mrs Pantelli.'

Meredith nodded – rather absently. He had just remembered that this particular Velasquez he had last seen when dining with its owner, a charming French *viticulteur* of classical tastes. 'Of course,' he said, '– the grey tones. Have you had this one long?'

But Mr Neff had pressed the button and they glided forward. 'And here, Mr and Mrs Pantelli, is my best Titian – though I have a better coming from London.' Mr Neff chuckled gleefully – and was immediately solemn once more. 'This is early, of course. You can see Carpaccio in it, I dare say. And it has the kind of softness of Palma Vecchio, hasn't it? Not that it could be anything but Titian, really. Look at the luminosity – and the saturation.' And Mr Neff, having delivered himself of this culture-patter from whatever manuals he was in the habit of studying, fell silent. He looked aside now at one picture and now at another – he had instinctively the connoisseur's distaste of gazing long at a single canvas – and then back at the Titian. 'It's the eye,' he said – abruptly and as if the thought had just struck him. 'Titian pleases *the eye*. And that isn't just what you would say of Mantegna there, or of Piero della Francesca.'

'No,' said Meredith, 'I suppose it's not.' Obscurely puzzled, he glanced at Mr Neff. There could be no doubt that Mr Neff had his natural-born sensibility about him still, and that not even reading popular treatises on the art of painting could blunt it. And yet about Mr Neff amid all this magnificence there was something different from what there had been before. It was as if here he

277

was always faintly puzzled without at all knowing why.

And even as this thought occurred to Meredith Mr Neff said something relevant to it. 'You know,' he began, 'one of the strangest things about art is that so often there's something that isn't quite right about it. I've though a lot about that. In the East, now – and I've been told this by more than one man who collects Eastern art big – the artists will always leave something imperfect. Maybe it's just a rug, and when you're going to buy it you think you see a flaw and try to bring down the price. Well, you're only giving yourself away. Because the flaw is there kind of deliberate. It's something to do with their religion.'

'*On earth the broken arc,*' said Meredith, '*in heaven the perfect round.* And I dare say some Eastern artists may believe perfection to be impious. But in the West the artist, I should say, simply regrets his inability to achieve perfection. Somewhere craft must fail him always – the state of affairs of which the broken pair of compasses is the symbol. *Deest quod duceret orbem.*'

Mr Neff received this speech with a good deal of attention. 'Well,' he said, 'there may be something in that. But still I can't figure it out. For instance, take the Masaccio –'

'Mr Neff' – it was Jean who interrupted – 'have you always had just the cartoons and things showing in the house?'

'More or less that, Mrs Pantelli – in order to be quiet, as I said, and no questions asked. But lately Flosdorf tightened up and made it quite a rule.'

'Perhaps since you had your talk in front of the Masaccio?'

'Why, yes,' said Mr Neff, 'it would be just about then, sure enough.'

Masaccio, thought Meredith, means something like Hulking Tom. Or Lubberly Tom ... he became aware that they were all three standing before Lubberly Tom's little panel of the Virgin and Child enthroned, and that Mr Neff was talking still.

'In a manner of speaking,' said Mr Neff, 'you go right into a picture like that and move about in it.' He turned with sudden challenge to Meredith. 'Isn't that so?'

'Oh, undoubtedly.'

'It's as if you were exploring it with all your muscles ever so slightly moving, so that there's a sort of dance going on way inside yourself that's like all the movements in the picture. Isn't that so?' And again Mr Neff looked challengingly at his guest.

Meredith was highly pleased. It was really remarkable, he thought, that this untutored person should so accurately describe what aestheticians call the theory of empathy. 'Oh, undoubtedly,' he repeated. 'Precisely so.'

'And then – quite suddenly – it's not like that any more. The dance kind of loses itself, and you feel like coming down stairs in the dark and taking a step that isn't there. That right?' And yet again Mr Neff looked at Meredith ... Was there some strange glint of apprehensiveness in his eye?

'Dear me, no. I should judge that to be a most unusual experience.'

'But it is like that!' Emphasis and something like the distant approaches of anger were in Mr Neff's voice. 'Art is beautiful – but nearly always there's something that isn't quite right about it. A picture like this' – and he gestured at the Masaccio – 'is like some fine piece of music with suddenly the player striking a false note. Don't I get art the way Flosdorf can't – and the way all those great experts come to see the cartoons and drawings do? So don't I know? I guess it's just that art is like most other things in life – always a fly in the ointment somewhere.'

'But not in the Leonardo, or the Dürers, or the Rembrandt etchings.' Jean spoke quietly, her eye fixed on the Masaccio panel. 'There's no fly in them. And that's why it's those that you keep about the house. They never let you down. They haven't got a missing step in the dark.'

'I don't know what you mean!' The vehemence of Mr Neff's protestation was matched by a growing panic in his glance. 'Haven't I found I understand art same as a kitten understands milk? And so if I see –'

'Really,' interrupted Meredith, 'I am altogether per-

279

plexed – and especially in point of what you say about the Masaccio here. For it appears to me to be a singularly faultless and harmonious composition. Particularly in the colour. Consider how the whole is toned to that lovely olive green in the draperies of the angel musician on the left.'

'Olive green?' said Mr Neff. 'Why, those draperies are a clear pale yellow.'

It was disconcerting, Meredith thought, that Mr Neff should prove to be colour-blind. Curious that one who so keenly appreciated the linear and spatial qualities of the plastic arts, who was laboriously learned, too, on grey tones and saturation and luminosity, should in fact –

Here Meredith caught Mr Neff's eye and abruptly ceased to speculate. Instead, a first glimmering consciousness of what this odd revelation meant to the man himself came to him. Mr Neff was standing quite still and beads of sweat were trickling down his forehead. His jaw moved but no words came. Very stiffly, and agonizingly slowly – rather as if some system of creaking pulleys were in operation – he turned his head and looked at the Masaccio 'Did you say green?' he asked.

'An olive green.' It was Jean who answered. 'You see it as pale yellow because – well, because you see some colours differently from other people.'

'Differently from what they really are?'

'That', interjected Meredith rather wildly, 'is a question with a good deal of metaphysical interest. Colour being a secondary quality, and therefore coming into being only in the eye of the beholder –'

'*Yes!*' said Jean. 'Quite definitely *Yes*. Normal people see those robes as green. Masaccio himself did. And the whole colour harmony of the painting turns on the particular greenness of that green. It is because you see a yellow that you think of that false note in music, or of the missing step in the dark.'

'So I can't ever be quite right about the coloured ones?'

'No – I don't think you can.' With an obscure sense of the need for pushing the affair to its crisis, Jean had decided on this frank exposition of the case. 'Not as far as the colour relations are concerned. And, of course, the planes and masses are in some way falsified for you too. Different passages of a painting than those which the artist designed will tend to withdraw or protrude. And colour-disposition is also, of course, a subtle balancing instrument. I dare say you feel one side of this Masaccio to be rather heavier than the other. But it isn't. And again –'

Mr Neff gave a shrill scream of rage; crouched; sprang. Meredith stepped hastily in front of Jean. But it was not she upon whom the disqualified connoisseur leapt; it was the Masaccio. He clawed it from the wall and for a moment held it before him – his complexion livid, his face twisted in fury. Then he hurled it to the floor. And just as the telephone had done, the Masaccio shivered into fragments.

Again Mr Neff inarticulately screamed. There was a slaver at his lips. His eye was bloodshot and gleaming. From a pedestal beside him he seized and swung a heavy bronze statuette. His scream deepened to a purposive roar of rage and thence crystallised into a single word. 'Yellow!' yelled Mr Neff, 'yellow!' His glance roved the gallery and fixed itself upon a picture which Meredith had not yet observed: a vast composition of elongated and apocalyptic figures like so many yellow and green and rose-coloured flames. It was an El Greco and one of the great paintings of the world. Mr Neff advanced upon it, his statuette flailing the air.

9

'STOP!'

Flosdorf was not by nature an authoritative person. But as he burst into the gallery at this moment desperation lent him power. 'Quit that!' he shouted at his demented employer. 'Quit it, I say! Don't you know that picture's worth close on one million dollars?'

And momentarily Mr Neff paused – as he had long been conditioned to doing when a really tidy sum of money was mentioned. Flosdorf seized his chance. 'Listen,' he said urgently. 'It's not as bad as you think by a long way. I can fix it. Only give me that darn statuette.'

'Fix it?' Mr Neff's reply was a snarl – but his hand was stayed. 'D'you realize, you damned Flosdorf, that you and your son-of-a-bitch Society sold me more than five hundred pictures I can't ever be right about – no, not even about the planes and the masses?'

'But I tell you I can fix it.' And Flosdorf turned to the door. 'Hey, you,' he yelled, 'come right in. Come right in and meet the patient.'

It was Higbed. Professional decorum and an abounding underlying vitality were alike indicated in his stride; his expression was that of one prepared to shed upon the *Kama-Sutra* and the *Anangaraga* – even upon the *Perfumed Garden* itself – the clear dry light of an impersonal science. He paused before a vast Rubens Rape of the Sabines – almost as if he supposed that these must be the ladies by whom his expository services were required – and then glanced in swift perplexity and distrust about the gallery. 'What's this?' he asked. 'I don't –'

But Flosdorf had taken him unceremoniously by the buttonhole and was leading him forward. 'Here's the guy will fix you up,' he said encouragingly to his employer. 'Properjohn and I had him shipped from England specially – and a whole library with him, too. No one with just his line in the States. Psychiatrist – deals with you when you're imagining things. And your kind of trouble in particular. Psychogenic visual disturbance – that right?' And Flosdorf turned to Higbed. 'Speak up, you.'

'I have certainly made some study of visual hallucinations in relation to the hysterias.'

'There!' Flosdorf was triumphant. 'And when I saw you had this trouble that time we looked at the Masaccio

I figured it you might get real mad as soon as you found out. So Properjohn and I read it up. Seems if you smoke too much you may come to see everything blue, and then the blue disappears and you just don't see any colours at all. Seems if you were a kid and were frightened by some dame dressed all in purple –'

'This is Mr Neff,' said Jean to the bewildered Higbed. 'He's colour-blind, and never knew, and now he's mad about it. And why they kidnapped you was to work a cure before he got madder and fired this Flosdorf and the rest. So get to work.'

'Colour-blind? Cure?' Higbed broke away from Flosdorf, seized Mr Neff by the arm and led him up to a Pinturicchio Madonna in Glory. He pointed at the Madonna's robe, in which there was a large area of sombre red. 'Now then, what colour's that?'

'Red,' said Mr Neff.

'And this?' Higbed pointed to a small patch of the same hue on the cap of a donor.

Mr Neff hesitated. 'Kind of dark yellow,' he said uncertainly.

'And what about this?' Higbed was pointing at the dull green of the donor's hose.

'Yellow. It's a pale yellow. Almost the same as the little yellow flowers in the foreground.' And Mr Neff, momentarily subdued and momentarily hopeful, looked almost timidly at his questioner.

'Nothing of the sort. It's green.' Higbed, it was evident, felt extremely disgruntled at the altogether uninteresting nature of the professional task to which he had been so unscrupulously dragged across the ocean. 'And there's no question of any psychogenesis. Your trouble is congenital and incurable. You'll go to your grave with it – and from your general condition I should say that will be in four or five years' time.'

'Congenital!' Flosdorf's voice rose to a scream almost like Mr Neff's. 'Didn't you write a book saying –'

'You don't know what you're talking about. Disordered colour-sensation is sometimes functional and likely to

283

yield to psychotherapy. But this is organic – some obscure condition of the nerve-endings. In fact, the man's a Dalton – a modified Dalton of the kind who may never know until they really get talking about colour – but a Dalton all the same.' And Higbed turned to Mr Neff. 'You're a Dalton,' he repeated rudely; 'just an ordinary modified Dalton.'

To Mr Neff, at once bemused and furious, this obscured insult was the last straw. 'You, Flosdorf,' he yelled, 'how dare you bring a man here calls me a Dalton!' And raising the bronze statuette he hurled it with all his force at his assistant's head. 'First you bring this girl says I can't ever know art not even the planes and masses, and then you bring this man says in four years I'll be dead.' Flosdorf ducked; the bronze crashed against a door; a second later the door opened and Mr Gipson, followed by Mr Neff's other friends and clients, entered the gallery.

'Hey!' said Mr Gipson. 'What's this?'

Mr Neff looked at him balefully. His breath was coming in deep painful gasps. 'Get out of this, Jeff Gipson!' he panted. 'Get to hell out of here.'

'Say! It's his pictures.' And Mr Gipson turned in delighted surprise to the followers. 'Now, just come right in and listen to the connoisseur talk about the stuff he got from the giraffes and dromedaries. Any more Ardos, Neff?' His eye fell on Higbed. 'And is this guy Berenson, or is he just Venturi?'

'I am Higbed.' The harassed psychologist considered this information so important that he delivered it at a sort of bellow, thereby momentarily drowning a surprising yowling and choking noise which was now issuing from Mr Neff. 'I am Higbed, and this screaming imbecile is I don't know whom. But he seems to have surrounded himself with a lot of pictures which are little more good to him than if he hadn't an eye in his head.' And as he made this malicious overstatement Higbed grinned nastily at Mr Neff, whom he plainly held accountable for his sundry tribulations and imprisonments.

'What's that?' Gipson's voice held a wondering delight. 'What's that you said?'

'The man can't see his own pictures right. He's colour-blind.'

'Great snakes!' Gipson gave a whoop of unholy joy. 'If that doesn't beat the band! Why, the poor cuss been and spent millions on them. Dotes on the things, too. It makes him feel all superior to reckon he knows art is beautiful. And all the time he couldn't tell a red-head from a brunette. Jeepers creepers, it's the cat's pyjamas!'

Mr Neff, thus grossly brought to bay, glared round him like a demented thing. And then manfully (so that, despite the shivered Masaccio, Meredith almost admired him) he lied. 'Pictures?' he said. 'Well, I never cared for them all that. A man like me must spend his money on something, and it's kind of natural to talk big about what you put a bit of cash in.' He waved a trembling hand round the gallery. 'But you can take the lot, if you care for them. For some time now, I've been figuring to collect a little old furniture instead.'

'Oho – so we can take the lot? I suppose that amount of money' – and Gipson too gave a wave around the gallery – 'don't mean anything to a man like you?'

'No, it doesn't. I'm through with the stuff', and suddenly Mr Neff's voice rose again to a betraying scream – 'I'm through with it, do you hear? And I don't care what becomes of it. I don't care, I say ... I don't care a damn!' Mr Neff spoke chokingly and with a mounting hate which made Meredith shiver ... For it came to him suddenly that it was hate directed, not against Neff's old rival Gipson, but against those rows and vistas of immortally beautiful things by which the wretched man conceived himself to have been betrayed ... 'Pitch 'em in the lake, if you like,' choked Mr Neff. 'Only take 'em out of my sight.'

'Your sight?' jeered Gipson remorselessly. 'Take 'em out of your screwy sight, eh? Well, as you're offering them round, we'll take one or two of the dirty ones – just as a memento of your old collecting days.' And Gipson, with a quick glance round the gallery, advanced upon the great Rubens canvas which had first caught the attention of Higbed. 'Come on, folks,' he said. 'Help yourselves. I'll take this bunch of dames.'

It was as Gipson's hands went out to the Rubens that sanity finally left Mr Neff. This second rape (as it were) of the Sabine women was too much for him. And when he acted it was with something like inspiration. Gipson, his friends and the fuming Higbed were all on the stationary conveyor belt. Mr Neff snatched up the little dial at the end of its flex and turned it. The conveyor belt moved forward. Mr Neff turned the dial again and the belt accelerated – with a rapidity so astounding that Higbed, the clients, and the unspeakable Gipson were in seconds a mere prone and supine mass, a congeries of waving legs and arms giving a momentary and nightmarish impression of some monstrous multi-limbed Hindoo god hurtling down the vista of Mr Neff's gallery like some out-of-the-way projectile on a garish pin-table. At the farther end was an open archway giving upon a downward flight of marble steps. And such was the impetus of their flight that the enemies of Mr Neff (including the still unfortunate Dr Higbed) went straight through and down like the rebel angels raining from the Empyrean. Their shouts of terror and howls of rage changed briefly to yells and screams of pain; then Mr Neff ran to the wall and pressed a button – whereupon a great fireproof door descended at the end of the gallery. Instead of the pandemonium of a dozen soft males bemoaning bruised bodies and broken limbs, there was only the stertorous and lunatic breathing of Otis K. Neff.

On all these disordered proceedings the dwarfs and grandees of Carreño and Velasquez, the peasants of van Ostade and the princes of Boltraffio, Botticelli centaurs and Duccio Madonnas, gallants by Watteau and wantons by Manet or Lautrec, Luini saints with their lurking and epicene Leonardo smiles, El Greco hermits nine feet high, impassively looked down. But not for long. Mr Neff had gabbled insanely but commandingly through a house-telephone; and now he was hurling himself with demoniac fury upon those silent witnesses of his sensuous frailty. Flosdorf had disappeared. So, Meredith with consternation discovered, had Jean. The conveyor belt had been reversed, and now the Rubens came down and was pitched upon it. Appalled, Meredith stepped forward to resist. But as he did so a small army of men-servants, scared but obedient, hurried into the gallery and began tearing the pictures from the walls and piling them on the belt. Mr Neff dashed frantically about, urging on the work, screaming for more speed in corridors and elevators, commanding that everything be hurried to some lower entrance giving on the lake. His hideous purpose was plain. Art might be beautiful, but it had let him down. And so he was going to drown it – or all of it he could lay his hands on – deeper than ever Prospero drowned his book.

'Stop!' shouted Meredith. 'He's mad, demented! The pictures are stolen; they are masterpieces which no one can ever replace!'

But these rational persuasions were in vain. Mr Neff, sustained by an uncanny access of nervous force, carried everything before him. 'Out with the lot!' he screamed. 'And those in the house too – plain as well as coloured! Don't forget the statues; don't forget that darn thing in the elevator; ring down to have the belts speeded up again; have the whole lot rowed out a good half-mile; anyone tries to keep anything on the quiet I'll skin him alive.' And Mr Neff charged at a Giovanni Bellini Doge as if he that instant recognized his deadliest enemy.

Helpless and aghast, Meredith watched the walls grow bare, the resplendent marble and gold gallery become an empty shell, the long procession of doomed paintings trundle ever more rapidly away down a vista of unending corridor. There was a strange wailing note in his ear, like defunctive music or the lament of the parting genius being with sighing sent: it issued from the mechanism of those conveyor belts which at the command of their inventor were sweeping more and more swiftly through the unending passages and colonnades of Dove Cottage.

Meredith made his last effort. He advanced towards Mr Neff with open and imploring hands. 'Stop!' he said. 'You understood those things – loved them. Your disability has been greatly exaggerated. When you are calm again you will realize the folly and horror of what you have caused to be done. I beg you to halt before it is too late.'

'And clear him out too.' Mr Neff pointed a quivering finger at Meredith. 'Pitch him in with the rest of the junk. And his wife if you can find her. Let them swim for it or drown.'

Meredith looked round for a weapon, but even as he did so he was seized by a couple of powerful men and pitched bodily upon the conveyor belt. It was travelling at a great pace; the backs and fronts of canvases and panels surrounded him; the corners of massive gilt frames gouged his ribs and thighs. He struggled and there was an ominous crack. He desisted, not knowing what damage he was doing to some priceless surface. It was true that both he and Mr Neff's late collection seemed alike doomed to a watery grave – nevertheless, he would not trample upon these things even in this moment of their common agony. So Meredith was hurtled down a corridor and into an elevator which dropped like a stone; thence he was ejected upon a turntable and trundled down a further cavernous corridor dimly lit – an incongruously human outcrop upon this monstrous funeral procession of pigment and bronze and marble, this glyptic and plastic twilight of the gods. And everywhere the attendants of Mr Neff, pervasively infected by the hysteria of their employer, like impatient mutes whose dinner awaits them, hurried the cortège forward.

The journey from level to level and end to end of Mr Neff's hypertrophied Cottage was dreamlike and endless, like a vast trans-Atlantic reflection of the troglodyte fantasies of Miss Dorcas Macleod; it wanted only the baying of Titian and Giotto to be like a fevered magnification of the hurtlings through Bubear's warehouse; it was altogether more perilous and confounding than Meredith's remotely kindred ride with the Flying Foxes over the crumbled battlements of Castle Moila ... Another turntable received him; he felt a jolt as the mechanism momentarily faltered; there was a small landslide among the objects of art surrounding him, and a marble object came down hard on his head.

After that mere confusion was about him. It was dark and there was a raw, cold air; he heard the plash of water and dimly knew that he was out upon some landing-stage where the immense abode of Mr Neff touched the answering immensities of the Laurentic Basin. There were low voices about him and a sound as of the straining of oars in heavily laden boats. He listened more intently and could hear too, from far out in the darkness, a steady intermittent splash which told of a succession of objects being dropped into the engulfing waters of the lake ... Meredith struggled to a sitting posture. It was quite dark except in one direction – and there he blinked at what was at first no more than a dazzle of light. But presently he saw that it was the vast front porch of Dove Cottage and that there stood Mr Neff himself, insanely dancing beneath the portico, his gold and ruby dove hovering above him while the solemn strains of William Blake's 'Jerusalem' floated down through the air.

'That's the lot; now get him in quick.' Meredith felt himself lifted and tumbled to the bottom of some small and rocking craft; he heard the creaking of oars and knew he was under way. The solemn strains of the massed choirs grew fainter. The *splash ... splash ... splash* of objects falling into water was louder in his ears. Interminably the rowing went on.

'... *green and pleasant land.*' The singing faded out. There was a gentle bump. Meredith was seized and heaved, not overboard, but up. Petrol vapour was in his nostrils.

'O.K.' said a familiar voice. 'Quit that splashing; we've got the old goat fooled. Jean, get out the barley-sugar. We'll be airborne in three minutes and I reckon there's nothing like glucose.'

10

THE flying-boat was up, and so was the moon. Mr Drummey looked at the water skimming a few feet beneath them. 'It's a load,' he said thoughtfully.

'Too much?' Sucking barley-sugar, Meredith peered out.

'Not if we don't meet head-winds ... and once get out of this blamed bay.' Drummey glanced at his instruments. 'Joc,' he called, 'we'll have to take the gap behind the house.'

'Sure.' Joe's voice was even more impassive than usual. Meredith and Jean sat still, aware of some early crisis in the final phase of their adventure.

They were higher now; to Meredith it seemed very high. But Drummey sat slightly frowning, and on the controls his hands were as sensitive as a musician's. He was a plain, snub-nosed man in the early thirties. But after all, thought Meredith, it is not only art that is beautiful – nor, among human kind, only the photogenic faces of Hollywood ... He caught his breath. Dove Cottage had appeared again in the moonlight. And it was hurtling at them like a projectile through the air.

'Right over the top,' explained Joe. 'Otherwise you're wrong for the line of the valley beyond.' He paused. 'Yards, this time.'

'Feet', said Drummey. Dove Cottage disappeared. 'Inches ... *hold tight!*'

The flying-boat jarred and violently rocked in air. A second later it was flying on its way on an even keel. Joe picked himself up. 'Hit it,' he said. 'Which is clean crazy. We ought to be dead.'

'Only that fool tank.' It was the young man called John who spoke. 'Plastic stuff, and we shivered it by catching the last centimetre of the top. Tricky materials always. Jiminy – have a look!'

Meredith and Jean scrambled to a point of vantage.

Vast and fantastic in the clear moonlight, Dove Cottage was veering away behind them. But it was no longer a swell home; it had become in an instant an inverted Niagara, a fountain a hundred times more gigantic than any ever conceived by Louis Quatorze or Kubla Khan. 'The swimming pool!' said Jean. 'And the sharks and octopode must be coming down like an unholy hail –'

'Or like frogs in China,' said Drummey without stirring 'But, of course, there it's tadpoles chiefly. Always a bit of exaggeration in travellers' tales.'

'But I don't see –' And Jean stared in perplexity at this sudden Eighth Wonder of the World, now rapidly diminishing behind them. '*All* that water –'

'Mains,' said Drummey. 'There's three mains goes up there with booster pumps behind them. Any of them can recharge the tank in five minutes with water at a temperature how you like. And if it's as you say, I reckon the valves must have gone when we got the tank. What's falling over the old man's palace is tens of thousands of gallons of cold water a minute. Dampening ... Well, we're clear. Nothing in front of us but the Mountains of Mayo and the Pennine Chain.'

Jean was still gazing backwards. Dove Cottage had shrunk to the dimensions of a toy, and presently the sides of the valley closed in and blotted it out – a tiny aqueous fantasy. 'Higgy's final indignity,' she murmured. 'The greatest shower-bath in history. And all because I took him on a petting-party to – what was it called? – Rest-and-be-thankful.'

For the first time Drummey looked up from his instruments. 'What's that?'

'He never got there. He was captured instead.'

'Sometimes,' said Joe sagely, 'it's pretty well the same thing.'

The Atlantic was beneath them; behind shone great Arcturus; to the south was Antares rising; the clear white light of Lyra hung at the zenith of the pale blue dome above; the nose of the flying-boat pointed into Cygnus, the cross of which was sweeping on its side through the eastern sky. Interminably John murmured of these stars, of Capella and Aldebaran; interminably he mumbled over the sums they set him; interminably the engines droned. But it was all a great improvement on Captain von Schwiebus's submarine. Meredith, rejoicing in this almost planetary progress, did not inquire whether headwinds were before them.

'But I'm still not at all sure', he said, 'just how it was managed. Coffee – and sandwiches? How very delightful.'

Drummey grinned. 'I jes' thought I'd keep in contact. You know, there must have been something about Miss Halliwell put it in my head.'

'Is that so?' said Meredith, slightly puzzled.

'We were to be out there, anyway, you know, tuning up for some fool trip to the Coast in the morning. But it couldn't have been done if Jea – if Miss Halliwell hadn't squared Flosdorf pretty quick.'

Jean set down her mug. 'It was eating candy,' she explained seriously. 'Flosdorf realized it just couldn't be kept quiet and that his best chance was to bolt. I dare say he's in Cincinnati or St Louis by now. But he realized too that the less of that stolen property was destroyed the less bleak it would be for him if he was finally nobbled. So he came round in under three minutes and fixed as many of the underlings as were necessary. But with all those belts going at the pace they did it was very much what you might call working against time.'

'And so we have virtually the whole collection on board?'

As Meredith spoke Joe squeezed himself through a hatch. 'There's just over five hundred paintings,' he said, 'and some of them about as big as a tennis-court. But that's nothing – nor all the etchings and things either. The real freight's the marbles and bronzes. Talk of blondes in your bomb-racks! We've got bevies of Venuses and the like cuddling themselves all over the ship.'

'It's a load,' said Drummey. 'But we'll make it...if this darn wind shifts.'

'I wonder' – Meredith was troubled – 'whether we are justified in taking this particularly venturesome course? After all, we need only –'

'We're going right across.' Drummey was again impassive. '*Britain delivers the goods* – remember that one? What you used to stamp on the crates when you sent on Lend-Lease pepper-pots and grand pianos to guileless neutrals. But it's *America delivers the goods* this time. John and Joe and I propose to hand you back your effects. Might make a little round trip of it: London, Amsterdam, Brussels, Paris.'

'I'm not sure', said Jean, 'that I wouldn't like to take Castle Moila and Carron Lodge in passing.'

'Likely enough', said Drummey, 'we'll be going that way.'

It was freezing, but the three young men were sweating as well as heavy eyed. The constellations had gone and with them the moon. Only just above the horizon northwards there was a faint white light, the faintest aurora, as if another moon was rising there. Meredith had learnt the meaning of the altimeter and the artificial horizon. The flying-boat was going down.

'Ought to have a crew of six', growled Joe. 'The old goat liked things on a tidy scale. But he liked economies too ... Going down? Sure we are.'

'In that case hadn't we better jettison some of those bronzes and marbles?'

'America delivers the goods.' Drummey's voice was resolute. 'But we're not going down willy-nilly – or not yet. It may be less dirty just skimming the big drink.'

'You really go as low as that?'

'Just so as to clear the smoke-stack of the *Queen Mary*. Eh, Joe?'

'Sure.'

'And the rollers. If the moon comes through you'll see them any time now. Rather flattened out when viewed from above. But not what you could call harmless-looking, all the same.'

'Wonderful guys, those on the ferry services,' said Joe

cheerfully. 'Nerve. And not just nerve. Nerve this week and nerve next. Chronic nerve, like some folks can run to chronic alcoholism or chronic love ... What was that?'

'I thought', said Jean, 'that it was a wave. At least it was green, and watery, and it rolled.'

Drummey nodded. 'Matter of fact, it was two waves – and us between. Ship's going crank. Nothing for it, I'm afraid, but to let a couple of tons of marble go after all. Jean, do you and Mr Meredith act as selection committee.' His eyes were fixed on the dials before him. 'And don't deliberate too long.'

'Folks,' said John suddenly – and Meredith awoke with a start – 'what's the height of Ben Nevis?'

'Four thousand, four hundred, and six,' said Jean promptly.

Drummey swung round, and for the first time his voice was sharp. 'John,' he said, 'd'you mean that?'

'Cloud by night and fog at dawn' – John's tone was disgusted – 'so what can I do? Fifty miles one way or another all round the compass. We may be over land by now.'

'Then get out more of those marbles. Stop short only when you come to Myron and Praxiteles. We need another three thousand feet.'

Meredith considered. 'There are two more that we might reasonably spare. One appears to be a St Bruno by José de Mora, a very strained piece of Baroque piety –'

'Turn it out.'

'The other is probably rather good – an allegorical group I can't quite make out, by a living Yugoslavian sculptor.'

'If he's living he won't mind help keeping us alive too. And he can chisel another one. Send it down.' Drummey was silent for some moments. 'There!' he said triumphantly. 'Climbing like a bird.'

'And, jiminy, there's the sun!' John grabbed his instruments. 'I'll have us sitting on the Clyde in under a quarter of an hour. Mr Meredith, you can be in London in time for dinner, same as the old goat was going to be.'

'London?' Meredith was again almost asleep. 'Well, it began there ... and with scraps of poetry –'

'Or almost poetry.' Jean dug for the last piece of barley sugar.

> 'Resolved at length, from vice and *London* far,
> To breathe in distant fields a purer air –'

Drummey shook his head. It was the first movement undirected to flying his craft that they had seen him make. 'Purer air? It's not distance will get you that. It's altitude ... Look at this.'

The flying-boat had risen from fog to cloud and from cloud to clear sky in which the dawn was breaking over endless vistas of blue and grey and gold. Drummey looked all round, loosened and threw off his helmet, set back his head:

> 'Before the starry threshold of Jove's court –'

Meredith came quite wide awake in his surprise. For all three young men were chanting in unison, and they were as beautiful as singing angels by Botticelli – or as any picture that Don Perez had ever stolen.

> 'Before the starry threshold of Jove's court
> My mansion is, where those immortal shapes
> Of bright aerial spirits live insphered
> In regions mild of calm and serene air,
> Above the smoke and stir of this dim spot
> Which men call earth ...'

Drummey had Jean's hand in his; he was looking now at Meredith and now at his instruments with an eye which had lost its strained look and taken on a glint of mischief. 'One of the advantages of the American language', he said, 'is its reams of poetry.'

'Dear me! I never heard before that Milton was an American.'

'He would have made not a bad one. But airmen, you see, must have a great deal of poetry by heart if they're not going to go to sleep. That's why between us we beat the *Luftwaffe*. They didn't have nearly enough poetry to keep awake on. Not even when they stretched a strict Aryan point or two and included Heine ... And now for the bonny banks of the Clyde.' Drummey was silent for several minutes. 'About Neff,' he said. 'Do you know, all that thieving and hoarding is beginning to make me feel mad?'

'And I, on the contrary, am coming to view it rather dispassionately.' Meredith looked at the young men, and at Jean, and smiled. 'All he stole was museums, after all. And although museums are important, they are not what is really important. What is really important is – well, what is going on. It's only if the museums help there that they begin to pay for what we spend on the lighting and the heating and the attendants.'

'But you can't get on without a tradition,' said Drummey, 'and a tradition has to be embodied in these material things.' He jerked a thumb towards the piled and ranked rows of pictures behind him. 'Neff tried to steal it and keep it to himself. That's what makes me mad – kind of ashamed to be an American.' He sat frowning into air. And then his brow cleared.

'Of course,' he said slowly, 'there's this to it. It all came of you people over here – all of you, from the Tagus to the Volga – getting in a mess. You couldn't help it, I dare say. But – well, you lost it and we brought it back.'

Meredith sighed. The flying-boat was dropping to a calm estuary and he was tired and well content. 'Yes,' he said; 'there's something in that. It isn't easy to bring back even now. But it would have been a hundred times more difficult if you hadn't come along ... And what about Jean? Is she going to be restored to us too?'

Drummey appeared to consider. 'Didn't somebody say something about Neff being a dragon? And isn't my craft bringing back the stolen treasure? You know what happens to the princess in stories like that.'

EPILOGUE

A LONG, melancholy wail rose, hung for a moment strident upon the ear, ebbed rapidly away. 'Tibbie,' cried Miss Dorcas Macleod, 'can this possibly be the second Thursday of the month?'

'Of course it is the second Thursday, Dorcas. And it is much to be hoped that Mrs Cameron has not forgotten the capers. She has been something disturbed since this distressing matter of Shamus. Pray hurry and welcome Captain Maxwell by the Seaway. I will meet you in the base-court, so that what we have in mind to show him we may go to at once.'

The throb of the *Oronsay*'s engine reverberated from the anchorage; sheep baahed and a dog barked; overhead the gulls screamed round a Flying Fox which hung, rusty and already derelict-seeming, above the ramparts. And Captain Maxwell, his formal salutation given from the bridge, stepped ashore and advanced with serious mien up the Seaway and past the grille to the precincts of Castle Moila. Miss Dorcas received him with hurried words, to which he listened with close attention, silent and unsurprised.

'... So it would seem', said Miss Dorcas, 'that the blackest magic must be in question once more. We had been given to understand that her power would not extend over water, but now we fear that Mr Properjohn's Foxes – which appear to have been out of order for some time – must have formed a fatal link.'

They walked to the base-court. 'We connect it, too, with the visitors who were here a month ago. They disappeared most unaccountably, after telling a strange story of how we were virtually besieged. Tibbie will say little about them, but it is my opinion that they were trolls.'

Captain Maxwell looked at Miss Dorcas doubtfully. 'I can't be saying that the lassie looked to me just like a troll.'

'But, Captain, have you ever seen a troll?'

'That I have not.'

'Then it is surely hardly possible for you to express an

297

opinion.' Miss Dorcas paused momentarily over this small logical triumph. 'And what is more likely than that Patuffa should have commerce with trolls? At her great age she must be far advanced in her arts. And it was the lad Shamus, we fear, who was first brought under a spell – on the very day marked by the appearance of our uncanny visitants. At first our opinion was this – that Shamus must have had an experience.'

'An experience?' asked Captain Maxwell uncertainly.

'A *religious* experience. He returned to the island much changed. Already we think that Patuffa had tried to ensnare him in that way. Some months ago – I do not know if we told you – a small statue was found in the Great Ditches. It was classical – indeed, it would be better to say pagan – in character; but whether a fawn or satyr I cannot tell. My Uncle Archibald, who was a virtuoso, and for long resided in –'

'Aye,' interrupted Captain Maxwell hastily, 'I've heard tell o' him many a time.'

'And it seemed to us that Patuffa must have sent this object – which was indelicately posed – with the intention of subverting Shamus's moral character and religious convictions. Now, of course, our speculation is confirmed. Having failed to wean him to paganism she has endeavoured, and we fear successfully, to convert him to popery – and by a similar resource. But here we are.'

They had arrived at a corner of the base-court, where Miss Isabella was already standing before a white marble figure which had been propped in the corner formed by a buttress and an ivy-covered wall. The representation was of a monkish person in an attitude of agonized piety, and anyone familiar with the art of the Counter-Reformation might have recognized it as the work of José de Mora. Captain Maxwell scrutinized it thoughtfully. 'Aye,' he said at length, 'there's no doubt that it's in the spirit o' them as is given to idolatry and false devotion. But we maun no' be ower-critical o' the lower forms o' Christianity. Only a few days syne the Reverend Wooley was saying to me –'

'And we have reason to believe', said Miss Dorcas in a low voice, 'that Shamus has been *praying* to it.'

Captain Maxwell shook his head. 'Have I no' always said', he asked, 'that ye hae but to take a Highlander outside the reformed Kirk and scratch him, and straightway ye come to a coarse Catholic creature underneath? Begging your pardon, Miss Macleod.'

The hereditary Captain of Castle Moila looked darkly at the writhing St Bruno. 'It is now some generations', she said, 'since our family has embraced the Protestant faith in its Presbyterian branch. And, of course, all our retainers have done the same. For instance, there is Mrs Cameron. She has just completed a sampler of the great red dragon, having seven heads and ten horns. Naturally, she is very perturbed. And so I fear there is only one solution.' Miss Isabella compressed her lips. 'Our brother must act decisively. It is, of course, an unpleasant thing to happen in a family. But there is no help for it. Great-aunt Patuffa must be burned.'

'Burned!' exclaimed Captain Maxwell.

'Certainly – and as soon as the necessary store of faggots can be collected. This may take a little time. For our countryside, as a visitor of some distinction remarked in the late age, is sadly deficient in timber. He is said to have been apprehensive lest we should steal his walking stick.'

Slowly Captain Maxwell drew a newspaper from his pocket. 'Miss Macleod,' he said, 'there's an auld proverb to the effect that it never rains but it pours. And I'm thinking that there's been more dropping from the skies than your uncanny kins-woman could contrive. Do you ever see the *Oban Argus?* As a journal o' opinion, it may be a wee bit more circumscribed than the *Scotsman* or *The Times*, but I've never had occasion to question the accuracy o' its reporting. So be pleased to listen to this.'

Captain Maxwell drew a pair of steel-rimmed spectacles from his pocket, inserted them between his bushy eyebrows and abundant beard, and read with slow emphasis:

'The death is reported, in obscure circumstances, of Mr Properjohn, senior, of Carron Lodge, Glen Carron. The deceased, who was an invalid of independent means residing with his nephew, Mr Amos Willoughby Properjohn, was found dead in bed on the morning of the 14th inst., having been crushed beneath the immense weight of a large marble statue which appears to have crashed with irresistible violence through the roof of the building. A fatality at once so mysterious and so awful has naturally aroused much speculation, but as no certain intelligence has yet been communicated by the investigating police we refrain from comment, and would at the same time warn our readers against giving any rash credit to the irresponsible conjectures of our sadly misnamed national Press.'

Captain Maxwell paused in his reading. 'It's no' a bad one, that,' he said. 'But now listen to this:

'Mr Nigel Fairbrother of the Scottish National Gallery, who chanced to be on holiday in the district, was called to Carron Lodge, and upon being shown into the dead man's study was surprised to observe a painting by the celebrated Jan Vermeer of Delft which, he declared, was indubitably the property of the Duke of Horton. It is believed that any explanation of this curious circumstance must await the return of Mr Properjohn, jnr, who is absent upon business believed to be connected with the box-making industry. Mr Fairbrother then proceeded to the scene of the fatality, and was the first to notice that at the moment of his death the deceased had apparently been reading *Der Untergang des Abendlandes* of the German idealogue, Oswald Spengler. Mr Fairbrother then identified the statue. It proves to be by a well-known contemporary Yugoslavian sculptor, and is an allegorical group known as the *Europa Rediviva*, or Europe Restored.'

Captain Maxwell took off his spectacles and folded the paper. 'What they ca' *The Decline of the West*,' he said. 'And then *Europa Rediviva*. Now, would ye no' be thinking there was some inwardness in that?' He shook his head. 'Awfu' times, Miss Macleod. Dances on Larra, and a Judgement in Glen Carron. Awfu' times, indeed.'

Discover more about our forthcoming books through Penguin's FREE newspaper...

It's packed with:

- exciting features
- author interviews
- previews & reviews
- books from your favourite films & TV series
- exclusive competitions & much, much more...

Write off for your free copy today to:
Dept JC
Penguin Books Ltd
FREEPOST
West Drayton
Middlesex
UB7 0BR
NO STAMP REQUIRED

READ MORE IN PENGUIN

In every corner of the world, on every subject under the sun, Penguin represents quality and variety – the very best in publishing today.

For complete information about books available from Penguin – including Puffins, Penguin Classics and Arkana – and how to order them, write to us at the appropriate address below. Please note that for copyright reasons the selection of books varies from country to country.

In the United Kingdom: Please write to *Dept. JC, Penguin Books Ltd, FREEPOST, West Drayton, Middlesex UB7 0BR*

If you have any difficulty in obtaining a title, please send your order with the correct money, plus ten per cent for postage and packaging, to *PO Box No. 11, West Drayton, Middlesex UB7 0BR*

In the United States: Please write to *Penguin USA Inc., 375 Hudson Street, New York, NY 10014*

In Canada: Please write to *Penguin Books Canada Ltd, 10 Alcorn Avenue, Suite 300, Toronto, Ontario M4V 3B2*

In Australia: Please write to *Penguin Books Australia Ltd, 487 Maroondah Highway, Ringwood, Victoria 3134*

In New Zealand: Please write to *Penguin Books (NZ) Ltd, 182–190 Wairau Road, Private Bag, Takapuna, Auckland 9*

In India: Please write to *Penguin Books India Pvt Ltd, 706 Eros Apartments, 56 Nehru Place, New Delhi 110 019*

In the Netherlands: Please write to *Penguin Books Netherlands B.V., Keizersgracht 231 NL–1016 DV Amsterdam*

In Germany: Please write to *Penguin Books Deutschland GmbH, Friedrichstrasse 10–12, W–6000 Frankfurt/Main 1*

In Spain: Please write to *Penguin Books S. A., C. San Bernardo 117–6° E–28015 Madrid*

In Italy: Please write to *Penguin Italia s.r.l., Via Felice Casati 20, I–20124 Milano*

In France: Please write to *Penguin France S. A., 17 rue Lejeune, F–31000 Toulouse*

In Japan: Please write to *Penguin Books Japan, Ishikiribashi Building, 2–5–4, Suido, Tokyo 112*

In Greece: Please write to *Penguin Hellas Ltd, Dimocritou 3, GR–106 71 Athens*

In South Africa: Please write to *Longman Penguin Southern Africa (Pty) Ltd, Private Bag X08, Bertsham 2013*

BY THE SAME AUTHOR

'A master – he constructs a plot that twists and turns like an electric eel: it gives you shock upon shock and you cannot let go' – *The Times Literary Supplement*

An Awkward Lie

'Mr Appleby,' Sergeant Howard remarks, 'you seem to be in a rather awkward lie.'

For Bobby – Sir John Appleby's engaging but naive son – is having a hard time proving his case. He did see a well-dressed corpse with a missing finger in the sand trap off the first green. And a very attractive girl did appear on the scene. But by the time he had telephoned for the police and returned, there was no girl, and no corpse . . .

Death at the President's Lodging

Inspector John Appleby has a difficult and delicate task when he investigates the murder of the unpopular Josia Umpleby of St Anthony's College. But with the unexpected aid of three precocious undergraduates, a subtle killer is unmasked and the devious dons find that the oddest thing about the case is Appleby himself . . .

The Daffodil Affair

While Inspector Appleby's aunt assigns her favourite cab-horse, Daffodil, to Scotland Yard's missing persons file, Mrs Rideout is equally distressed at the loss of her daughter Lucy. When a London house, said to be haunted, also vanishes in mysterious circumstances, the baffled policemen begin searching for a connection.

also published

The Journeying Boy
The Man from the Sea